Prai... t ...

"[In the D... ... night] shimmers with humor and
se... that only someone with ... ...sensi-
b... ...about the era and women's fantasies could
write. Here is the idle night's guilty pleasure."
—*Romantic Times* (4½ stars, Top Pick)

"Every page is pure satisfaction." —Lisa Kleypas

"A delicious and irresistible concoction, one part simple friendships, one part wicked delights, and all
parts wonderful!" —Connie Brockway

. . . and for Candice Hern's other novels

"Hern expertly infuses each encounter between her
delightfully appealing protagonists with delicious wit
and luscious sensuality." —*Booklist*

"Candice Hern will make you laugh and cry . . . and
then go back for more." —Sabrina Jeffries

"Ms. Hern brings historical details and witty characters to life. Pure fun!" —Judith Ivory

"A must read! An uplifting affirmation of the healing
power of love." —Mary Balogh

"Hern has done a masterly job. . . . Charming and
especially memorable." —*Library Journal*

Just One of Those Flings

Candice Hern

A SIGNET ECLIPSE BOOK

SIGNET ECLIPSE
Published by New American Library, a division of
Penguin Group (USA) Inc., 375 Hudson Street,
New York, New York 10014, USA
Penguin Group (Canada), 90 Eglinton Avenue East, Suite 700, Toronto,
Ontario M4P 2Y3, Canada (a division of Pearson Penguin Canada Inc.)
Penguin Books Ltd., 80 Strand, London WC2R 0RL, England
Penguin Ireland, 25 St. Stephen's Green, Dublin 2,
Ireland (a division of Penguin Books Ltd.)
Penguin Group (Australia), 250 Camberwell Road, Camberwell, Victoria 3124,
Australia (a division of Pearson Australia Group Pty. Ltd.)
Penguin Books India Pvt. Ltd., 11 Community Centre, Panchsheel Park,
New Delhi - 110 017, India
Penguin Group (NZ), cnr Airborne and Rosedale Roads, Albany,
Auckland 1310, New Zealand (a division of Pearson New Zealand Ltd.)
Penguin Books (South Africa) (Pty.) Ltd., 24 Sturdee Avenue,
Rosebank, Johannesburg 2196, South Africa

Penguin Books Ltd., Registered Offices:
80 Strand, London WC2R 0RL, England

First published by Signet Eclipse, an imprint of New American Library,
a division of Penguin Group (USA) Inc.

First Printing, August 2006
10 9 8 7 6 5 4 3 2 1

Cover painting: *Portrait of Madame Recamier (1777–1849)* by François
Gérard/Bridgeman Art Library.

SIGNET ECLIPSE and logo are trademarks of Penguin Group (USA) Inc.

Printed in the United States of America

PUBLISHER'S NOTE
This is a work of fiction. Names, characters, places, and incidents either are
the product of the author's imagination or are used fictitiously, and any resem-
blance to actual persons, living or dead, business establishments, events, or
locales is entirely coincidental.
  The publisher does not have any control over and does not assume any
responsibility for author or third-party Web sites or their content.

Dedicated with love to my father,
who always heaps high praise on my stories,
even as he tries manfully not to blush
at the sex scenes.

ACKNOWLEDGMENTS

Once again, I owe a huge debt of gratitude to my brainstorming partners, the Fog City Divas (www.fogcitydivas.com), who never seem to get tired of hearing, "And then what happens?" Thanks also to my editor, Ellen Edwards, for recognizing what was wrong with the first version of this book and helping me to fix it; to my agent, Annelise Robey, who was always there to buck me up when the going got rough; and to Krista Olson, who designed the gorgeous cover. Speaking of gorgeous, I'd like to publicly acknowledge Emily Cotler and her team at WaxCreative Design for their stellar work on the Extreme Makeover at www.candicehern.com. I love the new look!

The Heeramaneck Collection of Indian sculpture at the Los Angeles County Museum of Art served as the inspiration for Lord Thayne's collection. Many years ago, when I was studying Indian art in college, I had the pleasure of touring the storerooms that house the Heeramaneck Collection, and have never forgotten the sense of awe and wonder at seeing all those beautiful pieces up close and en masse. Lady Somerfield's instinct to want to touch them exactly echoes my own at that time. I would also like to mention William Dalrymple's excellent book *White Mughals*, which inspired some of Lord Thayne's experiences in India.

Chapter 1

He could not keep his eyes off her. Gabriel Loughton, Marquess of Thayne, had come to the Wallingford masquerade ball for the express purpose of surveying this Season's crop of beauties, but his eyes kept straying to the tall, elegant woman dressed as Artemis, the huntress.

She was no young girl in her first Season. In fact, given the way she closely watched the movements of a pretty blond shepherdess being led through a country dance with a plumed cavalier, Thayne would not be surprised to learn that his Artemis was the girl's chaperone. Or even, God forbid, her mother.

She did not, however, look like anyone's mother. The Grecian tunic she wore did little to disguise the shapely form beneath. Even the smallest movement sent the silky yellow drapery slithering and clinging in beguiling ways. Her arms were deliciously bare, save for a gold bracelet in the shape of a snake coiled high on one upper arm. Thayne had always found a woman's arms to be one of the most sensual parts of her body, and cursed British fashion or propriety or whatever it was that compelled most women to cover those intriguing assets with long sleeves or long gloves. Even at a masquerade, when a hint of boldness, or a hint of flesh, was generally forgiven, there were few bare arms to be seen. Whether milkmaid or queen, in Vandyke dress or Turkish garb, almost all the women kept their arms covered. Bosoms, however, were much on display, to Thayne's delight, and the occasional bare shoulder caught his eye. But very few arms were uncovered, and only one pair was of any interest.

His gaze feasted on those pale, slender limbs that moved so gracefully in gesture as she spoke. He wanted to touch them, to graze that white skin with his fingers, softly, very softly, and watch it prickle into gooseflesh.

Perhaps it was that very pale coloring that drew his attention. Her hair—or perhaps it was a wig; he could not be sure—was dusted with yellow powder flecked with gold that caught the candlelight. Her true hair might be dark, for all he knew, but he doubted it. Her skin had the translucence most often coupled with fair hair. And it was so very English. After eight years in India, where he'd been surrounded by dark, exotic beauties, Artemis's coloring was a treat to the eyes.

And yet, the room was filled with fair English roses with blue eyes and creamy complexions. There was something more that drew him to Artemis. The elegant coiffure intrigued him, to be sure. It was pulled up and back with gold combs, and crimped in waves reminiscent of the antique statuary his father collected to fill his gardens. There were many powdered heads among the guests, but all were dusted in the usual white. Artemis with her yellow powder would have been unique enough, but the gold flecks made her even more so. She was a woman of style and with the confidence of individuality that set her apart from the rest. One long curl fell over her shoulder and moved in a way that suggested it was her own hair and no wig. What he wouldn't give to see the rest of it hanging loose and then to bury his hands in it.

Damnation. His first night back in London and he was behaving like a randy schoolboy. With an effort, Thayne tore his gaze away from the fair huntress. He had no business ogling a woman who was certainly someone's wife, probably someone's mother. Not tonight. He hadn't come to the masquerade to find a mistress. As much as it pained him to admit it, he'd come here to find a bride. Or, more accurately, to see what was in store for him when his mother began, as early as tomorrow, trotting out for his inspection every eligible young girl with the requisite impeccable breeding and good looks. The duchess would, of course, have her favorites and she would try to push him toward one of them. But Thayne would not be pushed. He would make his own choice. Not that he had any strict requirements. So long as she was reasonably pretty and wasn't entirely empty-headed, he would be satisfied. He knew his duty. He just wanted to have a quick look around for himself before the matrimonial race began. Before anyone realized he'd returned.

Just as he had expected, a masquerade was the perfect venue to survey the field, which was precisely why he'd cajoled his sister Martha, Lady Bilston, into letting him use her invitation. Behind the security of their masks, not to mention elaborate wigs and costumes, the young ladies of the *ton* behaved with a little less restraint, less formality, less anxiety. Chaperones did not scrutinize their movements quite so closely. Thayne fully expected that he would have to choose a bride from among a group of girls so well protected by the strictures of Society that he would never really know her at all. At least tonight, when no one recognized him, he hoped to catch a glimpse of the real women behind some of those elegant masks.

He watched a pretty young brunette dressed in the long-sleeved gown and tall headdress of a fourteenth-century noblewoman, as she flirted with her dance partner. Her eyes sparkled coquettishly behind her mask and she ran a playful finger along his sleeve. She looked perfectly charming, but Thayne would be willing to wager she would never have behaved in such an alluring manner if it had been a normal ball, where her chaperone would be less forgiving. He would make a point of discovering who she was.

He continued to appraise potential brides from his position in a far corner, where he leaned negligently against a pillar. Several other pretty young women were worth a second look: a fair-haired milkmaid with an engaging smile, a Spanish infanta with masses of dark ringlets gathered on either side of her head like the ears of a spaniel, a girl with a magnificent bosom in a low-necked court dress from the time of Charles II.

Thayne would choose one or two to dance with, to discover if they were possessed of good conversation as well as beauty. Would one of them be worth a formal courtship, and potentially the role of his marchioness?

No matter where he looked, though, his gaze always came back to her. To the beautiful huntress with the tiny quiver filled with miniature golden arrows slung over her shoulder. Her body swayed slightly in time to the music, with the sensual grace worthy of a skilled *ganika*, one of the prized professional courtesans at the courts of India. But hers was not a studied grace. It appeared to come naturally, which made it all the more alluring.

She smiled as she spoke to the woman beside her, who was dressed in elaborate Elizabethan finery, with a bright red wig of tight curls and an enormous ruff around her neck. The stiff collar and heavy costume, which made it difficult for the woman to move more than her head and hands, was in sharp contrast with the natural drape of her companion's silky tunic. He was almost certain "Queen Elizabeth" was their hostess, Lady Wallingford, but he could not be positive since he'd arrived late in order to avoid formal introductions.

Who was Artemis, then? A friend? A Wallingford relation? Had he met her before, when he was on the town briefly in his youth? She was certainly someone of rank; else she would not be at such an exclusive gathering, nor would she be rubbing shoulders with their hostess.

He watched those fair shoulders rise and fall in a graceful shrug. Yes, it was definitely more than her coloring and unique style that drew his interest. The way she subtly, perhaps unconsciously, flaunted the fine-looking form beneath the Grecian tunic, the way she held her head at a slight angle, the way she smiled. And something more, something indefinable, an aura of sensuality that he could sense shimmering off her, even at a distance.

Her gaze swept the room and finally collided with his own. Elegant arched brows lifted above the gold mask as she looked at him, and one corner of her mouth quirked upward, as though she was pleased, or perhaps amused, by his scrutiny. Before he could return her smile, she moved away. It had been only an instant, but that winsome gaze had sent a shot of pure molten heat through his veins. Lord, she was magnificent!

Thayne smiled as a plan began to take shape in his mind.

He had come to the masquerade to ease his way back into Society without anyone knowing who he was, though he'd been away so long he doubted anyone would recognize him even without the mask and costume. He most particularly did not want potential bridal candidates to learn his identity just yet, and begin fawning and preening before the Marquess of Thayne. As he watched Artemis, though, he wondered if it might not be just as well to woo a *mistress* while in disguise, to encourage capitulation without laying his rank and fortune at her feet.

He couldn't take his eyes off her. It was time to do more than look.

Beatrice Campion, the Countess of Somerfield, adjusted the gilt girdle around her waist and fluffed the blouson that fell over it. She felt positively naked in this dratted costume. She didn't know what had possessed her to wear something so revealing—even her toes were bare in the gold sandals that laced up her feet—but then that was the fun of a masquerade, was it not? To be a little bold, a little shocking. Her niece, Emily, had certainly been shocked, but only because she feared Beatrice would draw attention away from herself. But it had taken little more than a moment before Emily realized that no one would take note of an elderly, widowed chaperone, no matter how provocatively dressed.

"After all," she had said, "you will be gathered along the wall with the other chaperones and dowagers, and no one is likely to take note of you. Indeed, I cannot imagine why you bothered to wear a costume at all when a simple domino would have sufficed."

"My dressmaker insisted it was just the thing," Beatrice had said in her defense, "that classical garb was exceedingly fashionable."

"And it would be," Emily said, "on someone not so . . ."

She appeared to have literally bitten her tongue. Beatrice laughed and then finished the thought. "So old?"

Emily shook her head, cheeks flushing prettily, and then changed the subject to the advantages of her own frothy costume and whether there might be too much lace at the neck.

Beatrice did not care what her niece thought. She was the mother of two daughters, but did not feel at all matronly or old tonight. Not in such a costume. In fact, even at the advanced age of thirty-five, something about the way the tiny pleats of yellow silk felt against her body made her feel quite . . . womanly. Sensual, even. Especially when a certain gentleman kept staring at her.

She wondered who he was. There was no clue to his identity beneath the exotic costume, which she presumed to be Indian. Did she know him? Is that why she so often found him staring at her? Even when her back was turned, she could feel his gaze on her, like a naked caress that sent a tingling through the fine hairs at the back of her neck.

What sort of man could make a woman's body react so, simply by looking at her? And what sort of brazen woman felt the urge to display that body to him with subtle movements she knew made the dress cling more closely?

Beatrice shook her head to clear it. This awareness of her body and how a man might perceive it was something entirely new. She had become acutely conscious in recent weeks of how men looked at her, and even more aware of her own reaction to them. She had been a widow for three years and missed the physical intimacy she'd shared with her husband. Though she had no wish to marry again, she had lately begun to feel a longing for that intimacy. And when a man looked at her in a way that left no question as to what he was thinking, Beatrice did not feel shock or outrage, as a respectable widow should. In fact, shameful as it was to admit, she found she rather liked it.

She blamed it on her friends, with all their frank talk of late about lovers and lovemaking. They called themselves the Merry Widows in private, though in public they maintained very proper respectability. When Penelope, Lady Gosforth, had confessed to taking a lover, she somehow managed to convince the rest of them to do the same. Or at least to make an effort to do so. None of them, so far, had actually succeeded. Except, perhaps, for Marianne Nesbitt, who was at that moment attending a house party at the estate of Lord Julian Sherwood, where she was likely to take him to her bed. That had certainly been her plan. The rest of the Merry Widows had also joined the party. Beatrice had to refuse her own invitation because of tonight's masquerade, which Emily had been determined to attend. Besides, the Wallingfords were the girl's aunt and uncle. It would have been bad form to decline.

Beatrice was rather glad she had come, after all, and that her dressmaker had convinced her to wear the Greek chiton. She had not deliberately worn the clingy silk dress in order to capture a man's attention—or had she?—but it had certainly done the job. She wondered if the unknown gentleman was going to ogle her from afar all night, or if he would ever actually speak to her, or even ask her to dance.

She watched a couple leave the room arm in arm—for a private tryst?—and thought again of her friends. Marianne would very likely return from the party full of the details of her own romantic encounter. That had been part of their Merry Widows' agreement, to be candid among themselves about their sexual activities. Penelope, who had wasted no time in finding a new lover in town, had certainly been candid. As Beatrice felt the eyes of the intriguing stranger on her again, all that frank speech came back to mind.

"He's coming!"

Beatrice pretended nonchalance at Lady Wallingford's urgent whisper, though her stomach muscles twitched in anticipation. "Who?" she asked in a disinterested tone

Lady Wallingford uttered a mocking little snort. "You know who. That striking-looking man dressed as a maharaja, the one who's been staring at you all night. The one you've been pretending not to notice. But I've seen your glance stray in his direction more than once."

Beatrice glared at her friend as if to deny that she'd done any such thing, but was undone by the knowing twinkle in the eyes behind the jeweled Elizabethan mask. She returned a sheepish grin and asked, "Who is he, Mary? Do you know?"

"I have no idea. We did not have a receiving line, as you know, so that everyone could keep their identities secret, if they desired. But he had to have an invitation to get past our majordomo. So I must have invited him."

"Unless he used someone else's invitation."

"He could have done that, I suppose," Mary said. "I certainly do not recognize him. But with the mask and the turban, he could be Wallingford, for all I know."

"I doubt your husband would look at me the way this maharaja has done."

"If he does," Mary said, "he'd better not let me catch him doing it."

Beatrice looked at her friend and they each burst into laughter at the thought of the portly, reserved Wallingford flirting with another woman.

"Dance with me."

Beatrice gave a start at the deep voice, then turned to find the unknown maharaja standing before her with a hand outstretched. He was even more intriguing up close. Mary was right about the mask and turban being an effective disguise. There were only a few hints of his true identity: dark eyes behind the mask, a well-shaped mouth below, a firm jaw, and a very slight cleft in the chin. There was also a bit of darkish hair in front of his ears, left uncovered by the elaborate turban. He was above average in height, though not overly tall, and had a powerful build set off by broad shoulders. Beatrice had the impression that he was about her own age. And extremely virile. Every inch of her skin, even to the very roots of her hair, tingled to be so close to him.

Who was he?

"Dance with me," he repeated, in that rich, deep voice, pitched low and mellow.

It was not a request. It was a demand. Or more like a fait accompli, as though he'd known she wanted to dance with him, as if she'd somehow willed him to her side.

Beatrice wanted nothing more than to take that proffered hand, but her gaze was inevitably drawn to the dance floor, where Emily danced with young Lord Ealing. She was charged with chaperoning her niece while the girl's mother, Beatrice's sister, Ophelia, was indisposed with a broken leg. At an event such as this, where the rules of propriety were loosened a bit, one really had to keep an eye on the headstrong girl. Beatrice wasn't here for her own enjoyment.

But those smoldering dark eyes beneath the mask beckoned.

"Go ahead," Mary whispered, giving her a discreet nudge.

Beatrice looked again at the tempting hand, then across the room to Emily. "You don't mind?" she asked Mary, though she continued to watch her niece, whose dazzling smile held her young partner in thrall.

"Of course not." She nodded toward the dance

floor as though to reassure Beatrice that she would keep an eye on Emily.

Beatrice could trust her to do so. Mary was the girl's aunt, too, after all. Her brother was Sir Albert Thirkill, Emily's father. But as Mary was a mere viscountess, Ophelia, always with an eye to the best advantage, had chosen her higher-ranking sister to act as Emily's chaperone.

"Go on and dance." Mary gave her another little nudge toward the maharaja. "Enjoy yourself."

"Thank you, Mary." Beatrice took a deep breath, and placed her hand in the maharaja's.

Since neither of them was wearing gloves—another one could risk at a masquerade, for the sake of the costume—the shock of skin against skin was momentarily disconcerting. He softly caressed her fingers in a manner that caused her breath to catch. Hearing that tiny gasp, he smiled, then brought her fingers to his lips. Instead of a chaste salute, however, he flicked the tip of his tongue over her knuckles, very discreetly, so that not even Mary would realize what he'd done. Unless she noted the sudden stiffening of Beatrice's spine and the involuntary shiver that danced along her shoulder blades.

Before she could entirely compose herself, the maharaja placed her still-tingling fingers on his arm and led her toward the dance floor.

Beatrice mentally ticked off all the dark-haired dark-eyed gentleman of her acquaintance, but could reconcile none of them with the man at her side. "Do I know you, sir?"

"I doubt it."

Though she, too, was masked, and her red hair powdered yellow, Beatrice was quite certain her costume was no disguise. Most of her friends had recognized her. "Do you know me?"

"You are Artemis, the huntress. A most beautiful huntress."

"Thank you, sir. But do you not recall what vengeance Artemis has been known to wreak against men who stare at her?"

He smiled. "Ah, yes. The unfortunate Actaeon. But you were not bathing in private, so you must forgive me. I was overcome by your beauty."

"You are not afraid, then? I do have a weapon, you know." She grinned and gestured at the quiver and bow on her shoulder.

"As do I." He indicated a large, jeweled dagger in his belt. "But mine is quite real, I assure you, whereas yours is merely decorative, I think."

"Then perhaps I am the one who should be afraid."

He turned to look at her, an intense expression in those dark eyes. "Perhaps."

Lord, who was this man?

"We have not met before?" she asked again.

"Unlikely."

It was an unspoken rule at masquerades that one was not required to reveal oneself until the unmasking at midnight, and he obviously was not going to be forthcoming with his identity. Beatrice did not press him, despite her curiosity.

As they approached the line of dancers, she caught a glimpse of Emily in the next line, smiling at Lord Ealing. Just at that moment, her niece reached up and flicked the large, curling plume on the young man's broad-brimmed cavalier's hat. Oh, dear. Beatrice hoped the girl was not getting overly flirtatious. Though she was supremely confident and self-possessed, Emily was still very young, not quite eighteen, and was really quite innocent.

She turned to find the maharaja watching her. "Let us dance," he said.

Heavens, even his voice could send shivers skittering down her spine. And make her forget all about her duties as a chaperone.

He took his place opposite her and let his gaze slide over her as they waited for the music to begin. She felt more naked than ever beneath that warm gaze as he studied the pleated silk that fell sensuously along her hips and thighs. She stood up taller under his scrutiny, stretching her spine and thrusting her breasts forward.

What was wrong with her? She'd never behaved in such a wanton manner in her life. When his eyes returned to hers, she was so enveloped in that warm, dark gaze that they might have been alone rather than in a crowded ballroom. She hadn't been so affected by a man's presence since Somerfield passed away. Her husband had sometimes had that same look in his eye. A look of raw desire. A look that made her feel alive and womanly and . . . sexual.

The music started and brought Beatrice back to earth. She loved to dance and tried to concentrate on the figures being set by the lead couple. But she was so thoroughly distracted by the exotic stranger that she tripped once or twice. His hand steadied her each time, distracting her even more.

When the dance called for their bare hands to join, it was nearly electric. Skin against skin, sending unspoken messages. Beatrice felt awash in pure, unfettered desire, the air around her heavy with it, so that every move was tinged with sensual promise. She had almost forgotten how potent such feelings could be, but at least she'd always had Somerfield there to take care of matters. Now . . . there was nothing to be done about this stranger and the way he made her feel.

When they weren't touching, Beatrice took pleasure simply in watching him. He moved with a powerful grace, like a large tiger she'd once seen at Polito's Menagerie, arrogant, full of masculine confidence. There were two or three other men in attendance who were dressed in Indian garb, but his costume was unlike any garment she'd ever seen, consisting of a long, skirted coat richly and elaborately embroidered with gold, worn over trousers that fell in loose folds around his feet, which were shod in slippers that curled up at the toe. There were jewels around his neck and on his turban. A long, colorful sash stitched with gold thread was tied around his waist, and the rather sinister-looking dagger was tucked inside it. Despite the skirt and the jewels, the total effect was surprisingly masculine. Perhaps it was the dagger. Or perhaps it was the man himself.

Beatrice thought once again about her friends, the Merry Widows. She had told them she had no time for lovers this year, not with Emily's Season to oversee, and her own two young daughters underfoot. But this man, this stranger, made her feel that she could make time.

When, at long last, the dance came to an end, the maharaja took her by the hand and led her from the dance floor. Beatrice lifted her brows in question, for there was one more dance left in the set.

"Come, Artemis," he said. "Neither of us is interested in dancing. At least, not this sort of public dancing."

His words sent a rush of heat through her veins, for she did not misunderstand their meaning. Her throat went hot and dry, so that she feared she could not speak.

He asked for no words, however, but simply led her out of the ballroom—which was in fact the long gallery converted for dancing—and through the doors that opened onto a terrace. He drew her outside. There were a dozen or so people standing about the terrace, ladies fanning themselves, couples in quiet conversation. The maharaja took quick note of it all, then captured her hand again and conducted her down the curving stone staircase that led to the formal garden below.

Chinese paper lanterns had been placed throughout the garden, and several couples could be seen strolling along the gravel paths. The maharaja guided her down a pathway, then doubled back and down another, and then another, apparently seeking privacy. Finally, he turned away from the formal pathways and plantings, and pulled her around to the side of the house.

It was quiet, save for the soft strains of the music inside, and thoroughly deserted. And very dark. The moon was hidden behind a thick bank of clouds and a stand of plane trees, and there were no lanterns nearby. The darkness was almost stygian.

The exotic stranger positioned himself with his back against the wall, then pulled Beatrice against him with a single rough jerk, wrapping one arm tightly around her waist. With his other hand, he stroked her arm. The brush of his knuckles against the bare flesh etched a path of desire in its wake. All her awareness followed his touch, every sensation enhanced by the darkness and the mystery of the man. She could not see his face, even the parts left uncovered by the mask. But she felt his firm body pressed to hers, and the unique scent of him, a masculine musk tinged with something else—sandalwood?—sprang sharp in her nostrils. She did not need to see him to be thoroughly aware of every part of him.

"I want you, Artemis."

"I know." Her voice came out raspy, breathless.

"And you want me."

"Yes." There was no denying it.

"Then let us have each other." He smiled, then lowered his head, and kissed her.

Chapter 2

His kiss was surprisingly lush and unhurried. After only a moment, he pulled back and loosened his hold on her.

"I think we should perhaps lay down our weapons, don't you?" He reached for the quiver and bow on her shoulder and slid them down her arm. He then removed the vicious-looking dagger from his belt, and dropped all of it to the ground near their feet.

He put his arms around her again and said, "Now we are ready for complete surrender."

He kissed her slowly—exploring, tasting, tantalizing in delicate assaults to her senses. He kissed her upper lip, the corners of her mouth, and finally took her lower lip between his and sucked gently. Beatrice grew giddy with sensation as she leaned back in his arms and savored every touch of his lips and tongue.

The pleasure was deep and all-encompassing, and yet there was beneath it a counterpoint of apprehension, of doubt. A niggling little voice inside her whispered that a proper, respectable woman would be outraged, that a proper, respectable woman would never allow a perfect stranger to steer her into the darkest spot on the grounds and kiss her into oblivion.

Beatrice told the little voice to be quiet.

The maharaja continued his slow and intriguing exploration of her mouth, and finally parted her lips with a gentle nudging from his own, and all at once the kiss became more urgent and deep. He became relentless in the ravishment of her mouth. He had said he wanted her and she felt it now, felt his desire like a palpable thing. His heat poured into her and through her until her own blood caught fire. She lifted and arched against him, kissing him back with a passion long buried, but never quite dead. She answered the bold thrusts of his tongue eagerly.

Without warning, he spun her in his arms and reversed their positions, pinning her to the wall, his hips pressed tight against hers, his erection obvious and hard against her belly. He kissed her again, drawing her tongue deeper into his mouth and caressing it with his own. Flushes of warmth continued to run through her veins, waves and waves of it, from her bare toes to her scalp, pooling finally in heat and dampness between her thighs, throbbing flesh that had not been so aroused in over three years.

His hands slid over the silk of her tunic, tracing the curve of her shoulder, spine, and hips, drawing her closer. Beatrice boldly explored him with equally inquisitive hands and fingers. It was still too dark to see him properly, but she needed no moonlight to discover the shapes and planes of his face and body. As her fingers traced the cleft in his chin, his strong jaw, and up the straight ridge of his nose, she realized he'd removed his mask. With a start, she became aware that her own mask was gone, as well, hanging down past her throat from its gold laces. Had she removed it? Had he? She could not recall.

Did it matter? It was too dark to see in any case, but why did it give her a twinge of apprehension that they might actually see each other?

Anxiety dissolved when his mouth found hers

again and plundered its depths, ripping her senses from her. When she thought she might go mad, his lips trailed lower, along her jaw, beneath her chin, and down the length of her throat.

"Your dress is quite . . . unusual. Not at all English."

She felt the breath of his words against her ear as he flicked his tongue on the sensitive skin along its outer edge. "It is supposed to be Greek," she said, somehow managing the words, though her brain seemed to have lost its mooring and sloshed drunkenly in her head.

"The ancients had a much better notion of dress than we do, did they not?" he whispered. "Whereas we modern English are not always comfortable in our bodies and go to great lengths to hide and bind them, Greek and Roman dress allowed freedom of movement. It did not confine the body, but allowed natural expression. You should always wear such a tunic, Artemis, which is so very un-English in its freedom."

He ran a finger under the shoulder where the yellow silk was gathered in pleats, and coaxed it over her arm. His warm hand stroked the exposed shoulder and traveled down over her chest. He reached inside the silk for her breast, and gave a soft groan when his hand met only whalebone and stiffening.

"Not so free and natural, after all," he said. "Very properly confined. Very British."

Though he could not know it, Beatrice's nipples had grown puckered and taut beneath the stays. How she wished she were not so tightly laced. She wanted to feel his hands on her breasts.

His hand gave up the quest and returned to stroke her arm, tracing the outline of her serpent bracelet. It was almost as good. Almost.

"And what of Indian dress?" she said, nodding

toward his own elaborate costume. "It looks as confining as any English gentleman's."

"On the contrary," he said. "Eastern dress is quite unrestrained."

And suddenly she felt a length of soft fabric tickle her face. She laughed as more and more fell about her. "What is it?"

"My turban. You see how easily it is unbound?"

"I cannot see it, but I feel it." Boldly, she reached up and found the turban was entirely gone, and her hands met soft, thick hair instead. "Oh." She threaded her fingers through it and he gave a gruff moan of pleasure.

He captured her hands and pulled them above her head. With the fabric of the turban, he tied them loosely and held them there while he kissed the undersides of her upper arms and the bend of her elbows. Ticklish, she giggled and fidgeted against the sweet torture of his tongue. With one twist of the fabric, her hands were free again and she wrapped them around his neck.

"And not only the turban," he said, "is easily removed."

She felt him reach inside the skirted coat, and with a flick of the wrist, his trousers fell loose and, with a soft whoosh, pooled at his feet. One more quick adjustment, and the weight against her belly was real and hot and thoroughly unconfined. He was naked below the waist.

If there was ever a time to call matters to a halt, it was now. Reason told her to retreat, to show some restraint before it was too late, but she did not. God help her, she did not want to. She wanted this. She wanted him.

He began to kiss her shoulder and neck, and her head fell back against the wall to allow him access. Her bones had turned to liquid. If she had not been pressed tight between the wall and his firm body, she would have collapsed. She was vaguely aware of the rustle of silk as he pushed up her chiton and slid his hand up her bare leg. Cool night air touched the skin of her calves, then her thighs, as he raised the hem all the way to her waist. The warmth of that bold hand against cool skin, the touch of his bare thigh against hers, and finally the velvety weight of his erection against her belly caused her to cry out. He muffled her cry with his mouth, taking her in a deep kiss.

What remained of her reason, her dignity, her sanity, evaporated in that moment. Yielding to her body's urgent demands, she brazenly pressed herself against him, adjusting her weight to take him inside her. She was wet and throbbing and ready for him. Impatient. Eager.

"Steady," he said. "Like this."

He reached down and grasped her behind one knee, lifting her leg and guiding it around his waist. Her sex was now boldly open to him, but he did not invade it yet. Instead, he teased it and fondled it, first with deft fingers and then with the head of his penis, until she was slick and aching and mad with wanting him. She let out a plaintive cry, and he moved his hand behind her and lifted her buttocks. And with a single swift stroke, he was suddenly deep inside her.

Desire tore away reason, dragging her down beneath shame, beneath propriety, beneath intellect. She squirmed against the wall and wrapped her leg more tightly around him. He set up a slow rhythm, pulling almost completely out of her before pushing all the way in again, and she arched up into the ecstasy he gave her.

Involuntary coos of pleasure escaped her with each breath, little moans of pure bliss that matched the cadence of his thrusts.

She felt his mouth smile against hers. Then he said something, a word she did not understand or could not quite hear over the rasp and pace of her own breathing. "What?" she asked between breaths, not really caring if he answered.

"*Jataveshtitaka*," he said, and increased the tempo of their rhythm. "The twining of a creeper."

She had no idea what he was talking about, but it did not matter. She lifted to meet every thrust and the faster the rhythm, the harder her spine was slammed against the wall. Apparently realizing she was being bruised, he reached both hands behind her and cupped her buttocks, holding her away from the wall.

The faster he moved, the more tension built inside her until she thought she would break into pieces. She would die of pleasure, surely she would die. And yet it drove her, this impending demise, for she knew where it led and, dear God, she wanted it. All thought, all awareness, was cast aside in an effort to end this unbearable ache. Her inner muscles gripped him tightly and he let out a moan. She pushed up against him, harder and harder, in search of completion.

And it came. In an explosion of sensation so powerful her entire body shook with it. Beatrice threw her head back and was about to scream when his mouth covered hers and muffled the sound. A few seconds later his frenzied thrusts came to a halt and he pulled out of her. She felt hot liquid dribble down her thigh.

Dazed and disoriented, she fell limp against the wall, her sex still pulsing. One tiny, lucid corner of her brain was grateful that at least one of them had the sense to consider the consequences of what they did. She had been too far gone to think so rationally.

"Dear God," he said, his breath coming in pants and puffs as he leaned over her, arms bracketed against the wall. "Or should I say 'dear goddess'? My sweet Artemis, you have killed me after all."

He kissed her softly, then stepped away. Beatrice closed her eyes and tried to make sense of what had just happened, what she'd allowed to happen.

She began to tremble a little in the aftermath. Or was it the cool night air? Or the sudden realization that she'd lost all sense of decency and been sexually intimate with a perfect stranger? Though her body still thrummed with the aftereffects of sexual release, her mind found clarity at last and understood the outrageousness of her behavior.

How could she have done such a thing?

How had she let it go so far? She knew when they went outside that she would be soundly kissed by the dark stranger, but had she expected . . . this? No, she had not. Had she? Heavens, she was so confused. She had enjoyed his obvious interest, wanted him to kiss her. But had she truly imagined it would lead to anonymous coupling up against a wall, for God's sake?

One thing was certain. She knew when a line had been crossed and the ultimate intimacy was about to occur. She could have stopped it; she could have said she did not want it. But she had not done so. Because she *had* wanted it. There was no denying she had wanted it. But to have given in to her desire, to have shown no self-restraint whatsoever, to have allowed a strange man access to her body, suddenly made her feel off-balance, stupefied and stupid.

She did not know whether she was overwrought with outrage, or outrageously thrilled. Should she feel shamefully disgusted, or deliciously wicked?

Yes, she had been intrigued by his interest, and attracted to him. And the masks, the music, the re-vealing costume, had all made her feel quite daring. The anonymity of the encounter, the sheer boldness of it, had excited her even more and had given her an odd sort of courage.

Courage to behave like a wanton. To allow herself to be seduced in a garden outside a ballroom with hundreds of people inside. People who knew her, respected her, even admired her for her work with the Benevolent Widows Fund. People who would be beyond astonished to know what she'd just done.

If Beatrice had ever imagined herself taking a lover, and such thoughts had indeed teased her of late, she had assumed it would be a discreet affair that took place in the privacy of a bedroom. But this . . . this rough, unbridled passion in the dark, against a wall, with people wandering about who might come upon them, with Emily just inside . . . this was not something she could ever have imagined. It seemed so sordid, so dirty.

So exciting.

Deep in her heart, she knew it was wrong. She ought not to have let it happen. The best thing to do would be to walk away. Now, while the entire business was still anonymous. Suddenly, it seemed imperative to protect her identity. She did not want this man to know who it was who'd given her body so willingly, and she did not want to know who he was, either. That would make it easier for her to accept the situation as a moment of madness, an anomaly that was thoroughly out of character. Surely this man would believe her to be a woman of loose morals, a woman who thought nothing of making love in the dark with a stranger. Like a prostitute in Covent Garden. She did not want it known that Lady Somerfield was such a woman.

Because she was not. She had never done anything disgraceful or improper in her entire life. She had never been with a man other than Somerfield.

All of these thoughts flew through her mind in an

instant, jumbled and confused, before she could even
stir herself from the wall. She was ready to move
away when she felt his hand lift her skirt again and
she jumped back with a shriek. No! She would not
allow him to importune her again. She would not
allow the moment of madness to stretch into two
moments, or more.

But he did not press against her again to initiate
further intimacies. Instead he used a piece of silky
fabric to wipe her legs. "Let me help you, Artemis."

But she squirmed against his touch. The thought
of his seed spilling down her legs, a sticky reminder
of what she'd done, only made her feel more acutely
aware of the coarseness of the encounter. She tried
to get away, but the stranger rose again and pinned
her to the wall. "Don't run away, my huntress." He
kissed her again and she pulled back, fighting her
body's treasonous attraction to him in an attempt to
end the situation.

"Let me go," she said, trying to sound steady and
controlled but fearing she sounded quite the opposite.

His hands immediately released her, and in that
moment she knew he would have done so at any
time if she'd only asked. He would not have forced
her. He *had not* forced her. She could not use that as
an excuse.

"Don't leave yet," he said. "I don't even know
your name."

And Beatrice intended to keep it that way. She
wanted to flee back inside the ballroom, collect Emily,
and make a quick exit. She was determined that he
should not know her identity. "I have to go." She
straightened her skirts and pulled up the shoulder of
the chiton. Her hands went to her hair, securing the
combs that had come loose and tucking a few way-
ward locks into place. She remembered his hands in
her hair and hoped to heaven it did not look as

messy as she imagined. When she went back inside, would everyone who saw her know precisely what she'd been doing?

Beatrice frantically brushed her shoulders and the front of her dress, hoping she was not covered in hair powder. At least it was yellow and would not show too badly against the yellow silk. The gold flecks were a different matter. Why had she thought to add that little embellishment to her coiffure? She brushed and brushed her hands over the dress and plucked at the pleats to dislodge any powder and gold flecks that had been shaken loose.

"You will not tell me your name?"

She stopped brushing but did not look up. "No."

"You wound me, Artemis. How can you give me your body so sweetly but not gift me with your name?"

"I'm sorry. I cannot. I must go."

He stood before her, blocking her exit, and she pushed him away so she could pass. He took a step backward. And in that moment, a shaft of moonlight broke through the trees and illuminated the wall beside her. She blinked against the sudden light.

Damnation! He might see her face.

She quickly stepped away from the moonlight and reached for the strings of her mask. Replacing it as she moved deeper into the darkness, she almost tripped over the discarded quiver and bow. She quickly retrieved them and made a mad dash toward the garden.

"But Artemis," he called, "when may I see you again?"

Beatrice lifted her skirts and ran through the dark edges of the garden until she reached an illuminated path, blessedly deserted. She stopped to compose herself as best she could. She wanted to hurry inside, find Emily, and leave the ball before the stranger found her, but she did not want to run inside looking flushed and . . . ravished. Besides, he would have to tie those odd trousers back on and replace his turban, which would surely take several minutes.

She paused a moment to slip the quiver and bow over her shoulder and fluff the chiton into a proper blouson over her waist. Turning her face into the night breeze, she let the air cool her cheeks and calm her spirits. She licked her lips, and the taste of the stranger lingered. Did she only imagine they were a bit swollen? She took one last deep breath before moving onto the path, and inhaled the scent of him still on her skin. Him, and the telltale smell of love-making. She recalled the soft fabric on her legs as he cleansed her. A hint of stickiness remained, but no one would know about that. The smell, though . . .

Blast. She looked around her frantically, then hurried down the path when she saw what she needed. One of the herbaceous borders included several large lavender plants. She plucked off a few spikes and rubbed them along her arms and neck, the friction releasing some of the aromatic oil from the tiny blossoms.

The sweet aroma had a calming effect. Her breathing became regular, her pulse slowed, and her clamorous conscience, which had been hammering loud reproof in her head, quieted a bit. Beatrice considered again what had just taken place, and wondered if she had been rash. She had wanted a lover, and had found a willing one. And while it was happening, dear heaven, she had enjoyed it. Should she turn around and go back to him? Remove her mask, stand in the moonlight, and boldly announce her name, then ask if he'd be willing to join her in a discreet affair?

A couple strolled past her and she pretended to be sniffing the sweet-smelling herb. Their presence reanimated her conscience, reminding her of the shame and embarrassment she would feel if anyone guessed what had happened a few yards away in the dark.

No, it was best to go back inside and pretend it had never happened.

If such a thing were possible.

Well, well, well. The evening had certainly taken a different turn than he'd expected. To have found such a woman and to have experienced such a passionate interlude with her quite took Thayne's breath away. He had thought only to have an opportunity to preview the bridal prospects, and instead . . .

Damn. He ought to have run after her, but his *salvar* trousers were still tangled around his ankles, inhibiting movement. Besides, Thayne did not care to imagine the picture he would make if seen running through the garden with his own arbor vitae on display.

She had wanted to get away, though, and the gentleman in him was forced to allow her to do so. After such a splendid performance, he wondered why she was in such a hurry to leave. Clearly, she had been afraid that the moonlight might reveal her face to him. And she had not wanted to give her name. She did not want him to know who she was.

Why? Was she someone important? Or the wife of someone important? Or just a woman who had become caught up in the passion of the moment and regretted it?

Thayne suspected it was the latter. There had been a touch of shame in the way she'd shrunk away from him as he'd tried to clean her legs, a hint of disgust in her voice as she'd refused her name. She had been a more-than-willing partner, but Thayne was fairly certain she was embarrassed by that very fact.

He had not forced her, but had he taken advantage somehow? Seduced her into more than she had been willing to give?

No, he did not think so. She had had ample opportunity to put a stop to it, but she had not once indicated that she wanted to stop. By God, she had been
every bit as aroused as he'd been, and she had given
as good as she got. She had seemed shocked at first
when he'd lifted her leg, even a bit awkward. She
had not been accustomed to such a position; he
would swear it. But soon enough she had been pressing her heel against the small of his back, driving
him deeper inside her, clenching her inner muscles
around him like a fist, as skillfully as a practiced
ganika. But Thayne knew in his gut that it was not
practiced. It had been natural. And her completion
had come too quickly and too powerfully for artifice.
He suspected she had surprised herself as much as
him. Still, she had known what she was doing and
had enjoyed it. Damn, but she had been spectacular.

And beautiful. True, he never saw her face completely in the light and was unlikely to recognize it
if he saw it again, but it had felt beautiful. The bones
of her cheeks rode elegantly high on her face, and
her nose was perfectly straight. The mouth, which
he'd had the pleasure of seeing quite clearly in the
ballroom, was lush and full-lipped and had taken his
breath away when it had moved so sensuously against
his own.

She had allowed him to feast on her luscious arms,
too. Thayne had a special attraction to a woman's
arms, and hers had been sheer perfection. Slender
but not too thin; delicate-boned with the merest hint
of soft, feminine musculature. Sweet-smelling skin as
smooth and silky as gardenia petals; the glint of a
ruby-eyed gold serpent coiling up one upper arm.
He knew her arms better than her face.

And there was her laugh. When he'd tickled her
with the fabric of his turban, when other women
might have giggled, she had laughed outright, glee-

fully and playfully. A clear, musical laugh like the sound of temple bells.

He had to see her again. He had to discover who she was.

He tugged up the *salvar* over his drawers and quickly tied them in place, then retied the laces of his *jama* and straightened its skirts. His *patka* had gone missing at some point and he found it on the ground next to the coiled length of muslin that had been his turban. He retrieved it and wrapped it twice around his waist, then knotted it in the front, making sure the fringed ends fell properly with the ornamental embroidery faced out. Then he set about the complicated business of twisting and tying the turban. Ramesh, his valet, would have fits when he saw it, but the English men and women inside the ballroom would never realize it was not tied correctly.

Finally, he reached for the mask that hung down his chest on long laces, placed it over his eyes and nose, and tied it behind his neck, just below the turban. He was as ready as he would ever be, without a mirror and Ramesh. He'd almost forgotten about the dagger until he stepped on the hilt. He bent to retrieve it when the moonlight glinted off something else in the grass.

A tiny gold arrow. A souvenir from Artemis.

Thayne slid the dagger inside the folds of the *patka*, and tucked the little arrow behind it. He would keep it as a memento of her passion, and how she had nearly felled him with it.

He made his way back through the garden paths and up the stairway to the terrace. He thought about all those young girls he had planned to dance with, to flirt with, to surreptitiously evaluate as potential brides. He had lost all interest in them. The only thing he wanted to do was find Artemis and coerce, cajole, or seduce her into revealing her identity.

If it turned out that who she was somehow prevented a liaison between them, he would have to accept that. He would be disappointed, to be sure, but he would never impugn or embarrass her in public. If there was any way at all, though, to see her again, to have her again, by God he would move mountains to do so.

Thayne entered the ballroom and made a slow progress around its perimeter. He studied the dancers in their lines, the clusters of young women standing along the walls, and the older ones seated in cozy groups. He dipped his head into the card room, the anteroom set aside for tea, and the salon arranged with long tables laden with covered dishes for the midnight supper. No matter where he looked, there was no sign of powdered yellow hair and slender, white arms.

There was no sign of the little blond shepherdess, either.

Curse it all, she had bolted. His Artemis did not have the courage of the huntress after all. She had fled rather than face him again. Damn and blast.

His gaze swept the dance floor again and picked out two of the pretty young girls he'd noticed earlier. He really ought to stay and try to talk with them, even dance with them. But he had no taste for innocent flirtation after the passionate episode in the garden. All the glamour of elaborate costumes, the festive atmosphere, the gaiety—all of it was lost on Thayne. His mind was full of one thing only: Artemis. Who was she?

He looked around at the room full of exposed bosoms and covered arms, and his mind was filled with images of *her* perfect arms and of his fingers and hands and lips upon them. No other arms enticed him. There was nothing more for him at this ball.

He was making his way toward the stairs when he was stopped by "Queen Elizabeth."

"You are leaving, sir?"

"I am afraid so, Your Majesty. Though it has been a delightful evening, I have other commitments I must honor."

"What a pity. You will miss the unveiling, at midnight, when masks are removed."

"Disappointing, to be sure."

"For us all," she said, and gave him a quizzical look. "I had most particularly hoped to see who lurked behind those exotic robes and turban."

Most particularly? Had Artemis said something to her before she left? "Ah, but how much sweeter the mystery," he said, "if I make an exit now."

She gave a disparaging huff. "I am plagued with early departures. How provoking. I must see to the rest of my guests. Good evening, sir."

She swept past him in her heavy velvet skirts before he could probe her about Artemis, perhaps unearth a clue to her identity. Would Good Queen Bess have told him her name if he'd asked?

But he would never have asked. Thayne would not jeopardize the privacy or reputation of Artemis. But damnation, he wished he knew who she was. There was nothing for it but to put her out of his mind, and consider tonight's rendezvous a onetime affair— a delightful interlude not to be repeated. It was certainly not the first time he'd enjoyed a woman's charms only once and never again. It was not even the first time the woman had been nameless.

So, he would proceed as planned, making known his return to town, and setting about the business of finding a bride. Life would go on in the usual manner.

He would try to forget her. But as he fingered the tiny golden arrow hidden in his *patka*, he rather suspected he was doomed to searching every *ton* event for a fair-haired huntress with a kissable mouth.

*   *   *

That night Thayne dreamed of India. Outdoors in the evening. The trickle of a nearby water fountain. The breeze scented with night-blooming jasmine. The cry of peacocks from the mango trees. A woman's voice rose in plaintive song. The heartbreaking strains of a *sarangi* and the sweet, clear notes of a *basuri* flute. The seductive rhythms of a tabla drove the sinuous movements of a nautch dancer. Thayne watched her dance as he lounged against bright-colored silk bolsters beneath the ornamental canopy of a *chattri*. The colors, the music, the heady scents, wrapped around him like hookah smoke, drugging him. The dancer came nearer, the tiny bells on her ankles jingling, calling to him like a siren's song. He wanted her. His body was on fire for her. She came closer so that the silk of her trousers brushed against him. The elegant mudras of her hands captivated him. When his eyes were finally able to gaze upward, he found her face partially veiled. But one long strand of yellow hair flecked with gold escaped the veil, and large blue eyes gazed down at him. He reached out to her.

Chapter 3

"How extraordinary." Beatrice looked at the women gathered in Grace Marlowe's sitting room, each one of them nodding her head to confirm that what she was hearing was true. Apparently Lord Julian's house party at Ossing Park had not turned out quite as expected. Marianne Nesbitt had indeed taken a lover to her bed, but it had not been their host.

In fact, she had not known who it was.

Beatrice could hardly believe that two of the Merry Widows had had encounters with perfect strangers. Beatrice had not yet revealed her story, but she could not help thinking of it, of her unknown lover, as she listened to her friends tell what had happened at Ossing Park.

The women had gathered for their regular meeting as trustees of the Benevolent Widows Fund, a charity organized by Grace to aid women who'd been left destitute when their husbands had been killed in the Peninsular War. Their most successful fund-raising efforts were the charity balls they sponsored during the Season. The balls had become very popular, and invitations were coveted, even though a sizable contribution was requested on acceptance. The balls were held every two weeks from April through the end of June, and so the trustees met frequently to ensure that all arrangements went smoothly.

But lately, their meetings had taken on a decidedly different tone. Ever since Penelope, Lady Gosforth, had convinced them all to make a secret pact to find lovers, and they had dubbed themselves the Merry Widows.

Marianne's story, it seemed, was not quite the same as Beatrice's after all. The youngest of the trustees, Marianne had been the first to fall into Penelope's plan. She had obviously wanted to pursue a lover, but had been rather shy and uncertain about how to go about it. They had all offered advice and counsel, and encouraged her to allow Lord Julian to win the day. But apparently something had gone awry. Marianne had thought Lord Julian was making love to her in the dark, but realized the next morning it could not have been he, as he had been injured the previous evening. She had fled the party after discovering that a stranger had tricked her and taken Lord Julian's place.

"Who could have done such a thing?" Beatrice asked, astonished that any man would have such audacity. At least her own masked lover had not pretended to be someone else. He'd simply been a maharaja-garbed man who'd clearly desired her. Beatrice had not stopped thinking about that desire, and her own, for days, and was still conflicted about it.

"As it happens," Marianne said, "I know who it was."

The trustees listened in amazement as Marianne revealed that her secret lover had been her closest friend, Adam Cazenove. Wilhelmina, the Dowager Duchess of Hertford, was the only one who seemed unsurprised by the news, claiming she had always suspected Adam was in love with Marianne.

The business of the Fund was cast aside as they spent the next half hour discussing Marianne's predicament. Each time Adam's lovemaking skills were mentioned, Beatrice felt her skin flush in reminiscence of her maharaja. She had to wonder if she would ever have considered going into the garden with him if the trustees had stuck to business and never become the Merry Widows. Their frank, and often racy, conversations had, she believed, primed her for seduction. She did not know if she should scold them for leading her astray, or thank them.

The discussion of Marianne's dilemma ultimately descended into silliness and laughter and talk of laying in supplies of juniper juice for contraceptive purposes. Even Grace, the prim and prudish widow of the late, great Bishop Marlowe, became caught up in the merriment of the moment.

Finally, Penelope turned to Beatrice, the movement causing her soft brown, fashionably cropped curls to bounce against her cheeks. "And what about you, Beatrice? What have you been up to while we were enjoying the interesting happenings at Ossing? I don't suppose you have found yourself a lover, have you?"

Her eyes twinkled with mischief. Penelope was bound and determined that they should all take lovers, as she had done, for the sake of their health and happiness. She had a new lover, Eustace Tolliver, and had regaled her friends with the details of his prowess in the bedroom.

Beatrice had given a great deal of thought as to whether or not she should confess to her garden encounter. She was still more than a little embarrassed about it. Yet at the same time, she was brimming with excitement over the pure boldness of it. In fact, it was that push-pull between mortification and delight that had finally convinced her to tell her friends what had happened. Perhaps they would be able to help sort out her feelings.

She took a deep breath and offered Penelope a halfhearted smile. "It is quite possible I have," she said.

Penelope gave a little shriek. "I knew it!" She pounded the tea table so hard that every cup and saucer and bowl rattled precariously. Beatrice and Marianne grabbed their cups before they could topple, and Grace steadied the table with her hands. Penelope was oblivious to it all. "I told the others you were up to something," she said, her face wreathed in a dazzling smile.

"I wasn't up to anything before you left," Beatrice said, "but something quite unexpected happened while you were gone."

And so, with encouragement from all four ladies, and with constant pressing for details from Penelope, Beatrice told her tale.

"I confess I have been torn apart by the whole affair," she said at last. "I have felt shame, delight, embarrassment, wonder. I haven't known whether I'm coming or going."

"It is rather shocking," Grace said, quite as one would have expected.

"I think it is frightfully exciting," Penelope said, with equal predictability. "I declare, it is more interesting even than Marianne's situation. But how extraordinary that you each found such pleasure in a stranger's arms. Perhaps there is something to be said for a bit of mystery. I wonder—"

"Don't get any ideas, my girl," the duchess said. "I don't want to hear of you dashing off with every stranger who makes eyes at you."

Penelope snorted. "No, I suppose Eustace would not like it."

"No, he would not," Grace said. "He cares for you, in case you had not noticed."

Penelope turned to her and beamed. "Do you think so?"

"But you have no idea," Marianne said to Beatrice, getting back to the point at hand, "no idea at all, who he might have been?"

"I am afraid not," Beatrice said. "Indoors, he was masked. And outdoors . . . well, it was very dark."

"I know the feeling," Marianne murmured.

"And up against a wall, no less," Penelope said, and heaved a little sigh. "How exceedingly daring of you."

"Or exceedingly cheap and vulgar," Beatrice said, "like a doxy in a dark alley."

"Do not be so hard on yourself," Wilhelmina said. "You are no doxy, and it does not sound as though he treated you like one."

Beatrice felt her face flush at the duchess's words. Though Wilhelmina had ultimately married a duke, it was easy to forget that she had started out life as little better than a cheap doxy. She was quite open about her past, but Beatrice knew that she sometimes felt the differences between her and the other trustees very keenly.

"You are right," Beatrice said. "It was not a slam-bang sort of affair. He took his time with me. He . . . he pleasured me. He did not treat me like a light-skirt. I have simply felt like one from time to time since that evening. I have never done anything like that before, and it is still unsettling to me."

"You were emboldened by the darkness, I daresay," Marianne said in a wistful tone that hinted it had been just so in her own case.

"The worst part, though," Beatrice said, "is that I was so determined he not see me and recognize me, or I him, that I bolted. It seemed the right thing to do at the time, but instead I have been driving myself mad every time I see a dark-haired, dark-eyed man of the same build, wondering if he was my maharaja. I can barely look a man in the eye for fear I will somehow recognize him."

"And what if you do?" the duchess asked. Wilhelmina was older and wiser than the rest of them, and she'd had a great deal of experience with men. Ever since their Merry Widows' pact, Wilhelmina's rather scandalous past and her knowledge of men and love affairs had become a useful resource. She was also the kindest and most generous of women. "Will you bolt again?" she asked.

"I don't know," Beatrice said. "I suppose it depends on how he reacts if *he* recognizes *me*. What will I see in his eyes? Mockery? Scorn?"

"I doubt that," Wilhelmina said. "He asked your name. That means he wanted to see you again."

"Yes, he said as much as I ran away."

"Silly woman," Penelope said. "What on earth made you run away from such a man?"

"Because she was shocked at what she'd done," Grace said, and they all turned to look at her. "Well, weren't you? I certainly would have been."

"I am sure you would," Penelope said, "and we would all have been equally shocked, I assure you."

"Grace is right," Beatrice said. "That is why I ran away. But I admit that for one tiny moment, I almost turned back. Even then, I was torn and confused. After all, I'd never done anything remotely disgraceful in all my life. I'd never been with any man other than Somerfield. I frightened myself, you see, and so I ran."

"The question is, will you continue to run if you see him again?" Wilhelmina asked.

Four anxious pairs of eyes turned to Beatrice. She wished she could oblige them with a firm answer. "I don't know. I truly do not know. I suppose a lot depends on who he is. He could be someone's husband, God forbid."

"What did he say to you?" the duchess asked. "Was there any hint about family or background?"

"Let me think. I asked if we had met before and he was quite sure we had not. Or so he said. And my costume and mask were not that much of a disguise, so it cannot have been a matter of simply not recognizing me."

"Assuming he was telling the truth," Penelope said, "then he must be new to London. Everyone knows you, Beatrice. He is either some undesirable sort from a different level of society, or he has lived a life somewhere outside of London."

"A country gentleman?" Wilhelmina asked.

"A soldier?" Penelope asked.

"I don't think so," Beatrice said. "Unless he was a general. He had a very confident, almost arrogant bearing."

"What about his costume?" Grace asked. "Was it truly Indian? Could he have just come from India?"

"He's a nabob!" Penelope exclaimed, clapping her hands together in glee. "Beatrice, you've found yourself a rich nabob. What fun!"

Beatrice laughed. "Don't be silly, Pen. His was not the only maharaja costume at the ball. I'm sure he must have got his from a theatrical company or some such place. Besides, would a nabob have somehow procured an invitation to the Wallingford ball? Mary suggested he might have used someone else's invitation to gain admittance, but then he'd have to have *ton* connections, would he not?"

"If he's rich enough," Marianne said, "he could find acceptance fairly easily, I should think. And a lot of men have made a great deal of money in India, some of them from very good families. He need not have been a struggling clerk who made a fortune in diamonds. He may be a gentleman."

"And if he's not," Penelope said with a shrug, "what does it matter?"

"You are all getting carried away," Beatrice said. "I don't think the costume had any special significance."

"And it *does* matter," Grace said. "If he is not an

honorable gentleman, he might resort to gossip if he ever learns your identity. Whether he is a nabob, a duke, or a laborer, we must hope that he is to be trusted."

"As a matter of fact," Beatrice said, "I have been a bit concerned about that. Besides worrying that every man I see might be him, I also have feared that he truly did recognize me and that now every man I see knows what I did with him. I *so* hope he is not one of those unscrupulous men who flaunts his conquests to the world."

"Like Lord Rochdale," Grace said, and gave a little shudder.

"Exactly. I would hate to endure what poor Serena Underwood went through. Rochdale's open acknowledgment of their affair, and then his public rejection of her, was worse than cruel."

"I think it best that we assume your maharaja did not know your identity, but that if he did, he is a trustworthy, honorable gentleman," Marianne said. "Unless and until we learn otherwise."

"And if he is," Penelope said, "and if you run him to earth again, by God you must keep him this time. Don't bolt like a green girl. Meet him as a woman, as a lover, and steal every moment you can. That is what our pact is all about—finding pleasure in a man's arms again, just because we want to."

"But with discretion," Grace said. "You must always be discreet and take care for your reputation."

"Of course, Grace. You must not worry that I will do anything to embarrass the Fund." Assuming she hadn't done so already, and that the fellow hadn't begun smearing her name in the betting books. "Besides, if I ever discover who he is, I haven't yet decided what I will do. It may come about that I do nothing."

Then again, if her body kept singing its sensuous

tune every time the stranger was mentioned, she might indeed have to do *something*.

"You are still determined to track her down?" Jeremy Burnett was ensconced comfortably in a large wing chair in Thayne's sitting room at Doncaster House, his lanky limbs sprawled in every direction.

"Of course," Thayne said from the depths of his own wing chair. "I intend to find her."

"In the name of your bridal quest?"

Thayne quirked a grin. "Not exactly. I had something else in mind."

He caught the brief flicker of interest in the eyes of Ramesh as he set out the hookah on a small table between the two wing chairs. The young valet had come with Thayne from India and was still trying to make sense of Western society. He had expressed some confusion about the relationships between English men and women, which seemed to him so much more complicated in their monogamy than the purdah and harems he was accustomed to in India.

"So you have two quests, then," Burnett said. "A bride and a . . ." He slanted a glance at Ramesh and smiled. "A bibi."

A glint of understanding lit Ramesh's dark eyes before he schooled them once again into the calm, disinterested manner of the invisible servant. He would understand the concept of the Indian bibi, which was what the British men in India called their native mistresses. Burnett, who'd spent the last seven years with Thayne in India, had used the term for Ramesh's benefit. But Thayne had no intention of setting up a separate household with a mistress and children, as was done with bibis in India. "No bibis," he said. "I just want to find the elusive Artemis and convince her to embark on a simple love affair. The bridal quest is another matter."

"But I thought you were committed to the plan?"

"I am. It was the bargain I made with my father when I turned twenty-one. He would allow me to indulge my passion for adventure and travel so long as I promised to return to England and take a bride before my thirtieth birthday. I am committed to honor that promise—I celebrate my birthday in December. I know my duty, but the whole business of selecting a bride is a daunting prospect. Especially as my mother has made it her business to trot out as many candidates as possible."

"Yes, mothers love that sort of thing."

"Especially mothers who are also duchesses," Thayne said. "They are determined that their successors are worthy of the title. In the end, it hardly matters what *I* want."

Ramesh wiped the hookah bowl with a clean cloth, then placed the tobacco in the bowl and slightly dampened it. He set the bowl aside and filled the base with water. It was a beautiful object, given to Thayne by a Hyderabad official, and made of the local bidri ware inlaid with silver. He watched as Ramesh handled it with care that was almost worshipful.

"Any promising candidates so far?" Burnett asked as he, too, kept an anxious eye on Ramesh's ministrations. The hookah was a guilty pleasure neither of the Englishmen had been willing to give up when they returned to London. It was too exotic to smoke in public, at their clubs, but here in Thayne's private apartments there was nothing to stop them.

"They are all pretty, well-bred girls," Thayne said, "but I have not yet singled out anyone in particular. But I will do so soon enough, I promise you."

"And the duchess? Has she a favorite?"

"She may have, for all I know, but I will not be manipulated. I will honor my promise to take a bride, and I know the sort of woman expected of me, but I will do my own choosing."

Ramesh finished filling the base of the hookah, then attached the silver neck, the bowl, and the smoking tube. He turned to the fireplace, where he'd set a small brazier on the flames, and removed a glowing coal with a pair of metal pincers. He placed the coal atop the tobacco in the bowl, allowed the tobacco to begin to smoke, covered it, and handed the amber mouthpiece to Thayne.

Thayne drew a few times on the pipe to ensure the tobacco was lit properly and the water in the base was bubbling, then drew in one long breath of cool, smooth smoke and exhaled with a sigh of pleasure. He much preferred the water-cooled hookah to cheroots or cigarillos, with their rough smoke that irritated the throat rather than soothed it. The hookah was only one of many aspects of Asian culture that Thayne found to be superior to European culture.

He placed the mouthpiece on the table for Burnett. He kept to the Indian etiquette, in which it was considered rude to pass a smoking tube hand to hand. Burnett picked it up and took a long draw.

"Will there be anything else, my lord Thayne?" Ramesh asked in the musical accents of Rajasthan.

"No, thank you, Ram. You may go."

The man made a crisp bow and left the room. Burnett smiled and said, "He's trying so hard to be a proper British gentleman's gentleman, is he not? Though he hasn't quite mastered the art of Western dress."

Ramesh continued to wear the loose trousers and long kurta he was accustomed to, but he generally topped it with one of Thayne's discarded waistcoats, the more elaborately embroidered the better. But when there was company, even someone as familiar as Jeremy Burnett, Ramesh donned a tailored British jacket. Even had he worn proper breeches and a starched linen neckcloth, his ubiquitous saffron-colored turban would always lend an exotic air.

"He does a fine job," Thayne said. "He always has. Can you even imagine that I could have left him behind?" He took another draw on the water pipe.

"Even had you done so, he would have followed."

Thayne shrugged and laid down the mouthpiece. "Yes, I believe he would have done, which is why I invited him to join me. He is an excellent valet. And where else would I find one who can prepare a hookah so expertly?"

Burnett gave a lazy chuckle. The smoke was affecting them both. They sank deeper into their chairs and conversation moved at a more desultory pace. Thayne closed his eyes and enjoyed the soft gurgle of bubbling water and the fragrant aroma that filled the room. Taking the hookah once a day was one of the few quiet moments Thayne could depend on amid the hustle and bustle of London at the height of the Season. There was nothing more relaxing than the smooth, aromatic, water-cooled smoke, and Ramesh made sure Thayne was not disturbed while he used the pipe. There was already enough gossip belowstairs about all the exotic objects to be found in Lord Thayne's apartments, not the least of which was his lordship's valet.

"So, the duke and duchess have been accommodating of all you brought back with you?"

Thayne took a long drag on the pipe and exhaled slowly. "Yes," he said at last, "for the most part. Mother would prefer it if I chose a valet from among the footmen, and she is not pleased about Chitra. But I introduced Father to the hookah, and he rather liked it. I may have to have one made for him."

Burnett took the mouthpiece and inhaled. A long moment later, he said, "The duchess will not be pleased that you are introducing His Grace to such exotic vices."

"I presented her with several bolts of Indian silk that pleased her exceedingly well, not to mention the pounds of tea and spices, so she can have no complaints."

"And what about your crates? How does she feel about all those statues? Have you unpacked them yet?"

"No, and I don't plan to until I move into the new town house."

"What new town house?"

"Didn't I mention it?" Thayne said. "I found a good house available in Cavendish Square. I don't choose to live here at Doncaster House with a new bride, though it's certainly large enough. I will inherit it eventually, of course, but not, God willing, for many years. I thought it best to have my own establishment here in town. I'd like my marchioness to be mistress of her own house."

"An excellent idea. When do you move in?"

"Don't know yet," Thayne said after another leisurely draw on the hookah. "There is quite a bit of work to be done. It's one of the older houses on the square and needs a fair amount of renovation. But I probably won't need it until next year, so there is enough time to have it done properly."

"Meaning you want it to be a suitable place to display your collections."

"That, among other more practical issues of leaking roofs and rotting plaster. There is, though, a fine gallery space for my statues." Thayne had collected a great many ancient stone sculptures of Hindu deities. He had developed a passion for the sensual lines and lush vitality of the carvings, and brought back enough pieces to fill a small museum.

"Your future marchioness had better not be too high a stickler, my friend. Some of those sculptures border on the erotic."

"If she wants to be my marchioness, then she will not object, for I will not tolerate it. I will be marrying out of duty, as will the young woman I choose for my bride. The right woman will understand her role as Marchioness of Thayne and future Duchess of Doncaster. She will be pleased enough with such rank and fortune that she will keep any objections to herself."

"Including objections to a certain Grecian goddess who might also share your bed? If you can find her, that is."

"Oh, I'll find her, you can be sure of it." His gaze traveled to the fireplace mantel where the tiny golden arrow lay as a reminder of his unknown huntress. He had not been able to stop thinking about her, about her leg wrapped around him and her hips moving in sensuous counterpoint to his own. He wanted her again, and was determined to have her. But first, he needed to discover who she was.

"But how will you recognize her if you didn't see her clearly? You're not even sure what color her hair is."

"I believe I will know her when we meet. I cannot explain how, but I think I might recognize her blue eyes. And I did catch the glimpse of a darkish eyebrow. At first I was convinced she was a blonde, but kept thinking I saw hints of darker hair beneath the powder. And it was beautifully waved. I suspect I am looking for a blue-eyed woman with wavy dark hair."

And there had been the way she moved. He was fairly sure he would recognize the sensuous sway of her hips and the supple grace of her arms. Yes, Thayne was quite sure he would recognize those arms again.

"In the meantime," he said, "I will keep the duchess happy by attending every possible *ton* event, allowing her to present me to any number of eligible young misses. And while I'm doing my duty, I will keep one eye on the watch for my Artemis. I shall find her, too. And if I can convince her to become my mistress, then yes, my marchioness will have to accept that situation, if she happens to learn of it. It is the way of things, after all."

Burnett chuckled. "You could build a zenana at the house on Cavendish Square."

"We are not in India anymore, my friend. I do not want a harem, but only one woman." One particular woman. And by God, he would find her.

Chapter 4

"And please try to be demure, Emily." Beatrice surveyed her niece from head to toe, fluffing her skirts, straightening the lace of her chemisette, adjusting the ribbons of her bonnet. "You look very pretty, my dear, but you sometimes put yourself too much forward. She is a duchess, you know. You must mind your place."

"Do stop fussing, Aunt Beatrice. I look perfectly splendid in this dress. And I do not put myself forward. I simply see no reason to pretend to be less than I am."

Beatrice loved her niece, but the girl was too much aware of her beauty. Emily was not yet eighteen but had none of the artlessness of youth. She was quite sure she was the prettiest girl in London, which was probably true. But she was still naive in ways she could not yet understand. Beatrice kept a sharp eye on her, for she was just the kind of headstrong girl to get into some sort of scrape through being over-confident. Emily was well aware that men admired her beauty, and she used it to keep a constant court of beaus at her feet. But she was not as sophisticated about men as she liked to believe. She was, in fact, completely innocent in that respect. Emily knew men wanted her, but Beatrice did not believe she had any idea what they wanted her for. As far as Emily was concerned, it was all about landing the best husband. The girl had no notion that a man might want her for anything but marriage.

"I hope the marquess will be there," Emily said as she examined herself in the hall mirror. "I have heard that he is actively looking for a bride this Season. And that he is quite handsome. Caroline Whittier caught a glimpse of him at the Douglas rout party and said so. It is most provoking that we have not yet seen him. But perhaps he has not been out and about much and I can still gain an advantage over the other girls by meeting him today. Indeed, I will be extremely vexed if he is not there."

"If he is there, you must promise me you will not flirt with him, Emily. It is not at all becoming in such a young girl."

"Fiddlesticks. If I find him pleasing, I shall try to entice his interest. Besides, I am the most sought-after girl of the Season. He could do no better than to offer for me."

He might do better to find a girl with less conceit, Beatrice thought. "Have a care, my dear. Such arrogance can be off-putting. And remember that most men would rather be the pursuer than be pursued."

"Oh, he will pursue me. You may be sure of it. Why should he be any different from every other man I've met this Season? The only thing is to make his acquaintance before he throws his cap at some other girl. So, let us be off."

Beatrice shook her head and wondered why she bothered at all to take the girl about and try to educate her in the fine points of negotiating Society. She didn't need a chaperone to tell her what to do. She knew exactly what she wanted and would go after it with a singular tenacity, whether her aunt approved or not.

It was a short drive to Park Lane and the weather was fine, so they took an open carriage. Beatrice

continued to prepare her niece, or try to prepare
her, for meeting a duchess and for behaving with
absolute propriety. Beatrice could not afford to have
the duchess displeased. Not today, when she was
on an important errand for the Benevolent Widows Fund.

"Remember, Emily, we are not going on a social
call. Not precisely. I am calling on the duchess simply to solicit the use of her ballroom for our last
charity ball of the Season. And I am only conde-
scending to bring you along because the duchess
could be a useful connection for you. Even if you
do not chance to meet her son, you could benefit
from future introductions once you have made her
acquaintance. So do, please, be on your best behavior."

Emily offered a bright, sweet smile and said, "Do
not worry. I know how important this visit is to you.
I will do nothing to embarrass you, I promise. After
all, I have you to thank for such an opportunity. If
Mama was my chaperone . . . well, I would never
have met a duchess, to be sure. You may count on
me to be a pattern card of good breeding and behavior."

Beatrice reached over and squeezed the girl's hand.
She was fretting over nothing. Emily's beauty would
always give her a social advantage, and she could be
perfectly charming when she wanted to be. Especially when she remembered what the Season might
have been like with her mother at her heels. Ophelia
could be something of a trial at the best of times.
Emily had never said as much, but Beatrice had no
doubt the girl worried that her mother's sometimes
strident and impetuous nature could be an embarrassment to her, and might even drive away suitors.

To make matters worse, Ophelia had recently become more shrill and demanding than usual. Emily

believed it to be no more than the frustration and confinement of having a broken leg, which would put anyone in bad spirits, and she seemed pleased to be away from her mother's contrariness at this crucial time.

"Poor Mama," she said time and again. "We must be sure not to put a strain on her nerves. She needs her rest."

These pronouncements were more frequent and heartfelt after a visit to her inquisitive mother, who regularly threatened to leave her couch and take over the supervision of Emily's Season when she thought matters were not progressing fast enough. Beatrice could well imagine that the very last thing Emily wanted was her surly, temporarily crippled mother escorting her about town.

In fact, Beatrice knew there was more involved in Ophelia's recent mood than the frustration of a broken leg. The truth was that Ophelia was desperate for Emily to marry a fortune. Her own lavish spending was compounded by a penchant for gambling and her debts had finally reached epic proportions. Sir Albert Thirkill, Ophelia's husband, was so far unaware of the impending crisis. He kept away from London, busying himself with an archaeological excavation on his Suffolk property. Something of a head-in-the-clouds scholar, he cared nothing for Society and allowed his wife to do as she pleased. But he would not be so complaisant if he was forced to mortgage his beloved estate.

"He will throw me out on my ear," Ophelia had wailed, "leaving me to my own devices. He will divorce me, mark my words."

"Albert will not divorce you," Beatrice had said, "and he is too kind a gentleman to beat you, no matter how much you deserve it."

"You will not be so glib, Sister, when he sends me

packing and files for a separation. I will be forced to rely on your charity, and move into your house as a poor relation."

"Dear God." The very idea had given Beatrice palpitations of the heart.

Ophelia had heaved a dramatic sigh. "I suppose I could be a governess to your girls. Once I am able to move about again." Her voice had dripped with tones of pathos.

There had been a great deal of hand-wringing, teeth gnashing, and theatrical swooning. But Beatrice knew her sister's melodramatic moods all too well. "We have a perfectly good governess, Ophelia, and you will move into my house only over my dead body."

"Then you must *help* me. You must find a rich husband for Emily."

Not entirely confident that Ophelia was bluffing about moving in with her, Beatrice had taken on the task of chaperoning Emily. And if she was ever in danger of forgetting her sister's threat, the notes Ophelia sent round several times a week never failed to remind her. It had not been for Emily's sake alone that Beatrice had taken her to all the best parties and introduced her to all the best people, including a good many eligible—that is to say, rich—young men.

Beatrice would not have been surprised to discover that her sister had deliberately fallen from her horse just so that Emily could take advantage of Beatrice's connections. The girl had no notion of the state of her family's circumstances and simply believed Ophelia's ambitions for her were the natural dreams of a fond parent, and Beatrice would never disabuse her of that notion. Besides, Emily had more than her own share of ambition and did not need her mother to tell her where to toss her cap.

Even so, Beatrice hoped the young marquess would make an appearance today. He would satisfy everyone's ambitions. He had arrived in London only recently and was already a major topic of conversation and gossip among the other dowagers and chaperones and guardians who were firing off young girls into the marriage mart. The marquess promised to be the catch of the Season. It was not clear to Beatrice where he had been that his return was so heralded, but there were whispers of diplomatic missions abroad. An air of mystery added to the appeal of his rank and title.

"I know you will behave very prettily, my dear," she said. "You must forgive me for being such a fusspot, but I barely know the duchess and want this meeting to go well."

"I know, Aunt Beatrice. Don't worry."

"And if you aspire to be a duchess yourself one day," Beatrice said, "assuming you bring the young marquess up to scratch, then I recommend that you pay close attention today. A grand ducal mansion is much larger than what you are accustomed to, and the running of it requires a very large staff. The mistress of such a house will have a great deal of responsibility, so take note of how the duchess behaves."

"Yes, ma'am, I will."

They were met at the grand gateway to the house by a porter, to whom the coachman gave Beatrice's name. After checking his list of expected visitors, the porter opened the ornate entry gates to allow the carriage to drive through to the large courtyard. By the time they reached the main entrance, the doors were already opened, and a stately butler and a liveried footman stood ready to receive them.

Beatrice and Emily were handed down from the carriage by the footman, and led inside by the butler. They walked into a large, elegant entry hall with a painted ceiling and a marble floor laid out in a geometric pattern. Two housemaids stepped forward and bobbed curtsies. Emily was helped out of her pelisse. Beatrice, however, did not relinquish her short spencer jacket, for the jaconet muslin dress she wore, with the double frill of Vandyke lace at the throat, did not look half as well without it. Both ladies removed their bonnets. Emily's bright curls framed her face charmingly, though she fluffed them a bit to make sure. Beatrice wore a cap beneath her bonnet, as all women of a certain age did, but it was a cunning little quartered foundling cap of lace with a silk flower pinned to one side. Just because she was long past her youth there was no excuse to be unfashionable. She smiled at Emily. They both looked fine enough to meet a duchess.

The butler led them through an arched colonnade of white veined marble, and up the grand staircase. Enormous portraits of the current duke and duchess met them at the landing; then twin staircases, equally grand, completed the ascent to the first floor.

Beatrice had been inside most of the important ducal mansions in London, but never this one. Its reputation as the grandest of them all was not unwarranted. It was a magnificent, palatial building that almost took one's breath away.

She looked at Emily and smiled. If things went well, this might all be hers one day. Mistress of all this grandeur. Her niece, a duchess! Beatrice's heart gave a little flutter of excitement at the possibility. What a coup that would be. Ophelia would probably drive Sir Albert into tossing her out just so she could move in here.

A footman stood guard at a pair of paneled mahogany doors polished to a high gleam. At a nod from the butler, he opened them to reveal a large saloon or sitting room. A tray-shaped coffered ceiling rose up at least forty feet above them, each coffer set apart with richly gilded molding and painted with classical figures. Gilt also decorated the ornate moldings around the windows and doors and fireplace.

The draperies and the furniture—which was elegant, expensive, and very much in the French taste—were done in shades of crimson. Sunlight poured into the room from windows that reached the ceiling, and enormous mirrors were placed between the windows. The room was filled with light, and though impressively grand in scale, it was also warm and inviting.

"Lady Somerfield, Your Grace," the butler announced. "And Miss Emily Thirkill."

The duchess rose from a small writing desk and smiled. Beatrice guessed that she was in her late sixties, based on the ages of her children, but she looked at least a decade younger. She was slender and elegant, with a crown of thick hair that was more silver than brown. Her face was not unlined, but the fine bones of cheek and jaw gave it a timeless beauty.

Beatrice made a deep curtsy and was pleased to note that Emily's was even deeper.

"Good afternoon, Lady Somerfield. How nice to see you again. And Miss Thirkill?"

"My niece, Your Grace. I am chaperoning her this Season for my sister and her husband, Sir Albert and Lady Thirkill. I hope you do not mind that I brought her along."

The duchess smiled at Emily, who, for once, actually did look demure. "Of course I do not mind. I am pleased to meet you, my dear. Charming," she said as she surveyed Emily from head to toe. "Quite charming." She gave a signal to the butler, who nodded and departed with a crisp bow. "Please sit down." She gestured toward two crimson-upholstered armchairs.

Beatrice and Emily took their seats and straightened their skirts. The duchess, quite obviously struck by Emily's exceptional looks, could not seem to take her eyes off the girl, who was quite aware of Her Grace's scrutiny and sat up straight and tall.

"I trust you are making the best of the warm weather," the duchess said. And several minutes of polite, inconsequential conversation about the weather and their good health followed.

A pair of housemaids was soon ushered into the room by a footman. One was carrying a tea service, the other a tray of dishes piled with a variety of sweetmeats and biscuits. The footman brought a tea table from a corner of the room and placed it in front of the duchess. The service was arranged with precision on the table, and another footman came in with a large silver urn on a stand and set it beside the duchess so she could easily refill the teapot with hot water.

She poured out cups of tea for each of them. One of the maids delivered their cups while the other passed around the dishes of sweets and biscuits. The duchess spoke a soft word to one of the footmen, who nodded and followed the rest of the staff out of the room.

"Now, then," the duchess said, "you wish to make use of our ballroom, I understand?"

"If it would please Your Grace," Beatrice said. "The Benevolent Widows Fund trustees have asked me to inquire if you would allow us to hold our last ball of the Season here. We understand you have a rather large ballroom."

"It was the Great Drawing Room at one time," the duchess said, "but the furniture was removed so often for balls that we decided to convert it permanently into a ballroom. There are several other drawing rooms, so it was no sacrifice to transform the largest of them. We have four daughters, you know, and when they were younger, one of them was always wanting us to host a ball for her."

Beatrice took a sip of tea and smiled. "I have two young daughters myself," she said, "and already they talk about the balls they will be wanting in a few years. They are certain to keep me busy."

The duchess nodded. "If they are anything like my girls, they will. But it is a great pleasure to fire off one's daughters into Society. And you are getting early practice this Season with your charming niece." She turned to Emily. "Are you enjoying your Season, my dear?"

"Yes, Your Grace," Emily said, "very much so. Thanks to my aunt, who takes me to all the best parties and balls."

The duchess smiled. "And a pretty girl like you never sits out a dance, I'll wager."

Emily lowered her eyes in a look so demure, so meek and modest, that Beatrice had to bite back a smile. If she didn't find a proper match for the girl, there was always the stage.

"Thank you, Your Grace," Emily said. "I have been very fortunate to dance so often. I enjoy dancing. Especially at my aunt's charity balls, which are the best of them all."

Well, bless her little thespian heart. It truly was difficult not to be charmed by the girl.

"Yes, the Widows Fund balls are quite popular," the duchess said, "and support a very good cause."

"The response to our balls has been most gratifying," Beatrice said. "We raise enough money to support a large facility where war widows and their children may stay while the staff helps them find respectable employment and permanent housing. We have been privileged to assist a great many women in getting back on their feet again. But this war makes more widows every day, and many of them are left with little or nothing. And so we continue to raise money for their support. We trustees are all widows ourselves, you see, but more fortunate in our circumstances. It seems only right that we should reach out to help women who don't have our advantages to recover from such a loss."

"You are to be commended for stepping up and doing what the government ought to be doing," the duchess said. "But the country is run by men, and they really have no idea how their wars affect the lives of women, do they? Your balls do a great service, Lady Somerfield. Of course you may use our ballroom. I am honored that you thought of it."

Beatrice gave a quiet sigh of relief. She had hoped the duchess would agree, but one could never be certain about such things. "Thank you so much, Your Grace. You are most kind. You cannot imagine how much this means to us. If your ballroom is large enough, we may be able to increase our number of invitations and therefore raise even more money."

"It is my pleasure," the duchess said. "When we finish our tea, I will take you to see the room, and you may judge for yourself how many invitations to send."

"The last charity ball of the Season has typically been a masquerade ball," Beatrice said. "Do you have any objections to a costume ball?"

The duchess smiled and her eyes twinkled with pleasure. "None at all. I haven't attended a masquerade in years. I look forward to it. I will even try to talk Doncaster into wearing his infamous Cardinal Wolsey costume. If he does, I shall dress as a nun." She threw her head back and laughed.

"What has you so amused, Your Grace?"

Beatrice looked toward the door to see three gentlemen enter. The speaker was the duke himself, a stately, still-handsome gentleman with a thick shock of bright silver hair. The other two men were much younger. One was tall and thin with light brown hair and twinkling gray eyes that found Emily and stared.

The broader, dark-haired gentleman had something of the duke's look about him as well as the noble bearing. Surely he was the marquess.

"Really, Doncaster. Must you barge in on our tea?" the duchess said, trying to look stern, though amusement lit her eyes.

"You must forgive me, Your Grace," the duke said as he approached his wife. "We could not resist the sound of your laughter. If you will share your amusement, we shall pay our respects to your guests and be off." He bent down to kiss his wife's outstretched hand.

The duchess wrinkled her nose. "Ack. You've been smoking with Thayne again. That horrid hubble-bubble thing."

"Yes, we've all three had a nice smoke," the duke said, and grinned at his wife. "Perfectly marvelous thing, the hookah."

"Perfectly horrid, if you ask me."

"I'm sorry, Mother." The dark-haired gentleman spoke. He stood ramrod straight, his shoulders thrown back in an almost military stance. Unlike the duke's, his countenance was dour, as rigid as his posture. "Perhaps we should leave you to your guests."

So he *was* the marquess, as she'd guessed. He was extremely good-looking, with dark hair and dark eyes. Why did it seem that every gentleman Beatrice met these days had that same coloring? She studied him for a moment, searching for signs of a certain maharaja. There were similarities in build and coloring, but the marquess was certainly not her unknown lover. There was too much cool reserve about him to have been her warm, seductive maharaja. And thank goodness. She could only imagine the awkwardness of pushing her niece into the arms of her secret lover. The very idea made her shudder.

"No," the duchess said, "as long as you are here you must all stay a while and give us your company. Come, let me make my guests known to you."

"I am already acquainted with Lady Somerfield, of course," the duke said. "It is good to see you again, madam."

Beatrice exchanged a few pleasantries with the duke. They'd met only once before, but he was one of those men steeped in social graces, who made a point of remembering personal details about every acquaintance. He asked about her charity work and about her daughters.

"But you have not met Lady Somerfield's niece," the duchess said, steering her husband toward Emily. "This is Miss Emily Thirkill."

Emily curtsied prettily and offered a fetching smile. Beatrice had to give the girl credit for not cowering or stammering in the face of so formidable a peer. The confidence born of extreme beauty served her well in such situations. She stood straight and proud, and looked the duke squarely in the eye as she responded in a clear voice to his questions about her Season.

Emily was no fool. She knew she had to win the approval of the duke and duchess if there was ever to be any hope of winning their son. Within minutes, she had the duke smitten. He never dropped his regal demeanor, but the tiniest gleam in his eye signaled his appreciation.

Well done, Emily.

"And this is my son," the duchess said, drawing that gentleman forward. "Lord Thayne, and his friend Mr. Burnett."

The Marquess of Thayne wore patrician detachment like a cloak, never cracking a smile as the duchess made introductions. He kept his hands behind his back and made a crisp bow to Beatrice. His dark eyes studied her for a moment, then moved on to

Emily. Beatrice experienced a sharp twinge of heat, as his eyes had looked into hers so intently. But it had been the same with other dark-eyed, dark-haired men lately. Damn that maharaja for making her so aware of—what? Male potency? Was she doomed to imagine secret couplings with every dark-haired man she met, even one as cool and distant as the marquess? Once again, she cursed herself for bringing on this confusion through one irrational moment in an unlit garden on a moonless night. Despite the encouragement of her friends, she regretted that encounter more with each passing day, and was now determined to put it behind her and concentrate on the delicate business of securing a rich husband for her niece.

She watched as the marquess made his bow to Emily, who tilted her head at a flattering angle and gave him her most dazzling smile, the same smile that had captured the heart of almost every man in London, or so it seemed. But so far, she had not allowed her own heart to be captured. She was holding out for the perfect match, which meant rank, fortune, and good looks, in that order.

Who better to meet Emily's ambitions than this handsome marquess?

But the gentleman seemed unaffected by Emily's charms. He acknowledged her with the cool arrogance of the true aristocrat. Emily would have to work hard to crack his shell. Beatrice hoped he wasn't the priggish sort who looked down his noble nose at the rest of the world. Did she really want Emily to align herself with such a cold fish? When she thought of how warm certain men could be—a certain man in particular—Beatrice wondered why anyone would give a second thought to a man like the Marquess of Thayne.

The long-limbed Mr. Burnett was quite the opposite of his friend. Boyishly charming with an open and friendly countenance, he quite won over Beatrice with his lopsided smile. She liked him at once. He tried to keep from staring at Emily, but his gaze was drawn to her like a lodestone.

"And will you finally tell us, my dear," the duke said, "what Lady Somerfield or Miss Thirkill has said to make you laugh so?"

"Lady Somerfield's charity is going to use Doncaster House for a ball," the duchess said. "It is to be a masquerade ball, and I was just musing over what we should wear. I believe we should unearth your Cardinal Wolsey costume."

The duke gave a bark of laughter. "A splendid idea!" He turned to Beatrice. "Her Grace knows how much I enjoy parading about as the old scoundrel, with a red cap on my head and a ridiculously heavy gold chain across my chest." Returning his twinkling gaze to his duchess, he asked, "And who shall you be, my dear?"

"I won't tell you," she said. "But I promise it will be an appropriate complement to your cardinal. Oh, this will be great fun, Lady Somerfield. Will it not, Thayne?"

"A masquerade?" His brow furrowed and an odd expression crossed his face for an instant, and then was gone. "Yes, of course. How delightful." His tone and stony aspect, however, did not evidence delight.

Beatrice tried not to scowl at the provoking man. Must he be so stiff and reserved? Emily didn't seem to mind. She continued to smile and preen, trying to attract his attention. His rank and fortune and good looks were enough for her, it seemed. It didn't matter that the man might be a haughty prig or a stern autocrat. It mattered to Beatrice, though. She knew firsthand what it meant to be married to an intractable husband. She hoped for more warmth and affection in her niece's marriage, and the marquess, at first acquaintance anyway, did not seem to be the man to provide it.

And yet, how contrary was it that such an aloof man could send a little flutter of heat low in her belly when he looked at her? Beatrice really had to rein in these absurd fancies and inappropriate physical reactions.

Damn that maharaja for awakening her sexual desire. It would surely be the death of her.

Chapter 5

It was not enough, apparently, that Thayne be introduced to young women at appropriate social occasions. Now his mother was bringing them home to meet him.

Miss Thirkill was certainly pretty enough to capture any man's attention, though she did seem to be rather too aware of her beauty. The duchess would have approved her connections before parading her before him, so he did not question her breeding. Her aunt was a countess, after all. And the girl had pretty manners, even if she was a bit forward. But Thayne knew he was seen as a good catch, so he could hardly fault a young woman for trying to draw his attention.

The aunt was an attractive woman, and as he did with all attractive women, he examined her for hints of Artemis. Lady Somerfield had blue eyes, but so did more than half the female population of London. Her hair was a rich shade of red and pulled back sleek and straight beneath a lace cap that was more stylish than matronly. It was lovely hair, but not the wavy brown he'd been seeking. Besides, she sat stiff-backed and prim as a governess, without a hint of sensuality. And she had the air of a fierce mother hen guarding her chick. It took only a moment to dismiss her as a potential Artemis.

He glanced again at Miss Thirkill, who lowered her eyes demurely, then slowly raised her lids halfway to gaze at him through the screen of long lashes. The girl was a flirt, by God. Intriguing.

She was more than merely pretty. She was, in fact, quite stunningly beautiful, with a heart-shaped face, guinea gold hair, a perfect complexion, a Cupid's bow mouth, and large blue eyes set off by darker lashes and brows. And she was well aware of her beauty. Every glance and gesture invited him to admire it.

And he did, in a dispassionate sort of way. She was too young to truly interest him as a person. But he did consider how she would look on his arm, and how handsome their children might be.

Burnett, on the other hand, appeared thoroughly moonstruck. Although friendly and charming as ever when addressed, he remained a step behind Thayne, not putting himself forward in any way. He knew Miss Thirkill was there for Thayne's inspection. If Thayne had known his mother's summons had been for the purpose of meeting a young lady, he might not have dragged Burnett and the duke with him. But they had been enjoying a hookah together and it had seemed quite natural for all of them to wait upon the duchess.

Thayne hated these introductions. He hated the whole ordeal of finding a wife among the Season's latest crop of young women. He had to don his best lordly manner, to demonstrate pride and arrogance appropriate to his position, for the young women and their mother hens were interested in the marquess, heir to a dukedom, and he must act the part. It was not an unnatural or a difficult role, to be sure. He was born to it. A certain level of arrogance and entitlement had been bred in him from infancy. But he'd discarded some of it the past eight years during his travels, and he was somewhat out of practice at playing The Marquess. He made the effort for his parents, who expected him to do his duty.

He glanced again at his mother's latest candidate. Yes, Miss Thirkill was definitely worth serious consideration. Assuming she did not turn out to be a complete ninny. He did not expect, or even want, a bluestocking for a wife. But he did expect a certain degree of conversation. He could not abide a silly woman.

He listened politely as the duchess continued to speak about the masquerade ball. The topic was one he would rather avoid, as it brought to mind images of yellow silk and powdered hair and uninhibited desire. Thayne made an effort to bank the heat brought on by such recollections. It would not do to embarrass himself in his mother's drawing room. He glanced at Lady Somerfield while his mother chattered on about costume possibilities for her and the duke, and about memorable masquerades from her youth. The countess kept her eyes on the teacup she held, but a slight frown furrowed her brow as though she, too, was remembering a masquerade, but much less fondly than the duchess.

His mother rose and said, "Perhaps we should show you the ballroom now, Lady Somerfield."

In a perfectly orchestrated maneuver, the duchess walked ahead with Burnett, and the duke walked alongside Lady Somerfield, leaving Thayne to escort Miss Thirkill.

"It is very kind of your mother," the girl said, "to allow my aunt and her friends to use the ballroom."

"I am sure she is pleased to oblige." He did not offer his arm, but walked with his hands clasped behind his back and kept his eyes straight ahead.

"I will have to have a new costume made, of course," she said. "Everyone has seen the pink shepherdess costume I wore at the last masquerade I attended. What costume do you think I ought to wear?"

"I am sure I do not know. Whatever pleases you."

"And what would please *you*, Lord Thayne?"

By Jove, she was a determined little flirt. "I am sure whatever you choose will be very pretty. Wear whatever you like, Miss Thirkill."

Out of the corner of his eye he saw her give a little shrug. "You are right," she said. "It really doesn't matter. The effect will be the same regardless of my costume." She gave a resigned sigh. "I don't mean to draw attention, but I always seem to find myself surrounded by gentlemen. I suppose I should be pleased to be so popular, but it really is a trial at times."

What a cunning little vixen. Did she really think his interest would be piqued by knowing that she was pursued by other men? Or was she trying to inspire a spirit of competition?

"I understand you are staying with your aunt for the Season."

"Yes, I am," she said in a bright tone. "She has been acting as my chaperone since Mother was injured in an accident and could not take me about herself."

"An accident? How dreadful. I trust it is not too serious an injury, and that she is recovering."

Miss Thirkill leaned toward him and lowered her voice. "She fell off a horse and broke her leg!"

She seemed to find her mother's misfortune amusing, as she began to laugh. It was a musical laugh, similar to one he remembered hearing on a dark night in a particular garden. Was he destined to be reminded of that sweet interlude at every turn? By every laugh and every pair of blue eyes, even when they belonged to an innocent who could not possibly have been his Artemis?

He steeled himself against the memory by employing his best Marquess of Thayne manner—polite, but haughty and formal. "I am glad it is nothing more serious," he said. "And how fortunate that you were not forced to postpone your Season, that Lord and Lady Somerfield were able to take you in."

"Oh, but there is no Lord Somerfield," she said. "I mean, there *is*, but he is not my uncle. The previous earl, my uncle Somerfield, died several years ago. Didn't you know? I thought everyone knew my aunt is a widow. She is, after all, a trustee of the Benevolent Widows Fund, the charity supported by the ball she wants to hold here at Doncaster House."

So the aunt was a widow. Not that it mattered, but he cast a glance in her direction as she walked ahead with his father. A certain sway of hip gave him pause for an instant, sent a brief jolt of fire through his loins, but only because it reminded him of another pair of hips that swayed in a similar manner.

Damnation. He had no business lusting after Miss Thirkill's chaperone. He could not go on much longer without finding his Artemis. She had stirred him in a way he hadn't been able to forget, and he saw hints of her in every pair of blue eyes, in every graceful arm, in every sinuous hip. He wanted Artemis and still meant to find her, and yet here he was wanting, even for an instant, someone else who only vaguely reminded him of her. He did not have the time for such distractions. He had other matters of more pressing urgency. He had to settle on a bride.

For all he knew, she could be walking beside him at that very moment.

The duke peppered Beatrice with questions as they made their way to the ballroom. He was obviously trying to discover if Emily would be a suitable bride for his son. His interest was gratifying. Beatrice provided all the points in Emily's favor, avoiding any mention of her mother's debts and sometimes rash behavior. Emily's extraordinary beauty was a significant asset, but breeding and connections were more important to a duke. One would expect the heir to a dukedom to marry much higher than a baronet's daughter, but His Grace seemed enchanted enough with Emily to pursue the matter. Thankfully, he was unacquainted with Ophelia. But he showed a keen interest in Sir Albert.

"Something of an archaeologist, is he not?"

"Indeed, Your Grace, an avid amateur."

"I do believe I have read an article or two by him. Am I thinking of the right man? Articles on Roman antiquities found in Britain?"

"Yes, that's Sir Albert. In fact, he was unable to come to town because of an excavation he is supervising. He found the remains of a Roman mosaic floor on his property in Suffolk."

"Did he? How exciting for him."

"Yes, you may imagine how thrilled he is. The delights of the London Season cannot compare with such a find."

The duke smiled. "I should think not. I spent some time in Rome when I was a young pup on my grand tour, and I quite fell in love with ancient ruins. I trust I shall have an opportunity to meet Thirkill, and his lady, one day soon."

Beatrice smiled. The duke seemed satisfied with Emily's background, despite the lack of blue blood in her family tree. Perhaps it was sufficient that her late uncle Somerfield had been an earl and her grandfather, Beatrice's father, had been a viscount. If the duke approved of Emily, and he certainly appeared to do so, then his opinion would surely carry some weight with the marquess. This excursion to Doncaster House was turning out to be more successful than Beatrice could ever have dreamed.

If only Lord Thayne were not so rigid and unapproachable. She could not imagine a girl of Emily's temperament being happy with such a man. But perhaps she was being unfair. She'd only known the marquess for a few minutes and was no doubt rushing to judgment. There might be more to the man than met the eye. She must get to know him.

"Here we are," the duchess announced, as a liveried footman—there seemed to be an army of them—opened the door to the ballroom.

For a brief moment, Beatrice forgot her concerns about the marquess. The room was magnificent, surely the largest and most imposing of all that had ever hosted a Widows Fund ball. The ceiling coved to a great height, and was elaborately coffered and gilded, with plaster medallions in the four corners. The long central compartment of the ceiling held three large, slightly concave circles that gave the appearance of shallow domes. Enormous crystal chandeliers hung from each of them.

The glint of gold was everywhere: on the coffered ceiling and the floral frieze below it, the overdoor pediments festooned with garlands of fruit and flowers, the ornate gilt frames of a set of enormous mirrors that lined two walls and made the room appear even larger. The fireplace, of white marble, was topped with a carved and gilded panel depicting the Three Graces that reached the edge of the ceiling frieze.

The only furniture in the room was a group of very fine chairs in the French style, upholstered in gold brocade, that had been placed along the walls.

"Well, what do you think?" the duchess said. "Will it do?"

"It is surely one of the most beautiful rooms I have ever seen," Beatrice said. "The ceiling quite takes my breath away."

Her Grace beamed with pride. "Yes, the ceiling

is one of the treasures of the house. We added the chandeliers when we converted it to a ballroom."

The duke also puffed up a bit, equally proud of the room. "I am not sure how the second duke, who built the house, would have felt about them," he said, "but I think the chandeliers look rather splendid."

"They do indeed." Beatrice turned in a circle and gazed all around her. "They must look especially beautiful when fully lit and reflected in the mirrors. Oh, this is marvelous. Perfectly marvelous. You are so kind to lend it to us for one night. It will surely be our grandest ball ever."

"We will do our best to make it so," the duchess said. "And you, Miss Thirkill? Do you like the room, as well?"

Emily was staring up at the ceiling with an awestruck smile on her face. No doubt she was imagining one day being the mistress of such splendor. Beatrice did not blame her. Who cared about the man when there was all this?

"My goodness," Emily said in a breathless voice, "it is quite spectacular, is it not? I don't think I've ever seen anything so wonderful. Everywhere you look, there is some perfect detail. What do the medallions represent?"

The duchess smiled and took Emily's arm. "They are various scenes from Greek mythology. Let me show you."

The duke joined them, as did Mr. Burnett, but Beatrice held back and stood beside the marquess. She was determined to discover what sort of man came with the spectacular house. Who lurked beneath that regal presence?

"You must have missed all this," she said.

"I beg your pardon?" He actually glared down his nose at her.

Beatrice was tall, for a woman, and though he had several inches on her, he did not tower over her. But the upward tilt of his chin gave the impression of greater height. She suspected he would have appeared tall even if he were a head shorter than she. It was all a matter of bearing. That aristocratic carriage.

Perhaps he was simply accustomed to people kowtowing to him. How would he react to someone who did not?

"I understand," she said in a breezy voice, "that you have been away for quite some time, Lord Thayne."

"That is correct." His tone was clipped, almost brusque. "I have been out of the country for the last eight years."

"Eight years?" It was no wonder he was such a novelty this Season. He had not been seen in all that time. Had he come home to marry? And if so, would he put roots in English soil or gad about the globe all his life? "My goodness, such a long time. I cannot imagine being away from home for so many years. Were you traveling for pleasure, or perhaps on government business?"

His eyes narrowed slightly as he continued to look down at her. "A bit of both."

She bit back a groan. Clearly he was not going to be forthcoming with details. What an odiously taciturn man. "It must have been interesting to see different countries. I should love to travel, I think. I have never been beyond our borders, I'm afraid. Unless one counts Scotland as a foreign country, which, of course, it often seems to be. Especially the farther north one travels. The Highland accent can sometimes sound like a foreign language. What parts of the world did you visit?"

"India, mostly. And the Punjab, Persia, Afghanistan, Java, Burma. Central and South Asia for the most part."

"Heavens, how exotic! It must have been fascinating."

"Yes."

"But after such a long time away, it must feel good to be back on sturdy English soil. And to be back in this grand house."

"Yes, it is good to be home."

"Do you plan to settle in England now?"

He arched a dark eyebrow. He did not misunderstand her probing. "I hope I have the opportunity to travel again one day. But yes, I plan to stay in England and . . . settle."

"Do you have a home of your own, Lord Thayne, or will you continue to reside here at Doncaster House?"

The other dark eyebrow lifted to join the first. "So many questions, Lady Somerfield."

And so few answers.

"Forgive me, my lord. I do not mean to be impertinent. But I am . . . interested in such things, you understand."

His eyes glinted with the faintest hint of amusement. "I do understand. You are a doting aunt to Miss Thirkill, I believe."

Beatrice felt her cheeks heat with a blush. She really was being an impertinent busybody. But it was worth it just to see that tiny crack in his reserve.

"But I shall tell you what you wish to know," he said. "I have an estate of my own in Northamptonshire. It is not quite as grand as the ducal seat at Hadbury Park, but large enough. And I have purchased a town house on Cavendish Square, which is in the process of renovation. I have fortune enough to support both houses . . . and a family. I plan to take my role in Lords seriously and hope one day to have an official position in foreign affairs. I collect art, primarily sculpture. And I enjoy hunting and shooting. There. Now you know all there is to know about me. Do I pass inspection?"

Beatrice smiled. "I shall have to get to know you better before I can say."

"I look forward to it." His gaze became more intense, and Beatrice felt her knees go weak. She had to look away. She did not want him to misunderstand. It was not for herself she asked all those questions.

"But on first meeting," she said, not daring to look at him, "it seems you have led a full life and have an impressive future ahead. Now, let me see what the duke is telling my niece about the ceiling."

Thayne watched her walk away and wondered what had just happened between them. He was bewildered by his reaction to her. His thoroughly sexual reaction. She was a striking looking woman, to be sure, with the palest alabaster skin set off by hair the color of a Titian Madonna. But she had not been flirting with him. He was quite sure she was not. She was merely a tenacious chaperone looking to him as a suitor for her niece.

He'd faced many a hopeful chaperone already this Season, but none who'd made his blood run warm.

This would not do. He should be paying more attention to the beautiful Miss Thirkill, who already appeared to have the duke wrapped around her pretty little finger. Lady Somerfield engaged his mother in a discussion about the ball—a masquerade, of all things!—and how to set up the room, while her niece laughed delightedly at something his father was telling her. They were all of them conspiring to set her up as his future marchioness. He supposed he ought to feel apprehensive, that the situation had spun out of his control, but he did not. Not yet. He had no objections to the girl, after all.

But as he watched the four of them, his eye was more often drawn to her aunt.

Burnett had strolled over to join him and now stood at Thayne's side.

"Well, what do you think?" he asked in a low whisper. His eyes never left Miss Thirkill. "I do believe the duchess has come through with a winner. Have you ever seen such a pretty girl?"

Thayne followed his gaze. "She is very beautiful, to be sure. She knows it, too."

"How could she not? She must surely look into a mirror now and then. You do not like her? You think she is too self-assured?"

"No, she is quite charming."

"She can't help being beautiful, Thayne. Such good looks must surely give her a degree of confidence other young women may lack."

"Yes, and I think that is why the duke and duchess are so taken with her. She has the poise and confidence that suits a marchioness and future duchess."

"She has thoroughly seduced them both," Burnett said as he watched her. "They will be wanting an announcement soon."

"They will have to wait. I am not ready to commit myself to any young woman until I know her better." Thayne chuckled at the recollection of similar words from her aunt. "Lady Somerfield must agree. She quizzed me like a schoolmaster."

"Did she? I would think your rank and fortune speak for themselves. What else does a hopeful mama, or aunt, need to know?"

"I got the impression she was taking my measure, trying to determine what sort of man I am. She was almost impertinent. But I . . . I like her. It is somehow refreshing to think that she cares for more than my rank and fortune."

At that moment, Miss Thirkill looked in their direction and smiled. She turned to speak to her aunt, who nodded, and then came tripping across the room to join them.

"Lord Thayne," she said, bringing the full force of her smile on him, "I simply won't take no for an answer."

"To what question, Miss Thirkill?"

"To an invitation. My aunt is hosting a barge party on Thursday. We are going to sail—or whatever a barge does; they have no sails, do they?—down the Thames while having a leisurely breakfast. We're going to Kew, to walk around the gardens a bit. You must join us, Lord Thayne, you simply must. It will be great fun, I assure you."

"It sounds delightful," Thayne said. "I shall be pleased to join Lady Somerfield's party."

Miss Thirkill clapped her hands together. "Excellent! Oh, and you must come, too, Mr. Burnett. If you are free."

"As a bird, Miss Thirkill," Burnett said, "as a bird. It sounds marvelous. I wouldn't miss it."

"That's settled, then," she said. "We gather at the Palace Yard Stairs near Westminster Bridge at one o'clock on Thursday. I look forward to introducing you to some of my friends, Lord Thayne."

"As do I, Miss Thirkill."

"Of course, many of us will be at Lady Wedmore's rout party tonight. Will you be attending, as well?"

"Yes, I have accepted Lady Wedmore's invitation. As did Mr. Burnett. We have planned to attend together."

"Excellent! Perhaps I will see you there. I hope so. I believe we shall be arriving close to eleven o'clock. Who knows how long it will take us to reach the door, of course? It's bound to be a mad crush."

Thayne took her message. Guests arrived and left

at all hours at a rout because one never stayed very long. If he wanted to see Miss Thirkill, or honor her obvious wish to see him, then he now knew when to arrive.

Miss Thirkill returned to her aunt's side, and the two ladies departed a few minutes later, with Burnett tagging close behind.

And so it begins, Thayne mused as he watched them go. That young woman would publicly attach herself to him as early as that evening. Their names would begin to be linked. Soon enough, there would be expectations of a match. It was all happening rather more quickly than he'd expected, but perhaps that was for the best. He would satisfy his bargain with the duke by marrying the most beautiful girl in London.

"By God, what a beauty!" his father exclaimed when they'd returned to the red drawing room. "What an excellent mother you have, my boy, to find such a delightful young woman for you."

"I did not find her," the duchess said as she arranged herself in her favorite chair. "I never laid eyes on the girl before today. She came along to keep her aunt company while we discussed plans for the charity ball."

"I think the countess is more shrewd than that," the duke said. "She knew precisely what she was about by bringing Miss Thirkill. I will admit that I had hoped for a higher match for you, Thayne, but the girl comes from good stock. She would make a perfect marchioness. What a lucky dog you will be to have such a beauty on your arm. I presume you have no objections to the girl?"

"I have only just met her, Father. Besides her being a beauty, I know little about her."

"What else is there to know? She has looks and breeding and is perfectly charming. Don't you agree, my dear?"

"I was quite taken with her," the duchess said. "She has a well-developed air of assurance for one so young. I believe she would wear the coronet as well as anyone. I would certainly approve a match."

"Last week you were singing the praises of Lady Emmeline Standish," Thayne said. "And Lady Catherine Villiers. And Miss Elizabeth Fancourt and a few others. Have they all been stricken from your list, Mother?"

"They would all do very nicely for you," she said, "but I find myself quite partial to the lovely Miss Thirkill. She is the prettiest of the lot, to be sure."

"She is indeed," Thayne said. "Well, then, I shall give her serious consideration. We attend the same rout party this evening, so perhaps I will be able to spend some time with her."

"And observe how she behaves in public," the duchess said. "I have no doubt she is a pattern card of propriety. Lady Somerfield will have seen to that. But it is best to make certain."

The mention of the countess reminded Thayne of the unwelcome stir of desire she had wrought in him. He had better get that desire under control if he was to seriously court her niece. How ridiculous it would be to court and perhaps marry the younger, more beautiful girl while harboring a foolish lust for the older woman.

He supposed he should blame it on his unknown Artemis. She had not been a young girl whose sensual nature had needed coaxing and patience to awaken. She was a sexually experienced woman who had been thoroughly uninhibited in her desire, and in her response to his own passion. Since he had not yet found Artemis, he was no doubt seeing such potential in other attractive women. Like Lady Somerfield.

But if he was going to court her niece, then he

would have to seek out some other woman and get the red-haired countess out of his mind.

If only he could find Artemis, he could forget all about Lady Somerfield.

Chapter 6

"The Marquess of Thayne?"

Emily watched her mother's eyes grow huge with excitement, and felt her own stomach twist into a knot of anxiety. If Mama managed to ruin this opportunity for her, Emily would surely die.

Lady Thirkill was stretched out on a chaise in her sitting room with a mountain of pillows at her back and several paisley shawls draped over her legs. Even among family, she did not like to have her splinted leg on display. "The Marquess of Thayne!" She rubbed her hands together with glee. "And you had several minutes of private conversation with him?"

A plate of almond biscuits had been placed on the small tea table between Emily and her aunt. Emily reached for one and said, "We were not alone, so it was not entirely private. But we did speak together several times. Probably for twenty minutes altogether." She was more than pleased with her first meeting with Lord Thayne and it was only natural that she should share the news with her mother. But it was best if she banked her own excitement in hopes that Mama would not feel obliged to "help" to encourage his lordship's interest.

"Wonderful!" Her mother practically bounced on her chaise, her enthusiasm already too much to con-

tain. She would likely have danced around the room
if her leg were not broken.

Please, please, Mama, do not ruin this for me.

"You are to be commended, Sister, for doing your
niece such a good turn. No other girl will have had
the advantage of private conversation with him in
his own home. And for twenty minutes!" Emily's
mother fanned a hand rapidly before her face. "Bless
me, I feel quite flushed. My daughter, a marchioness!"

"Really, Ophelia," her aunt said, "that is quite a
leap from a single meeting, don't you think?"

Her mother lifted her chin at a determined angle
Emily knew well. When Mama got a notion in her
head, nothing could dislodge it. "I have heard the
marquess is looking for a bride," she said. "Everyone
says so. Who better than our Emily?"

Though Emily was inclined to agree, she did not
like to see her mother get too attached to the idea of
Lord Thayne's courting her. One never knew what
she might say or do to jeopardize the possibility of
a match. Thank heaven she was confined to her
couch, for she would surely dog the poor marquess
until he ran screaming in the other direction. If all
went according to plan, Emily would not introduce
Lord Thayne to her mother until he had declared
himself and it was too late to back down.

In truth, she wished her mother had stayed in the
country with Papa, where it would have been more
difficult for her to interfere. But she had insisted on
coming to town, to stay in their house on Bedford
Square, even if she could not go about. "I must
keep a sharp eye on things," she'd said, "and make
sure your aunt does everything that is required."
Mama had several friends who called on her frequently and kept her abreast of all the news. And
every Tuesday afternoon, at her insistence, Emily
and Aunt Beatrice paid a call on her and reported

on all their activities. If they did not, Emily was quite sure her mother would have risen from her couch and somehow made her way to Brook Street to see for herself what was going on. When Emily had not found a husband in the first two weeks of the Season, her mother had begun threatening to take over the supervision of Emily's Season herself, broken leg or not.

And that was the very last thing Emily wanted.

She hated to harbor such disloyal thoughts, but Emily knew she was better served by her mother's absence from the Season. Aunt Beatrice not only had better connections but was well respected and admired. Everyone liked her. Mama, on the other hand, could sometimes be too loud, too excitable, too shrill. Her social skills were not as polished. Aunt Beatrice was sometimes overly concerned with proper behavior, but Mama seemed sometimes to have no discretion at all.

Though God may not approve, Emily nonetheless thanked Him every night for the injury that kept her mother confined to her couch.

"You must find an excuse to call on the duchess again soon," her mother said, wagging a finger at Aunt Beatrice. "And you must somehow contrive to attend all the same functions as the marquess. It is imperative that we throw these two young people together at every opportunity."

"There is no need to fret, Mama. Lord Thayne has accepted an invitation to join my aunt's barge party on Thursday. And he will be at Lady Wedmore's rout party tonight, so we may see him there, as well. Rest assured that I shall make the best of each opportunity. I am as anxious to bring him up to scratch as you are, Mama."

"Do whatever it takes to secure his interest, my girl. *Whatever* it takes."

"Ophelia!" Aunt Beatrice scowled at Emily's mother and shook her head.

"She will not likely have such an opportunity again," her mother said. "Wealthy marquesses do not grow on trees, you know."

"You're right, Mama. But don't worry. I have every intention of succeeding. I will be the most charming girl he has ever met. He will not be able to resist me."

Aunt Beatrice continued to frown. Emily did not understand what had upset her. Surely she wanted Lord Thayne to court her? She had said as much several times before they arrived at Doncaster House.

"Just be sure you behave with strict propriety with him at all times," her aunt said. "One false step and the duchess will withdraw her approval."

Propriety! It was a constant litany with her aunt. "Of course, Aunt Beatrice. You need not worry on that account."

Her mother *harrumph*ed and Aunt Beatrice shot her a look. Emily wished she understood what her aunt was so worried about. "The duke and duchess both seemed to like me," she said. "I did my best to charm them."

"You did indeed, my dear," her aunt said, and smiled again. "I declare, the duke was quite smitten with you. They both questioned me rather thoroughly, Ophelia. Emily's rank is significantly beneath Lord Thayne's, and they clearly wanted to be sure she was worthy of him. I gave a glowing report, of course. The duke has read some of Sir Albert's articles, by the way, and seemed to approve of his archaeological endeavors."

"Well, that is something," her mother said. "You don't suppose they will look too closely into . . . certain matters, do you?"

"What matters?" Emily asked.

"Simply matters of connections and such," her aunt replied, reaching over to pat her affectionately on the knee. "Nothing of any consequence. And they seemed quite satisfied with what I told them, Ophelia. I spoke with the marquess myself for some time, as well. He is excessively proud and rather too haughty, if you want my opinion. Emily will have her work cut out for her to pierce that steely reserve. But I did notice he warmed up a bit when talking of his travels in Asia. You might keep that in mind, my dear."

"Then I shall ask him all about it," Emily said. She did not need to be told that men liked to talk about themselves. She had learned that trick when she was still in the schoolroom. "And I shouldn't be concerned about his haughtiness. He's the heir to a duke, after all. Who has a better right to be haughty?"

And once she married him, she would be equally haughty. Why should she not be? She would have snared the matrimonial prize of the Season.

If only Mama didn't manage to ruin things.

Thayne was looking for Miss Thirkill and her aunt when he saw her. *Artemis.* He had found her. Here at the very crowded Wedmore rout, he had found her at last. He was quite sure of it.

The large town house was teeming with guests. The rooms had been emptied of furniture and were now filled to bursting with people. If there was food or drink, Thayne hadn't seen it. Just throngs of people coming and going, moving from group to group, talking and laughing. It had taken him almost half an hour to make his way up the stairs.

And that was when he saw her. She was standing near one of the windows of the drawing room. She had very fair skin and very dark hair set in soft waves and gathered at the back of her neck. Her eyes were the purest blue. She moved with an unconscious grace, a gentle sway of hip and shoulder that was very like the attitude of his elusive huntress. She even wore a yellow silk gown that fell softly over the curves of her body. Her arms were covered, though, to his disappointment. The tops of her gloves met the edges of her sleeves, so not a hint of flesh could be seen. But he was sure they were *her* arms. His Artemis.

Who was she?

"Do you see the woman in yellow?" he asked Burnett, who stood several inches taller than anyone else in the room and would have a better vantage. "Do you know who she is?"

Burnett craned his head in her direction. "Can't say that I do. Pretty woman, though. Hold on. You think she might be . . ."

"I feel sure she is. Everything about her is right. It is *her*, I tell you."

Thayne shouldered his way through the crowd, making such a determined progress toward her that people stood aside and let him pass. She seemed to sense his approach and looked his way. Her eyes widened slightly. He held her gaze, willing her to recognize him, to acknowledge him. But instead she flushed and turned away.

Perhaps his urgency had shown too well in his eyes. He had frightened her. She moved closer to a man standing nearby, who smiled at her and took her arm. She clung to it like a lifeline. It seemed his Artemis was indeed a married women, and she did not wish to acknowledge what had passed between her and Thayne that night in the garden.

Damn. He had suspected that might be the case when she'd bolted so quickly and refused to give her name. She'd been ashamed and even a bit fearful, despite having minutes before melted in his arms. The masquerade had allowed her to be bold and she had ultimately done something rash. As he watched her, he could imagine how out of character the sexual encounter had been for her. There was a demure air about her, almost a shyness, as she clung to the man who must be her husband. She would not want Thayne to approach her, to acknowledge, even with a look, what had happened between them.

Bloody hell.

Disappointment slammed into him with the force of a tidal wave. He had been determined to find his huntress and entice her into a love affair. He could see now that it would never happen. She would not allow it. She would not even speak to him.

Thayne had come to a halt in his progress and Burnett almost crashed up against him before he realized it. "What is it?" he asked. "Why have we . . . ? Ah. I see. Bad luck, old man. Married to Vernon, is she?"

Lord Vernon? Dear God.

"Well, perhaps she would be interested in a discreet bit of dalliance," Burnett said, grinning. "My father is well acquainted with Vernon and I've met him a time or two. Do you know him? If not, I could introduce you. Then you'd have an excuse to speak with Lady Vernon."

"Good God, no. Damn and blast. Let's move on. Let's get out of here."

It seemed that all the possible bad situations he'd imagined had come to pass. She was worse than merely married. She was married to an important minister in Lord Liverpool's cabinet. Thayne would never dare to dally with the wife of such a man. He could hardly believe he'd already done so. God help him if Vernon ever found out, though it appeared his wife would never let on. She would not want her formidable husband to know she frolicked in dark gardens with masked strangers.

Even worse, Lord Vernon had Liverpool's ear. If

Thayne ever hoped for a ministry post of his own, and he did, he could not afford to have Vernon speak against him to the prime minister.

Thayne turned and walked away, his disappointment now overshadowed with relief. It had been a very near thing. He might have been seen to importune Lady Vernon and lose all chance at a political career. It was unfortunate that he could no longer dream of a love affair with his huntress. But there was nothing for it. Their one mad moment together would simply be a sweet memory, never to be repeated.

"Ah, there is Miss Thirkill," Burnett said. "She has seen us. You know what they say, Thayne. One door closes and another opens. Forget about Lady Vernon. The prettiest girl in the room is smiling at you."

Burnett was right. Thayne had no time to pine over the loss of a lover. He had to woo a wife.

Miss Thirkill, however, did not need wooing. Radiant in shades of pink, she was surrounded by a group of young men who might have been admirers, or simply other guests conveniently crushed into her vicinity. She gifted Thayne with her brightest smile as he approached. He glanced to her side to see Lady Somerfield. She was even more attractive in evening wear, fashionably dressed in a shade of deep green that set off her beautiful hair. She smiled, too, but there was a hint of challenge in it. Had she sensed his attraction to her that afternoon, and was warning him off?

That awkward stir of heat in his loins flared again at the sight of her. Dammit, he must get those blasted urges under control. Why could he not direct them toward Miss Thirkill? Her beauty dazzled the eye, and yet she awakened not the tiniest twinge of hunger in him. Not like those jolts of raw desire that her aunt caused to shoot through his vitals. He was no doubt regretting the loss of Artemis, but if his traitorous body thought there was a possibility of replacing her with Lady Somerfield, it was dead wrong. How could he, when he was about to pay court to her niece?

What the devil was the matter with him, lusting after women he couldn't have?

The fact was, Thayne was not accustomed to being denied what he wanted. But he was generally not foolish enough to want what he could not have. What had happened to him? Had India changed him somehow?

Perhaps he simply needed a woman. It was time to find someone else to satisfy his urges. And soon.

"Lord Thayne!" Miss Thirkill snapped open her fan and fluttered it before her face. She raised her voice to be heard above the cacophony of hundreds of other voices. "Is this not a terrible squeeze? We will never be able to have a conversation amidst such a din. What good luck that we were able to speak together earlier today at Doncaster House."

Clever girl. She made sure those near her would know of their prior acquaintance, and that she had been to his family's home, which hinted at greater intimacy. Thayne had to admire such skillful management of the situation. Miss Thirkill was a force to be reckoned with. No wonder the duchess liked her.

"I am pleased to see you again, Miss Thirkill. And Lady Somerfield." He sketched a bow to each of them. "You remember Mr. Burnett."

His friend stepped forward and made his bows. "Ladies. It seems an age since we last met, does it not?"

Burnett's lopsided grin had won many a female heart during their years abroad. But the single-minded Miss Thirkill was not moved. She ignored Burnett and continued to smile at Thayne as she moved even closer to his side.

"I do not believe you have met some of my

friends," she said, touching his arm ever so briefly with her fan. "Allow me to present them to you, if I may."

And so Thayne was introduced to several young ladies and even more young gentlemen. It was done with a subtle possessiveness, as though Miss Thirkill wanted to make it clear, particularly to the other ladies, that he belonged to her.

Amazing. Thayne had spent his entire life in command of everything around him. Except for the bargain with his father eight years ago, he had never allowed anyone to manipulate him or any situation that involved him. He was a man who liked to be in charge. But he'd had no experience of the marriage mart. The female players in this game—young ladies and their mamas alike, or their aunts, not to mention his own mother—had him easily dancing to their tune like a marionette. He had lost all control of the situation in an afternoon.

And they called women the weaker sex!

Thayne had a niggling notion to take back that control somehow, to let it be known that he was his own man and would make his own decisions. But when he looked at Miss Thirkill, he thought better of it. In the first place, he was loath to embarrass her publicly in any way. In the second place, he doubted he would find a better bridal candidate on his own, so why not let her—and her aunt and his mother—have their way in this one matter? Once he was married, his bride—whoever she might be—would discover that he would not be so easily manipulated.

Thayne and Burnett stayed and chatted with the group for several more minutes. To be perfectly honest, Burnett did most of the chatting, charming all the ladies into laughter and wide-eyed interest with brief anecdotes of their travels. With the constant shifting of people through the room, Thayne found himself suddenly at Lady Somerfield's side. A rotund gentleman made his way past and caused her to brush against Thayne.

And there was that surge of heat again.

He muttered an apology and stepped away quickly, putting a decorous distance between them.

Lady Somerfield smiled. "If you insist on apologizing to everyone you bump against, you will have no time for other conversation, my lord. Such accidents are unavoidable in a crush like this."

"Undoubtedly," he said.

"You are a man of few words, are you not, Lord Thayne? Your friend is full of tales of India, and yet you say very little."

"It is difficult to converse in such a crowd."

"Indeed. But I still mean to get to know you better, my lord. I shall insist on a lively conversation during my barge party on Thursday."

He cracked a small smile. "I cannot promise to be lively, Lady Somerfield, but I shall try, once again, to answer all your questions."

She laughed, and it reminded him of temple bells. And of another woman he could not have. "You no doubt think me an inquisitive old busybody," she said.

"On the contrary. I do not think you at all old."

She laughed again. "You are too kind, sir. But I see you do not deny that I am a busybody. It does not matter. I will expect a conversation on Thursday in any case. Do I have your promise?"

"Of course. I look forward to it." And he found that he did.

But for the proposed conversation, or for the chance to stand close to her again?

Beatrice looked about her with the pride of a successful hostess. She could not have been more pleased. The barge was lovely, the river calm, and the weather glorious. It was a perfect day for cruising leisurely down the Thames.

"What a splendid idea this was, Beatrice." Penelope was one of only two of the Fund trustees, the Merry Widows, who had been able to attend, though they'd all been invited. "Whatever made you think of it?"

Beatrice gave a little shrug. "I don't know. I wanted to do something different for Emily. We've been to so many breakfasts and garden parties and such, I couldn't bear to host another one myself. When I learned that some of the livery companies rent out their ceremonial barges when they are not in use, it occurred to me to hire one. Isn't it simply gorgeous?"

The small shallops one could rent from various bargehouses could accommodate no more than six or eight passengers, whereas the ceremonial barges were enormous and could hold as many as fifty. The one Beatrice had hired for the day was all polished wood and gilt, with eighteen liveried oarsmen. It was a magnificent vessel, and she was very proud to have acquired it.

"It rather makes one feel important to be on such an elegant barge," Penelope said. "Very queenly. I almost feel like waving to the masses as we sail by in such splendor."

"It definitely outshines every other vessel on the river," Beatrice said. "Even in lesser boats, though, I have always enjoyed river travel. It is rather relaxing, don't you think?"

"Delightfully so." Wilhelmina, gracefully ensconced on one of the velvet-cushioned benches, held up her glass of champagne and saluted Beatrice. "Kudos to you, my dear."

Beatrice raised her own glass in acknowledgment and took another sip. She'd paid an exorbitant amount to obtain the French champagne. It was almost certainly smuggled into England, though the wine merchant pretended he'd had several pre-war cases on hand. But Beatrice had had her mind set on champagne and strawberries, and was pleased to have both in abundance. Huge silver bowls of ripe strawberries were placed about the cabin, along with pastries, cheeses, and other fruits, while footmen kept everyone's glasses filled.

"I know this party is for Emily and her young friends," Wilhelmina said, "but I am pleased you invited a few of us elders."

"They do make one feel one's age," Beatrice said as she glanced around the cabin, "do they not?"

"Nonsense," Penelope said. "I wouldn't want to be seventeen again for any amount of money, if such a thing were possible. I'm much more content with my life now."

"Yes, so am I," Beatrice said.

"So tell us," Penelope said, lowering her voice to a whisper. "Have you had any luck locating your masked lover?"

"No, and I have stopped looking. I have too much on my mind with Emily to think about secret lovers. Besides, I have become more regretful of that incident and rather prefer to forget it."

"But I thought you enjoyed it," Penelope said.

"I did. But it was madness. I should never have done such a thing. It has only served to make me crazy, worrying that some dark-haired gentleman will recognize me and announce to the world what we did together. I prefer to forget it ever happened."

"Silly woman!" Penelope said. "You should not forget it. You should find the fellow and partake of his lovemaking again. Perhaps you will be more inclined to do so once some young man has taken Emily off your hands."

"It looks to me as though that might be sooner than later," Wilhelmina said. "Lord Thayne is very attentive, is he not?"

"If you call that stiff formality of his attentive," Beatrice said. "But Emily seems determined to have him."

"Who can blame her?" Penelope said. "The man is exceedingly handsome. And a marquess. Every girl's dream, I should say."

"Emily's dream, to be sure," Beatrice said. "But I must confess I would prefer a man to show a bit more warmth of feeling. Lord Thayne is so reserved with her, so aloof. And he is terribly arrogant and proud. Even a bit intimidating. An aristocrat down to his toes."

And one who had the unfortunate ability to make her own toes curl up in her slippers when she merely looked at him. That, of course, was the worse problem, but it was *her* problem, not his or Emily's.

"Of course he is," Penelope said. "He is a marquess, the heir to a duke. What did you expect?"

Beatrice shrugged. "I don't know. I suppose I am worried that all his highborn detachment suggests an intractable, severe nature. He might be a difficult, demanding husband. I would not wish that for Emily."

"You are imagining troubles before you have cause to do so," Wilhelmina said. "Give him a chance. You barely know the gentleman."

"Actually, I announced to him quite boldly that I wanted to get to know him better. I have been trying to goad any kind of a response from him that is not strictly formal and impersonal."

"And have you succeeded?" Wilhelmina asked.

"I have caught a glimpse or two of something beneath that patrician restraint, but only a glimpse. I really do want to get to know him better. For Emily's sake. She is too young to understand that a rigid temperament could make for a less-than-happy marriage."

"I don't think you have anything to worry about with Emily," Wilhelmina said. "She will use her beauty as a tool to get what she wants from her husband and from life."

"And what happens when her beauty fades?" Beatrice rose from her chair and shook out her skirts. "I made Lord Thayne promise to have a conversation with me today. It is time I called in that promise. Excuse me, ladies."

Beatrice made her way carefully to the front of the cabin, threading through groups of chattering young people, both seated and standing. She stopped to speak with each group, ensuring they had all the refreshments they wanted and were enjoying themselves. She was roundly congratulated for a splendid time on the river, which made her feel rather smug with self-satisfaction.

Lord Thayne stood near Emily, who was smiling and chattering gaily. The charming Mr. Burnett was on her other side; Lord Ealing, Sir Frederick Gilling, and Lord Ushworth also stayed nearby, in hopes, no doubt, that she would favor them with a smile. But Emily's smiles were, Beatrice knew, for one man alone.

His lordship's demeanor was as formal as ever, his expression inscrutable. He nodded now and then in acknowledgment of something Emily said, and once went so far as to offer a tight-lipped smile. Beatrice wondered what it would take to receive a full-blown smile from the man. She suspected it would suit him better than his usual dour dignity.

And probably cause her knees to buckle, blast the man.

She spoke to Emily first. "Are you enjoying the day, my dear? Would you like more strawberries?"

"Thank you, no, Aunt Beatrice. Everything is wonderful." She looked at Lord Thayne. "Just perfect."

The girl had hardly left Lord Thayne's side the whole trip. Every gesture, every word, was calculated to let the rest of the party know that Lord Thayne was her property, so to speak. And since this was *her* party, no one dared to disagree. A match between them seemed so right—the prettiest girl and the most eligible gentleman—that most everyone seemed to accept it as inevitable.

Thank heaven. Ophelia would be pleased.

"I'm glad you are having a good time," Beatrice said. "We shall be at Kew shortly and will be able to stretch our legs a bit. I'm sure the gentlemen will enjoy that."

She turned her attention to Lord Thayne. He gazed out the open-air cabin, through the tall, pillared arches, watching the passing scenery. The entire party had stood at the arches or stepped outside the cabin to admire Fulham Palace as they'd passed, and several other places before that. Since then, the riverscape had been gentle and quiet, with no great houses or other marvels to be seen, and so most of the guests had retired to seats inside the cabin.

Beatrice moved to stand near Lord Thayne. "There will not be much to see until perhaps Brandenburgh House, which is lovely but not terribly grand. Then Chiswick, of course, shortly before we arrive at Kew."

"There is always something to see along the river," he said.

"Yes, that is true. Perhaps, sir, you would give me your arm for a few moments and step outside with me. The view is better and the weather is fine."

And there it was again, that half smile, a mere twitch of the lips. "It would be my pleasure." He offered his arm, and led her to the deck outside.

There was not much of a deck, only a small area between the cabin and the oarsmen. These barges were built to carry passengers inside, not outside. But one small bench had been placed against the cabin wall, and Lord Thayne held her hand steady while she took a seat. He released her with unflattering speed, as though her touch burned him. She was mortified to think it may well have done so. Every time she was near the wretched man, heat pooled low in her belly. Had he felt it, even through the fine leather of her gloves?

Thayne turned his face into the breeze, hoping to cool his blood. He wished he could control his reaction to Miss Thirkill's aunt, but he seemed helpless to do so. What was it about her that set him off like that? She was very attractive, of course. Even beautiful. Not in the way of her niece, whose beauty was fresh and fine and nearly perfect. Lady Somerfield's beauty was more . . . smoldering. Perhaps that was why his blood heated every time he saw her. Her beauty singed him.

His only recourse was to impose whatever control was left him. He stiffened his spine and held his shoulders back and his head high.

"You promised me a conversation," she said.

It would be churlish to keep his back to her, so he turned to face her, lifting his chin a bit. "I am at your disposal, my lady. What questions do you have for me today?"

She smiled up at him from beneath the brim of a fetching bonnet trimmed in the same shade of blue as her spencer jacket. The costume enhanced the color of her eyes, which twinkled merrily at him. "A whole list of them, I assure you."

"Do you wish to know the value of my land holdings? The number of acres given to farming? A report of my investments?"

She laughed. "That would certainly be interesting. But another time, perhaps. On such a day as this, I believe I'd like to hear more of your travels."

"What would you like to know?"

"Whatever you would like to tell me. Your favorite places. Your most interesting adventures. Anything."

"There were so many places, it is hard to choose a favorite."

She gave him an exasperated look. "Try."

"Well, I spent a lot of time in Hyderabad. I liked it there a great deal."

"Why?"

And so he told her about the citadel of Golconda and Maula Ali's shrine, about the Chaumhala Palace and Purani Haveli, about the beauty of Hussain Sagar Lake and the Banjara Hills, about the new British Residency building and the parade grounds. About elephants and tigers, about gardens and gleaming white palaces.

He stopped when he noticed her staring quizzically at him. "What is it?" he asked. "I have bored you."

"On the contrary. I am quite fascinated, I assure you. It is just . . . well, you really did love it there, didn't you?"

"Yes, I did."

"Do you know that your eyes light up when you talk about it? That your face is transformed from the stern aristocrat into . . . something else? Something more—forgive me for saying so, but it is true—something more alive."

He gave a start. "Egad. I had no idea you thought I was dead. No wonder you are concerned for your niece."

She burst into musical laughter. "That was a poor choice of words, I fear. I must apologize for my impertinence, my lord. I seem to have turned into one of those care-for-nothing widows who says exactly what she feels. I never thought you dead. Just a bit . . . reserved. But you allow that reserve to slip away when you speak of India."

"Do I?" He supposed he *had* got a bit carried away, lost in fond memories of Hyderabad.

"Yes, and I quite enjoyed it. You must do so more often, my lord. With a wistful look in your eye and an abstracted smile on your face, you seem much more . . . approachable. I will make a confession to you. I have been deliberately provoking you. I have wanted to draw you out, to see what sort of man you are."

He arched an eyebrow. "Or what sort of husband I'd make?"

She laughed again. "You must forgive me, Lord Thayne. I am thoroughly transparent, am I not? Emily is a vibrant young lady, but also very innocent of the world. I am twice her age—dare I admit it?— and have seen all different sorts of marriages. Some are loving and affectionate, with equal partners sharing in all aspects of their lives. Some are quite unequal, with the wife totally subservient to the husband. Some husbands are bullies. Some are indulgent. Some are indifferent. Some are heavy-handed and autocratic—they do not allow their wives to make even the simplest decision, and do not ask for their input on any decisions the men make for their families."

Her voice had become quite animated. Was she speaking of her own marriage?

"Emily is a beautiful girl with a great many suitors," she continued. "I just want to make sure she is happy."

"She is a very lucky young woman to have so caring a chaperone. But I do not know if I can tell you what sort of husband I would be. I rather suspect somewhere between overly indulgent and autocratic.

I will have certain expectations due to my rank, of course. Beyond that, I cannot say."

"You are very obliging to say as much as you have. And I am a shrew to be asking such questions." She gave a sheepish grin. "You must blame it on that look in your eye when you spoke of India. You made me think I could say anything to you."

"I hope you will always feel so, Lady Somerfield."

Devil take it, he really did like this woman. It would have been easier if he despised her. Then he might be able to control those damnable yearnings that crept up on him again as she spoke. He would have to try harder to suppress them. Then perhaps they could be friends. He hoped so.

"Ah, look." She rose from her bench and put up her hand to shield her eyes. "There is Chiswick. We are almost at our destination."

The rest of the party realized it, as well, and began to stir about in the cabin. A few wandered out onto the small deck. Lady Somerfield was called away by other guests, and Miss Thirkill took her place at his side. The pink ribbons of her bonnet fluttered in the breeze as she smiled up at him and began to chatter cheerfully about how much she looked forward to strolling through the gardens of Kew. He paid little attention to what she said, his mind still on the conversation with Lady Somerfield. Perhaps over time, Miss Thirkill would grow into the sort of woman her aunt was. He would be pleased to have such a wife.

When the oars were lifted and the barge was pulled to the dock, the gentlemen handed the ladies out onto the Kew river stairs. Thayne helped Miss Thirkill to alight, but allowed Burnett to lead her up the stairs. He waited for Lady Somerfield, who, as hostess, was the last to leave. After giving instructions to the footmen, she was ready to disembark. She seemed surprised, though pleased, to find him waiting for her. He wanted her to know that he had not minded her blunt questions, and had enjoyed their conversation.

She held out her hand to him. He took it, looked her square in the eye, and smiled broadly.

He had to catch her by the elbow when her knees seemed to buckle and she lost her footing.

Chapter 7

The next Benevolent Widows Fund ball was held a week later at Hengston House. Beatrice had left an invitation with the Duchess of Doncaster, and tried to convince herself it was because she could expect a sizable donation to the charity from Her Grace. And that she had included the marquess in the invitation only for the sake of Emily. But if she was perfectly honest with herself, she simply wanted to see him again.

It was not as if she did not encounter him often enough. They'd met at practically every social event she and Emily had attended. Since he now went about more frequently, he'd caused something of a stir among the ladies of the *ton*. Beatrice often observed the reaction whenever he entered a room. Handsome, rich, and with aristocratic arrogance oozing from every pore, he was a formidable presence. Women of all ages watched him with interest. Beatrice had begun to worry that Emily might face some stiff competition, as some of those interested ladies had pedigrees longer than her arm. But in the end, she trusted in Emily's determination and the girl's own brand of arrogance to win the day. In fact, Thayne had been most attentive to Emily, and expectations were running high.

At each social function, however, Beatrice had

grown to look forward to the few minutes she might have to share a word or two with the marquess. He had indeed loosened up his tight manner a bit. At least with Beatrice. He still behaved with strict formality around Emily.

In the last week, since their conversation on the barge, a sort of friendship had developed between her and Lord Thayne. And Beatrice found she quite enjoyed it. There was still that little spark of something between them. She had finally concluded that it was definitely *between* them and not on her side alone. That had become clear when she had almost fallen into his arms when she stepped off the barge, his smile unsettling her, exactly as she'd predicted. She tried her best to extinguish that spark, and felt sure he was doing the same. Eventually, it would pass and they could be friends. Which would be the only proper thing if he married Emily.

Until such time, however, that tiny spark still flared hot, and Beatrice was helpless to fight it.

In fact, she had dressed with extra care for the evening, wanting to look her best. Beatrice always tried to look her best, but tonight he would see her in her own element, at *her* ball, and so she tried a little harder. Poor Dora, her lady's maid, must have thought she was mad as she discarded one dress after the other before settling on just the right one. It was a new dress of celestial blue satin scooped very low at the neckline, with very short, full sleeves finished at the bottom with knotted beading. The hem was ornamented with the same beadwork. Over the dress she wore a Polonese robe of gossamer net trimmed with lace and more knotted beading. Dora had fashioned her hair into an elegant twist at the back of the head, confined with a wreath of lace and pearls.

Beatrice thought she looked quite splendid. Not at all like a middle-aged dowager.

Later, as she and the other Merry Widows stood in line with Lord and Lady Hengston to receive their guests, Beatrice waited anxiously for Lord Thayne's arrival. But there was no sign of him. She was gratified when the duke and duchess came through the line. They had never before attended a Widows Fund ball, and their appearance was quite a coup for the trustees. Grace had looked ready to swoon at the size of their contribution to the Fund, but had quickly composed herself and accepted it with polite gratitude.

"Will Lord Thayne be joining us, as well?" Beatrice had asked.

"He would not miss it," Her Grace said. "If he has not yet arrived, I am certain he must be delayed. He will be here, Lady Somerfield. You may assure Miss Thirkill of it."

Beatrice was pleased to be assured of it, as well.

She joined the dancing toward the end of the first set, partnered with Emily's uncle, Lord Wallingford. She sat out the second set and acted the good patroness, mingling with the guests and making introductions. She found Emily in the center of a circle of admirers. Lord Thayne was not among them.

Standing near Emily's court were Adam Cazenove and Lord Rochdale. Adam was frowning furiously, and Beatrice guessed why. Marianne was playing a dangerous game with him, and Beatrice hoped they would soon resolve their differences. Adam was so obviously in love with her.

The notorious Rochdale, on the other hand, wore a roguish smile as he surveyed the room. He made no attempt to disguise his salacious scrutiny of certain women. Women whose charms were more abundantly displayed than others. Beatrice instinctively reached up to cover her own exposed bosom.

Her blood ran cold, though, as she watched him choose his next object of interest. Emily, with her perfect beauty and her deceptive demeanor of sophistication. Rochdale was a cad of the first order, his seductions numerous and very public. There had been a terrible scandal the year before when he'd been quite public in his seduction of Serena Underwood, then just as publicly rejected her. The poor young woman had been ruined and no one had seen her since. And there had been rumors of a child.

Beatrice would not let the scoundrel get within an inch of Emily, if she could help it. The girl had no notion of his reputation. Beatrice must be sure to warn her to avoid the man. She expelled a sigh of relief when he looked away and found another target of interest. But for the time being, Beatrice would keep a close watch on her niece. Just in case.

She looked down to see her glove had come unbuttoned, and reached up to correct it.

Thayne arrived later than he'd wanted, but he'd got caught up in a game of cards at his club and lost track of time. He missed the receiving line altogether, which was disappointing. He had especially wanted to express his thanks to Lady Somerfield for the invitation. Well, he would see her soon enough. All he had to do was locate Miss Thirkill and her aunt was certain to be nearby.

He looked about for the famous guinea gold curls and easily found them across the room. As ever, Miss Thirkill was surrounded by a court of swains. He wondered if he had any serious competition. Unless one of them was a duke, he supposed it unlikely.

He made his way toward her, and was stopped dead in his tracks.

A woman in pale blue with her back to him was in the process of removing her glove. As she rolled it down her arm, baring the palest perfect flesh, his breath caught in his throat and his heart began to pound rapidly in his chest.

Something about that arm.

It could not be. Could it? It was definitely not Lady Vernon. This woman's hair was quite red, so perhaps he was wrong.

And then he saw the bracelet. A gold serpent coiled about that pale upper arm. If he moved closer, he was almost certain it would have ruby eyes.

He approached slowly, wanting to be absolutely sure. She made some adjustment to the glove and tugged it slowly back up her arm, driving him quite wild with desire. He watched that arm closely. Lithe and supple as a willow, almost boneless in its soft lines. Beautiful, and very, very familiar. A stab of white-hot passion speared through him with a ferocity that almost knocked him off his feet. He could barely breathe.

The glove left a narrow expanse of alabaster flesh exposed beneath the tiny puffed sleeve. Just enough flesh to contain the gold serpentine bracelet.

This time he was absolutely sure. Those same arms had intoxicated him once before.

As he moved closer, as he studied her hungrily, he became aware that it was more than just her arms that was familiar. The elegant column of her neck arching up from her shoulders. The way she held her head at a slight angle. The glorious red hair.

Red hair? Could it be?

He stopped mere inches behind her, then reached out and tentatively touched her arm. She turned, and his heart skipped a beat.

Their eyes locked. The air between them shimmered with an elemental charge so potent it threatened to explode.

"Artemis," he whispered.

A look of pure horror came over her face, and

Lady Somerfield spun on her heels and dashed away.

Beatrice sped through the crowd, not caring who she pushed aside or what slippers were ruined as she trod on them. Her only thought was to get away. Away from him.

Somehow she found the terrace doors and rushed outside. She leaned against the railing and the cold night air washed over her. She took deep gulps of it to calm her racing heart.

Dear God. How could she have missed it? Dark hair. Dark eyes. A slight cleft in his chin. A connection to India. An uncontrollable attraction. Had she been *blind*?

Her heart flip-flopped wildly in her chest. She tried to compose herself, as there were others on the terrace, but one thought kept spinning in her head. She had had sex up against a wall with the Marquess of Thayne. The same young man who, she was quite sure, would very soon make her niece an offer of marriage.

Bile rose in her throat and Beatrice was seized with panic.

Good Lord, what was she to do?

Hurried footsteps sounded on the flagstones. He'd found her, of course.

"Lady Somerfield." Even the voice was familiar, if she had but listened.

"Go away."

"No. We must talk. Please turn around."

"I have nothing to say to you, Lord Thayne."

"Do you not?"

He touched her arm and she flinched as though scorched. "Go away. This is not the time or place."

"We are quite alone, Lady Somerfield."

She turned to look, and saw he had spoken the

truth. The others had returned inside, leaving her alone with Lord Thayne. Her maharaja.

"You cannot imagine how hard I have searched for you, Artemis. And to think, it was you all along. Did you know it was me?"

"Of course not. Do you think I would have allowed you to court my niece if I'd known?"

"Why did you run away from me that night?"

For a thousand reasons. For no reason at all. How was she to answer him? "I had to."

He gazed at her so intently she was forced to look away.

"Why? Not because of Miss Thirkill. I had not yet met her. If you had but made your identity known to me, I would have stayed away from her."

"But you did not stay away from her, and now it is too late."

"I have not yet made her an offer. And now I will not."

"You cannot back down now, Lord Thayne. Everyone in London expects you and Emily to marry."

"Then they will all soon discover they are wrong. I will remove myself from her court."

"And have all the world think you have jilted her? She would be ruined, my lord." And Ophelia would have her head.

"Emily has a thousand other suitors. She will not be ruined."

"Socially embarrassed, then. Please. Do not do this to her. We will never speak of what took place between us. We will forget it ever happened."

"That is impossible. Even if it were not, I don't wish to forget. I would trade a dozen Emilys for another night with you. It was a magical night, Artemis."

At last, ironically, she was seeing the warmth and passion she had always hoped to see in him. The same passion he had demonstrated that infamous evening in the garden.

She would give anything to have that chilly reserve back again.

"It was not magical," she said. "It was madness."

He did not speak for a long moment, and then said, "If it was madness, then let us be mad. I said it to you at the masquerade ball and I will say it again. I want you. And I recall quite clearly that you said you wanted me. We are two adults attracted to each other. Why should we not be together?"

Beatrice snorted. "You really *are* mad. Even if I wished for it, how could we possibly be together now? It is absurd."

"Is it because you *know* who I am now? Do you only give yourself to strangers?"

She almost raised her hand to slap him, but remembered that someone else might walk onto the terrace at any moment and see them. "How dare you?" she said through her teeth.

He shrugged. "It is the only explanation I can think of."

"The *only* explanation? You are being despicable, my lord. I am not that sort of woman. I am not a . . . a loose woman. I am respectable. At least, I have always behaved respectably. What happened that night . . . I have never done anything like it in my life. You must believe me. I do not know what came over me. But I can assure you it will not come over me again. I implore you to forget it ever happened."

"I can't," he said. "Every time I look at you, I remember. And I want to create more memories with you. We could be so good together, you and I, in a proper bed instead of up against a garden wall. You *know* it would be good."

Lord, how she wished he would not say such things, encouraging a fantasy she could no longer indulge. He reached out to touch her again, and she brushed him away. She must have unconsciously realized it had been him all along. His touch, his very presence, had plagued her from the start.

"I am a brute," he said, his voice as softly caressing as his fingers. "I do not think you a loose woman. I *know* you are not. You were seduced by the masks, the music, the darkness—and me—into behaving out of character. I apologize if I encouraged you to act against your will. My only excuse is that I found you irresistible, Artemis."

She sighed. "It was not against my will, as you surely know. But it was most certainly out of character."

"Since you admit you were not coerced, then you must forgive me if I try to convince you to act out of character again. No, not tonight. It is enough that I have discovered at last who you are. But I give you fair warning. I will not give up trying."

"Please . . ." There was a plaintive edge to her voice she could not control. She drew in a deep breath and let it out slowly. "Please, don't."

"You are killing me, Artemis."

"Stop calling me that."

"Then you are killing me, *Lady Somerfield*. You must know how much I want you. I will do anything to have you."

She almost collapsed in frustration. Though his voice was edged with passion, he was still the arrogant aristocrat determined to have his way. Gripping the railing behind her, she said, "You know it is impossible. Emily expects an offer. Her mother expects an offer. *Your* mother expects an offer."

"But I shall not make one. Never."

"You cannot back down in order to have an affair with Emily's aunt. How would that look? My own reputation would be in shambles."

He took her hand and would not let go when she tried to pull away. "I would never do anything to hurt you, Artemis. I know how to be discreet."

"No. I cannot do it. I *will* not do it. Do not press me on this, Lord Thayne."

He pulled her closer and began to stroke her arms with his free hand. Oh, how she wished he would not do that.

"Have you not felt it?" he asked. "That surge of desire every time we touch? Every time we speak? I know you have felt it as strongly as I have. But I didn't understand it until tonight when I saw your . . . bracelet. It makes perfect sense now. Our bodies knew what our minds could not accept. We are meant to be together."

He had ever so subtly pulled her closer so that mere inches separated them. She couldn't bear it. Her whole body shivered, and she was quite sure it was not because of the cold. Why was he doing this to her?

"We cannot," she said. "We cannot. There is Emily to—"

"The devil take Emily! It's *you* I want in my bed."

"The duke and duchess expect—"

"They expect me to marry, but I will choose my own bride. There are any number of girls I can choose. It doesn't have to be Emily. There have been no words between us on the subject, no understanding of a future offer. We have known each other little more than a week, after all. I will not pull away from her abruptly, if you prefer. I will do it slowly and no one will think anything but that I am fickle or that Emily has changed her mind."

"But she is perfect for you. You know she is."

"And how would I bear it every time I had to see her aunt? Do you expect me to pretend indifference?"

"Yes! As will I."

"Well, I won't do it." He glanced over his shoulder as though making sure no one was watching, then pulled her tight against his chest. "I won't do it."

He set his lips to hers and he kissed her, ravishing her mouth, ripping the senses from her. And she allowed him to do so, allowed him to draw her tongue deeper into his mouth, allowed her world to start spinning.

When her wits returned, she pushed him away and stood back.

"You truly are mad."

"I want you, Lady Somerfield, and I always get what I want."

"Do you? Well, perhaps not this time." She turned and walked back into the ballroom. She heard his voice behind her.

"We shall see, my lady. We shall see."

Beatrice had hoped the day's activities would help her to forget what had happened the night before. When her world had slipped off its axis and spun drunkenly out of control. But nothing could make her forget. Her mind was full of Thayne and his kiss and the implications of his identity as her masked lover. She had almost made herself ill with worry and had thought to bow out of today's commitment. But that would not be fair to her friends.

All five of the Fund trustees had gathered at Marlowe House, a large set of buildings in Chelsea that had once been almshouses and now served as a halfway house for as many war widows and their children as could be accommodated. Initial contributions to the Benevolent Widows Fund had been used to purchase the buildings and renovate them to house families of soldiers killed in the war. Subsequent contributions maintained the house and all its associated charitable functions, such as employment agents, schoolrooms, staffing, food, clothing, and such.

The trustees had insisted it be named for Grace, whose idea it had been, and who made sure everything ran smoothly. They visited Marlowe House as a group at least once a month to meet with the families and the staff. Today they had come to inspect the herb gardens and the new stillrooms.

The gardens were lovely, planted and maintained by the families and one hired gardener, and Beatrice always enjoyed strolling about them. But today she might as well have been in a desert for all she noticed of the plantings. Her mind was so thoroughly elsewhere it was a wonder she knew to place one foot in front of the other.

"Why such a long face?" Penelope asked. "The gardens are so pretty and fragrant today, but I would be willing to bet you haven't noticed, Beatrice. What on earth has you so glum? You haven't spoken more than a few words since you arrived."

Beatrice heaved a sigh that came out rather shuddery and pathetic, and sat down on a stone bench placed in a corner of an especially pretty knot garden. "I am sorry, everyone. I can't think straight. I'm so—"

And before she could stop it, a sob welled up from her throat and she burst into tears. She was mortified, but could not seem to stop crying.

Marianne sat down beside her and placed an arm around her shoulders. "What it is, my dear? What has upset you so?"

Beatrice leaned her head on her friend's shoulder and tried to control her tears. She felt so foolish. Such an emotional display was unlike her. She took several deep breaths to compose herself. The choking sobs finally ebbed, though tears continued to well in her eyes and stream down her cheeks. She brushed at them and tried to speak.

"I have d-discovered the identity of m-my maharaja," she stammered.

"Good heavens," Penelope said. "Who can it possibly be to make you so upset?"

Beatrice took another deep breath and let it out slowly. "Lord Thayne."

There was a moment of stunned silence, and then they all spoke at once.

"No!"

"You don't mean it!"

"Dear heaven, is he not courting your niece?"

"Are you certain?"

"How did you find out?"

"Does *he* know?"

"Does Emily know?"

"What if he marries her?"

"How will you bear it?"

"What are you going to do?"

"Please." Beatrice lifted a hand for them to be silent. "Imagine all those same questions roiling in my head since last night, and you will understand my state of mind."

Grace sat down on the small space of bench on the other side of Beatrice and placed a reassuring hand over Beatrice's trembling fingers.

"Tell us what happened," Wilhelmina said in her kind, gentle voice. She reached out and wiped away a tear from Beatrice's cheek. "Something last night?"

"I was looking after Emily, making sure that dreadful Lord Rochdale was not importuning her, when I felt a brief touch on my arm. I turned around to find Lord Thayne staring at me with the most intent look in his eye. There was something in the air between us in that instant. Something powerful and almost frightening. And then he called me Artemis. And I knew."

"Artemis?"

"I was dressed as Artemis at the masquerade ball. That is what he called me that night, as I would not give him my name. It seems he had only that moment recognized me. I was wearing the same serpent bracelet and he said he remembered it."

"So you both learned just last night," Marianne said, "that you had been each other's secret lover?"

"Yes. And I have been frantic with the knowledge ever since. He *has*, in a way, been courting my niece. His name has certainly been linked with hers. And, God help me, I have encouraged it."

"And so now you will have to *dis*courage it," Wilhelmina said, "for your own peace of mind."

"That is what Lord Thayne says. He wants to give her up and begin an affair with me. Can you believe it?"

"Of course I can," Penelope said. "And you should allow him to do so."

"To be seen to jilt poor Emily? To publicly embarrass her by his apparent rejection? No, it is too late. There are already expectations. His parents are pressing for the match. The duke is enchanted with Emily and the duchess finds her charming. Emily's mother is dead set on the match and will have my head if he is not brought up to scratch. Emily certainly makes it clear that she will entertain an offer from him. She publicly favors him above all others. It's out of control, you see. The marquess can't back down now, though he is determined to do so."

"And he is right to do so," Grace said. "Even if you do not embark upon an affair, the fact that you have been intimate with him, even once, will make it awkward if he marries your niece."

"Believe me, I have thought of little else. It is making me crazy." Tears welled up in her eyes again.

Marianne squeezed her shoulder. She had never let go. "You poor thing. It is indeed a difficult situation. More than awkward. But Wilhelmina and Grace are right. It is best if he removes himself from Emily's circle."

"I do not want Emily hurt," Beatrice said. "The *ton* can be vicious, as we all know. There will be talk if he backs down now."

"That may be so," Marianne said, "but it will pass."

"And when it does," Penelope said, "you can take him for your lover without concern."

Beatrice shook her head. "No, never. It would always be awkward. It would seem as though I stole my niece's suitor."

"If you are discreet," Wilhelmina said, "no one need know."

But Beatrice would know. And would feel guilty and ashamed. "It seems poor Emily is bound to be hurt in this, no matter what I do. Lord Thayne will never make her an offer."

"Then you must convince her not to expect one," Wilhelmina said. "Give her the chance to make it look as if *she* is the one backing down."

Beatrice considered the idea for a moment and wondered if it might be possible. Though how to convince Emily to change her mind about Lord Thayne was something Beatrice could not imagine. The girl was determined on her course, and it would require a prodigious effort to shake her resolve. But it must be done. Her friends were right. Beatrice had to make this work out somehow. And if it did?

I want you, Lady Somerfield, and I always get what I want.

She thought of his kiss and how she had melted into it so easily. Would they eventually be sharing more than a kiss in the moonlight? Did she want more?

God help her, she did.

Chapter 8

"May I have a word, Countess." Thayne could not allow her to ignore him, or what had happened between them, as she seemed determined to do.

"The soprano is about to begin her aria." Lady Somerfield looked away from him and appeared to watch the guests taking their seats in Mrs. Verey-Nicolson's drawing room, which had been arranged for a musical evening. Thayne had already sat through an interminable harp solo. He did not think he could bear another assault to his ears.

"Yes, she is," he said, "but I wonder if you would mind if we sat it out in the refreshment room. We have things to discuss, you and I."

"Yes, I suppose we do. But I must return for the glee. Two of Emily's particular friends will be singing, and she would be disappointed if I missed it."

"It shall be as you wish, Artemis."

"Please do not call me that."

"I have no other name for you. 'Lady Somerfield' is much too formal for such *intimate* friends."

She rolled her eyes to the ceiling, but smiled, which gave him hope. "Tea is being served in one of the anterooms, I believe. It is this way."

They walked in silence through several connected rooms, stopping occasionally for Lady Somerfield to exchange a word with one of the guests. A few begged introductions, and Thayne was faced with more than one stammering, blushing young girl. He turned on his best aristocratic hauteur and, in most cases, offered no more than a nod and a how-d'ye-do. However, one overbearing mother hen with a chest like a ship's prow managed to manipulate him into asking her pale-faced daughter to reserve a dance for him at the Oscott ball two days hence. The poor girl almost fell into a swoon.

But Artemis was calm and poised. There was a self-possession about her, an easiness one seldom saw in younger women. Her niece, for example, who had lost no time in running him to ground this evening. Ever since he'd decided he could not court her, he'd become more aware of her flaws. She was full of forced animation, always conscious of her beauty, posing to her best advantage. Her conversation was overly cheerful or tinged with boredom, depending on her audience. She always seemed to be *on*, like a performer, which must be exhausting.

Her aunt, on the other hand, was a picture of serenity in contrast. Equally confident, but more comfortable in her skin. There was nothing forced or false about Lady Somerfield.

He bent and whispered in her ear, "I don't suppose there is a dark corner we could slip into?"

"No, my lord, there is not."

"Damn. No gardens, either, I take it."

"No gardens. This way, if you please."

She led them, at last, through a door into a room set up with several tables, all of them filled to capacity with others who preferred to skip the soprano. More guests stood about in groups. Footmen threaded their way between the tables, pouring tea and, he was thankful to note, wine.

"Oh, dear," Artemis said. "This was not the best idea, it seems."

"Over there," he said, and gestured to a window

seat where a man and woman stood and looked ready to leave.

They shouldered their way toward the window just in time to claim the vacated bench. Lady Somerfield sat, and Thayne was tempted to remain standing, where he could look down on her beautifully exposed bosom. But the noise of a dozen conversations, not to mention the music from the drawing room, made it difficult to hear, and so he sat beside her. Which was even better, as it turned out. The narrow width of the bench meant that her thighs and hips brushed up against his.

Thayne procured two glasses of wine from a passing footman, and held his up in salute. "To serendipity," he said, and touched his glass to hers, "which brought us together that night at the masquerade.

"I am glad you agreed to speak to me." He leaned in close on the pretense of not wishing to be overheard. But in fact the din of conversation was too loud for anyone to hear them. "I wasn't sure you would. I am hoping you have reconsidered what we discussed when we last met. About us, I mean."

"No, I haven't reconsidered. Well, not entirely."

He grinned. "Not entirely? I am hopeful, then."

"Lord Thayne, I—"

"Please, no more lording me. We are beyond that, you and I. In private, at least. My name is Gabriel, though only my mother ever uses it. I have never liked the name, in fact. My friends simply call me Thayne." He leaned in even closer. "But you may call me 'my love' or 'darling' or anything you like."

She smiled and pulled back slightly. "I shall call you Thayne. But please, do not sit so close. I do not wish for us to be the subject of gossip."

He shifted his position a bit. "It's a narrow bench. I will attempt a decorous distance, but I'm afraid parts of us are fated to . . . touch."

She arched an elegant brow and looked at him over the brim of her wineglass, but did not comment.

"And what of you?" he asked. "You will not allow me to call you Artemis, though it suits you. Will you honor me with your Christian name?"

She looked at him for a long moment before responding. "Beatrice."

"Ah, Beatrice. One who brings joy. You are certainly that, my lady. And I live in hope that you will bestow more joy upon me in the very near future."

She frowned. "Please. This is madness. There is still Emily. She is still determined to bring you up to scratch."

"And she will have no success in doing so, as I have told you before."

"But she will continue to try, and that makes it awkward for me. Don't you understand?" Her brow puckered and she gazed at him intently. "Yes, I will admit I am attracted to you, Thayne. You know that I am. But until Emily ceases to view you as a potential suitor, it just doesn't feel comfortable for me."

He took a long swallow of wine. "Damn the girl. Do you know she attached herself to me almost as soon as I arrived? She made it quite impossible to avoid sitting beside her during that wretched harp solo."

"You see what I mean?" She sliced the air with her hand, and her voice rose in frustration. "She will keep trying until she has worn you down. I wish you would do something to discourage her once and for all."

"If that is what it takes to have you in my arms again, I will publicly reject her."

Her expression softened. "Oh, no, Thayne. Please, nothing so harsh as that. But her vanity could use a bit of bruising. Perhaps if she sees that you are immune to her beauty, her pride will force her to give up the cause. But that will never happen if she keeps charming you into doing her bidding."

"It was not charm. I simply did not wish to appear churlish before so many onlookers."

"It is all the same. She will be seen sitting beside you and dancing with you, people will continue to link your names, expectations will mount, and before you know it, you will have been cajoled into making her an offer."

He laughed. "You must have more faith in me than that. No one—not Emily, my mother, or anyone else—is allowed to order my life for me. No one."

"Emily will try. Believe me. I know her well."

"But I see that you have decided I am right about backing away from her. The last time we met, you seemed determined that I should court the girl. I am glad you have changed your mind."

Her lips pursed into a tiny grimace before she spoke. "I simply cannot accept the notion of my niece marrying a man with whom I've . . . been intimate."

"Which is precisely why I will never marry her. Even if I wanted to, I could never do that to you, Beatrice. What she needs is a distraction. What if we threw another attractive suitor at her head?"

She gave a little snort. "Do you not see the court of admirers that always follows in her wake? There are any number of potential suitors littering my drawing room almost every day. But none of them is an heir to a duke."

"Are there any other dukes available? I have been away so long that I have no idea."

Beatrice smiled and shook her head. "The only other bachelor duke is Devonshire, and he's deaf as a post. There are always the royal dukes, I suppose. Clarence, for example."

"Is he as fat as I remember?"

"They're all fat. No, I think we will have to come up with something else."

Thayne surreptitiously pressed his knee against hers. "I will contrive a plan, I promise you. And you must have more faith in my lionhearted resolve against one troublesome young chit. We shall be together, you and I, if I have to pay someone to abduct the wretched girl and drag her to Gretna Green."

Thayne had lost no time in putting a plan in action to deal with the problem of Miss Emily Thirkill.

"You don't mean it." Jeremy Burnett stood beside him in the shadows of a large classical statue in one corner of the room. "How the devil am *I* supposed to capture her attention away from you?"

"With your infamous charm. And by staying at my side. Even if the girl does not make her usual effort to track me down, I fully intend to speak with her aunt. If Miss Thirkill is not with Lady Somerfield at that precise moment, you may be sure she will lose no time in returning to her aunt, ready to flaunt her beauty in my face. She is persistent as a fly on a hound's nose."

"She's devilish gorgeous, that's what she is."

"Which should make your job all the more easy." Thayne watched his friend and knew that look in his eye. The girl's looks had had him smitten from the first.

"I agree it is no great effort to spend time with her," Burnett said. "But if she has her sights on a marquess, what makes you think she'll deign to show interest in a plain mister?"

"Your father's an earl."

"But *I* shall never be, unless you have some sinister plot to remove my two elder brothers. No, there is nothing to recommend me to that sort of girl."

"Nonsense. Your fortune alone is a powerful recommendation. And you forget that I have seen how you charmed your way into every zenana in India, not to mention the bedrooms of every British woman there under forty. Besides, I am not asking you to marry the girl, or even to seduce her. Just to be there to aim some of that charm in her direction while I attempt to depress her hopes with my most imperious condescension. She's a tough little nut, though. Alone, my arrogance makes no impression on her. But your good nature can act as a counterpoint to my rudeness. When she is angling for me to request a dance, you step in and request it first. Think of it as being a sort of bodyguard. Keep her away from me as much as possible."

"A bodyguard, eh? I might require a hefty fee for such strenuous employment."

"What sort of fee?"

"Hmm. I just might want to rid you of one of those Hindu statues."

"If you can get that damned girl to give up any notion that I'll make her an offer, you may have as many statues as you want."

"You think this will work? That she'll give up if I keep her away from you?"

"She will not like to be seen pursuing a man who has no interest in her. It would be too wounding to her pride. Hopefully the girl will eventually let it be known that she has no interest in *me* and never did have. But it is a two-man job, I assure you. It will take me twice as long to be rid of her without your help. And the sooner the girl picks up her cap and walks away, the sooner her aunt will agree to an affair."

Burnett looked across the room at the two ladies in question. "I can see why you are in such a hurry. She's a stunning woman. Always thought so. Funny how she turned out to be the very woman you sought."

"She is indeed stunning, in every way. And with your help, I intend to have her again, and soon. If Miss Thirkill shows even the smallest sign of irritation with me, I shall have my opening. I depend upon you, old chap, to help her to see what a pompous ass I am."

Burnett grinned, displaying the full force of the boyish charm that had captivated women from Calcutta to Madras. "That should be no trouble at all," he said.

"Hmph. Let us make ourselves more visible."

They stepped from the shadows and began to move about the ballroom. Almost at once, they encountered Lady Emmeline Standish and her mother, Lady Frome. Lady Emmeline had been presented to Thayne by his mother, who was enthusiastic in her assessment of the girl's suitability as a potential bride. He had no objection to the young lady, who had glossy dark curls and a pretty mouth, and who did not seem as diffident as some of the other candidates. He should make an effort to get to know her. His request for a dance later in the evening was accepted.

"Seems a nice girl," Burnett said as they moved on.

"Yes, I like her. She doesn't fawn over me or simper or stammer. Her father's an earl; her mother is the daughter of a marquess—the blood's blue enough to suit even my mother."

Burnett stopped him with a hand to his arm. "That's it! There's your solution."

"What?"

"Miss Thirkill's blood is not blue enough for your exacting standards. Her father is merely a baronet. You wouldn't dream of introducing such an insignificant bloodline into the family."

Thayne's eyebrows rose in interest. "By Jove, it's brilliant. And credible. You have my permission to paint me as the loftiest of highborn snobs."

Burnett snorted. "Oh, *that's* a stretch."

"Remember that statue you wanted?"

"Yes, yes."

"Aha. Here they come. Get ready to exert your best charm."

Beatrice and her niece were walking toward them. Emily was beaming a dazzling smile at the young men who buzzed around her like bees. Thayne caught Beatrice's eye, and desire surged through him with a ferocity that left him breathless.

God, how he wanted her. He tried not to stare, but probably failed. She was clad in a green dress trimmed in gold that clung to her curves in a most provocative way when she moved. Her full bosom was on display, to his delight.

He was hard-pressed not to grin like a fool at the sight of her, but if his plan was going to work, he must retain his aristocratic reserve. And so, with an effort, he kept his lips tight, his face calm and rigid as a mask, his chin high. He turned away from the slow approach of the ladies and pretended to survey the room.

"There he is, Aunt Beatrice," Emily whispered. "He has seen us. Let us take our time. I do not wish to appear overly eager."

"A wise idea, my dear. It would not do to have people think you are chasing after him."

"I do not chase," Emily said in an indignant tone. "But I have saved a set for him."

Several young gentlemen stopped them and requested dances from Emily. She obliged them all with promises for later in the evening, but gave no one the next dance. Clearly, she wanted her first appearance on the dance floor to be on Lord Thayne's arm. Beatrice glanced at him again, and was pleased that he was no longer watching them approach.

He had donned his best toplofty demeanor, she noted, which came so easily to him. But there was something else, too, a contained energy about Thayne, as if the room, the starched neckcloth, all of Society even, were too small for him.

Had that lordly hauteur she'd once been so concerned about really been something else altogether? Beatrice sensed a feeling of confinement, a suppressed urge to bust loose and take life by the horns, on his own terms. That was probably why he'd spent so many years traveling in India, to fuel his restless spirit, to stretch the boundaries of his world. Yes, he would do his duty to his title and family, but he did not seem the sort of man to be constrained by that duty. He would reach beyond it somehow, to grab more from life.

It was one of the things she found most attractive about Thayne. He was so different from Somerfield, who'd been so rigid, so thoroughly fixed in his view of the world. He would never in a thousand years have traveled to India. It was too different, too alien, a place that did not conform to the rules he understood.

But a man like Thayne who explored new lands and new people and new ideas appealed to Beatrice. Perhaps it was merely a reaction to her years with Somerfield, but she was drawn to this young man with his strange dichotomy of upright nobility and restless spirit.

And the way he looked at her, with open desire. She had succumbed to that desire in a moment of madness and had subsequently hoped it would be enough to assuage that persistent hunger she'd felt ever since Penelope had pressed that wretched Merry Widows' pact upon them. It might have done, if she had never discovered his identity and been thrust into his company so often. The one wild evening had, in fact, done nothing to silence her body's urges, but had intensified them. She would fight them for now, or at least try to do so until she and Thayne sorted out what to do about Emily.

Beatrice noted with concern that Lord Rochdale had come to hang about on the fringes of Emily's court of admirers. His intense gaze was worrisome at best. She could not believe his intentions were honorable. All the world knew he did not have a principled bone in his body where women were concerned. He caught Beatrice's eye and arched a black brow. She glared at him and he finally moved away. She would have to warn Emily about him. Though he was too old for her, he did have rank and fortune that might appeal to the girl. Or, God forbid, to Ophelia.

For the moment, however, Emily was taking aim in another direction. They had made their way to where Thayne stood, and Emily stopped directly in front of him.

"Lady Somerfield," he said, and sketched a bow. "And Miss Thirkill." He gave a crisp nod in Emily's direction.

"Good evening, Lord Thayne," Beatrice said.

"Is it not a lovely ballroom?" Emily exclaimed, her blue eyes sparkling, her smile brilliant. "I plan to dance every dance. I've already promised several sets, and hope to have them all promised very soon. I hate to sit out a dance, don't you?"

"You remember Mr. Burnett, of course," Thayne said, completely ignoring Emily's not very subtle suggestion that he dance with her.

Mr. Burnett made an elegant bow. "Miss Thirkill, may I be so bold as to reserve one of your remaining sets? I promise not to tread on your toes too often."

"Oh."

Emily looked at Thayne, apparently hoping he would claim the set instead. The marquess, however, affected a demeanor of supreme disinterest and said nothing.

Beatrice gave Emily a discreet poke in the ribs.

"Why, yes," she said, plastering a brittle smile on

her face, "I'd be happy to dance with you, Mr. Burnett. As it happens, I have the next set free."

Again, she darted a glance at Thayne, for she had surely been saving her first set for him. But there was nothing she could do about it now.

"Excellent," Burnett said. He smiled broadly and offered his arm. "Shall we dance, Miss Thirkill?"

He led Emily onto the floor, where several lines were forming for the first country dance. Thayne shot Burnett a significant look, and Burnett nodded in response before taking his place in the line. What signal had just passed between them? What were they up to?

"There, see how easy that was?" Thayne said. "Burnett will keep her occupied for a while."

"It is only a dance, my lord," Beatrice said, "not a betrothal."

"You are not to *my lord* me anymore, remember? Anyway, Burnett has promised to fill the girl's head with accounts of the worst aspects of my character."

"Ah, so that is your plan. But what makes you think he can capture her interest, when she has all but ignored him up to now?"

"Because he has the power of love to drive him—he is besotted with the girl—plus the promise of a statue. His primary goal is to convince her that I am not worthy of her attention, that I am too toplofty and will never condescend to court her. Only a baronet's daughter and all that. While he's blackening my name, I have no doubt he will try to woo her for himself. He has always had a way with the ladies. I've known a dozen women or more who've fallen in love with the fellow based on little more from him than a smile."

"He is rather attractive," Beatrice said, "in a lanky, boyish sort of way. And that smile *is* devastating. He quite charmed me with it the first time we met."

"He is meant for your niece, my Artemis, not for

you. I want you all to myself. In fact, come with me."
He turned to walk back toward the entrance. Surely
he did not mean to seduce her here, at another ball.

"You are not to take me into the garden, Thayne.
We cannot do that again."

"Not the garden," he said. "But I took time to
learn the lay of the land here at Oscott House before
you arrived. There's a nice, dark little alcove just
around this corner."

Beatrice understood what he meant to happen in
that alcove. He was going to kiss her, at the very
least. She ought not to allow it. One dance with Mr.
Burnett did not relieve them of the problem of Emily,
and Beatrice had been determined to resolve that
issue before allowing herself to be seduced again by
Thayne. And yet here she was, abandoning all her
best intentions to accompany him to some dark corner so that he could kiss her. Her desire for the
wretched man was too powerful to resist.

Thayne casually strolled toward his destination,
not touching Beatrice or even standing close. At least
he maintained propriety in public. When the few
people wandering about had disappeared into the
ballroom, Thayne pulled her into the dark recess beneath the stairs.

He tugged her against his chest, and kissed her.

She resisted at first, instinctively, without thought,
as though the wrongness of it was elemental. He felt
it, and pulled back, lifting his head and staring down
at her with eyes so dark they appeared black.

"Why?" He kept his arms around her, holding her
close. Her hands were pressed flat against his chest.

"Because we should not be together."

"Why? And don't tell me it's because of your
niece. We have settled that business. She has nothing
to do with us."

"I can't help feeling guilty. You were seen to be

her suitor and it feels wrong to be with you. But that is not the only reason."

"Then why?"

"We're wrong for each other. I'm too old for you—"

"Don't be silly. You are *not* too old."

"I am a respectable widow with children—did you know I have two daughters?—and you're the Marquess of Thayne, Society's golden prize, the gleam in every hopeful mother's eye. Everyone knows you are looking for a bride."

"I am not offering matrimony to you, Beatrice."

"I know."

"Is that what you want? An offer of marriage?"

"Good God, no. I have been married. I am done with marriage."

"Then there is no problem, is there? Yes, I will marry before the end of the year, probably to one of the girls in the next room. But in the meantime, there is us. There is this."

And he kissed her again, in slow, succulent bites as though savoring a sweetmeat. This time, just as instinctively as she had closed up and rejected him before, she now opened like a new blossom and welcomed him. Her hands slid up his chest and over his shoulders, finally wrapping around his neck and pulling him down. She opened her mouth and touched her tongue to his. He accepted the invitation and set up a dance between their tongues more lush and exciting than anything happening in the ballroom next door.

She had tried so hard to make this attraction to him wrong, but it felt so right. Her mind spun back to the garden, the darkness, the cool night air, his flesh against hers, and suddenly she knew she had to have him again. Age, be damned. Emily, be damned. Everyone and everything, be damned.

His mouth left hers and trailed lower, over her arched neck and down to the tops of her breasts, pushed up into firm mounds by tight stays. His tongue dipped into the cleft between her breasts, and she let out a little groan.

"Stop, please," she said, though it was truly the last thing she wanted. "Not here. Please. Someone may walk by."

He lifted his head and loosened his arms. He looked down at her with eyes so full of raw desire she felt weak in the knees. "No," he said in a rough whisper, "not here. But somewhere. Yes?"

She studied his face, almost drowning in the depths of his dark eyes. Lord, how she did want him. Could she really do this? Could she put aside all the objections she knew to be reasonable and right and take him as her lover?

"Yes?" he repeated.

"Yes."

And suddenly, his face broke into a wide grin, slightly smug, as if to remind her that he always got what he wanted. He brought one of her hands to his lips, then made a sort of growl. "Blasted gloves." He bent to kiss the end of her nose instead, and it made her giggle.

"You have obsessed me, you know. I think of nothing but you."

"Oh." She smiled at such earnest passion.

"When?" he asked. "How soon? Tonight?"

"No, not tonight. And I have so many obligations as Emily's chaperone. Oh, I cannot begin to imagine how we will manage it."

"There are twenty-four hours in the day, my huntress. Surely we can find one or two for ourselves. Leave it to me. But where? Your house?"

"Oh, dear. No, no, we cannot go there. Emily is staying with me, for one thing, and I have two daughters underfoot, as well, not so many years younger than Emily. How am I to teach them propriety if they find me in bed with a man? No, I cannot risk bringing you home."

"And I am staying at my father's house. It is big enough to hide in, as you have seen, but it would be difficult to get you in unnoticed. There are too damned many servants about. I trip over one every time I turn around. And the gossip belowstairs is rampant, and tends to make its way upstairs eventually. And the duchess is everywhere. One never knows when one might run into her."

"Oh, no, that would not do. I would hate to come out of your bedchamber and crash into your mother."

"Egad, no. I have bought a house on Cavendish Square, but it is not ready to move into yet. There are carpenters and plasterers everywhere—the place is littered with ladders and scaffolding and paint buckets and lumber. I'm afraid we can't go there yet."

"Oh." The deep disappointment she suddenly felt was rather comical when one considered that only a moment ago she had been entirely opposed to the business of a love affair with him. Now, after only a few kisses, she could not wait for it.

"I'll think of something," Thayne said, and led her out of the dark alcove and into the hallway. "I promise. I will send round a note when everything is arranged."

Beatrice was almost bursting with anticipation and hoped that note would not be long coming. And she hoped they would not have to resort to some tawdry hideaway. Or another garden wall.

As they entered the ballroom again—keeping a decorous distance between them so no one would guess they were anything more than acquaintances—they came upon Wilhelmina and Penelope, who were standing just beyond the entrance and involved in what looked to be a serious conversation. Penelope caught Beatrice's eye and waved her over. Thayne followed.

"Good evening, ladies," Beatrice said. "You remember Lord Thayne?"

Penelope smiled brightly and cast a quick, knowing glance at Beatrice before addressing the marquess. "Of course. It is good to see you again, my lord."

Thayne demonstrated his impeccable breeding by remembering each of their names, and making an elegant bow before them. "Your Grace," he said to Wilhelmina. "I am pleased to meet you again. And Lady Gosforth. You are both looking exceptionally lovely this evening."

"Bosh," Penelope said. "Beatrice—Lady Somerfield, that is—puts us all in the shade with that marvelous Pomona green dress."

"Have you two been dancing?" Wilhelmina asked. "You are looking a trifle flushed, my dear."

Penelope placed her fan over her face to hide a giggle.

"No, we were only . . . talking," Beatrice said, though they would both know what had really been going on. "But I am a bit parched. Perhaps I ought to track down some punch."

"Allow me," Thayne said. "And you, Lady Gosforth? May I bring a glass for you, as well?"

"I'd like nothing more, thank you," she said.

"And you, Duchess?"

"No, thank you, but I will walk along with you, if you do not mind. I need to speak with Lord Ingleby, who is on the other side of the room."

"It will be my pleasure," Thayne said, and offered his arm to Wilhelmina. She took it, and they walked off together.

"Heavens, but he *is* attractive," Penelope said after they'd gone. "And that was very kind of him to offer his arm to Wilhelmina. She is so often ignored at these events, despite her title."

"People can be very cruel," Beatrice said. "Her blood may not run blue, but she has more character in her little finger than anyone in this room, our duchess does."

"But what about Lord Thayne?" Penelope's voice grew excited, though she kept it pitched low. "What is happening between you? It is obvious that you have just been kissed."

"Is it so obvious?" Beatrice lifted a hand to her cheek.

"To one who knows you. Well, then, if you've been kissing, then you must have decided to take him as your lover after all."

"I have, God help me. Oh, Penelope, I hope I am not making a fool of myself."

"Of course you aren't. The man can't tear his eyes from you. You are not a fool. You are a lucky woman. So, when is it to be?"

"We have not yet contrived a plan. Neither of us can bring the other home and flaunt our relationship to our families."

"That's true. But you'll figure something out."

"That's what Thayne said."

"Then trust him to do so. He looks like a man who generally gets what he wants."

"Yes, he is." *And he wants me.* Beatrice began to laugh, feeling almost giddy at the thought that such a beautiful young man wanted her.

Perhaps she was not so very old after all.

Chapter 9

"What is it, Mama? Bad news?"

Beatrice looked up at her youngest daughter, who sat across the breakfast table, slathering jam on a slice of buttered bread. Beatrice made an effort to school her features, to affect an air of nonchalance, when she felt quite the opposite. Charlotte, at thirteen, noticed altogether too much. She had certainly caught the brief moment of anxiety Beatrice had felt upon opening the note that had just been delivered by a footman. In fact, very little got past that girl. She had the sort of curiosity that had been landing her in one scrape after the other from the time she could walk. The last thing Beatrice needed was for Charlotte to discover the contents of the note in her hand.

The note from Lord Thayne.

"No, dear," Beatrice said, "not bad news. Just a bit of a disappointment regarding a . . . a contribution we had anticipated for the Benevolent Widows Fund. Nothing to worry you. In fact, the only thing you should be fretting about is that classical essay Miss Trumbull tells me you haven't yet finished."

"Oh, bother," Charlotte said, and rolled her eyes. "Who cares about a bunch of silly old gods and goddesses anyway?"

"You should care," Beatrice said as she surreptitiously slipped the note into her sleeve. "Every well-educated person should have some knowledge of classical mythology."

"Then perhaps you ought to take me with you to the opera tonight," Charlotte said, tilting her chin at a defiant angle. "Emily says it is all about that Orpheus chap dashing down to Hades to rescue his wife. It might help me to make more sense of it if I saw it onstage."

Emily, at the other end of the table, suddenly came alive. "Oh, no, Aunt Beatrice. Please do not inflict the infant on us tonight. I am going to wear my brand-new pink dress and try to catch a certain gentleman's eye. Charlotte would ruin everything with her constant chatter and her total lack of decorum."

"I have decorum!" Charlotte said. "Loads of it, if only I were given a chance to display it." She turned a plaintive look on her mother.

Beatrice smiled. "Of course you have decorum, my love. You can be a very proper young lady when you want to be. But you will have to wait a few more years to show off your good manners to Society."

"Does that mean I do not get to go with you tonight?"

"Why should you?" Beatrice's quieter daughter, Georgiana, finally spoke up. "I'm two years older than you and I don't get to go. You must wait your turn just like everyone else."

Charlotte sank back against her chair and pouted. The poor girl was so anxious to be grown-up. Having Emily around this Season, to see how full and exciting a young woman's social life could be, had been exhilarating for both girls. Charlotte, though, had become a trial for her governess, preferring to hear about Emily's evenings out than to study history and French and music.

"Don't be so glum, Charlotte, my love," Beatrice said. "You and Georgie may join me tomorrow in the drawing room when I am at home to visitors. That is, if you finish your essay. Would you like that?"

Charlotte's blue eyes grew wide with excitement. "May I? Truly?" She loved it when Beatrice allowed her to mingle with visitors. She was much more gregarious than her older sister, and was not the least uncomfortable chatting with visitors. But she was just as likely to sit quietly and listen, hoping to pick up bits of gossip. Charlotte loved gossip. Beatrice supposed it made her feel more a part of Society, to know everything that went on, but she worried that the girl would hear things she was too young to understand and had no business knowing.

"If you promise to put on your best manners and sit quietly. And not to speak unless you are specifically addressed."

"I promise."

"And *if* you finish the essay."

"I'll finish it! I will! I promise."

"Then you had better get to work, my girl."

"Yes, ma'am." She got up quickly, her red curls bouncing, and moved away from the breakfast table. "C'mon, Georgie."

After the girls left, Beatrice turned to Emily. "What are your plans for the day?" she asked.

"Caroline Whittier wants me to go shopping with her. Then that odious Mr. Burnett has invited me to drive in the park with him this afternoon. He simply would not take no for an answer. But he is Lord Thayne's particular friend, so I shall get him to talk about the marquess and perhaps I will learn how best to keep his interest."

"Mr. Burnett seems a perfectly charming young man," Beatrice said. "You seem to have attracted his particular interest."

Emily gave a dismissive wave. "He does not matter. It is Lord Thayne I intend to have."

"But, my dear, you cannot force the marquess to

take an interest in you. It might do you well to look elsewhere."

"Why are you suddenly so set against the marquess?" Emily asked in a peevish tone. "At first you were determined that I should bring him up to scratch. Now you seem determined that he will not come around, but he will. Eventually. And his mother likes me. She will sing my praises to him, I have no doubt. I don't mean to sound vain, but there are no other eligible girls as pretty as me. Lord Thayne will recognize that soon enough. He will tire of that odious Lady Sarah Addison, who has been practically throwing herself at him. Or Lady Emmeline Standish. None of them are as pretty as me."

"Perhaps beauty is not as important to him as it is to some men," Beatrice said. "You know, my dear, that your father is merely a baronet. Lord Thayne's father is a duke. He may be looking higher. His recent lack of interest may have nothing to do with *you* at all, but only with rank."

Emily gave an unladylike snort, but then grew pensive as she finished her breakfast. Hopefully she was beginning to see, at last, that Lord Thayne might actually be unattainable, despite her beauty. Beatrice prayed that was so, and not only for her own sake, but for Emily's. The girl needed to learn that she could not always rely on her looks to get her everything in life she desired.

If only she could make Ophelia believe it, as well.

After breakfast, Beatrice returned to her bedchamber and closed the door. She sat on the bed and slipped the folded note from inside her sleeve. She had not had a moment to contemplate its message while surrounded by three young girls. In fact, she had read only the signature and the first line before Charlotte had noted her anxiety. Beatrice had refolded the note without reading beyond that rather stunning first sentence.

It is arranged.

He had done it. Somehow he had contrived a plan for them to meet, to be together again, to make love.

It had probably been for the best that she had received the note while in the company of the girls, for she had not had time or opportunity to dwell on its import. Now that she was alone, she could give in to every anxious, excited, nervous twinge that had been stifled in the breakfast room.

She opened the folded parchment and her eye was first drawn to the large and forceful "Thayne" scrawled across the bottom. His penmanship was a perfect reflection of his personality: arrogant, resolute, powerful. She read on.

It is arranged. We will meet tonight.

Tonight? So soon?

Do not change your plans for the evening. Go to the opera. I will see you there. Dress your hair simply, for I intend to take it down.

That last line sent a little shiver across her shoulders. She fell back against the bed, flung her arms out wide, and grinned up at the canopy.

And so, it was to happen. The oh-so-proper Lady Somerfield was about to embark upon her first love affair. She felt a bit wicked. Certainly more worldly than ever before. She supposed she ought to feel foolish for succumbing to this ridiculous passion for a younger man. But she did not. Instead, she felt alive, invigorated, rejuvenated. Yes, she felt young again. And something more. A new air of confidence filled her, made her feel strong and invincible.

It was similar to the overwhelming sense of independence she'd felt when she'd made her first financial decisions after Somerfield died. He had never allowed her to be involved in anything regarding money, despite the fact that she had a head for figures and took a real interest in markets and investments. Whenever she had offered an opinion, her husband had given her an indulgent pat on the cheek and told her not to worry her pretty head about such things that were beyond the understanding of the female mind.

Beatrice had hated that condescension from him, and it was the source of a great many arguments over the years. She had so wanted to be involved in investment decisions, not out of any sense of entitlement, but because she enjoyed it and was good at it. But Somerfield had been intransigent on the subject. He had been conservative to a fault in regard to their finances. He'd inherited a profitable earldom, but had done almost nothing to increase that profit, to build his fortune. He was too afraid of losing it. Beatrice, on the other hand, had seen that they had quite enough money to risk an occasional interesting investment, but Somerfield would not budge.

After his death, when a sizable fortune had been left in her hands—thanks to her father's sound management of her marriage contract—Beatrice had begun to dabble in a few schemes that had paid off handsomely. For the first time in her adult life, she had taken risks.

And now she was taking another one with Thayne. A very big risk. To make such a decision by herself, *for* herself, to be so completely in charge of her own destiny, made her feel . . . powerful. She was quite giddy with it, in fact. She even felt confident that everything would work out satisfactorily where Emily was concerned. Some other rich young man would win the day.

But for now, Beatrice could think only of one particular rich young man who was about to win the night.

She clutched his note to her breast and giggled like a girl.

Where was he?

Beatrice was growing jittery waiting for Thayne to show up at the opera. His parents were in a box on the opposite side of the stage, but Thayne had not joined them yet. She supposed he was waiting until close to the end to make an appearance. *Orfeo ed Euridice*, though one of Beatrice's favorites, was a very long opera. How was she to be expected to maintain her composure for several hours until it was over? And then what? Was she simply to walk away on his arm, begging Emily to excuse her while she went off to make love with Lord Thayne?

That would certainly spike the girl's guns. And send Ophelia into a murderous rage.

No, he must have something else in mind, though Beatrice could not imagine what it was. She would have to trust in his resourcefulness and his discretion. He was too much of a gentleman to manage things in a way that might damage her reputation.

She had dressed with extra care this evening, wearing one of her most revealing dresses. Not that she needed to entice the man further, but it enhanced her confidence to know that she looked desirable. And she had done as he'd asked regarding her hair. She wore a simple coiffure gathered up at the back of her head and fastened with two small combs. If Thayne took her hair down, and she had no doubt he would do so, she was fairly certain she could re-create the hairstyle easily enough afterward. It would not do to return home with her hair hanging about her shoulders.

Her thoughts were interrupted by a soft wail beside her. Beatrice turned to find Wilhelmina bent over, her face buried in her hands. The duchess had been looking forward to seeing this particular opera for some time, and had been pleased to receive Beatrice's invitation to share her box. But she had been quiet and reserved all evening. Was she ill?

Beatrice slipped an arm around her friend's shoulder. "Wilhelmina?" she whispered. "Are you all right?"

The duchess shook her head but said nothing.

"Are you ill?"

After a few moments, Wilhelmina raised her head and Beatrice was startled to see tears streaming down her face. "My dear, whatever is the matter?"

"I am not feeling myself tonight, I fear," Wilhelmina said in a shaky voice. "Forgive me."

"You must go home, then," Beatrice said. "You are not well and should not sit through this long performance."

Wilhelmina choked back a sob. "You are right. I should go."

"Of course you must. Let me help you. I'll go downstairs with you and see you to your carriage."

Wilhelmina clutched at her arm. "Oh, Beatrice, I don't think I could bear to be alone tonight. I do hate to trouble you, but . . . would you go with me? Would you take me home? I am afraid I shall need a shoulder to cry on."

The poor woman was overset about something. Beatrice wondered what could have happened to so discompose her even-tempered, normally unflappable friend. Was it something to do with Lord Ingleby, the man with whom Wilhelmina was carrying on a discreet love affair? Had he thrown her over?

"Of course I will come with you," she said, "and stay with you as long as you need. Just let me make arrangements for Emily to be taken home later."

Beatrice experienced a momentary pang of regret that her plans with Thayne, whatever they were, would have to wait for another night. She would not leave her friend alone when she was so upset.

She spoke quietly to Lady Billingsley, who was there with her daughter Sarah, a particular friend of Emily's, and told her the duchess was unwell. "I would like to see her home, and to stay with her a while to make sure she is all right. Would you mind terribly looking after Emily for me?"

"Not at all," Lady Billingsley said. "I am sorry Her Grace is ill, but you must not fret over Emily. I will keep an eye on her and see that she gets home safely."

Beatrice had a word with Emily, who was properly concerned for the duchess, but was pleased to stay behind with her friend. "May I still go to the card party at Drake House after the opera? Sarah is planning to go, I am certain."

"If Lady Billingsley does not object, you may go. But you must stay with her, as she is to bring you home. Ah, the first act is over. Blast. I had hoped to get the duchess outside without everyone gaping at her. I must hurry before the corridors become too crowded."

Beatrice grabbed her shawl and helped a listless Wilhelmina with her wrap. They made their way to the door of the box just as it opened and several young gentlemen entered. One of them was Mr. Burnett.

He bowed, offered his endearing grin, and said, "You are leaving, Lady Somerfield? What unfortunate timing. I was just coming to pay my respects."

Beatrice smiled at the young man as she tried to usher Wilhelmina through the door. "Do not worry, sir, Miss Thirkill is not leaving with me. You may pay your respects to her instead."

As she and Wilhelmina stepped into the corridor, Beatrice overheard Emily say, "Ah, Mr. Burnett. And where is your friend Lord Thayne tonight?"

"He is not here, I am afraid," Mr. Burnett replied. "He had other business this evening."

So Thayne hadn't even planned to come to the opera. Beatrice wondered for a moment what exactly his plan had been, but she concentrated on her friend, who kept her head bowed as they walked through the crowded corridor and down the main staircase.

When they reached the entrance and walked out into the cool night air, Beatrice was just about to ask a footman to call her carriage when Wilhelmina placed a firm hand on her arm.

"No, this way," she said in a steady voice.

She moved quickly, tugging Beatrice behind her, and there was no longer the slightest indication that she was ill or upset. The plumes in her yellow hair bobbed jauntily as she hurried along to the rows of carriages that stood waiting.

"What is going on?" Beatrice asked, somewhat breathless as she tried to keep up.

Wilhelmina stopped in front of an elegant carriage, and the door swung open from the inside. "Go on," she said. "Step inside."

Beatrice walked to the open door and saw a dark figure inside the carriage. It reached out a hand. "Come on in, Artemis."

Beatrice gasped, then turned to Wilhelmina, who was beaming. "Go on," the duchess said. "He is waiting."

Beatrice smiled at her friend, who had obviously been instrumental in Lord Thayne's plans. "So, all that weeping and drooping about was merely an act?"

"Remember, my dear, that for a short time many years ago I trod the boards. Ha. It seems I still have a bit of the thespian left in me. What fun! Now, go. Have a lovely time with your young man. I have my own carriage waiting, with my own gentleman inside. Go. Go!"

Beatrice took Thayne's hand and stepped into the

carriage. Wilhelmina smiled as she shut the door, gave a signal to the driver, then waved as she walked away.

"At last," Thayne said. He reached across Beatrice and pulled down the window shade. "At last."

He gathered her into his arms and kissed her.

Now that there was no hindrance to their passion, no guessing where it might lead, they each fell into the kiss with raw, unbridled hunger before the carriage even moved.

When the carriage finally lurched forward, they were already entwined, reaching and groping as they kissed and kissed and kissed. After a while, Thayne pulled Beatrice onto his lap and buried his face in her full cleavage, dipping his tongue into its depths. One hand, warm and ungloved, reached up her skirts and stroked her bare thigh. She gave a moan of pleasure, and Thayne took her mouth again. He eased her down until she was lying on the soft velvet of the squabs, her skirts hiked up around her thighs and Thayne urging them apart with his knee.

His hand crept higher until it found the damp place between her legs. His fingers had just begun to work their magic when the carriage came to a jolting halt.

"Damn." Thayne removed his mouth from hers and pulled away. He tugged down her skirts and lifted her upright again. "We need not be in such a rush when a soft bed awaits us. I believe we have arrived."

A bit flustered for having so completely forgotten herself in the carriage, Beatrice adjusted her clothing and hair. She looked at Thayne, who was smiling.

"You look adorably rumpled," he said, and touched her cheek with the backs of his fingers. "I cannot wait to see you even more thoroughly undone."

Thayne opened the carriage door, jumped down,

and offered his hand to Beatrice. She stepped out and looked around to see where they'd been taken.

"Why, this is Wilhelmina's house," she said, recognizing the handsome brick home on Charles Street with its classical white pediment and elaborate ironwork.

"The duchess sensed our dilemma," he said, "and offered it for our use. She will be spending this night . . . elsewhere, or so she told me."

"Really? She did this for us?"

"She is an excellent ally, your duchess. A remarkable woman."

"You do know who she is, do you not? Or who she was?"

"Yes, of course. I remember infamous tales from my university days. But she's risen above it all and made a good life for herself. I quite like her."

Beatrice laid a hand on his arm. "I'm so glad. Many people are still cruel to her. She pretends not to care, but it cannot be easy."

He laid his hand over hers. "You are a good friend to her. And, heaven be praised, she is a friend to us both tonight. She has given all but one servant the night off, and he is said to be the soul of discretion. Come, my huntress."

A butler held open the front door. Beatrice had been to Wilhelmina's house several times before and knew that face. It was not easily forgotten—large, crooked nose, heavy brow, and long scar running across his chin. He would surely recognize her, as well. She must remember to tip him handsomely to further ensure that he kept quiet about this little rendezvous.

"Good evening, my lady." He might have the face of a thug, but he had the voice of a refined gentleman. It always surprised her. He made a crisp bow. "And my lord."

"Good evening, Smeaton," she said, and walked through to the entry hall.

"Her Grace has told me to expect you. Follow me, please."

Thayne took her arm and they followed Smeaton up two flights of stairs. He led them to an open doorway and gestured that they should enter. Beatrice stepped into the bedchamber—not Wilhelmina's, but a guest chamber—to find a cozy fire burning and a heavily canopied bed with the coverlet turned down. Beside the fireplace was a table that held a decanter of wine and two glasses, as well as a plate of fruit and cheeses. Bless Wilhelmina's heart, she had thought of everything. Beatrice turned to Thayne and smiled.

"Perfect," he said, and placed something in the butler's hand. Smeaton nodded and left, shutting the door behind him. Thayne looked at Beatrice with open desire. "Perfect," he repeated.

He pulled her to him and kissed her, then went to work on her clothes. "I promise more finesse the next time, but I am too eager to go slowly just now."

She was equally eager, and so they quickly undressed each other, flinging bits of clothing this way and that until they both stood naked in the firelight. Good Lord, but he was beautiful. Broad shoulders and a well-muscled chest, a tapering waist and slim hips, a rampant sex, fully erect and large—he was the picture of masculine perfection. His chest was covered in dark hair, as were his legs and forearms, and a thick, dark cushion surrounded his sex. Somehow all that dark hair, not to mention the robust erection, dispelled any notion she might have had that he was too young a man for her. Thayne was no boy.

He was staring at her body with the same curiosity, and Beatrice suddenly lost some of her confidence. She knew what he saw. Her waist had begun to thicken slightly and her stomach was not flat as it had once been. Her breasts were no longer pert and plump, but had graduated into matronly fullness. She could never pass for a young girl again.

She made an instinctive move to cover herself. But he grabbed her hand and held it out to her side.

"You are magnificent," he said, and lifted his other hand to her hair. He removed one comb, then the other, and a few hairpins later, her hair fell loose about her shoulders. He stood back and gazed at her. "Positively magnificent."

"No, I'm not. I'm not young anymore. My body has aged. Oh, how I wish you could have seen me before I had two children, before I lost my youth."

"I like you just the way you are, Artemis. You have a woman's body. A beautiful woman's body." He swooped down and lifted her into his arms. "Now, let me worship it."

He deposited her on the bed, lay down beside her, and began to do precisely that. With mouth and tongue and hands and eyes he explored—worshipped—every inch of her, using all the tricks he'd learned in India to pleasure her. Her hair was glorious and skeined red across the pale linen of the bedsheets. He combed his fingers through it and buried his nose in it, inhaling the sweet fragrance of soap and lavender.

Her skin was a marvel. Creamy white and flawless, it felt like silk against him. He couldn't get enough of it, wanted to wrap himself up in it. He rubbed his cheek against the silky skin of her belly, and moved his way upward. Thayne adored her breasts. They were full, though not too large, and amazingly soft. He kneaded them with his thumbs and teased them with his tongue until the nipples were taut pebbles. She squirmed and moaned beneath him, and set him on fire.

He wanted to take more time. She deserved more time. But he could wait no longer. If he did not bury himself in her now, the consequences could be embarrassing. And so he nudged her legs apart and positioned himself at the entrance to her sex. "I'm sorry, Beatrice. I want you too much. I want you now." And he plunged inside her with a single stroke. She was slick and warm and welcoming. He almost came at once, but steadied himself and breathed the way he'd been taught in India.

When he had himself under control, he began to move in her, slowly at first. She lifted her legs to give him better access, and wrapped them around his back. And then she began to move with him, rocking and bucking against him with uninhibited passion. God, he loved the way she moved, the way she unashamedly sought her own pleasure. No woman, not even the skilled courtesans of the Punjab or Hyderabad courts, had ever moved like this, with such open, honest, unrestrained desire. They had always been working hard to please him. Strangely enough, Thayne found it infinitely more arousing that she greedily took as much pleasure as she gave.

He tried to give her more, driving faster, pressing himself hard against the nub of her sex, the center of pleasure. With a supreme effort of will, he held himself back until he felt her climax build, until he felt the tension in her body coil tight and finally spring loose into a hot, pulsing release that had her crying out and writhing beneath him.

"Oh my God, Thayne! Oh my God, oh my God. Gabriel!"

The sound of his name on her lips, unexpected and intimate, drove him harder. He thrust faster and faster until he could hold on no longer. With a groan, he quickly pulled out, convulsed violently, and spent himself on her white belly.

* * *

It had been worth it. Beatrice was not going to regret a single moment of this night. After a second, more leisurely bout of lovemaking, she lay curled up against Thayne. Gabriel. She would think of him now only as Gabriel. She was not sure why his name had burst from her lips in the throes of a sexual climax. Perhaps she had felt so connected to him in that moment of ultimate sharing that only his most intimate name seemed right. And it *was* right.

After the first loving, Gabriel found a basin and water—bless Wilhelmina, again—and gently cleaned her, then pulled her from the bed to sit by the fire. They had drunk the wine and eaten grapes and figs, and finally fell into lovemaking again, right there on the floor. They lay there still, her back against his chest, his arm wrapped around her and softly fondling her breasts.

"I adore your body," he said. "It reminds me of my favorite works of sculpture from India. Full and round here"—he cupped a breast—"narrower here"—his hand slid to her waist—"and softly rounded here"—he laid his hand flat against her belly. "I have several crates of stone-carved goddesses shaped exactly like you."

"I am glad you like my body, but it is not the ideal you find in your sculpture. I'm quite sure your stone goddesses have firm breasts." She giggled. "Well, of course they do. They're made of stone!"

He laughed and she bounced against his chest. "I love your breasts," he said, moving his hands to cup them again, "just the way they are. Soft and pliable. It will be an effort to ever take my hands away from them."

The dear boy. He really seemed to mean it. Though why he should prefer soft, middle-aged breasts to firm, perky younger ones was a mystery. "You make me feel beautiful, Gabriel."

"You are beautiful," he said in a matter-of-fact tone that made her believe him.

She reached behind her and touched his face. The

rough prickle of beard marked his jaw. "That is why I was so drawn to you at the masquerade," she said. "You looked at me in a way that made me feel beautiful, desirable. I could not resist you, the way you looked at me. I had not felt such open desire from a man in . . . well, I don't know if I ever have, actually. I believe it made me a little crazy that night."

"I have been away from England too long," he said. "Some sort of sea change must have taken place in the male population while I was away. Or they have all gone blind. How could a woman like you have never felt a man's desire before?"

She hunched a shoulder. "I felt it from my husband."

"But no other?"

"No. But perhaps I wasn't paying attention. Until I saw you."

His hand crept lower until his fingers threaded through the copper curls between her legs, setting off tingling sparks of sensation. "Are you paying attention now?"

"Oh, yes." She smiled to think that he was ready for another round of lovemaking. It seemed there was, after all, a singular advantage to taking a younger man for one's lover. "Very close attention, indeed."

And she turned in his arms and kissed him.

Chapter 10

"Thayne? What the devil are you doing here?"

He muttered an oath and turned to face his mother. "It is nice to see you, too, Your Grace."

She gazed at him quizzically as she handed her parasol to a housemaid. It had never occurred to Thayne that she would come to call on Beatrice, but here they both stood in her entry hall along with a few others who'd dropped by. Beatrice had told him this was her "at home" afternoon, and he'd decided he couldn't wait to see her again, even among a small crowd of visitors. Since they had left the Duchess of Hertford's house last night, he had thought of little else but when they might be able to meet again.

"You surprise me, Thayne," his mother said. "I thought you were not interested in the Thirkill girl, but I am very pleased to see you have changed your mind."

"I have not changed my mind. I am only here because Burnett dragged me along. He is the one with a partiality for Miss Thirkill. I have come to support him, to see that he doesn't make a cake of himself."

In fact, it was quite the other way around. Thayne had pleaded with Burnett to accompany him, knowing that if he arrived alone, others would make the same assumption as his mother. Now that there was a full-blown love affair between him and Beatrice, the very last thing he wanted was to be linked again with her niece. They had spoken about Emily at some length as they'd lain cocooned together under a blanket in front of the fire. Beatrice was very concerned about the girl's continued interest in Thayne and asked him to keep his distance. She would not welcome his appearance here today, but he had not been able to stay away. Besides, he had no intention of allowing a headstrong young girl to dictate his movements.

"Burnett?" The duchess craned her neck to see who was climbing the stairs. "I do not see Mr. Burnett."

"He is already upstairs, Mother. In his eagerness, he dashed on ahead when I stopped to speak to you. Come, take my arm. We shall go up together."

The duchess looked all about her as they ascended the stairs. "This is a rather elegant balustrade, is it not? The ironwork is quite splendid. I can see that Lady Somerfield's good taste is not limited to her wardrobe. It's a lovely house."

"Yes, it is." He generally paid little attention to such things as balustrades, but now that he looked around him, he could see that the house was a reflection of its mistress. The furnishings, the pictures, the window draperies—everything was tasteful and refined, as elegant as Beatrice herself.

They had talked a great deal the night before, getting to know each other's mind as well as body. He liked that about her, the fact that she wanted to talk. He'd had a notion that their relationship would be solely physical. He was looking for a bride this Season, after all, and sought nothing more from Beatrice than her body.

He ought to have known better. They had begun a sort of friendship when he'd still been interested in Emily. He had always enjoyed her forthright conversation.

And now he found himself remembering things she'd said last night as much as he remembered things they'd done together. As he led his mother toward the open doors of the drawing room, he was looking forward to speaking with her again. Almost as much as he anticipated making love to her.

He was very much afraid this was not going to be the simple, carnal love affair he'd expected.

Beatrice was listening politely to Lady Tewkesbury's mindless chatter while attempting to keep an eye on all three of her charges. Her daughters were behaving quite properly, even Charlotte, who was in one of her more watchful moods today. She had been complimented several times on the girls, who were both dressed in pretty spotted muslin dresses. Golden-haired Georgiana, though still a bit angular, showed all the signs of becoming a true beauty. Charlotte hadn't yet blossomed, though she reminded Beatrice very much of herself at that age, with bright red hair and freckles. She sat ramrod straight with her hands folded demurely in her lap. Miss Trumbull's deportment lessons must be working, at last.

Then Charlotte broke into a wide smile as one of Emily's swains stopped to speak with the child. Beatrice could only hope she would not talk the young man to death. The girl could chatter endlessly, barely pausing for breath.

Beatrice's gaze swept the room and happened to catch Emily, who was positively beaming. Her pretty face was wreathed in a dazzling smile and a glint of excitement lit her eyes. But that sparkling gaze was not aimed at young Lord Ushworth, who sat beside her, trying so hard to impress her, or at Mr. Burnett, who stood nearby and smiled patiently, awaiting his own turn with her. Emily was looking toward the door. Beatrice followed her gaze.

And gasped.

Gabriel! Good heavens, what was he doing here? Theirs was to be a discreet relationship. He should not be showing up in her drawing room like this, setting off a sudden pulse of heat in her loins. And in her face. She felt the idiotic heat of a blush. How mortifying.

Blast the man, he would become linked with Emily again!

But how wonderful to see him.

And the duchess! Good God, he'd brought his mother. Beatrice took several steadying breaths, trying to pull herself together, to still her racing heart. Was Her Grace here to press for a match with Emily?

Gabriel had told her last night that he had made it clear to his parents that he had no interest in Emily, that he was looking elsewhere. They had been disappointed, Gabriel said, especially the duke, who was very fond of Emily—or simply captivated by her beauty—and had looked forward to a match.

Had Gabriel been wrong about the acquiescence to his decision? Was Her Grace determined to overrule him?

"Please excuse me, Lady Tewkesbury, but I have new guests I must greet. Do you know Her Grace of Doncaster? Yes, of course you do. Come, let us welcome her."

Beatrice kept her eyes, and her smile, on the duchess, doing her best to ignore the woman's son. She subtly maneuvered Lady Tewkesbury between her and Gabriel, shamelessly using her ladyship as a buffer, for Beatrice feared her reaction if she got too close to him. And feared that people would notice her reaction.

"Good afternoon, Your Grace." Beatrice dipped a

modest curtsy. "How lovely of you to call on me. I am so pleased to see you again. And Lord Thayne. Thank you for escorting the duchess."

"Oh, but I did not drag Thayne with me," the duchess said. "I tripped over him in your entry, Lady Somerfield. He claims to have accompanied Mr. Burnett."

"And so he did, Your Grace." Jeremy Burnett took the duchess's hand and kissed the air above it. "I came to call upon Miss Thirkill. And Lady Somerfield, of course."

"Did you? Ah, Miss Thirkill. Don't you look lovely in that shade of blue?"

Emily had wasted no time in attaching herself to the duchess, and by extension to Gabriel. In fact, most of the visitors had gathered around Her Grace to offer greetings. She was an important lady, and everyone wanted a moment with her. Beatrice made a few introductions, initiated conversation on general topics, and soon found herself quite unnecessary as her guests enjoyed themselves.

Emily, however, had not left Gabriel's side. All the other gentlemen who'd come specifically to see her were ignored, and stood about looking lost and forlorn.

"We should lock him up somewhere so the rest of us can have a chance." Mr. Burnett had come to stand beside Beatrice. They both watched as Emily turned the full force of her charm on Gabriel. Worse, Beatrice saw that her niece affected a deliberately proprietary air, standing just a shade too close to him, touching his sleeve once or twice.

That was the most important reason he should have stayed away. People would get the wrong impression, the impression that Emily was trying her best to give them.

"This will not do," Beatrice muttered to herself.

"Indeed not," Mr. Burnett agreed.

He looked at her in a way that suggested he knew what was between her and Gabriel. But then, Gabriel had told her that he'd engaged Mr. Burnett to distract Emily, so perhaps he knew why that was necessary.

And yet, as he turned to look at Emily once again, Beatrice thought there was something more going on. "Mr. Burnett, I know what Thayne has asked of you. But it seems to me that you do not find his assignment a hardship. You are fond of my niece, I think."

"Yes, God help me," he said, and turned his engaging grin on her. "I'm as big a fool as every other man in London, apparently. But she will never notice me as long as Thayne is around, no matter how cool he is to her. He is a marquess, after all. And I am merely a younger son."

Beatrice continued to watch Emily, growing increasingly uncomfortable as the girl seemed to want everyone to believe Gabriel belonged to her. The only solace to be found in this provoking scenario was that he was not playing along. He stood rigid and unsmiling, giving no indication that he had any feeling for the wretched girl. In fact, if one watched long enough, it began to look a bit of a farce. Gabriel would subtly inch away from her, but she moved with him each time. It was like a dance—he stepped left, she stepped left. In ten minutes' time, they would have circled the room.

Beatrice had to put a stop to it before tongues began to wag again. "Emily must not be allowed to monopolize him," she said, "or to ignore her other guests. We must try to extricate him from her somehow."

"Mama?"

Beatrice had not noticed her daughter's approach. How much had she heard? "Yes, Charlotte?"

"I should very much like to meet a duchess, Mama," Charlotte said. "I have never met one, you know."

"Yes, you have. You've met the Duchess of Hertford on more than one occasion."

"But she is a dowager duchess, and I don't think that counts. I would love to meet a real duchess. An important duchess. Do you think I might?"

Beatrice touched her daughter's cheek and smiled. "Of course, my love, I shall present both you and Georgiana to Her Grace. But first, allow me to introduce Mr. Burnett."

"Oh, we've already met," Charlotte said.

"Yes, we are old friends," Mr. Burnett said, grinning down at her.

They must have become acquainted while Beatrice was busy with other guests.

"He's been to India, you know," Charlotte said. "And has even ridden an elephant!"

"Has he? Well, that is most interesting, Mr. Burnett."

"Lord Thayne and I rode in a caravan halfway across India once, perched upon elephants the whole trip."

"My goodness!" Charlotte said, wide-eyed. "How frightfully exotic. And Lord Thayne, as well? He is the one Emily is—" She clamped a hand over her mouth and gave Beatrice a chagrined look. She recovered quickly, however, and said, "Well, if Lord Thayne has ridden an elephant, I should like to meet him, too."

"Then it shall be done," Mr. Burnett said. "Come, Lady Charlotte, and allow me to introduce you." He looked over Charlotte's head and sent Beatrice a brief wink. He would use Charlotte to detach Emily from Gabriel's side.

Beatrice followed. The duchess was closer, and so she stopped first to present her daughter. Charlotte curtsied beautifully and said all that was proper. Beatrice beamed with pride when Her Grace complimented her daughter's pretty manners.

They moved on to the court of admirers that had gathered around Emily. Mr. Burnett was taller than the rest of them and somehow managed to forge a path to her side.

"Ah, Thayne," he said. "You must allow me to introduce you to a delightful young lady."

Beatrice saw Emily's eyes narrow momentarily as Gabriel was coaxed away from her side by Mr. Burnett. But her attention was soon drawn by Lord Newcombe, who eagerly took Gabriel's place.

"May I present Lady Charlotte Campion?" Mr. Burnett said. "Lady Somerfield's daughter. Lady Charlotte, allow me to introduce Lord Thayne."

Gabriel dropped his somber, aristocratic reserve a bit and smiled. "I am charmed, Lady Charlotte." He took her hand and bowed over it, causing Charlotte to giggle. "How good of your mother to allow us to meet you."

"Mr. Burnett said you rode an elephant halfway across India."

Gabriel nodded. "So he is already filling your head with tales of our travels, is he?"

Charlotte's face fell. "Tales? It's not true, then?"

"Oh, it's perfectly true. I'll wager you would enjoy riding an elephant, Lady Charlotte. They are twice the height of a horse, you know, so one feels quite above the world atop one of them."

Charlotte's eyes grew wide as saucers. "Oh, how utterly, absolutely, thoroughly wonderful! I should like nothing more. Does everyone ride elephants in India?"

"Not everyone can afford to own an elephant," Gabriel said. "But I met a king once who had a stable that housed one hundred and twenty elephants."

Charlotte gasped. "One hundred and twenty? My goodness, that must have been a prodigious big stable."

Gabriel chuckled. "It certainly was."

"How I wish I might travel to India one day," Charlotte said, and heaved a wistful sigh. "It would be exceedingly interesting, would it not, Mama? Oh, there is my sister, Georgie. We must tell her about the elephants." Charlotte began waving wildly at her sister, and Beatrice despaired of any further decorum from her youngest daughter that afternoon.

Georgiana came over and Beatrice made the introductions. The sound of new arrivals and departures recalled her to her duties as a hostess, however. "Please do not allow my girls to monopolize you, gentlemen. Georgiana, five minutes. Do you understand me? No more than five minutes, then allow Lord Thayne and Mr. Burnett to take their leave of you."

Beatrice caught Gabriel's eye and smiled ruefully. He returned her smile and nodded. He was being an awfully good sport. Charlotte could be wearying in her enthusiasm. He seemed pleased, though, to spend time with her girls. Or maybe it was simply a matter of not having to spend any more time with Emily.

But he ought to have known how it would be. It was foolish of him to risk renewed expectations from Emily. And from everyone else in attendance who might spread new gossip about them. He really ought not to have come.

Beatrice turned toward the new arrivals, pleased to see Wilhelmina, to whom she owed a great deal of thanks for last evening. She welcomed the opportunity to tell her how grateful she was. Penelope followed close behind, and then Grace, too, entered the drawing room. All the Merry Widows, save one.

Beatrice quickly greeted other guests and bade farewell to those departing, then allowed herself to be pulled into her group of friends, each of whom seemed very excited about something. She sent a silent thank-you to Wilhelmina, who nodded, but was not given a moment to say anything before Penelope began speaking in an anxious whisper.

"You will never guess what has happened," she said. "Never."

"No, I never will," Beatrice said, "so you had better tell me. What is it?"

"Marianne and Cazenove are married."

"Married?" Beatrice smiled and shook her head. "That *is* surprising. But I do think they are very much in love, don't you? When did this happen?"

"Yesterday," Wilhelmina said. "Grace was a witness."

"Yes," Grace said, "I was there. Mr. Cazenove had procured a special license and convinced Marianne to marry him right away. It was very romantic, if you ask me. Marianne sent for me to stand up with her, and Lord Rochdale was there for Mr. Cazenove."

"Rochdale?" Beatrice gave a little shudder. "I do not like that man. I have seen him look at Emily in a way that makes me very uneasy."

"He looked at me that way all through the ceremony," Grace said. "It was most unsettling."

"He flirted with you?" Penelope sounded as though such a thing were impossible, but Grace was a remarkably beautiful woman, even if she was prim to a fault.

Grace nodded and her mouth twisted in distaste. "I suppose it comes from being the only woman in the church besides Marianne, and he couldn't very well flirt with her at such a time. He stood altogether too close, and whispered things in my ear. It was horrid, I tell you. But it was worth a bit of discomfort to see Marianne so happy. She was perfectly radiant."

"Then I am pleased for her," Beatrice said.

"But *marriage*?" Penelope said. "I thought she only meant him to be her lover. Do you not find it a bit shocking, after all we have said about not wanting to marry again? You especially, Beatrice."

"Well, it is not me who has got married. But yes, it is rather unexpected. But I have to think they will be happy together. You can see how much he loves her. Let us wish them the best and not question Marianne's decision."

Penelope heaved a sigh. "Well, at least we know she'll be happy in the bedroom. Remember what she told us about his lovemaking?"

"Penelope, hush," Grace said. "That is not proper conversation for Beatrice's drawing room, especially when she has other guests."

"Thank you, Grace. You are quite right, of course. We must keep those sorts of discussions to ourselves. And ladies, I have much to tell you in that regard."

"No!" Penelope's face lit up like a candle. "Lord Thayne?"

"Shh. He is right over there, talking to my daughters. So please, let us discuss it later."

"You can be sure we will," Penelope said. "I want details, my girl, details."

"Later," Beatrice said. "I must see to my guests now. But I will tell you this, Penelope: you were right."

"I liked Mr. Burnett best," Charlotte said.

The three girls and Beatrice were all sitting on Emily's bed sorting through fashion plates. It had been a busy afternoon with more guests than usual, and Beatrice was fatigued. But her daughters, especially Charlotte, were still agog with all the people they'd met. Georgie was a bit dazzled at having met the Duchess of Doncaster, though the fact that her own mother was a countess did not seem to impress her much.

"I thought Lord Ushworth was rather nice," Georgie said. "And quite handsome. Do you like him, Emily?"

Emily gave an indifferent shrug. She often affected an air of ennui when talking to her younger cousins about her social life. Beatrice was always pleased to note, however, that both of her daughters tended to ignore Emily's often superior attitude. They knew her too well and did not allow her to get away with it for long.

"I have no particular opinion of him," Emily said, and tossed aside a few fashion plates. "I suppose he might be seen as a good catch for some people, but he is nowhere near the top of my list."

"What about Sir Frederick Gilling?" Georgie said. "He seemed quite taken with you."

"And he had a splendid set of watch fobs," Charlotte said. "Did you see them? One of them had an actual Roman intaglio. I was dying to ask for a closer look."

"Thank heavens you had the good sense not to do so," Beatrice said. The image of her daughter reaching for a man's watch fob, which hung below his waist, was enough to induce palpitations.

"And what of Mr. Jekyll?" Georgie asked.

"He's too short," Charlotte said. She picked up the discarded fashion plates and thumbed through them. "I still like Mr. Burnett best."

"He is *very* tall," Georgie said. "And has a wonderful smile."

"He certainly does," Beatrice said, pleased to champion the charming young man. Gabriel had assured her that Mr. Burnett was in possession of a tidy fortune, despite his position as the younger son of an earl. Such were the benefits of India. Ophelia might prefer a grand title for her daughter, but in the end it was the fortune that mattered. "I should think most girls would swoon to have Mr. Burnett's smile turned on them."

"Mr. Burnett does not make *me* swoon," Emily said. "He is too much of a tease. Not at all a serious gentleman."

"But he's ridden an elephant," Georgie said, grinning at Charlotte. "How many gentlemen do you know who can claim that?"

"Well, there's Lord Thayne, of course," Charlotte said.

"Oh, my, but he *is* handsome," Georgie said in a wistful tone than sent a shudder down Beatrice's spine. "Surely the most handsome of all the gentlemen we met today. Do you not think so, Emily?"

"I suppose so."

Beatrice gaped at Emily. She supposed so?

"I think he's positively divine," Georgie said. "Even handsomer than you said he was. I can see why he is considered the catch of the Season. I do think it would be exceedingly romantic if you married him, Emily."

Beatrice picked up another stack of fashion plates and pretended to study them. She did not like the direction of this conversation. To hear her own daughter describe Gabriel as divine—Gabriel, the man who had just the night before held Beatrice naked in his arms—was almost more than she could bear.

Emily held up a fashion plate showing an evening frock with a demitrain. "This one," she said, and handed it to Beatrice. "Yes, Lord Thayne is handsome enough, but the more I see of him, the more I wonder what all the fuss is about. There are handsomer men, taller men, probably richer men, too."

"I thought he was at the top of your list," Charlotte said. "He is a marquess, after all, the heir to a duke."

"Yes, but I have discovered that I cannot like him. I find him rather tiresome, and excessively dull."

"Dull?" Charlotte squealed. "He's been in *India* and ridden *elephants*. How is that dull?"

Emily shrugged and handed Beatrice another fashion plate. "I like this pelisse," she said. "And I am sorry, Charlotte, but I have no interest in elephants. Perhaps if Lord Thayne is still looking for a bride when you grow up, he will marry *you*, and you can ride off on an elephant together."

"I should like that," Charlotte said, quite seriously.

"Well, *I* should not," Beatrice said with feeling. It seemed that she no longer had to worry about Emily and Gabriel, thank God, but the last thing she needed was for one of her own daughters to pine after him. "He is too old for you, my girl, and will be even more so by the time you are ready for your comeout."

"Yes, I know," Charlotte said. "He is faaaar too old. I was only joking, anyway. And I still like Mr. Burnett best."

Beatrice rose from the bed and straightened her skirts. "You are seduced by the exotic, my love. I fear an ordinary country gentleman will never do for you."

"Never!" Charlotte burst into giggles.

"What about this one?" Charlotte asked, holding out a fashion plate with a bold-colored opera dress.

Emily took one look at it and shuddered in horror.

"That would not suit Emily," Georgie said. "Those colors would not look at all well on her."

"Thank you, Georgie," Emily said, nodding an acknowledgment to her cousin. "I declare, I despair of you, Charlotte. If you cannot see how that shade would not suit *my* coloring, how on earth will you ever pick out your own dresses? That red hair will always be a trial, you know."

"Mama will teach me," Charlotte said. "She has the same coloring. Sort of."

"Still, you will need to take care," Emily said.

"You cannot afford to wear something that does not flatter you."

Charlotte snorted. "You think because I am not beautiful that I will need all the help I can get."

"We should all dress in styles and colors that flatter us," Georgie said.

Emily smiled. Georgie was by far the prettier of the two, with coloring closer to her own, but always made sure that the fact was not tossed in poor Charlotte's face too often. She was very protective of her younger sister, though if there was ever a person who did not need protecting, it was Charlotte.

"You needn't worry about me," Charlotte said. After her mother had left she had stretched out on the bed, lying on her stomach with her knees bent and her feet stuck in the air. "You may have been born beautiful, but I will grow into my looks. Mama says so. She says I look just as she did at my age, but that eventually my freckles will fade and my body will fill out and maybe I'll look like her one day. I hope so. I think Mama is the most beautiful woman in all of London."

Emily laughed. "For an older woman, she is indeed very handsome." *And besides*, she would like to have added, *everyone knows that I am the most beautiful woman in London.*

"For any age," Charlotte said. "Don't you notice how certain gentlemen look at her?"

"No, I cannot say that I have noticed," Emily said. What a silly girl, to think that men would be attracted to a woman her aunt's age.

"Didn't you notice, Georgie? Today, I mean, when all those gentlemen were here."

"I don't know, Charlotte. I was too nervous around so many people to notice much. The Duchess of Doncaster, for heaven's sake. She's practically royal."

"Well, *I* noticed," Charlotte said. "And if you had

been paying attention, Cousin, you might have figured out why Lord Thayne is not interested in you."

Emily gave a contemptuous sniff. Not interested in
her? What did it matter? She did not care two figs
for Lord Thayne. He was practically rude to her
today. Not that he'd ever been the least bit warm.
He'd been polite, but little more. She had no time for
a man who did not appreciate her.

"Since I am not interested in Lord Thayne," she
said, "whatever you have figured out is of no consequence to me."

"That's a good thing, then," Charlotte said, "since
he is completely besotted with Mama."

What? Emily's mouth dropped open and she
glared at her cousin.

"Don't be a goose, Charlotte," Georgie said.
"That's just silly."

"It is *not* silly. It's true."

"It is perfectly silly," Emily said, chuckling softly.
"Your mother may be attractive, but she's *old*. A man
like Lord Thayne would never in ten million years
be besotted with Aunt Beatrice. It's . . . ridiculous."
She started to laugh, and Georgie joined her. Soon,
they had both fallen back on the bed, laughing so
hard that tears poured down their cheeks.

Charlotte sat up, leaned against the bedpost, and
crossed her arms over her thin chest. She screwed
her face into such a frown that it made them laugh
even harder.

Aunt Beatrice and Lord Thayne? Truly, it was the
funniest thing Emily had ever heard.

Chapter 11

He saw her everywhere. Their level of Society was exclusive enough that one tended to see the same people at almost every event. Even if Thayne had wanted to avoid Beatrice, which he did not, it would have been difficult to do so. He was ostensibly looking for a bride, so he attended events where he could meet and spend time with eligible young women. And she was chaperoning a young woman looking for a husband. They were bound to meet each other now and then. As it happened, they met frequently.

And not just at *ton* events. With the help of the Duchess of Hertford, Thayne had orchestrated two more nights in Beatrice's arms. It was a complicated business, though. Besides devising excuses for Beatrice to absent herself from whatever event her niece was scheduled to attend, they had to contrive increasingly complex ways to avoid being seen together. They arrived at the duchess's house separately, and departed at different times.

Despite the hoops they jumped through in order to be together, the time spent making love with her was worth the effort. Beatrice was a superb bed partner, uninhibited and adventurous. He had taught her many of the positions and movements he'd learned from some of the best *ganika* in India, and she had been more than willing to experiment.

He was grateful for his aristocratic upbringing, that steely reserve bred into him from boyhood that allowed him to see her at *ton* events and, with little effort, pretend there was nothing between them. He did his best to ignore her entirely, since to do otherwise also brought him into Emily's orbit, and he wanted to avoid any hint of a possible future there.

Fortunately, Emily seemed to have given up the chase. She was as cool toward Thayne as he was toward her. In fact, she made something of a show of her disdain for him, making it obvious to everyone that she had not the least interest in him. Beatrice had been right about the girl, apparently. She did not wish for anyone to imagine she harbored a partiality that was not returned. It would be too lowering to her vanity.

Even so, Beatrice was even more determined that their affair remain a secret. As a trustee of an important charity, she had a reputation to maintain, and she guarded it fiercely. She kept an impressively cool demeanor around him, even when he knew she must be thinking of the same thing that never left his mind: when would they make love again?

He often wondered, though, if they were both fooling themselves, and their desire for each other was plain to everyone who saw them.

It was sometimes amusing to see Emily and Beatrice at various events, each of them flaunting their indifference for him, but for very different reasons. What would the niece think if she knew the truth about Thayne and her aunt? Which one of them would she want to murder first?

And there was the dratted bridal quest hanging over him like a dark cloud. His mother had got a bee in her bonnet that he should be ready to announce his betrothal at the Widows Fund masquerade ball to be held at Doncaster House at the end of

June. She thought it a very cunning notion to unveil such an announcement just at the moment when the masks were removed at midnight.

Thayne was willing to cooperate, if only he could manage to narrow the field and fix his interest on one particular young woman. But his heart was not in the quest. He almost did not care whom he married, so long as she was suitable, reasonably biddable, and not painful to look at. But so far he had been unable, or unwilling, to single out a candidate or two, though his mother was relentless in her questioning and prodding. He could not disabuse her of the idea of a masquerade announcement, and so she persisted in pressing him to make a decision. She had even gone so far as to show up at several balls, something she rarely did since his sisters had all been fired off.

"I do not want to see you disappearing into the card room with the duke," she had told him the first time she had unexpectedly appeared at a ball. Thayne's father, who suffered such events only because he could count on a spot of cards to make the evening pass, had already gone in search of the games. "You can gamble at your club," his mother had said, "but a ball is for meeting young women and getting to know them better. Dancing allows you to see how gracefully a girl moves, how comfortable she is with other people, even how good her conversation is." She poked him, actually poked him in the chest with a finger, and said, "That is why I keep thrusting all these ball invitations at you, my boy. There is no better place to meet your future bride, and since you will not have Miss Thirkill, you must find someone else. And soon. Now, stop this idiotic standing about and dance with someone."

On that occasion, Thayne had put a spoke in her wheel by taking her hand from his chest and leading *her* onto the dance floor. She retaliated afterward by dragging one poor girl after another to him and forcing him to reserve a dance with each of them.

Since then, he had preempted any further motherly interference by choosing his own partners. Though he had settled on no one yet, he danced with several young women at each ball, never more than once. Lady Emmeline Standish continued to impress him, as did Yarmouth's eldest daughter, Lady Sarah Addison, and Viscount Wedmore's daughter, Miss Elizabeth Fancourt.

The problem was that he simply could not muster up real enthusiasm for any one of them. It had no doubt been a bad idea to embark on a passionate love affair at such a time. His thoughts were consumed by a certain red-haired countess. Compared with her, every other young woman seemed incomplete—less vivid, less self-assured, less genuine. But that was not a fair comparison. Beatrice was a mature woman with more experience of life. She'd been married and had children. He should not compare her with young, innocent girls who hadn't yet lived.

Besides, the whole point of picking a young bride was precisely that she *was* unformed, so that she could be molded into the perfect marchioness, the perfect wife and mother. It was something he ought to anticipate with pleasure, to have the chance to help bring a young woman into her full and complete self. He really ought to make more of an effort to find the right girl, but he found little joy in the prospect and was simply impatient to get on with it.

Tonight, having just arrived at yet another ball in a seemingly endless round of them, he spotted Miss Fancourt standing with her mother at the other end of the room, and decided he would pay his respects and request a dance. But, as so often happened, his gaze found Beatrice in the crowd and all thoughts of

Miss Fancourt were swept from his mind at the sight of her.

He maintained his customary detachment, a haughty aloofness, but still could not keep his eyes off her. The thing was, he never tired of looking at her—the way she moved, the elegant line of her neck and throat, the deep red of her glorious hair, which he could not wait to loosen once again. And oddly enough, since he seldom noticed such things, he liked the way she dressed. She had a certain style about her, a flair that was uniquely hers. She had often complained about the burden of red hair, but Thayne suspected that it was her attempts to flatter her coloring that had allowed her to develop a style of her own over the years. Dark colors suited her, and bright jewel-like tones of green and blue. She looked especially striking tonight in a deep russet-colored gown that almost exactly matched the color of her hair. That was one thing he liked about her. She did not fight her red hair, which she must surely know was one of her best features, but embraced it and even emphasized it with the right colors. The russet silk was a bold declaration. She looked magnificent.

But it was not simply a matter of color. She knew how to set off her body's best assets. The current high-waisted styles showcased off her slender form—it was not, as she so often claimed, thickened with age to any degree that he noticed—while revealing to advantage those curves he knew so well. Ivory breasts mounded above the russet neckline. Soft and round and perfectly fitted to his hand. Not overly voluptuous, but quite full and pushed tantalizingly upward by her stays. She called them matronly. Thayne called them wonderful.

Damn. He could not look at her without becoming aroused.

He ought to wrench his gaze away and make

straight for Miss Fancourt or some other young woman. But his feet did not listen to reason and led him instead toward Beatrice. She narrowed her eyes as he approached, as though to warn him off, and he paused, thinking she was probably right.

"Come along, old chap." Burnett had sidled up beside him without Thayne even noticing. "It will not be so obvious if you approach her with me at your side. You can always claim that I dragged you along against your will."

It was an excellent plan, and Beatrice could not fault Thayne for supporting a friend in the throes of infatuation. "Ah, so you are after Miss Thirkill again this evening?" he said. "You are quite the persistent puppy, are you not?"

"Hmm. What is that old saw about the pot and the kettle?"

"Touché. But you know, Burnett, Miss Thirkill has completely thrown me over, so there is really no need for you to keep hanging about her."

"Oh, do shut up, Thayne. It has nothing to do with your damnable plan for me to distract her. I am afraid she has turned the tables and quite distracted me instead."

"You are serious about her, then?"

Burnett shrugged. "I do not know about serious. I do not stand a chance with her in any case, so it is rather blockheaded to try. But besides her extraordinary beauty, I have once or twice caught a glimpse of cleverness, a hint that there is a brain lurking beneath all those blond curls. But I believe she goes to lengths to hide it, and relies too much on her beauty, which will not last forever."

Thayne stared at his friend. "Egad, man. You think to change her?"

"No, that would be foolish. She will learn the truth as she grows older, that beauty is less important than character. I would just like to be there when she realizes it. Ready to catch her if she falls. But I sincerely doubt I will have the opportunity. She flirts outrageously with every man but me. I am not worthy of her flirtation, as a mere mister without a lofty title."

"But like a dog with a bone, you will not give up."

Burnett grinned. "Not yet. It is much too early in the game to quit the field. I may not have a chance of winning, but I shall enjoy the play."

"Then lead on, MacDuff."

"And damn the man who gives up on his woman first and says 'enough.' "

They elbowed their way toward Beatrice and Emily, who had her usual court of admirers dancing attendance. Thayne nodded at Beatrice and tried not to smile.

"Lady Somerfield," he said, and bowed, "and Miss Thirkill."

"My lord," Beatrice said. Her tone was curt and she would not meet his eyes.

Emily gave a theatrical sigh and said, "Lord Thayne. And Mr. Burnett, of course."

"Of course," Burnett said, and flashed his famous smile. "I am here to claim my dance."

"What dance?" Emily glared at him.

"Have you forgotten? You promised last evening that I might have the first reel tonight, and I do believe it is about to begin."

Emily's brow puckered into a frown, but then she immediately schooled her features into a bland smile. She was either very much aware that a frown was not a flattering expression, or she did not wish to encourage wrinkles and lines on her brow.

"I confess I had indeed forgotten," she said. "I am sorry, Lord Ealing, but it seems I have a prior commitment. But I still have the next-to-last set free, if you care to wait."

Once Burnett had led Emily onto the dance floor, the ubiquitous swains disappeared, leaving Thayne standing alone with Beatrice. They both watched the dancers and did not look at each other.

"You are incorrigible, my lord," she said in a soft whisper that he barely heard over the sound of the musicians tuning their instruments. "I ask for discretion, and yet you always seem to make your way to my side at every ball or party."

"I cannot help it," Thayne said, biting back a smile. "You are positively irresistible in that gown. Quite delicious, in fact. I want nothing more than to take a bite of you."

"Stop it," she said. The corners of her mouth twitched upward, giving lie to her words. "This is too dangerous."

"I miss you. It's been two nights."

"I know. But I cannot feign another illness. We'll have to think of something else."

"But soon."

She looked at him at last, and the smoldering fire in her blue eyes sent a blast of heat through his vitals. "Yes, soon. I cannot wait, either."

She did not have to wait as long as she'd expected. Serendipity, which Gabriel often claimed had so far ruled their relationship, took matters in hand the very next day.

Beatrice was out alone, running a few errands and enjoying an afternoon without three young girls underfoot. Emily was spending the day shopping with Sarah Billingsley and a few other friends, and Miss Trumbull had taken her charges on an excursion to Polito's Menagerie, where Charlotte was determined to get a close look at an elephant.

Beatrice entered a watchmaker's shop in Aldersgate and almost ran smack into a very familiar chest. "Gab—that is, Lord Thayne. What a pleasant surprise."

And it was. She had developed such a voracious

appetite for the man that to see him at all was a pleasure. But to see him at last in a more casual setting, without the eyes of all the world upon them, was a pure delight.

He beamed a smile at her. "Lady Somerfield. A very pleasant surprise indeed." He looked behind her and said, "And without your charges in tow."

"It is probably very bad of me to say so, but I am grateful for an afternoon without them. Three energetic girls can be exhausting. Emily is shopping for bonnets with her friends, and my girls have gone to have a look at an elephant."

"An elephant?"

"It is all your fault, you know, and Mr. Burnett's, for filling Charlotte's head with tales of India. There is said to be an elephant at Polito's, along with lions and tigers and other exotic creatures to thrill my daughter."

Gabriel smiled. "I trust Lady Charlotte will be suitably impressed."

"And I trust that she will soon tire of elephants. Then perhaps she will stop spinning tales of how she will go adventuring in India and Africa when she's old enough."

Gabriel laughed. "A girl after my own heart. I was about her age or even younger when I started pestering the duke with pleas for adventure. He finally gave in after I'd finished at university."

"It is not the same for girls."

"No, of course not. But what brings you here? A new clock, perhaps? I have just ordered a longcase for the entry hall in my new house. It's a beauty, with a revolving moon phase above the dial."

"It sounds wonderful. But I am here on a more modest errand. My favorite watch had been running slow and I brought it in last week for Mr. Gray to clean and reset. I am here to pick it up."

Gabriel did not leave, but followed her into the

shop and waited, chatting quietly with a shop assistant while she conducted her business with the watchmaker. He then took her into the adjacent showroom where clocks of all kinds were on display—shelf clocks, longcase clocks, lantern clocks, figural mantel clocks, as well as barometers and chronometers and other instruments—and pointed out the clock he had ordered. It was enormous, with the clock face a good foot above her head.

"It's very handsome," Beatrice said, "and very . . . large. But it suits you, Gabriel."

He laughed. "I will take that as a compliment. But it needs to be large. I want it for the entry hall in my new town house, which has soaring ceilings. I did not want a clock that would be dwarfed in such a space. Would you like to see it? The house, I mean. If you have no other pressing plans for the afternoon."

To spend an afternoon alone with Gabriel would be better than wonderful. "I would like very much to see your new house."

His face lit up like a boy's. "Excellent. You are certain you have no other plans? You must know how much I would enjoy spending the afternoon with you, but if you have something more important . . ."

Beatrice was always enchanted when Thayne's latent boyish nature overcame his more formidable bred-from-the-cradle lordliness. He could skewer a person with a single arrogant lift of his brow, but in private he let down his reserve and allowed the charming young man to take over. And very occasionally, as now, he let slip the merest hint of vulnerability. He wanted to show off his new home to her, but also wanted her approval of it.

"I have no plans that cannot wait for another day," she said. "I had thought to visit my solicitor to discuss a few matters of business, a bit of investment strategy, but I would much prefer to see your new home."

"Investment strategy? Your solicitor manages your funds for you?"

Beatrice smiled ruefully. Everyone always assumed a woman could not possibly understand such things. "No, I manage my own funds. But he acts as my agent. I tell him what to buy and when to buy it. Or when to sell it. As it happens, I wish him to sell a portion of my bank stocks and use the proceeds to increase the investment in one of my mining stocks."

The look of complete astonishment on Gabriel's face made her laugh. "Do not be so shocked, my lord. Some women *do* manage their own money, you know."

"Yes, I know they do. I just never met a woman who actually cared about bank stocks or mining stocks."

"Well, now you have. Believe it or not, I actually find it all very interesting. And, if I may be allowed to boast a bit, I am quite good at it."

He smiled. "Are you indeed?"

"I am. I have always had a head for finances. One of the things I love about being a widow is that for once I can actually make my own decisions, investing where and when I choose. It is what I have always wanted." She paused and frowned. "I am sorry. That was badly said. I do not mean to imply that I wished poor Somerfield dead so I could play on the Exchange. I only meant that being his widow has provided me with an amount of freedom I never had as his wife. Freedom to manage my own money, for example." She smiled again. "And to be with you, of course."

"You are a remarkable woman," he said. "The head of a businessman and the body of a goddess. What a potent combination. Perhaps I should consult you on my own investments." He grinned, and she knew he was only joking, patronizing her. Like Somerfield, he would be unlikely to trust a woman's judgment on financial matters.

"I can offer a few bits of advice, if you like," she said. "Beeralstone Lead and Silver Mines. And Holloway Waterworks. Look into them both."

His brows lifted in surprise. "I shall have my man of affairs do so. In the meantime, shall we have a look at my house?"

"Yes, please."

"I warn you, though, that it is rather a mess. There is still a lot of work to be done. You might find plaster dust raining down on your head and drop cloths tangled at your feet. Did you come in your own carriage?"

"No, I took a hackney."

"Then I shall take you up in mine."

Beatrice frowned. "Do you think that is wise? We might be seen."

"You worry too much, Beatrice. I doubt anyone here in Aldersgate will pay us the least mind. And when we reach Cavendish Square we'll dash inside before any nosy neighbor or passerby can see us. Besides, that bonnet of yours will hide your face if you keep your head down."

They left the showroom and Gabriel was approached by the shop assistant, who handed him a small package. Gabriel thanked him and slipped it in his pocket, then led Beatrice outside. His carriage, which she ought to have noticed before, stood across the broad thoroughfare. Gabriel signaled to his coachman, who nodded and touched his hat brim. A liveried groom had been minding the horses and he leaped up on the back of the carriage as it pulled away. The coachman waited for traffic to thin, then turned the carriage around and drove it to where they stood in front of Mr. Gray's establishment.

Once inside the coach, and bouncing along through

the crowded streets, Gabriel took her hand, removed her glove, and kissed the tips of her fingers. "An entire afternoon with you, Artemis. The Fates smile upon us once again."

"They do indeed." Oh, the bliss of making love to him again. How had she ever thought to survive without physical passion? "But we cannot go to Wilhelmina's house without warning her. She may be busy. Or have visitors."

"We do not need the duchess's hospitality today. We have my house. If you can bear the clutter and noise. I am anxious for you to see it, and to see you in it. I have missed you, Artemis. You have become like a drug to me, and I fear I am quite addicted." He leaned over and kissed her softly. Then he put his arm around her shoulder and pulled her close against him, and said, "I have enjoyed our time together."

Beatrice's stomach gave a tiny lurch at the hint of finality in his words. Was he going to end their affair? So soon? But surely not yet. Not yet. "So have I, Gabriel. Very much."

"I want to give you something." He reached into his coat and pulled out the package from Mr. Gray's. "It is not much, but I want you to have it."

She took it from him and tried not to give in to the wave of sadness that had washed over her. She was not ready for this passionate ride to end. She had always known, of course, that it was a temporary thing. Once he became betrothed, she would not allow their affair to continue, and she had told him so many times. It would be unfair to his bride, and Beatrice would have no part in such a betrayal. But she had thought they had more time.

She opened the package to find a beautiful gold chain. It had alternating large and small links, the larger ones finely engraved in a scroll pattern.

"It is for your watch," he said.

"It is lovely. How thoughtful of you, Gabriel. Thank you."

"I would prefer to give you emeralds and sapphires, but I suspect you would not accept them from me."

"No."

"But I have wanted to give you *something*. Something to celebrate what we have together. It is not much, but you cannot reject a simple gold watch chain. No one need know it was a gift from me."

To celebrate, not terminate. Thank heaven.

"*I* will know," she said. "And I will treasure it, Gabriel. Thank you."

She kissed him, and though it started out tender and warm, it soon grew hotter. But her blasted bonnet was in the way. Gabriel untied the ribbon at her chin and removed the bonnet, placing it on the opposite bench with his own hat. He took her in his arms again and set about ravishing her mouth. The bouncing rhythm of the carriage served to increase their passion, until Gabriel pulled away with a groan. He took her hand and placed it on his crotch.

"You see what you do to me, Beatrice?"

She traced the outline of his erection with her fingers, and he groaned louder. She quite literally held him in the palm of her hand. He was completely under her control. She could do anything, and was all at once giddy with her own power.

She deftly unbuttoned the fall of his breeches and felt his body tense.

"Beatrice?"

"Hush. Let me please you."

She reached inside the open flap of his breeches and pulled at his smallclothes until his erection sprang free. She ran her fingers up and down its velvety smoothness, and he threw his head back and clenched his teeth. A tiny bead of moisture escaped from the tip of his cock as she brushed it with her fingers. She bent and licked it off with her tongue. He gave a sort of growling moan, and shouted aloud when she took him completely into her mouth.

Gabriel arched against her, thrusting his hips up and down with the rhythm of the carriage, his breath ragged and loud. She delighted in the pleasure he took from her, and she gave it gladly, enthusiastically, basking in the wonder that they could share their bodies so freely with each other. She felt his climax coming as he rocked faster and thrust deeper. Suddenly, he pushed her roughly away and jerked a silk handkerchief from his coat.

Beatrice held him as he groaned and spilled his seed into the white silk.

Chapter 12

"This is where the new clock will stand," Thayne said, "against the wall behind the scaffolding." He was still a bit unsteady on his pins after what had taken place in the carriage. But Beatrice was as composed as ever, looking elegant and refined and not at all the sort of woman who would pleasure a man while driving through Holborn, or tell him afterward that he need not have resorted to the handkerchief. That was one of the things he liked best about her. Not only that she knew how to pleasure a man and did not shrink from doing so, but that she was so full of surprises.

She certainly was not what he'd expected, though he could not say precisely what that was. Beauty and refinement, he supposed. But there was so much more to her than that. He loved her self-possession, how she knew who she was and what she wanted from life. Once again, it might have been simply a matter of maturity. He really needed to stop comparing her with all the young women he was supposed to be courting, but he could not help himself. Any one of them—Lady Emmeline Standish, Miss Fancourt, Lady Catherine Villiers, any of them—might in time mature into the kind of woman Beatrice was. But how was he to predict such a future, and would he be willing to wait?

One thing was becoming more and more clear to him. He wanted more from Lady Somerfield than an uncomplicated affair.

"It's lovely, Gabriel." She studied every corner of the room, which was rather grand in size for an entry—not as imposing as Doncaster House, but more so than the average town house.

He smiled. "How can you possibly tell when everything is in such disarray?"

"Oh, it's easy enough to see the potential of the space. I like the openness of this hall. There is so much light. It is very welcoming, while still retaining an impressive grandeur."

"I like open spaces," he said. "I had two walls torn down—here and here. It was too dark and small before. This way, we take advantage of the windows, which were doing little good in the smaller anterooms. You will see that throughout the house I have had several walls torn down and rooms combined. I despise cramped spaces and lots of little rooms heading this way and that, like a rabbit warren. I prefer to spread out a bit. Fewer rooms, but each one more spacious. I hate to feel . . ."

"Confined."

"Yes." He studied her face, astonished again by her insight. "Exactly."

"From the time we first met," she said, "I sensed that you were not a man who could be bound to a place, constrained from reaching farther. You have such a large presence, Gabriel. A small house or even a small room would never suit you. It would be too insulating, and you would be bursting to get free. I am not surprised that you have been consolidating rooms here. I suspect you will be knocking down walls all your life."

He gazed at Beatrice in wonder for a moment. Then, without thought, he pulled her to him, battled for a moment with the brim of her bonnet, and kissed her. He didn't care that workmen were watching. He had to connect with her right then, in that moment, when she seemed to have looked straight into his soul.

She kissed him back, but then gently extricated herself from his arms. "You should not do that," she said. "Not here." Her mouth was set in a disapproving line, but the sparkle in her eyes told him she wasn't truly angry.

She turned away from him and studied the ceiling. "I am glad you are having the plasterwork restored. It is very fine. How will you have it painted?"

He looked up to where the classical moldings and coffers were being brought back to life. The decoration was not at all modern in style, having been done in the middle of the last century. But he liked it well enough and thought it suited the room, so he had hired the best stucco and plaster workers to restore it here and throughout all the main rooms. "I hadn't thought about color," he said. "I assumed it would be white."

"May I make a suggestion?"

"Of course."

"Introduce a subtle bit of color in the grounds. You see this acanthus pattern?" She pointed to a heavy molding around the edge of the ceiling decorated with a scroll of acanthus leaves alternating with a more elaborate floral element. "The small bits of ground, the flat areas behind the raised patterns, could be painted in the palest gray in order to set off the scrollwork. Or blue gray. Or even a pale sage green. That way the eye is more clearly drawn to the intricacy of the plasterwork. It's a subtle but effective trick."

"I see what you mean."

"And if you are inclined to add gilt—"

"How did you know?" He grinned.

"I have seen your father's house, my lord." She

returned his smile. "As for the gilt, I would recommend that you use it sparingly. Allow the beauty of the plasterwork to stand on its own. Those floral bunches, for example, between the acanthus leaves— you might use gilt on the ribbon that ties them together. It would be restrained, but still elegant enough for the home of a marquess."

He looked up at the molding and tried to imagine what she suggested, and found he liked the idea. "You have a good eye for decoration, Lady Somerfield. It shall be done. I will talk with the head plasterer tomorrow. Now, let me show you the rest of the house. I'd like your opinion on a few other matters."

He walked toward the staircase, but she did not follow, and he turned to find her brow furrowed into a frown. He placed a hand on her arm. "What is it, Artemis?"

"You ought not to be asking my advice, nor should I be giving it. You are to be married soon. Your bride will be the one to consult, not me."

He stiffened and dropped his hand. "I have not yet chosen a bride."

"Then perhaps you should wait on some of these decisions."

"I do not wish to wait. I want it done now so I can move in as soon as possible." He moderated his tone, which had become autocratic even to his own ears. But dammit, he did not want to think about his future bride when he was with Beatrice. And she really did have a good eye. "I would very much appreciate your advice," he said, and infused the merest hint of seduction in his tone. "My architect has merely been following my requests without suggesting alternatives. I fear I must intimidate him, but I am not so vain to think I have perfect taste. I have *expensive* taste, to be sure, but I am willing to entertain any recommendations to make Loughton House the best it can be."

"Loughton House?"

"Yes. That is our family name, you know. And I want the house to honor that name. So any advice you may have would be more than welcome. Truly."

Beatrice reluctantly agreed, but seemed circumspect at first as he took her from room to room. Soon, though, she was offering more suggestions. Some were simple, such as the type of fabrics for the window coverings or where a mirror should be placed to add light to a room. But some were more complex, such as replacing a wall with a pillared screen, or moving a chimneypiece from one wall to another.

More than once, he agreed with her and stated, "It shall be done." But in truth, Thayne paid more attention to Beatrice than he did to her suggestions. Her blue eyes were lit in one moment with enthusiasm for some proposed alteration, in another moment softened with admiration for the carving of an overdoor or the pilasters placed between windows.

It was as if she belonged here. She loved the house. Thayne sensed it more than merely believing her words of admiration. She loved it. She would make it a beautiful home. If it were hers.

She caught herself more than once, and reminded him that he must save some decisions until after his marriage. But as he watched her, Thayne had a difficult time imagining anyone else in the house. Still, she was his mistress, not his wife. He must remember that.

He left the gallery for last, one of the few rooms that did not have workmen wandering about or perched on ladders or scaffolds. They were quite alone, finally, and in his favorite place. "This is where I plan to display my sculpture collection. Some of it, anyway. I could not possibly fit it all in this room."

Plinths and platforms were being built specifically for certain pieces. Sections of wall had been demolished and scooped out, and niches were being installed to house other works. It was as messy as the other rooms, but here, at least, Thayne's vision was complete and unalterable. He knew precisely what he wanted.

"I am afraid," he said, "that some people will be outraged to see such alien artwork on display. But I have developed quite a passion for it, and I want it where I can see it."

"In hopes that others will develop an appreciation for it, too."

He smiled at her, pleased once again at how well she understood him. "Yes, that is my hope. In fact, I have a larger plan in mind. Shall I tell you?"

"Please."

"I hope to build a public gallery one day where the bulk of my collection will be on display for everyone to see and appreciate. Such beautiful art should not be kept from view simply because it is unfamiliar."

"What a splendid idea, Gabriel."

"Do you think so?" Her praise made him feel like a schoolboy. His chest swelled with pride. How foolish that the opinion of his mistress should mean so much to him.

"I do," Beatrice replied. "I shall be very disappointed if you do not build your gallery. You must educate the rest of us to better understand what is alien in style or in religious context. How much did you bring back with you?"

"Over two hundred pieces."

Her mouth gaped in astonishment. *"Two hundred?"*

"And a bit more. Some are quite small, though, so it is not as large a collection as it sounds."

"Where do you keep it?"

"Here. I have two temporary storerooms filled with crates."

"Are any unpacked?"

"Some."

"May I see them?"

He gazed at her, trying to determine if she was patronizing him, but he saw only genuine interest. "I'd like to show you, if you are truly interested."

"Of course I'm interested. Everything about you interests me, Gabriel."

He slipped a hand around her waist. "Everything? And here I was thinking it was only my body you craved."

She pressed herself against him. "Everything. I want to know all your passions."

He reached down to kiss her, but the damned bonnet was in the way again. He dipped under the brim and gave her a quick kiss, then went to work on the ribbon beneath her chin. "I am tempted to forbid you ever to wear these things in my presence. They're a damnable nuisance."

She removed the bonnet and laid it on one of the plinths along with her reticule, then walked into his arms. "A lady must always wear a bonnet in public," she said as she gazed up at him. "You cannot forbid that."

"But this is not public. This is just you and me, alone. With no bonnet to keep us apart." He kissed her, but kept it gentle. He was not assuaging a hunger. He was savoring something precious.

He put her away from him after a moment, and said, "Come. Let me show you a few pieces from my collection."

He took her into one of the storerooms off the gallery. Crates were stacked everywhere. Some were open and empty, the statues unpacked and standing against one wall.

"There is no chronological or historical logic to what you see," he said. "Most are Hindu, though some are early Buddhist. Some are perhaps two hundred years old; others are over a thousand. When I have a true gallery, I will impose some sort of order. But here, in my home, I will display a variety of pieces."

"Your favorites."

"Yes."

He did not explain what any of them represented. He simply allowed her to look. She stood quite still, her gaze sweeping the room.

"My goodness," she said at last. "I can see what drew you to them. They are so very different, so . . . earthy."

He chuckled. "They are indeed. You see this one?" It was a large carving of one of the Apsaras, a celestial female spirit, a sort of nymph, which had once graced the outside of a temple. She wore nothing but a thin strip of fabric around her waist and a series of necklaces that hung between and over her extremely voluptuous breasts. "This is what I meant when I said you reminded me of Indian sculpture." He reached out to touch the smooth sandstone, his fingers tracing the nymph's curves as he spoke. "Full breasts, small waist, elegant flare of hip, a slight softness of belly. If this was white marble instead of weather-darkened stone, it might be you."

She laughed merrily, and the sound reminded him again of temple bells. "I do *not* look like her! No human female looks like her. Those perfect round globes are an Indian man's fantasy. Breasts that size, no matter how firm, would sink to the waist on a human woman. I am pleased that I remind you of such an ideal form, but honestly, Gabriel . . ." She paused to laugh again. "You cannot tell me you have ever seen a real woman with a body like that."

"Yours comes very close." He came up behind her and wrapped his arms around her full breasts. "Very close."

She leaned back against him, and in that moment Thayne thought he never wanted to let her go. He was falling in love with her. Had fallen.

The realization shook him to the core for an instant, then settled upon him with ease. Nothing in his life had ever felt so right.

"Aside from her rather spectacular body," Beatrice said, oblivious to Thayne's epiphany, "it is really a beautiful carving. There is so much movement in the lines of her body, the way one hip is cocked and one thigh slightly forward, the arm raised. Is she a dancer?"

"Yes, she is."

"I can see why you had to have her. And what of this pair?" She moved out of his arms to study another piece.

He watched her with new eyes. Or eyes finally awake to what she had become to him. A part of him wanted to throw himself at her feet and pledge his eternal love, now that he recognized it for what it was. The more rational part of his brain told him she would not appreciate such a declaration. Nor, in truth, was he ready to give it. Only a fool fell in love with his mistress. He would keep his feelings to himself and simply enjoy being with her, loving her.

"This is a stone icon of Shiva and Durga from Uttar Pradesh," he said in his most pedantic, unloverlike tone. "It dates from the eleventh century."

"Really? How extraordinary to think such . . . sensual sculpture was being created in India while our ancestors were being represented in the stiff, formal manner one sees at old churches and tombs. It truly defines the difference in our cultures, does it not? I do not know who Shiva and Durga are, but can you imagine one of our eleventh-century kings sitting like this with his queen? It is rather moving, actually, the way they sit together with their arms wrapped around each other and her leg resting on his, so natural and human. There is such an open sexuality, is there not? And yet so much affection."

Thayne could not have been more pleased with her reaction. Without the least comprehension of the religion or culture that had created these works, she understood them as human expressions. Perhaps he had underestimated the open-mindedness of the English. He rather suspected, though, that such understanding was unique to Beatrice.

She walked from one piece to the next, commenting on each and asking a few questions. She came at last to a sculpture that had already been attached to a base for display. It was the first one Thayne had unpacked, the one he loved more than all the others. It was the figure of a woman in the red Sikri sandstone of Mathura. In a similar state of dress, or undress, as the voluptuous nymph, this woman was missing her head, feet, and one arm. Though incomplete, she was still beautiful.

Beatrice studied the statue silently for a long time, then asked, "May I touch it?"

"Of course."

She reached out and ever so gently ran her fingers over the belly of the woman. "I almost thought it would be pliable," she said, "that the stone would give. It looks so . . . tactile. Even without a head, she looks so alive. I do believe this is one of the most beautiful things I've ever seen."

"She is my favorite," he said.

"I can see why. I see that she is ready to display. Will you . . . oh, my goodness!"

Thayne grinned. She had caught sight of one of the erotic carvings. It was a corner piece from the exterior of a temple, and showed a standing couple, entwined around each other, making love, their genitals clearly displayed. It was actually one of the less graphic poses. He had seen temples covered in couples and threesomes engaged in every act and every position imaginable. This piece was rather tame by comparison.

"Does it not look familiar? It is *Jataveshtitaka.*"

She looked at him quizzically.

"The twining of the creeper," he said, and winked.

"Oh! You said that word to me when . . . when . . ."

"Yes, when we made love the very first time, standing against that garden wall. You see? This is the position we used. The woman is wrapped around the man like a creeper around a tree. It is called *Jataveshtitaka.*"

He pulled her to him, grabbed her skirt, and hiked it up to her waist. Running a hand along her bare thigh, he said, "Shall we try it again? Or perhaps just a little prelude."

His fingers reached higher and found her sex, and he smiled at how moist and warm she was already. He slipped a finger inside and stroked her gently while he nibbled his way up the elegant neck now arched in passion. When he felt her muscles tense, he used his thumb to massage the taut little nub at the core of her pleasure, until her whole body jerked once and then trembled as she cried out.

He held her close as her tremors subsided, stroking her hair and nuzzling her ear. Loving her.

"You are too good to me," she murmured against his shoulder. "Good *for* me."

"Nothing is too good for you, my huntress. Come. The afternoon is still young and there is one more room I want to show you."

Beatrice lay panting and spent in his arms, her back pressed against his damp chest and her neck arched to rest her head on his shoulder. "Is there a name for that one, too?" she asked in a breathless voice.

He tightened his arms around her. He breathing

was equally ragged. The final few minutes of lovemaking had become extremely energetic. "It began as
the *Dhenuka*, the Milch Cow, but I believe we created
something entirely new."

Beatrice chuckled. "Milch Cow? I'm not sure I like
the sound of that."

"All the positions in which the man takes the
woman from behind are named after animals. For
obvious reasons."

"I don't suppose you care to tell me how you
learned such things?"

"No, I do not."

"Well, I can guess, anyway." No doubt he had
been with numerous Indian courtesans. She could
not imagine that the ordinary people of India had
codified their sexual behavior. But the courtesans
would have been well trained and skilled, and would
have taught him the terminology.

Her breath slowed and her body relaxed. She wig-
gled against him like a kitten. She loved the way his
firm, warm body felt, and the way the coarse hair on
his chest and legs teased her skin. It would be too
easy to become accustomed to such bliss. Accustomed to Gabriel.

She looked about the room, which she had been
too preoccupied to notice earlier. There were boxes
and crates neatly stacked along one wall. More sou-
venirs from India? A strange jarlike object with a
hose attached stood on the floor near a chair. Beatrice
guessed that it was a hubble-bubble, a sort of water
pipe that she had read about. A small bronze statue
of a dancing figure with many pairs of arms stood on
the mantel, over which hung an unexotic, perfectly
English portrait of a woman. Beatrice was fairly certain it was the Duchess of Doncaster in her youth.

The walls were freshly painted, and the moldings
and wainscoting were so pristine they must have
been recently restored. Thayne would at least have a

bedchamber ready to use, even if the rest of the house was still in disorder. The bed they lay in was a simple four-poster stripped of its hangings. He was probably having special bed hangings made with coronets as finials for the top corners. A marquess would require an important bed. Beatrice was rather glad that for this afternoon, anyway, it was incomplete and plain. She would feel less like she had betrayed his future wife in this bed than she would if his crest and coronet were staring her in the face.

She turned in his arms and lay on her side, facing him.

"I won't ask about how and from whom you learned all these exotic moves," she said, "but I am interested in how you know the Indian names. Did you learn the language while you were there?"

"I was there for over seven years, so I was bound to learn a thing or two." He grinned and stroked her arm with a finger. "I picked up Hindustani while there, and studied Persian before I left. I've always had an ear for languages. It's one of the reasons my father finally capitulated and allowed me to leave England. He knew I would be able to manage on my own with so many languages in my kit."

"He did not want you to go?"

"Of course not. I am his only son, his heir. He worried that I would get myself killed and never return." He continued to run his fingers slowly up and down her arm. "But I was dead set on having an adventure, and so we struck a bargain. First, I had to promise that before I reached the age of thirty, I would return to England and take up my responsibilities as his heir, which primarily meant finding a wife and setting up my nursery. He would allow me seven or eight years of adventuring, but no more."

"That is why you returned now? Because you are about to turn thirty?" Heavens, was he only twenty-nine?

"Yes, I am honoring my part of the bargain. But there was a second ducal caveat. I could go only with purpose and not strictly for random adventure. So he arranged for me to go to India on assignment for the government."

"What sort of assignment?"

"There had been considerable concern about French encroachment into India and about a possible threat of a Franco-Russian invasion through Persia. I was to be a sort of watchdog, to make sure the East India Company stood firm against a French threat."

Did that mean he had been a government spy? Beatrice did not ask, for she suspected he would not answer. "Does the French threat still exist?" she asked.

"No. Or at least it does not appear so at the moment." He moved her arm aside and began to trace a line with his fingers from the side of her breast, down her waist, over the curve of her hip, and back again. "When Lord Minto became governor-general," he went on, watching his fingers stroke her body, "he was adamant that any such threat be squashed. He sent out missions in all directions with the task of negotiating treaties with every important leader. I went along with Metcalfe to Punjab, where we were finally able to settle a treaty with Ranjit Singh. I sat with the Amirs of Sind for a time, and also traveled into the Afghan. And I was sent to Java with Raffles. I saw just about every part of the region while I was there."

"Traveling by elephant."

He grinned and kissed the tip of her nose. "Sometimes, yes. And also on camelback. Or horseback."

"It was a grand adventure after all, then? It was everything you had hoped for?"

"The thing about adventures is that you never quite know what to expect, so I embarked on my travels with an open mind. But yes, it was a very grand adventure. I loved it, every minute of it. I only hope I will have a chance to visit India again one day."

"Tell me about India. What is it like?"

He looked at her intently, his brown eyes searching hers as though he believed she was merely making conversation and not truly interested. But she was. She had led a pedestrian, unadventurous life. In fact, lying here with Gabriel was the most adventurous thing she'd ever done. In more ways than one, he made her realize how much she had missed. She gave him a nod, prompting him to respond.

"How shall I describe India? Vast. Intoxicating. Colorful. Hot. Sticky. Monsoons so powerful that entire villages are swept away in an hour. Sand that stretches as far as the eye can see, but also fertile farmlands edged with palm groves and guava orchards. Field after field of white-budded cotton. Majestic mountains in the north and tropical beaches along the coasts. Bulbous white domes of temples and palaces. Crowded streets and noisy souks. Foods spiced with curries and peppers that both enflame and delight the tongue. But mostly it is the colors I will remember. The land is so often lacking in color that the people compensate by creating vivid hues everywhere you look. Nothing muted or pale. Everything is brilliant, jewel-like. Reds and greens and blues and purples that dazzle the eye. You cannot imagine it, Beatrice. It is like nothing you will ever see in England. We have color in our landscapes, but in India, it is the people who bring color to the land."

"In their clothing? Their fabrics?"

"Yes, the textiles are stunning. The way the women wrap themselves in such brightness is quite startling at first. And the men, too, with turbans of every color. The textiles are not only for clothing, though. Every bazaar stall is draped in brilliant shades of red

and green and blue. Every pleasure pavilion is tented
in vivid shades. And the wealthy people have fantas-
tic gardens, forcing color into their landscape. Inside
their palaces and pavilions and temples, the walls are
set with vibrant tiles. In the Mughal courts, the tiles
are decorated in floral and geometric patterns in glorious hues. I brought back stacks of miniature paint-
ings that portray all the color I'm talking about. I
will show them to you one day, when I have discovered where I packed them."

"I would like that. In fact, you make it sound so
beautiful I am tempted to visit India myself."

He gave a sheepish smile, as though embarrassed
at the effusiveness of his description. He reached out
and cupped her face in his hand. "The Indian sun
would be a punishment to this skin. You would have
to cover yourself from head to toe to protect it."

"It would be worth it, I think, to experience all
that color."

"I do have a bit of Indian color I can show you
right now."

He rolled over and out of bed, and walked to one
of the crates. He was gloriously naked, and Beatrice
feasted on the sight of him—the movement of sleek
muscle along his back and shoulders as he re-
arranged the crates to reach one at the bottom, the
taut flexing of his buttocks and thighs as he lifted
the crate and placed it atop another, the swell of
muscle in his arms as he pried open the lid and
tossed it aside. The pure animal beauty of his firm,
young body set her heart racing.

What lucky star had she been born under, to have
such a man want her?

He reached inside the crate, pulled out a length of
bright red silk, and tossed it to her. Then a bolt of
brilliant blue muslin worked with gold thread. Then
deep purple with a green and gold paisley border.

And gold silk. Orange muslin. Turquoise silk. And more and more. Gabriel flung them all on the bed until she was covered in a rainbow of fabric.

Laughing, she dug her way out and stood beside the bed, gazing down at the array of vibrant, luxurious textiles. "Oh, Gabriel, how beautiful. All of them. Such colors! What are you going to do with all these wonderful fabrics?"

"Wrap you up in them." Gabriel came up behind her and wrapped a length of bright emerald green silk around her body. It slithered sensuously against her bare skin. "These are just the sort of colors that suit you, Artemis."

"Not all of them. That lovely deep rose-colored muslin clashes rather badly with my hair. But the rest . . . how lovely. What a splendid afternoon you have given me, Lord Thayne."

He spun her around in the green silk until she was facing him, gathered her in his arms, and kissed her passionately. When he lifted his head several minutes later, he said, "I am glad to have pleased you, my huntress. You have certainly pleased me."

She reached up and stroked his jaw. "It has been a lovely day, Gabriel. Though I admit I was feeling very sad at first, when you gave me the gold chain."

"Sad? Why?"

"I thought it was a token to mark the end of things. I thought the affair was over. I am very pleased that it is not. Yet."

He used the silk to tug her closer and cocoon them both. "Never. I adore you, Beatrice."

Her heart skipped a little at his words. "Oh, don't say that, Gabriel. It cannot last forever—we both know it. I have told you that it will be over for me when you become betrothed."

"I am not betrothed."

"Not yet. But soon. And we will have to end it. I will regret it, though, Gabriel, very much. I will miss days like this. I have never known such passion. I will miss it when we part, but I will always remember that it was you who showed it to me, showed me how to open myself to it."

She felt strangely bashful, saying such private things to him, and looked away.

"You did not need showing. You had it in you always." He took her chin and gently turned her face to look at him. "I never knew a more passionate woman, Beatrice. You just needed someone to share it with."

"I am glad to have shared it with you, Gabriel. I shall never forget you."

"And I shall never let you," he said, and kissed her. Desire flared between them once again, and they fell back onto the bed, enveloped in a tangle of vibrant Indian silks.

Chapter 13

"He said it was called the Milch Cow. Can you imagine? But, oh, my dears, it was wonderful." Beatrice smiled at her friends, gathered around a tea table in Grace's drawing room for another meeting of the Benevolent Widows Fund trustees. As usual, the conversation strayed to more personal subjects. In fact, they were not really meetings at all anymore. They did eventually discuss Fund business, or develop the guest list for the next ball, or write out the invitations. But the gatherings had long ceased to be merely for business. Ever since they had dubbed themselves the Merry Widows.

"Goodness," Penelope said, her eyes wide with interest, "I feel as though I should be taking notes. Eustace is an excellent lover, but not nearly as adventurous as your young man, Beatrice. Of course, he has that special thing he does with his thumb."

"Thayne knows that one, too," Beatrice said. "When he did it to me, I almost shouted out, 'Oh! That is Penelope's thumb trick!' But I fear it would have broken the mood."

Penelope giggled. "No doubt. But I am pleased you are enjoying yourself. Did I not tell you how beneficial a lover could be to your health? Look at her face, ladies. She is positively aglow."

"I do feel rather fit, from all that stimulating exercise," Beatrice said. She used a pair of silver tongs to pick up a lump of sugar and drop it into her teacup. Just for good measure, she added a second lump. "And I cannot seem to stop smiling," she said, and grinned to prove it. "It is like being on top of the world."

"You see?" Penelope said, bouncing slightly in her chair. "I told you so!"

"And you were right," Beatrice said. "*So* right." She stirred her tea until the sugar had dissolved, then took a sip. "But it is Marianne who truly glows. You still have that blissful look of a new bride, my dear."

"I can't help it," Marianne said, beaming. "I *feel* blissful. I've never been so happy in my life. Oh, I know you all think I have betrayed our pact, but we did not actually promise we would never marry. We only agreed that we would not allow our families or anyone else to *force* us into another marriage. No one forced me. I went quite willingly. I never did a more right thing in my life."

Beatrice reached over and patted Marianne's hand. "You did not betray us. All any of us want is to be happy. I am delighted you and Adam have found such joy together."

"Thank you, Beatrice. We may each find happiness in different ways. You have your young man, and he has certainly put roses in your cheeks."

"That he has," Beatrice said. "I confess I cannot stop thinking of him. In truth, I am quite astonished with myself. Such lust! I have never felt anything like it, even with Somerfield. I enjoyed physical intimacy with him and enjoyed his body. But this new lust— this is quite different. I suppose it is because Thayne is younger than I am, and that makes me feel ever so slightly wicked. Or perhaps because it is all so secret, as though he were forbidden fruit. Or maybe because I know it is temporary. Whatever the reason, I cannot stop thinking about him, wanting him. Is it the same with you and Eustace, Penelope?"

"There is lust, to be sure," Penelope said. Grace passed her a full cup and she took it, sloshing a bit of tea into the saucer before she could put it down. "But Eustace is not my first lover, as you know, so there is not quite the obsession that you are experiencing with Lord Thayne. The whole business is still something of a novelty for you, but that will pass eventually, and you will be less consumed by it all. You will be more ready to take on the next lover."

"The next?" Beatrice shook her head. "I cannot imagine anyone else but Thayne. I know I am being foolish, but I dread facing the end of the affair. I realize it must end soon, but I fear it will break my heart."

Wilhelmina, who'd been rather quiet, cast her an appraising glance. "*Is* your heart involved?"

Beatrice shrugged. She had tried not to face that question. It would be rather absurd, at her age, to fall in love with a handsome young man. "Only insomuch as I have an affection for him," she said. "I like him immensely. And I remember what Penelope once said about her first lover. She told us he was like a tonic to her. That is how I feel right now with Thayne. He makes me feel young and beautiful. He actually likes my body, my poor past-its-prime, middle-aged body. Or so he tells me. Rather often, in fact." She chuckled as she recalled those Indian sculptures with the impossible breasts, and how he liked to compare her to them.

"He sounds like a prince," Penelope said, stirring milk into her tea.

"Besides all that," Beatrice continued, "Thayne is a fascinating man. I could listen for hours to his tales of India. He also has a sharp mind and a sly wit, not to mention a powerful sense of honor and duty. He is committed to finding a bride this Season to honor a pledge to his father. Of course when he does our affair comes to an end."

"Is your niece still pursuing him?" Marianne asked. "That could be awkward."

"More than awkward, it would be disastrous. But no, Emily has apparently decided it would tarnish her image if she were seen to favor a man who does not favor her."

"Has he singled out any other young woman yet?" Wilhelmina asked.

"No, but it won't be long. He has set his mind to it, and he is a very strong-willed man."

"You don't suppose he will make *you* an offer, do you?" Wilhelmina asked. "When I spoke with him that night at the Oscott ball, he seemed very much infatuated with you. And determined to have you."

Beatrice put down her teacup and laughed. "Make *me* an offer? How ridiculous. Of course he will not. I am his lover, for the moment, that is all."

"Then you must simply enjoy it while it lasts," Penelope said. "And take notes."

"Please do," Marianne said. "I believe I shall want a copy. Even Adam hasn't tried some of those positions."

They all laughed, except for Grace, who merely smiled. She no doubt found all the talk of exotic love-making embarrassing. Grace was terribly prim and never very comfortable with their candid discussions about sex. "We must see what we can do to find Grace a lover," Beatrice said. "She is the only one of us not glowing with good health."

Grace flushed prettily. "I am perfectly healthy, thank you. I am just not like the rest of you . . . in that way. I could never . . . well, you know. Besides, I am not the sort of woman to attract that kind of attention from a man. Thank goodness."

"Nonsense," Marianne said. "Men look at you

with admiration all the time. Even I noticed how Rochdale could not keep his eyes off you at our wedding."

Grace shuddered visibly. "What a horrid man. He simply found it entertaining to flirt with me. I hate the way he looks at me, as if he were undressing me in his mind."

Marianne laughed. "He probably was. But if it makes you feel any better, Grace, he looks at most women like that. I do not believe you have anything to fear from him. Adam tells me that despite that ugly business with Serena Underwood, Rochdale does not typically seduce unwilling women."

"I am safe, then," Grace said, "for I am certainly unwilling. The man is a libertine and a gamester. And a cad, considering what he did to poor Serena. And heaven only knows who else."

"There are lots of other gentlemen out there, Grace," Wilhelmina said. "Not all of them are cads, you know."

"I know," Grace said. "And I am pleased, truly I am, that all of you have found nice gentlemen to . . . to make you happy. But I have no such inclination. And even if I did, I don't have the time. Besides the Fund business, I have a new project taking up my spare time."

"Another charity?" Wilhelmina asked, and passed her teacup to Grace.

"No, something altogether different." Grace smiled as she refilled the cup and handed it back to Wilhelmina. "I have decided to publish a collection of the bishop's sermons. I am in the process of editing them now, reading through his notes and determining what should go in the collection. It is rather a large effort."

"Yes," Penelope said, "I should imagine it is." She caught Beatrice's eye and lifted her own gaze to the ceiling. Beatrice covered her mouth to keep from giggling.

Later, when they were gathered in the entry hall retrieving bonnets and gloves and pelisses before departing, Wilhelmina pulled Beatrice aside.

"I thought I should tell you, my dear," she said, "that Ingleby will be away for the next fortnight. I am afraid my house will not be vacant in the evenings until he returns."

"Oh." A wave of disappoint swept over Beatrice. Two weeks without Thayne's lovemaking? How could she bear it?

"Of course, you may still use my guest bedchamber, if you like."

"No, no," Beatrice said, "I would not impose on you like that. You have been more than generous with your hospitality. In fact, I owe you so much, Wilhelmina. I don't know what we would have done without you."

"Lord Thayne is a resourceful young man. He would have managed somehow. And he will again. Perhaps you can arrange another afternoon in his new home."

"Afternoons are very difficult," Beatrice said. "Emily is forever needing to go somewhere or to meet someone, and there are my own girls to worry about. With our busy evenings, the afternoons are often the only time I have with them. But you are right. We will contrive something. Do not worry."

"I am terribly sorry, my dear. But it is only two weeks. When Ingleby returns, I shall be spending most nights with him, I trust. Until he tires of me, of course."

"Don't be silly," Beatrice said. "The man is besotted with you. He is unlikely to tire of you in the near future, if ever."

"Perhaps. But if he does throw me over, I shall not

go into a decline. I have had a good deal of experience in these matters, you know. My heart is well guarded."

"Are you suggesting mine is not?"

"Is it?"

Beatrice hunched a shoulder. "I don't know, to be honest. I like him a great deal, and his lovemaking takes my breath away. He has taught me how important physical passion is, and has made me crave it. But when we part, which we will, I shall just have to find another lover. I do not think I will be able to give up that part of my life again."

"You think it will be that easy?"

"To find another lover? Why not? London is full of eager gentlemen."

"I meant giving up Lord Thayne. I do not believe you will find that as easy as you think."

"But what of Lord Thayne?"

Emily's mother was ensconced in her chaise with the mountain of pillows at her back and the paisley shawl, as usual, covering her legs. Mama seemed to think no one would know of the wooden splint beneath, which amused Emily, since everyone knew she had a broken leg. She certainly did not allow them to see her being carried downstairs, which Emily's maid, Sally, told her took two footmen to accomplish, with Mama screeching the whole time about how they were going to drop her. She was already comfortably disposed on her chaise each time they arrived. She wore her best lace cap, as well. And it was not as though Emily and Aunt Beatrice were real callers. They were family, after all, but Mama had her standards.

"Emily?"

She jerked to attention. "Yes, Mama?"

"I asked you about Lord Thayne. You have mentioned Lord Ealing and Lord Newcombe and Sir

Frederick Gilling. But what of the marquess? Will you be able to bring him up to scratch?"

Emily looked at Aunt Beatrice, who had a frown on her face. She always frowned lately when Lord Thayne was mentioned. For some inexplicable reabson, she seemed to have taken a dislike to him. Emily had no idea what had changed her aunt's mind. She had certainly been in favor of him earlier, when they'd first met him. Perhaps it was because she sensed he was looking for someone higher than a aronet's daughter, and she did not want Emily to make a cake of herself over a man who would never offer for her. Emily had no intention of doing such a stupid thing, however. She could have no interest in a man who had no interest in *her*. Even though she would make a better marchioness any day than that pasty-faced Miss Fancourt. But what had happened to change her aunt's mind so decidedly against him? It was a mystery Emily hoped to solve one day.

"I have no interest in bringing Lord Thayne up to scratch," she said. "Did Mrs. Gadd make jam tarts today?"

"What?" Her mother's voice rose almost to a shout and she pounded the cushion at her side. "What do you mean, *no interest*?"

"Just that," Emily said. "There are plenty of other gentlemen who are equally eligible." And who appreciated her beauty as something out of the ordinary. Lord Thayne had never given the least indication that he even noticed. For a time, Emily had even entertained the notion that the man was shortsighted. It seemed the only explanation for not finding that glint of admiration in his eye that she saw in every other man, whether he was eighteen or eighty.

"What about those tarts, Mama? Do you think she could send some up?"

"Equally eligible?" her mother said, ignoring the jam tarts. "I think not, my girl. I have not heard of another heir to a duke paying his attentions to you."

"But neither has this heir to a duke," Aunt Beatrice said. "As extraordinary as it sounds, Ophelia, Lord Thayne has shown no interest whatsoever in our Emily."

Mama glared daggers at Aunt Beatrice. "That's ridiculous. Every man shows an interest in our Emily. How could he not? What have you been about, Sister, that you have so badly managed things? Maybe it is time I took Emily in hand and relieved you of the duty. *I* would see to it that the marquess was brought in line, you may be sure of it. I shall rise from this couch at once and—"

"No, Mama!"

"Please do not get up, Ophelia," Aunt Beatrice said. "There is no need for you to hobble about on your crutch in public. Emily is doing quite well. She has several very eligible and very *rich* young men interested in her. I have no doubt she will receive several offers before the end of the Season."

"But . . . but what of Lord Thayne?" her mother said, sputtering in her agitation. "You cannot give up on him. He is the biggest prize of the Season."

"Recall, Ophelia, that as pretty as Emily is, she is only the daughter of a baronet. He may be looking higher, and if so, there is nothing we can do about it. Besides, he truly is not showing an interest."

"I do not believe it for a moment," her mother said. "It makes no sense. Emily is too beautiful to be overlooked."

"Perhaps the man has no taste," Aunt Beatrice said, and smiled at Emily.

"That would account for it," Emily said.

Her mother uttered a dismissive snort. "That is no reason for Emily not to encourage his attentions.

Even if he is a dolt without the sense God gave him, he is still a marquess."

"I think it best if she does not encourage him," Aunt Beatrice said. "And wisely, she has not done so. I believe our Emily knows how odd it would look if her encouragement was not addressed with a returned interest. You would not want your daughter to be an object of pity, would you?"

"How could anyone pity such a face?" Emily's fond mother said.

"They would not pity her face, Ophelia. They would pity her heart, thinking Lord Thayne had broken it with his indifference."

Though Emily would never dream of admitting it, Aunt Beatrice was right. She could not bear even to imagine the public humiliation of being rejected, and so she chose to ignore Lord Thayne altogether.

"My heart is in no danger of being broken," Emily said. "But my stomach is in danger of growling aloud. If there are no jam tarts, ginger biscuits would do. May I ring for some?"

"No, you may not," her mother replied. "You must watch your figure, my girl. Once you have landed a husband, then you may grow plump as a Christmas goose, if you wish. Until then, you must not risk any potential blemish to your beauty."

Emily was more likely to risk fainting from hunger. She would ask Aunt Beatrice if they could stop at a pastry shop on the way back to Brook Street.

"As for Lord Thayne, I think you are wrong," her mother said to Aunt Beatrice. "Shall I tell you the gossip I have heard?"

"About me?" Emily thought it horribly vulgar to be the subject of gossip. Unless, of course, it was something flattering.

"About you and Lord Thayne. More than one person has told me that he is frequently found at your side at every ball you attend. And that he has more than once been seen in your drawing room, Beatrice, on those afternoons when you receive callers. Several people of my acquaintance seem to be under the impression that his lordship does indeed have a tendre for our Emily."

Aunt Beatrice gave a soft groan.

"What I think," her mother continued, "is that you have mistaken his aristocratic bearing for disinterest. A man of his upbringing is not likely to be ardent or effusive in public."

"No," Aunt Beatrice said in a definitive tone that Emily found rather irritating. It was irksome that her aunt was so determined that Lord Thayne was not attracted to her. Even if it was true, did she have to hammer the point home so forcefully?

"I am not mistaken," her aunt said. "I can assure you Lord Thayne is not interested in our Emily. He is often seen with us because he is in the company of Mr. Jeremy Burnett, his particular friend. It is Mr. Burnett who is smitten with Emily, not Lord Thayne."

Emily rolled her eyes.

"Mr. Burnett?" her mother said. "Mr. Burnett? I have never heard you speak of a Mr. Burnett, my girl. Who is he?"

"He is nobody," Emily said. "Just an annoying gentleman who lurks about altogether too much. He does his best to draw my attention, but I will have none of him."

Especially not after some of the things he had had the temerity to say to her. He was forever teasing her and charming her with that lopsided smile, and he frequently made her laugh. But the last time she had seen him, he had told her she was too beautiful for her own good. She would admit that she had been flirting rather outrageously at the time with Viscount Ealing, who also happened to be heir to an earldom, and his lordship had been exclaiming about her extraordinary beauty. She had mentioned how thirsty she was, and Lord Ealing had sped away quick as a bunny to procure her a cool drink. Mr. Burnett had dropped his usual amusing banter and actually scolded her.

"You use your beauty to get all that you want in life," he'd said.

"Heavens, sir, it was only a drink."

"It is more than a cool drink. You believe your beauty entitles you to everything, that it will ultimately bring you happiness in life. Well, it won't, you know. Not because it is a fleeting thing—which it is, of course; you fool yourself if you think it will never fade—but because it is not important."

"Not important?" she'd replied. "How can you say such a thing? How many plain girls do you see winning a rich, handsome, titled husband? How many girls with spots? How many plump girls with extra chins? Of course it is important, you silly man."

"No, it is not," he said. "It does not define your character, your intelligence, your talents and abilities. You should be looking for a man who is not content merely to have your beauty at his disposal, as an ornament to his pride. You need a man who wants to know who you are, what you believe in, what's important to you, what you dream about, what makes you laugh. Those are the essential things. For if you lost your beauty tomorrow, all the rest will still be there. The parts of you that truly matter."

"I suppose you are exactly that sort of man, the sort you think I need, the sort who doesn't care whether or not I'm pretty?"

"I am drawn to your beauty just like every other man with eyes in his head. How could I not be? But I care equally about the other things, about who you are. And so, yes, I am indeed the sort of man you need, for I would love you even if you fell victim to the pox and your face was forever marked by it. But I cannot offer you a title, so you will never have me. Will you?"

She had told him he was impertinent, turned on her heel, and walked away. But she still remembered every word of that strange conversation. It was the most unusual declaration of love she'd ever heard, and she'd heard scores of them.

And he'd been dead wrong about the importance of beauty. Of course it was important. It was everything. It was her path to fame and fortune, and her escape from being under Mama's wing.

"Emily?"

She was jerked back to the present by her mother's loud voice.

"I am talking to you, my girl. Get your head out of the clouds."

"Sorry, Mama. I was woolgathering. What were you saying?"

"I was asking about Mr. Burnett."

"Oh."

"He is a perfectly charming young man," Aunt Beatrice said, "with the most engaging smile you will ever see. My Charlotte is very fond of him and he is indulgent of her when he calls. He was in India with Lord Thayne, you know. Such things fascinate that girl and she is apt to plague him to death with her endless questions."

"You are foolish to allow your girls to mingle with your guests on your afternoons at home. They are too young."

"It is good practice for them," Aunt Beatrice said, "and they are perfectly well behaved. Charlotte does tend to get excited about tales of elephants and such. Mr. Burnett is kind to her, and much infatuated with our Emily. His father is the Earl of Mottisfont, by the way."

"Mottisfont?" A sudden spark of interest lit Emily's mother's eye.

"He is a younger son, Mama, so do not get your hopes up. There are two brothers ahead of him in the succession."

Her mother heaved a sigh. "How provoking. Well, never mind then. You must not waste your time with him."

"I am *not* wasting time with him. He is the one wasting time, hanging about like an idiot, thinking I'll toss my cap at him one day. Ha!"

"Good girl. Well, as long as your Mr. Burnett seems always to be in the company of Lord Thayne, there is still hope in that quarter."

"No, Ophelia, there is not. Allow that bee to fly out of your bonnet, if you please. Otherwise you will have your daughter seen as a flirt, if she pushes herself at Lord Thayne, and that will not do."

Once again, Emily had to wonder why her aunt was so dead set against the marquess. Was there some sordid tale she did not want Emily to know? And Mr. Burnett was forever warning her off, as well. More subtly than Aunt Beatrice, to be sure, but he always seemed to imply that Lord Thayne had interests elsewhere. Emily could not imagine who the object of his interest might be, since he never singled out any girl in particular.

"Confound it, Beatrice, you are being positively pigheaded about this." Emily's mother pounded at the pillows again, stirring up a flurry of dust motes. "Do not stand in the way of a brilliant match or I swear I will leave this couch, hobbling or not, and take care of it myself. Let the girl encourage the marquess, for God's sake."

"I have no intention of encouraging him, Mama."

"Do as you are told, my girl. You will thank me one day, when you are a duchess."

There was no arguing with Mama when she got a notion stuck in her head. Thank goodness she was not acting as Emily's chaperone. She would be one of those embarrassing mothers who forced their daughters upon unsuspecting gentlemen. Emily did not need that kind of assistance, thank you very much. She would do very nicely on her own. There were plenty of perfectly eligible gentlemen who made calf's eyes at her every day, including the impertinent Mr. Burnett. She did not need to force herself upon Lord Thayne. True, he was a marquess, and marquesses were not exactly springing up like weeds all over London. Striking him from her list represented a significant compromise in her objective, but there was no way in blazes she would allow herself to be thought to chase after a man who ignored her.

Perhaps she could wheedle out of Mr. Burnett the identity of the woman who apparently *had* captured Lord Thayne's interest. Emily suspected he knew that secret, and she was dying to know who it was. Just as a matter of curiosity, of course.

"And what's this I hear," her mother said, "about that dreadful Lord Rochdale hanging about? You must definitely *not* encourage that one, my girl."

"I keep an eye on him," Aunt Beatrice said. "More than once I have sent him off with a stern look. I cannot imagine why he continues to come around."

"Even a scoundrel has an eye for beauty," Mama said. "Our Emily is bound to attract all types, some of them less respectable than others. But I trust you to keep any objectionable men away from her, Beatrice. Or will you fail me in that regard, as well?"

"I do my best, Ophelia." Her voice had grown angry, and Emily could hardly blame her. Aunt Beatrice was a thousand times more cautious a chaperone than Mama would ever have been. "Rochdale has so far done no more than loiter about the edges

of Emily's court of admirers," Aunt Beatrice continued. "He hasn't even got close enough to speak
with her."

"I danced with him once," Emily said.

Aunt Beatrice stared at her openmouthed, then
said, "When? I have taken note of every partner who
ever led you onto a dance floor, and I never saw you
dance with Rochdale. I would not have allowed it."

"I should hope not!" Her mother looked thoroughly aghast at such a notion. "Good God, Sister, I
cannot trust you to do anything right. Dancing with
Rochdale, indeed!"

"It was at Aunt Wallingford's masquerade ball."

Aunt Beatrice grew pale.

"Dear God," her mother said. "What on earth was
Mary thinking, to invite such a person? May I assume that you did not know his identity when you
agreed to dance with him?"

"I did not know who he was," Emily said. "He
was dressed as a pirate and I did not recognize him.
But he told me who he was when I asked. I didn't
expect him to tell me—one isn't required to do so at
a masquerade, you know. But he did. I meant to tell
you afterward, Aunt Beatrice, but you had disappeared and then said you weren't feeling well and
that we must leave. Poor Aunt Beatrice has been ill
again several times since, Mama. I think I have been
overtaxing her, with all my parties and such."

"Is that true?" her mother asked. "Have you been
unwell, Beatrice? Why didn't you tell me? No wonder you are falling off the job."

Aunt Beatrice appeared oddly flustered. Perhaps
Emily should not have mentioned anything about her
being ill. But she really felt guilty about it, running
the poor woman ragged, dashing from ball to ball,
party to party. It must be hard on someone of her
age.

"I have not been unwell," she said. "Only a headache now and then. Nothing to be concerned about, I assure you. I shall not shirk my duties, Ophelia."

"Good. Then you must be sure to keep Lord Thayne in our Emily's orbit. I am persuaded there is still hope in that direction."

And Emily was persuaded that her mother was doomed to disappointment.

Chapter 14

Two weeks! Thayne would go mad if he had to wait two weeks to be with Beatrice again. He craved the pure, white perfection of her skin, the smell of her hair, her incredible breasts, everything. Desire for her lived in him now like a constant ache. She had become necessary to him. Two weeks without her would surely kill him.

But she could not promise another afternoon anytime soon, claiming she had too many commitments with Emily or her own daughters. He could not bring her to Doncaster House. Burnett was of no use, as he kept bachelor rooms at Albany. And Loughton House, such as it was, did not offer much hope, either. His bed had been deemed too small by his father, who had taken it into his head to buy Thayne a new one. The old bed, the bed where he had last loved Beatrice, had been dismantled and the new bed, properly grand enough for a duke's heir, had not yet been delivered.

It seemed the Fates that had once been so kind had turned against him. He wanted, *needed*, to be with Beatrice again. He could not wait for the accommodating Wilhelmina Hertford to be free to lend them her house a fortnight later. Thayne wanted Beatrice tonight. But how to manage it?

He wasn't sure what he was going to do, but he had to do *something*.

There was something else he was going to do, as well. Thayne had given it a great deal of thought and had come to an inevitable conclusion. It was so obvious, and so perfect, he felt an idiot for not having thought of it before. It had taken that day at Loughton House—the entire afternoon, not only the time spent making love to her—for him to fully accept his feelings for Beatrice. He loved her. He wanted her in his life, not just temporarily but forever.

It was useless to continue halfheartedly pursuing all those pretty young girls of eighteen or twenty who had nothing to offer but their potential. And what if he chose wrong? What if the girl who appeared to have the most promise turned into a shrew or a dullard or a featherbrained ninny? He would be stuck with her for a lifetime.

No, it was much smarter to choose a woman whose character was already fully matured and thoroughly admirable, who would offer no terrifying surprises after the wedding, either in the bedroom or the drawing room.

Thayne had more than his share of self-confidence and self-worth. He knew he tended to loom large, to intimidate, to take charge. He did not always like those aspects of his character—which he realized many people interpreted as supreme arrogance—but he could not change who he was. And although he might enjoy a pretty, young, biddable wife for a while, he knew without question that he would soon grow tired of a woman who offered no challenge, who acquiesced to his every desire, who let him rule every aspect of her life. He preferred a woman who could meet him on more equal terms, who would not acquiesce but might battle instead. He would ultimately have the upper hand, of course, but he preferred a bit of a challenge to get there.

The funny thing was that he'd only just discovered all this about himself. He'd always assumed a biddable young bride was what he wanted, an unformed girl who could be molded to suit his requirements as a wife, as a marchioness. But Beatrice had changed all that. He'd come to realize that *she* was the sort of woman he really wanted. Needed. A woman like Beatrice. No, not *like* her. *Her.* He wanted Beatrice.

He watched her across the room at another card table. Lord and Lady Marchdon had set up their large drawing room, and several other rooms, with tables for cards, and many members of the *ton* were in attendance, including Beatrice and Emily. There was no serious gambling involved. It was all very proper with only pennies for stakes. Thayne had never much enjoyed playing whist, and he was having difficulty concentrating on the play. Lady Emmeline Standish was his partner, and though she must surely be aggravated at his mistakes, she was every inch the proper young lady and never complained. In the last hand, he'd led trumps when he had only one trump card, causing them to lose the hand. Thayne muttered a Persian oath, but his partner merely smiled and gave a resigned shrug.

Somehow he managed to finish the rubber and paid their losses to the other couple. He was too wound up to play any more, and so he excused himself from the next hand, and invited Lord Newcombe to take his place. Lady Emmeline's eyes brightened. Did she have a tendre for the fellow, or was she simply happy to have a partner who would be awake to every play?

Thayne had once considered Lady Emmeline as the one he might choose as his bride. He liked her. She was very pretty and would have made a fine marchioness, he had no doubt. But he had other plans now, and was anxious to put them into motion.

If only this damned party would end.

Some time later, it did begin to break up and
guests began departing. He watched Beatrice and
Emily make their farewells, and Thayne did the
same. He took a moment to apologize to Lady Emmeline for being such a disappointing partner, claiming his mind had been elsewhere.

"No need to apologize, my lord," she said. "I quite
understand." Her eyes had darted toward the doors,
where Beatrice and Emily had just passed.

Good God. Did she know? Was he so transparent
in his desire for Beatrice?

No, it was more likely she thought his mind was
on Miss Emily Thirkill. Thayne stifled a groan. Was
there still gossip about them? Expectations he
thought had long been squashed?

Damnation. He had to make matters right, and
quickly. Tonight.

When he found his carriage among the throng of
vehicles, Thayne impulsively gave the driver Beatrice's Brook Street direction. He wasn't sure what
he was going to do, but he had to speak privately
with her.

When the carriage turned into Brook Street Thayne
experienced a twinge of panic. What if she hadn't
gone home? What if they had gone to another
party instead?

He heaved a sigh of relief when he saw her carriage pull away. She was home.

Now what?

He alighted from his carriage and sent the driver
back to Doncaster House. Thayne could walk the
short distance later.

After he'd done what? Come to her door at one
o'clock in the morning and announced himself? No,
that would not do. He was being foolish. He ought
to begin that walk to Park Lane now, and be done
with it.

But as he stood across the street, watching the

house like a moonstruck idiot, he saw her. Only for an instant, but candlelight most definitely glinted off red hair in one of the third-floor windows.

Her bedroom.

His groin tightened. She would be in there undressing, letting her hair down, getting into bed. How he wished he could be there with her.

And then he noticed it. The large tree right outside her window. The tree with thick, sturdy-looking branches within easy reach.

Thayne smiled. Serendipity again.

He waited for what seemed like hours, but was probably only twenty minutes, until all candlelight had been extinguished. Then he made his move.

Tap tap tap.

Beatrice sat bolt upright in bed. "Who's there?" She had not been quite asleep when she heard a sharp tapping. She tossed back the cover and slid out of bed.

She opened the door, but found no one there. She stepped into the corridor but saw nothing. All the other bedroom doors were closed, and no telltale light shone beneath any of them. How odd. Perhaps she really *had* been asleep and only dreamed she'd heard something.

She was about to crawl back into bed when she heard it again.

Tap tap tap.

It wasn't the door at all. Someone was tapping on the window. Good heavens. Had Charlotte been up in the tree again? At this hour? She would have that child's guts for garters, by God. What was she thinking?

She went to the window and flung back the curtains, ready to do murder. She unlatched the casement, pushed it open, and said, "Charlotte, is that you? I swear I will—"

"No, Beatrice, it is me."

Gabriel! Here?

Sure enough, there was his dignified lordship perched on a branch just outside the window. His teeth gleamed in the moonlight as he grinned like a fool.

"Gabriel, what the devil are you doing here? Get down from that tree at once."

"I could not wait two weeks," he said. "Or even another day. Step aside, my love. I'm coming inside."

And before she could stop him, he'd swung himself with athletic grace from the limb to the window ledge, and climbed through the window. He pulled the heavy curtains closed behind him, brushed off his waistcoat and breeches, then stood smiling and pristine as though he'd just entered a ballroom.

He reached for her, but she brushed him away. "Are you mad?" Anger spread like a fever along her shoulders and down her back. "How dare you, Gabriel? How dare you come to my house, to my bedchamber, when my daughters are asleep just across the corridor? My *daughters*, Gabriel! What if one of them hears you or sees you? For God's sake, what were you *thinking*?"

He reached for her again and captured her this time. He imprisoned her against him, her hands flat against his broad chest. "I was thinking I could not wait another moment to be with you again. I was thinking that if we were very careful and very quiet, no one would know I had been here. I have been thinking of nothing else for days but how to contrive to be with you. But most of all, I have been thinking I could not live another day without holding you in my arms. Without kissing you."

He bent his head and did just that. Despite all her misgivings—and they were legion—she found herself melting into his kiss, everything within her dissolving into liquid. Traitorous body! She could not resist him, even in her anger. His tongue found hers, tangling wet and urgent in a kiss so potent her knees almost buckled.

He broke the kiss at last and nibbled his way along her jaw and throat and neck. "Gabriel," she said, drawing out the first syllable in a kind of moan. "We should not be doing this. Not here. It's not right." She was angry with him for being so reckless, so rash, so arrogantly heedless of her perfectly reasonable objections. And yet she arched her neck to give him better access and snaked her hands into his thick, dark hair as his teeth nipped and scraped along her throat.

"It is always right between us," he said between nibbles, "and always will be."

So persuasive. So irresistible. Her wits deserted her entirely when his hands slid down her ribs and around to cup her bottom. She felt his arousal straining against his breeches, and wanted it, wanted him. She no longer cared where they were or how wrong it was. She wanted him. Now.

"All right," she said. "All right. You win. But only this once, Gabriel. I will not risk it again. And we must be *quiet*."

Beatrice tugged up her nightgown, pulled it over her head, and tossed it on the floor. She shivered when the cool air hit her skin. Or maybe it was simply in anticipation of what was about to happen.

"I want to see you." Gabriel went back to the window and pulled the draperies aside. Moonlight poured into the room. "Ah. Beautiful. Your skin is like polished marble in this light. Your hair like burgundy wine. But please, no plaits tonight. Let your hair down, my huntress."

She unbraided the thick plait that hung down her back while Gabriel undressed. She shook out her hair as he stood before her, naked, perfect, gloriously male. He gathered her loosely in his arms, his proud erection rearing between them.

"Let me love you," he said, and kissed her tenderly.

He took her hand and led her to the bed, pulling her down beside him. They already knew each other's bodies well, and Beatrice entwined her legs with his almost without thought. They kissed and stroked and fondled, leisurely, savoring each other without hurry. Finally Gabriel rolled on top of her.

"I adore your breasts," he said as he squeezed them together and flicked the tip of his tongue over each nipple. "I love the way they feel, the way they move, how deliciously soft they are. Why are you laughing?"

"They're soft and they move because they're no longer young and firm, and yet you seem to find that an asset."

"I do. They're perfect. Womanly, not girlish. Like you."

He made love to one breast, then the other, licking, stroking, sucking, taking the whole nipple into his mouth and curling his tongue around it. Beatrice felt her pulse race against his mouth.

He did not stop with her breasts, but used his lips and tongue all over her body. By turns tender and ravenous, he lavished her flesh with miracles such as she could never have imagined before he came into her life, miracles she now craved with a desperate hunger. She gave herself up to the pure, mindless sensation that coursed through her veins, hot and bright.

Finally, he trailed his tongue down her belly and into the crisp curls covering her sex. Parting her, he thrust his tongue deep inside her, and Beatrice arched up into his mouth, dizzy with sensation. His finger—no, two fingers—replaced his tongue, which he set to pleasuring the tiny nub just above. His tongue on that oh-so-sensitive spot made her squirm, but he held her legs apart, forcing her to accept the pleasure.

An agony of tension gripped her body, savage in its power. Then all at once the spike of pleasure speared into her, sharp and hot, emanating from that delicate nub of flesh he circled with his tongue and radiating to every inch of her body from her toenails to the roots of her hair. She bucked and twisted and clamped her lips together in a valiant effort not to cry out in her helplessness.

He held his mouth in place until he felt her go limp. Then he crawled up her body and kissed her, allowing her to taste herself on his tongue, to share in his pleasure of her.

He lay atop her and molded her softness against his harder frame, loving the feel of her beneath him, skin to skin, hers silky smooth, his . . . not. He grasped her hands and lifted them to rest on either side of her head, threading his fingers through hers. Gripping her hands tightly for support, he shifted his hips so that the tip of his cock was pressed on the same spot where his mouth had just been.

Her eyes opened and looked into his. A low hum of passion sounded in her throat as he moved against her.

"I shall die again," she murmured. "How many little deaths can a person withstand?"

"A thousand. A hundred thousand. A lifetime of *les petites morts*." He shifted again so that he was at the opening of her sex, her *yoni*. "At least once more tonight." He pushed inside her, slowly, until he was buried to the hilt in the sleek, hot wetness of her. He closed his eyes and savored the simple pleasure of being fully joined with her.

There would be nothing fancy tonight, nothing exotic. Tonight was about love, about connection, about sharing. Just a simple, pure, exquisite loving. He held himself above her, still gripping her hands. He looked into her eyes as he began to move. Slowly out. Slowly in. She smiled and moved with him. She rotated her hips and squeezed her inner muscles in a way that almost pushed him over the edge. He increased the tempo slightly, still holding her gaze and her hands.

"More," she said. "Harder."

And he complied. He drove faster, setting up a rhythmic, damp timpani as their hips met, retreated, met again. He felt her body tense. She gripped his hands tighter and arched her neck. Her face twisted into a grimace and her breaths became shallow. His own panting became more ragged as he thrust harder and faster. But he never let go of her hands and he never stopped watching her. And so he had the singular joy of watching her face as she reached her climax. Eyes closed tight, teeth bared, every muscle tense. And suddenly she was transformed. Her eyes opened wide, her mouth formed a perfect O, and a sort of wonder suffused her face as her body writhed and peaked beneath him, while he pumped and pumped and pumped.

His own release came quickly. He was so enraptured by hers that he almost did not pull out in time. He pressed his cock against her belly, still pumping, as his climax ripped through him.

Beatrice lay nuzzled against Gabriel's shoulder, content as a kitten in a basket. He had cleaned her up, as he always did, then slid under the sheets with her and tucked her up against him.

"I should be angry with you," she said, "but that was so lovely I almost forgive you."

"Almost?"

"It was still a bad idea, Gabriel, and you must promise you won't do it again. What if Charlotte or

Georgie were to wander in and find us like this? It's too dangerous."

"You're right," he said. "But I have an idea for making things easier for us." He turned on his side and lay facing her. "Marry me."

Beatrice gave a little jerking start. He could not be serious. But she gazed into his brown eyes and saw that he was. "Oh, Gabriel."

"You know that I have promised to marry this year, and you are the only woman who suits me, the only woman I want."

She was shaken by his sincerity. Despite Wilhelmina's suggestion that he might make her an offer, Beatrice had never expected it. Never.

"You know I care for you," he said, "and I think you must care for me a little."

She lifted a hand to his face. "You are very dear to me, Gabriel. You have brought a great deal of joy into my life. But I am not the wife for you. You are sweet to offer, but you cannot truly want to marry me."

"Yes, I can. I do."

"Gabriel, my dear, you are meant to marry some young virgin bride of good family who will provide you with an heir and a spare. Not a woman who has already been married, has children, and will be thirty-six on her next birthday."

"You worry too much about your age. It has never mattered to me. You know that."

"It may not bother you now, but I guarantee you it would make a difference over time. I will age faster. I will lose my looks and my hair will turn silver while you are still in your prime. A man like you doesn't marry a woman like me. You marry one of those pretty young girls on the marriage mart. You need someone younger, my dear. Young enough to have your children. I am too old for you."

His dark brows drew together in a frown. "I have

some degree of mathematic ability, Beatrice. I can count. I am twenty-nine. You are thirty-five. I believe that means a mere six years separates us. Not such a vast number. And not too old for children. My mother had my youngest sister when she was forty. Besides, I have discovered that I prefer a woman six years older than one six years younger, who hasn't two thoughts to rub together and doesn't yet know her own mind. I don't want a girl. I want a woman. I want *you*. Marry me."

"Oh, Gabriel."

She rolled onto her back and sat up, propping pillows behind her. Gabriel followed suit, and they sat side by side in awkward silence while Beatrice pondered how best to respond to such an extraordinary proposal, to make him understand how impossible it was.

"I want to be with you in the light of day, Beatrice. Legitimately, openly, and not in dark corners and secret assignations. You deserve better than that. We both do. I know you care for me." He stroked a finger up and down her arm. "You are not indifferent to me."

"No, of course I am not. You are very special to me, Gabriel. I . . . I adore you, I really do." She more than adored him, in fact. "But I thought you understood."

"Understood what?"

"That I do not *want* to marry again. When we first began this, you were not offering matrimony and I wasn't looking for it."

"I changed my mind."

"Why?"

"Because you have become more than a lover to me. You have become a friend. I've told you more about my years in India than anyone else since my return. You're the only one who has seen and appreciated my sculptures, the only one who truly understands the changes I am making to Loughton House. I sometimes feel that you see right into my soul." He picked up her hand and kissed the tip of each finger. "You have become more dear to me than I could ever have imagined. I want you for more than a lover, and for longer than a few months. I want you forever, as my wife."

Such a speech! And from such a man. It was almost heartbreaking. Oh, to be younger, when he might have swept her off her feet with such words. "Oh, Gabriel, that is a lovely thing to say. And you have become dear to me, too. I am overwhelmed that you should make me so splendid an offer. But I have had my marriage and my family. I am not looking for that again. I have only ever wanted . . . this. A love affair. A lover. Physical passion. I am too young to give up that aspect of my life, but too old to be a proper wife for you. You should find a nice young woman who will give you an heir, a biddable young woman willing to be dominated by her grand husband. I am not that woman. I will not do that again."

"What do you fear about marriage?"

"Fear?"

"Why are you so dead set against it? What do you fear?"

Beatrice uttered a little huff of exasperation. "Where to begin?" She got out of bed and retrieved the nightgown that had been tossed on the floor, then pulled it over her head and let it skim over her body down to her ankles.

She turned to face Gabriel, who had moved to sit on the edge of the bed. He was still completely naked, and she wished he would cover himself. His body was too distracting and she did not want to risk being seduced into accepting his proposal. She moved to look out the window instead.

"What did I hate most about marriage? Taking

orders. Being told what to do, or more often what not to do. When I was married, I learned to be secretive and sly, to agree to whatever was asked, and when it was something I despised or disapproved of, I deviously worked my way around it somehow. Marriage did that to me, made me artful and scheming. I have been a much better person since poor Somerfield died. My own person. And it wasn't Somerfield's fault. It is the way things are, the way wives are expected to behave. We take a vow to obey, you know."

She heard Gabriel move off the bed and turned to face him. He was pulling on his breeches. A good sign that he was ready to accept her refusal. He would be less likely to seduce her again with his clothes on.

"I hated being dominated," she continued. "I could not leave the house without Somerfield approving my dress, my bonnet, my destination, my companions. And he would not allow me to take a step outside without a maid or footman to accompany me. I was never allowed to do anything on my own, even something as insignificant as driving a one-horse gig."

"Forgive me, Beatrice, but he sounds like an insufferable bully."

"He was just an ordinary man. No different from most other husbands I've known. *I* was the problem, not Somerfield. I was not a good wife. I tried to be biddable, but it was not in me to be that kind of wife. And as much as I hated being dominated, I hated being ignored even more. I was allowed no part in any decision that affected our family. I have told you of my interest in financial matters. Somerfield would not even listen to me. He thought it unseemly for a woman to concern herself with such things. Ha! If he only knew how many times over I have increased my fortune in these last three years!

I chafed for thirteen years under a husband's authority. I will never put myself in that position again."

"You cannot judge all men by Somerfield's behavior," Gabriel said as he pulled his shirt over his head. Then he came and took both her hands in his and gazed intently into her eyes. "I would never treat you like that, Beatrice. I would want a marriage of equals, a partnership."

"Would you, really? Are you so very different, then, from other men? You would allow your wife to do as she pleased?"

"Within reason, yes. You would bear my name and my title, however, and a certain consideration for that position must be respected. Otherwise, you would have a significant degree of independence to do as you wanted."

Beatrice pulled her hands away. "But *you* determine that degree, don't you? You would still be in control of everything, wouldn't you? My behavior, my money, my . . . everything."

"That is a husband's responsibility, to protect his wife and children," he said as he tucked his shirt into his breeches. "And you must be reasonable, Beatrice. There are certain expectations from a wife, any wife, but especially the wife of a future duke."

"But you see, it is those expectations that I find objectionable. No, I won't marry again." Beatrice crossed her hands over her chest and looked down at her feet. "It has nothing to do with you, Gabriel. I would find it objectionable with any man. I am simply not willing to give up my freedom again."

He reached out and placed a knuckle under her chin, lifting it so she had to look him in the eye. "Not even for me?"

That voice. He was trying to seduce her with that voice. Damn him. She cocked her head away and he released her. "I'm sorry, Gabriel. I do not want a husband in my life again. I treasure the freedom my widowhood has brought me. I like being able to act and speak without the watchful eye of a possessive man, imposing checks on my behavior. I never want that again, never want another person to have such power over me again."

He picked up the waistcoat he had flung across the room and slipped it on. "You're being mulish, Beatrice. You think all men are the same. We're not. And as you are so fond of saying, you are not a young woman anymore, as you were when you married Somerfield. You are mature and self-possessed with a strong streak of independence. I doubt any man could have much power over you. I would not."

Beatrice snorted. "Of course you would. Look at what you did tonight, forcing your way into my house against my wishes, risking exposure of our affair to my young daughters. You had no consideration for my feelings in the matter. You just barged in and seduced me into capitulation."

He reached for his coat and glared at her, a glint of anger flickering in his eyes. "That is not how it was." The deep, seductive tone was gone and the lordly arrogance was back. He was Lord Thayne now, no longer Gabriel.

"Of course that is how it was," she said. "You always get what you want. You told me that the first moment you realized I had been the one at the masquerade. And I am to believe you would not try to control me? To dominate me? When you have just demonstrated that is precisely what you would do?"

He struggled into his coat and picked up the boots that stood by the bed. Anger radiated from every inch of him. His body was tense with it, and a muscle twitched in his jaw. "And so those are my sins, Beatrice? Youth? Arrogance? Or merely that I am a man? I think we have said enough on the matter. I am sorry I troubled you. I shall not do so again, I assure you. And do not worry. I will not disturb anyone in the house as I leave. I will go the same way I came."

He flung open the window, and was gone.

Beatrice stood in the middle of the room, stunned at what had just happened. After a perfectly wonderful interlude of lovemaking, it had come to this. Anger and bitterness. The end of her love affair.

Ironically enough, she had only just come to realize she was a little bit in love with Gabriel. More than a little. Why did he have to ruin everything by asking her to marry him?

She lay down on the bed, buried her face in the pillows, and wept.

Chapter 15

It was the last place he wanted to be tonight.
Thayne had no desire to see Beatrice after she had
so vehemently rejected his proposal last night. He
did not know what possessed him to allow Burnett
to drag him to this damnable ball. *Her* ball. One of
her blasted charity events. Meeting her in the receiving line had been difficult at best. Tension stretched
between them so thick you could cut it with a knife.
Even her friends had seemed uncomfortable. The
Duchess of Hertford was the only one to give him a
warm smile.

And did Beatrice have to look so bloody beautiful?
She wore a dress of brilliant turquoise that reminded
him of the sari he had wrapped around her that day
at Loughton House. The day that had been one of
the happiest of his life. He wished he could forget it.
He wished he could forget *her*.

He ought to hate her for all she had said, but he
did not. He could not stop loving her that easily. He
was angry with her, to be sure. She was as mule-
headed as any woman he'd ever met. How foolish
to allow that dolt of a husband not only to make her
unhappy while he lived, but to ruin the rest of her
life, as well. Thayne had wanted to shake some sense
into her. But he suspected she would never change
her mind. She was determined that marriage was lit-

tle better than a prison and that he would be the worst of jailers.

Damn her!

Had she never witnessed a happy marriage in all her life? Thayne thought of his own parents, who loved each other fiercely. If Beatrice thought he was domineering, she ought to have grown up with the Duke of Doncaster. And yet his mother had always held her own against him, would not allow him to bully her. That is the sort of marriage he had hoped for with Beatrice—that she would fight with him, butt heads with him, challenge him, and ultimately love him, all with equal passion. But she could not even comprehend such a marriage, and so she had dismissed him out of hand.

Damn her!

He still was honor bound to find a bride this Season, but how was he to do so now? He had made his choice. What the devil was he to do when that choice was not allowed him? Thayne had spent a lifetime making his own choices and decisions with little or no objections and no obstacles in his way. He had been totally unprepared for Beatrice to toss this decision, the most important of his life, back in his face. He had almost no experience in being denied something he badly wanted. It made him feel unsteady, like foundering in unknown waters. He did not like the feeling. It made him angry. *She* made him angry. Being at this damned ball made him angry.

But Burnett was determined on pursuing Emily Thirkill, and equally determined that Thayne should be there to support him. Whereas Thayne had once asked Burnett to fill Emily's ears with a recital of all his faults, Burnett appeared to believe it was Thayne's turn to exclaim his virtues to the girl. Since he barely ever spoke to Emily, Thayne did not know how such a thing was to be accomplished. But Burnett was top over tail in love with the girl and had begged his friend for help.

And if he was brutally honest with himself, Thayne supposed he would have to admit that he had in fact wanted to see Beatrice again. He still wanted her, God help him, and perhaps he hoped for one more twinkling of serendipity to bring them back together again. But overriding any glimmer of hope was a hot anger at the scene she had enacted for him the previous evening.

Damn her!

Burnett was at that moment chatting with the fair Emily. He seemed to have made headway among her circle, which was as crowded with lovesick puppies as ever. Thayne kept his distance, since Beatrice stood at her niece's side. She refused to look at him, and cast her gaze about the room.

Suddenly her eyes widened and her mouth dropped open in a look of complete astonishment. Thayne followed her gaze to the entrance, where she had stood earlier in the receiving line. A slightly stout, fair-haired woman was making her way across the floor with difficulty. She hobbled uncertainly on a crutch, a liveried footman at her elbow helping her along. The crowd that milled about the dance floor waiting for the next set parted to let her pass.

The woman wore an angry look, or perhaps she was in pain. In any case, she did not appear happy. Thayne was surprised to see Emily hurry across the floor to meet the woman. Beatrice followed close behind. Who was she? Could it be Emily's mother? It must be. The girl was speaking in a very animated manner, and at one point looked in Thayne's direction and nodded.

And then the most astonishing thing happened. The woman hobbled most determinedly toward him, her furious gaze boring straight through him as she approached. By the time she stopped a few feet in front of Thayne, all eyes were upon them and a hush had settled on the crowd.

The woman lifted a hand and pointed to him. "*You!*" Her voice rang out clear and shrill in the almost silent room.

Puzzled as to what she wanted, he made a crisp bow. "Ma'am?"

"You are Lord Thayne?" she asked.

"I am. But forgive me, I do not believe I have had the pleasure—"

"You scoundrel!" She made as though to strike him, but tottered on her crutch and was forced to balance herself. "Do you dare think you can get away with ruining my daughter?"

What the devil? Thayne shot her his most intimidating glare. "I beg your pardon, madam?"

"Mama, *please.*" Emily had come up beside the woman and clutched her sleeve. "What are you doing?"

"I am seeing to it that this so-called gentleman does right by you. I know what has happened. You have seduced my poor girl, sir, and by God you will marry her."

Hell and damnation. Did this shrew mean to entrap him?

He heard Beatrice gasp.

"*Mama!* What are you talking about? Don't *do* this. You're embarrassing me. Please, let's go." Emily tugged her mother's arm, but the woman—Lady Thirkill, he presumed—was not to be budged.

"I am afraid you are mistaken, madam," he said in a tone dripping with icy disdain. "I have not seduced Miss Thirkill. You wrong her by stating so."

"How dare you deny it, sir, when you were seen? Only last night, though how many other times you may have imposed upon her, I do not know. But last night, or more precisely the wee hours of this morning, you were *seen.*"

Last night? *Bloody hell.*

His eyes instinctively sought out Beatrice, whose face had gone pale as death.

"Aha!" The woman's shrill voice had reached a crescendo. "You do not deny it."

"Mama, *please.*" Emily looked ready to burst into tears and clung to her mother's arm. "I don't know what you're talking about."

"Don't you, my girl? The man was seen leaving your aunt's house, her dark house, in the early hours of this morning, climbing from a window with his boots in his hands. Skulking away like a thief in the night, down a tree, no less. And in his stocking feet. Everyone knows he has been chasing after you all Season. It seems he got what he was after. And by God he will pay for it."

Thayne could barely breathe. She might have plunged a red-hot poker into his chest. *What had he done?*

Emily's face had grown scarlet, her eyes bright with unshed tears. "You're being ridiculous, Mama. Please, don't *do* this. It was some other house and some other man, I assure you. Lord Thayne was not at my aunt's house last night."

"Yes, he was."

Silence rolled over the room like an ocean wave. Beatrice stepped forward, and it almost broke Thayne's heart to watch her. All she had ever asked for was discretion, and that was all blown to hell now. Every person in the room was watching.

Thayne went to stand at her side. He would not allow her to suffer this alone. He noticed that her friends, the other ball patronesses, had come to stand behind her.

"Yes, Ophelia," Beatrice said in a clear, steady voice, "Lord Thayne was in my house last night, but it was not to seduce Emily. He was with me."

"With you?" Lady Thirkill's face was a mask of

incredulousness. "*You?* All this time I was hoping to secure a match for our Emily with Lord Thayne and *you* were his lover?"

Beatrice closed her eyes for a moment and seemed about to collapse. Before Thayne could reach out to her, she opened her eyes and schooled her features into a semblance of composure.

"Yes," she said, and nothing more.

"Dear God." Lady Thirkill clutched a hand to her breast and Thayne watched it slowly squeeze into a fist.

"Aunt Beatrice! How could you? How *could* you?" Emily's voice had become a wail, and she covered her face with her hands.

The room erupted with a dozen whispered conversations. Thayne could feel Beatrice trembling at his side. She kept her head high, though her mortification was almost palpable. Her reputation had been shattered. As he studied her expressionless face, Thayne felt as if his heart had been ripped from his chest. He could not bear it. He could not bear to watch her pain.

Thayne took her limp hand and placed it on his arm. "You must forgive us, Miss Thirkill, for keeping it a secret, but your aunt and I are engaged to be married."

"Married?" Emily lifted her face and looked thoroughly confused, as if such a thing were impossible.

"Well!" Lady Thirkill said. "You might have told me, Beatrice."

"I did not tell you," Beatrice said as she removed her hand from Thayne's arm, "because it is not true. Lord Thayne is being presumptuous. We are not to be married. Now, please, let us remove ourselves to a more private area. We have made enough of a scene for one night."

Beatrice walked away, apparently with purpose, and so Lady Thirkill, Emily, and Thayne followed

her. She led them to a small, private anteroom. He
wished he could speak with her alone, to convince
her that marriage to him was the only way to salvage
her good name, but she did not give him the opportunity. She turned on him at once.

"How dare you try to force my hand in so public
a manner? After all I said to you last night?"

"I was only trying to save a wretched situation,"
he said.

"Oh, yes. You wasted no time at all in turning an
ugly scene to your advantage. Well, by God, sir, you
have picked the wrong woman to manipulate. I will
not have it!"

"I was not trying to manipulate—"

"Weren't you? You manipulated me last night and
look where it got us. If you had given even one moment's thought to my wishes, to the possible consequences of your actions, none of this would have
happened. And now you decide we should marry
and announce it to the world. *You* decide. I have no
say in the matter. You are controlling me already and
I am *not* your wife. You see why I can't marry you?
You'd be a worse bully than poor Somerfield ever
was. It would not surprise me to discover you had
orchestrated the whole thing, just to force me to
your will."

"See here, Beatrice, I never—"

"All your life you have expected to be obeyed, to
be in charge, to control everything. You give no
thought to what *I* want, or anyone else, for that matter. You just charge ahead with what *you* want, determined to carry the day, to command everything and
everyone. Well, sir, you will not command me. I
would rather suffer a sordid scandal than to marry
you."

She might as well have slapped his face. Fury
welled in Thayne's chest. How could she toss out all

those barbs when she must know he had been trying to help her? The ungrateful bitch. Damn her!

He pulled himself up to his full height and glared down his nose at her. "I am sorry to have caused you any distress, Lady Somerfield. My fault is in my stupidity, not manipulation. I orchestrated nothing tonight, I assure you. Rather than cause further distress, however, I shall remove myself from your presence. Good evening to you all."

He turned on his heel and stormed away.

Beatrice sank into a chair and dropped her face into her hands. She shook with anger. She had never been more furious or more mortified. What a bloody farce they had played out for all the world to see. She lifted her head to find Ophelia and Emily staring at her in openmouthed astonishment.

She waved a hand in the air. "Stop gaping, you two. Yes, I had an affair with Thayne. And thanks to you, dear sister, everyone and his brother knows about it."

"You astonish me, *Sister*," Ophelia said in her chilliest tone. "No wonder you were so adamant that Lord Thayne would not make a match with our Emily. You *stole* him from her. You stole the one man I had marked as the perfect husband for my daughter."

"I did not steal him. Emily never had him. Thayne and I were lovers before she even met him."

"Dear God, you are shameless. And now you have brought us all into disgrace by publicly admitting to the affair."

"You gave me no choice, Ophelia. Was I to stand by and allow you to ruin your own daughter's reputation with a lie? You forced my hand, and as a result . . . well, my name is now ruined. Dear God, I would like to wring your neck, Ophelia! Or break that other leg of yours. What on earth possessed you to haul yourself to one of *my* balls and make such a spectacle? And poor Emily. There is no excuse for what you have done to her."

"I have never been more humiliated in my entire life," Emily said. She paced the length of the room, and flung her hands in the air, gesturing wildly as she spoke. Tears slid down her beautiful face. "I hope you are satisfied, Mama. And you, too, Aunt Beatrice. You have each put a nail in the coffin of my future. I am ruined. *Ruined!* Who will want anything to do with me now, with a mother who insults me in public and an aunt who is having an illicit affair with a man too young for her? How am I ever to show my face again?"

"Everyone will know there had been a mistake and you were not seduced by Lord Thayne," Ophelia said. "There is no shame for you in all this."

"Except the shame of having a mother who was willing to ruin my name in public in order to snare a fine husband for me. Don't bother denying it, Mama. I know that is what you intended. And so does everyone else who witnessed your tirade."

"I only wanted to make sure that he did right by you," Ophelia said, "*if* he had seduced you."

"You ought to have trusted me, Mama, not to allow myself to be seduced. I cannot *believe* you thought I had done such a thing."

"What was I to think," Ophelia said, "when I heard of Lord Thayne leaving Brook Street in the middle of the night with his boots in his hand?"

"Who told you?" Beatrice asked.

"Phoebe Littleworth was at my door this morning with the tale. Her husband had been returning from his club—or more likely from his mistress, if you ask me—when he saw Thayne sneaking out of your house. Really, Beatrice, you ought to be ashamed. Carrying on with a man at least ten years younger."

"Six."

"And in your own house, when Emily and your own daughters might have bumped into him in the hallway. Or, heaven forbid, walked in on you during the act. If you insist on having a lover, you might consider being more discreet. Only look what has happened. How many people do you think heard that story from Phoebe before we straightened it out tonight?"

"Oh, God!" Emily wailed. "I really *am* ruined."

"And if you must know, Beatrice, it is a good thing you are not marrying Lord Thayne. Phoebe told me something about him that gave me pause."

"Not that it matters, but what?"

"Well," Ophelia said, in that snide tone she often used when reporting a delicious bit of gossip, "the house next to hers is being let by Henry and Rebecca Padgett."

"Never heard of them."

"Neither have I. They have been out of the country for some years. In India."

Beatrice's interest was suddenly piqued. "India?"

"Yes. As it happens, they returned on the same ship as Lord Thayne. And his lordship apparently had company on that journey. A young Indian slave girl."

"A slave girl?"

"You know what sort of slave I am talking about." She narrowed one eye in a knowing look. "A pretty dark-eyed girl, very young. He brought her back from India with him and keeps her in his apartments at Doncaster House."

A knot twisted in Beatrice's stomach. "I don't believe it." Even if there *was* a girl, she could not imagine the duchess allowing her to stay at Doncaster House.

"Apparently it was common knowledge among the passengers that Lord Thayne had brought a few slaves back to England with him, including that interesting young girl who is said to—" She paused and glanced at Emily. "Well, you know better than most what sort of service she provides him. They say those Indian woman are very skilled at . . . certain activities."

Dear God. Was it true? Was that where he had learned all those positions and their names? From his own slave girl? No, surely not. Beatrice was furious with the man but knew him to have a core of honor that ran deep. It did not make sense that a man like him would purchase slaves. It was illegal, wasn't it? British ships could not transport slaves.

"I don't believe it," she said. "He would not do anything so reprehensible."

"The Padgetts will swear that he brought slaves back with him to England. They particularly mentioned the girl called Chitra."

"Chitra." She had a name. She was not an anonymous vague rumor. She had a name. She was real. Beatrice's stomach roiled. She did not want to believe any of this.

"It is very interesting to me, Mama," Emily said in a haughty tone, "that you knew all this about Lord Thayne and still wished to force me to marry him."

"He may be a scoundrel," Ophelia said, "but he is still a wealthy marquess, and will be a duke one day. Society overlooks transgressions by men that high up in the aristocracy."

"So you not only tramped into the ball on your crutch," Emily said, "and announced to the world that I had been ruined, but were willing to marry me off to a man who keeps slaves."

Emily stomped to the door and turned to face them, hands on her hips. "I hate you both. I hate you with every fiber of my being. You have ruined my life, both of you, and I shall never, *ever* forgive you. I swear I will pay you back one day for this. I will make you both suffer as you have made me suffer tonight. I promise." She spun around and left the room in a flurry of pink muslin.

"And it only gets worse," Beatrice muttered. "Well, Sister, you have done a good night's work, ruining your entire family. I hope you are pleased with yourself."

"Tell me," Ophelia said in a conspiratorial tone, "why in heaven you refused that young man? You could have been a marchioness!"

Beatrice stood and walked to the door. "I will find your footman and send him to you. Then I trust you will take your leave. You were not invited, after all. Do not worry about Emily. I will do my duty as her chaperone, despite her hatred for me. I will find her a rich husband who will pay off your debts, and then I do not want to see you again for a very long time. I have had enough of you, Sister."

Beatrice left Ophelia alone in the anteroom. The long-suffering footman waited in the corridor and Beatrice sent him in to her. What a mess Ophelia had made of everything. She had no idea how much damage she had done.

Beatrice felt the stares of a hundred eyes as she reentered the ballroom. She held her head high, but her heart was heavy and her hands were still shaking. Her life had changed this night in so many ways. Her reputation was in shatters. She would now be a disgrace and a burden to the Widows Fund. Tonight's ugly scene might do real damage to their cause and future fund-raising.

And then there was Thayne. Had he really thought she would try to save herself by marrying him? She was not as fragile as all that. She would survive. Things would be different, but she would survive.

It was Emily who concerned her. The poor girl might never be able to rise above tonight's fiasco. Beatrice sincerely hoped some nice young man would overlook Emily's impossible mother and her infamous aunt and offer her a good life. She did not deserve what she had been put through this evening.

Beatrice searched the room for her niece, and groaned aloud when she found her. She was already delivering on her promise. She was dancing with Lord Rochdale.

The scandal spread like wildfire. Neither Beatrice nor Emily could show her face in public without whispers and stares following in her wake. Two days after the infamous ball, Beatrice had dared to visit Hatchards bookstore, and was snubbed by Lady Morpeth.

She was well and truly ruined. She did not care so much for herself, but worried about Georgiana and Charlotte. Beatrice hoped to God the scandal would blow over and be forgotten entirely by the time of Georgiana's first Season.

The girls knew something was wrong, but neither Beatrice nor Emily told them what had happened. Emily barely spoke a word to anyone. She had grown morose and surly, and seldom left the house. Beatrice's heart ached for the poor girl, who'd had such a brilliant Season up until now. The only caller they'd had was Mr. Burnett, who did his best to cheer up Emily, but she just sat there with a glum face and the occasional curt remark. It was left to Charlotte to keep up the conversation, which she was pleased to do.

On the night of the disastrous ball, the other Merry Widows had all pitched in to make the rest of the evening enjoyable and to downplay the scandalous scene. They had huddled around Beatrice like four mother hens, protecting her from staring eyes until she was able to grab Emily and spirit her away.

Beatrice had not spoken to any of them at length about what had happened, nor about her concerns over the effect the scandal might have on the Fund. But she had given it a great deal of thought, and when she arrived at their next meeting, she told them of her decision.

"No, Beatrice," Grace said, "you must not feel you have to resign. It is not at all necessary, I assure you."

"I think is it for the best," Beatrice said. "The scandal is still fresh and I would hate for it to have an impact on fund-raising. I fear some people might not come to the next ball if they believe I will be there."

"I think you exaggerate the effect of what happened," Marianne said. "I cannot imagine people would refuse our invitations on your account."

"In fact," Penelope said, "they might come in droves to get a glimpse of the infamous Lady Somerfield, who publicly rejected the most eligible bachelor of the Season."

"Either way," Beatrice said, "it does not reflect well on the Fund. And you may think I exaggerate, Marianne, but only yesterday Lady Morpeth gave me the cut direct in Hatchards."

"She didn't!"

"I assure you, she did. So you can understand my concern. If this storm blows over, perhaps I can rejoin you next Season. But only if I can be assured my name will bring no harm to the Fund. As I fear it will for the remainder of this Season."

"What an utterly outrageous, idiotic situation," Wilhelmina said, her voice infused with righteous indignation. "If you do not mind my saying so, Beatrice, your sister should be taken out and shot. What an unholy mess she has made of things."

"If you have a gun," Beatrice said, "I just might be willing to do it myself. What she did to poor Emily is beyond comprehension."

"I fear I must take some of the blame for all this," Wilhelmina said.

Grace gave her a quizzical look. "You?"

"If I had been able to offer you someplace else—"

"No, it is not your fault, Wilhelmina," Beatrice said. "If anyone is to blame, it is me. I should never have allowed him to come to my house. Never."

"I will confess," Wilhelmina said, "that I thought him more resourceful than that. Did he really climb a tree? It was a reckless thing to do at best. And at worst . . . well, we have seen the worst."

"I thought it rather wonderful when he stepped forward and claimed you were betrothed," Grace said. "Very honorable and gentlemanly."

"No, Grace, it was very manipulative," Beatrice said. "I had refused his offer of marriage the night before. We had quarreled over it, in fact. When he was seen creeping out of the house, it was after a bitter, final parting. It was over between us."

And she had wept buckets over that parting. She'd been miserable over it.

"I am sorry to hear that," Marianne said. "You seemed to be getting on so well. But we all sensed the tension between you that evening."

"We *had* been getting on extremely well, until he proposed marriage and ruined everything, the stupid man. He had no understanding at all of why I refused him. I do believe he'd never been refused anything in his life."

"Hertford was like that," Wilhelmina said. "It is part of their breeding, that arrogance. They cannot help it, poor dears."

"And he tried to convince me," Beatrice said, "that he would not dominate me if we married. He hadn't the slightest notion that he was dominating me in that very moment. And that is what he was doing when he publicly claimed we were betrothed. Trying to control me. To get what he wanted."

"I think you may have misjudged him in that," Grace said. "I believe he was doing the only thing possible to save your reputation."

"I am not a green girl whose virtue had been compromised," Beatrice said. "I did not need Thayne to rescue me. No one expects a widow to be a nun. My reputation will survive."

"And yet you find it necessary to remove yourself from the Fund," Grace said, "for fear of tainting it with your reputation."

"True, but I am resilient and will get through this."

"Brava, Beatrice." Penelope put an arm around her shoulder and squeezed. "Don't let a bit of scandal broth get you down. If you ask me, most women are probably green with envy that you had that gorgeous young man in your bed. I'll wager any number of them would have given their best diamonds to have Lord Thayne sneaking out of *their* houses in the middle of the night."

Beatrice noticed Grace absently tapping a quill against one of the Fund ledger books and realized there was still business to conduct. It was time to leave. If she was going to resign her trusteeship, she must do it now.

The good-byes were more difficult than she had imagined, with a great deal of hugging and more than a few tears. One would think she was leaving the country, never to return.

"I am not disappearing," she said, swiping at her own tears. "We shall still see one another. I hope you visit me in Brook Street now and then on Thursday afternoons. In fact, I shall depend upon it. You may be my only callers for a while."

"We shall be there," Grace said.

"Depend upon it," Marianne added.

"We are still the Merry Widows, after all," Penelope said. "Nothing shall change that."

Beatrice became rather emotional during the drive home. She loved those women. The dearest friends a woman could ask for. The Merry Widows. Only a few days ago, Beatrice had been the merriest of them all, basking in the glow of a thrilling love affair without a care in the world.

How quickly things could change.

She had barely set foot inside her front door when she was accosted by both her daughters.

"Mama, you will *never* guess what has happened."

"It is quite shocking, Mama."

"I never thought she would do such a thing."

"She has been so quiet lately."

"And so down pin."

"We have been worried for her."

"And all the time she was planning this."

"The little sneak."

"She could not have been thinking straight."

"To get into such a scrape as this."

"It is too bad of her, really, Mama."

Beatrice held up her hands. "Stop! Please. One at a time. Georgie, take a deep breath and tell me exactly what has happened."

Her daughter did precisely as asked, and blew out her breath in a loud whoosh. "Emily has bolted."

"And with that dreadful man everyone talks about," Charlotte said. "She has run away with Lord Rochdale."

Chapter 16

"Thank God you are still here."

Beatrice had dashed back to Grace's house as soon as she'd had the whole tale from her daughters.

"What has happened?" Grace asked, and came forward to grasp her hand. "You are shaking."

"Emily has run off with Lord Rochdale."

"Dear God."

"You don't mean it."

"Rochdale!"

"I came here to ask your help, Marianne. Adam is Rochdale's friend, is he not?"

"Yes, he is. How may I help?"

"I have no idea where they've gone," Beatrice said. "You know Rochdale well enough to realize there is no question of an elopement. If Emily has run away with him, it is not for marriage."

Surely the girl knew that. This was her vengeance. She would complete the ruin her mother had started. But she was so young, so innocent. She likely had no idea what it meant to be truly ruined.

"I fear you are right about Rochdale," Penelope said. "He will be out for seduction, not marriage."

"I am hoping," Beatrice said, "that Adam will have some idea where Rochdale might take her. She has been gone less than an hour. There may still be time to catch up with them and try to redeem the situation before it is too late."

Marianne stood and shook out her skirts. "I shall go at once, and return here as soon as I have news."

"Not here," Beatrice said. "I must go home. I want to be there in case the silly girl changes her mind, or sends word, or someone else sends word, or . . . I don't know. I am at my wit's end. I cannot let that poor girl ruin herself over what happened at our ball. I shall be at home, Marianne. You may find me there."

"You should not be alone," Grace said. "Let me go with you."

"We'll all go with you."

And they did. The four of them waited anxiously for Marianne's return. The others spoke quietly on innocuous subjects while Beatrice wore a path in the carpet as she paced back and forth, silently cursing herself for not anticipating such a scheme. Emily had warned them she would exact her revenge. She would make them suffer. Beatrice ought to have kept a closer watch on the girl. How had she managed it? She must have been in secret communication with Rochdale. Stupid, stupid girl! She had chosen him, of course, because Beatrice and her mother had specifically warned her against him. But she could have no idea why. She was too naive to understand about libertines and what they did. Beatrice only hoped they could find Emily before it was too late.

Where was Marianne?

The sound of voices below brought her pacing to a halt. Thank God. Now maybe they could take action and resolve this miserable business.

But when the drawing room doors opened, it was not Marianne who entered, but Jeremy Burnett. Oh, no. Why now, of all times? Cheevers ought to have told him she was not at home to visitors.

And there was worse to come. Gabriel followed Jeremy into the room. What the devil was he doing here?

Jeremy's usual cheerful smile had been replaced with an angry scowl. "Have you found them yet?"

Good God. He knew.

"What do you know of this situation, Mr. Burnett?"

"I know that Rochdale has made off with Miss Thirkill, and I intend to track him down and kill him for it. I have brought Thayne as my second."

Dear heaven. It was not enough that a young innocent girl had run off with a scoundrel. Now there was to be a duel, as well. Beatrice groaned and sank into a chair.

"May I ask," she said, exerting every ounce of control to keep her voice even, "how you came to hear of this, Mr. Burnett?"

"Lady Charlotte told me."

"*What?* Charlotte?"

"She sent me a note," he said. "Said that Emily— Miss Thirkill, that is—had been abducted and had need of rescue. Does anyone know where he's taken her?"

Beatrice would strangle Charlotte. When this was all over, she would surely strangle the child. What had got into her, to send a note to a gentleman, a note airing yet more family scandal? Would this nightmare never end?

"We are awaiting word from Mrs. Cazenove," Grace said. "Her husband is a friend to Lord Rochdale and may know where they have gone."

"And we may as well disabuse you of one notion, Mr. Burnett," Beatrice said. "She was not abducted. My daughter misled you on that point. Emily went willingly. I rather suspect the whole thing was her idea."

"Foolish, foolish girl," he said with feeling. "She believes her reputation is ruined and so she might as well finish the job. But she can have no idea. . . ."

"You are right, sir. I fear she has no idea. I hope to find her before it is too late."

"Forgive me, sir," Wilhelmina said, "but may I ask what your interest is in this matter? And why Lady Charlotte thought to inform you of it?"

"I love her. Miss Thirkill, that is. Lady Charlotte must have guessed it. She is a very perceptive young lady."

"Ah. I see," Wilhelmina said. "Then we may trust in your discretion. And Lord Thayne's."

"Yes, please," Beatrice said, and glanced at Gabriel. "We have had enough scandal. I know you gentlemen will not spread the tale of this situation once it is resolved. If it is ever resolved. Where the devil is Marianne?"

"I believe she has just arrived," Penelope said as she looked out the window. "Yes, it is Marianne."

"Thank God," Beatrice said.

Within minutes, Marianne rushed into the room. "I am so sorry," she said breathlessly. "Adam was not at home and I had to track him down. Here." She handed Beatrice a sheet of paper and glanced quizzically at Jeremy and Gabriel. "Rochdale has a small villa in Twickenham where he sometimes has . . . entertainments. Adam believes he will have taken Emily there. This is the direction," she said, and pointed to the paper. "It is no more than a two-hour drive, if that. I am afraid they will have already arrived by now. I'm sorry, Beatrice. But perhaps it is not too late to . . . to do *something*."

Beatrice gave her friend a quick hug. "Thank you, Marianne. Without your help, we should not have known where to find her at all. Please give my thanks to Adam."

"For what it's worth," Marianne said, "Adam says

this chicanery is out of character for Rochdale. He does not seduce innocent young girls, as a rule."

"Unless that innocent young girl throws herself at him," Beatrice said. "She is taking her revenge on her mother and me. We had warned her against Rochdale, you see, so naturally she chose him for her ruin."

Jeremy muttered an oath.

"I must hurry," Beatrice said, and reached for the bonnet and pelisse she had kept ready. "There is no time to waste."

"I'm coming with you," Jeremy said.

"That is not necessary, sir," Beatrice said. "You have seen that this is likely Emily's doing, that she was not abducted. There is no need for you to call out Rochdale over it."

"We don't know that," he said. "I do not trust the bas— the fellow. I intend to see that no harm has come to her. I take leave to kill the man if he has laid so much as a finger on her."

"Please, Mr. Burnett. Do not add more fire to this scandal with a duel, I beg you. I am in no mood for such foolishness. I have enough troubles."

"You cannot travel so far all alone, Beatrice." Thayne spoke up for the first time. Naturally, it was to issue orders. "Allow us to escort you, at least."

"An excellent idea," Wilhelmina said. "I did not like to think of you chasing after those two all by yourself."

They all conspired against her to add one more element of agony to this nightmare. She was to ride in a carriage for several hours with Gabriel.

"You must not travel alone with two gentlemen," Grace said in a tone that suggested they were all shockingly remiss in forgetting such a thing. "It would be highly improper. I shall go along with you."

Dear heaven, it was to be a crowd.

"Four of us, then," she said, and glanced again at Gabriel. "Let me call for the town coach instead of the chariot."

"There is no need," Gabriel said. "My own traveling coach is waiting outside, and the horses are fresh. There is more than enough room for all of us."

Beatrice ought to have guessed he would want to take charge of the situation. But she was in no mood to argue. They had to get to Emily as quickly as possible.

"All right, then. Thank you, my lord. Grace, let us be off."

She began to shrug into her pelisse when Gabriel stepped behind her to help her into it.

"I am sorry," he whispered. "I know you have no desire to be in my company, but let us make a temporary peace for now. You can scratch my eyes out later, after we have plucked Emily to safety."

"This is all your fault, you know."

He sighed. "I know."

"And mine, too. I should never have allowed . . ." She shook her head and walked ahead, leading the way downstairs to his awaiting carriage. The four of them piled in, ladies on the front-facing seat, gentlemen opposite. When the horses took off, Gabriel's knees knocked up against hers.

It was going to be a long ride.

"There it is," Jeremy said. "And there is light at the windows. Rochdale is there."

Thank heaven. It had been a miserable journey, and Beatrice would hate to think it had been for nothing. Hardly a word had been spoken among them during the entire time. It was odd, but even a week ago, Beatrice would have enjoyed it, traveling with three of her favorite people. But there had been no enjoyment on this journey. Only awkward silence, and the constant shifting of positions so one's knees did not brush up against someone else's.

But if Emily was inside the house, it would be worth it. Even if they were too late and she had sacrificed her virtue for revenge, there was still the possibility of salvaging the situation, of keeping it secret. Unless Jeremy insisted on putting a bullet in Rochdale. There would be no keeping that secret. She must not allow such a thing to happen.

The carriage came to a halt in front of a tidy little Palladian building of five window bays and two stories above the ground floor. The moonlight—for it had grown dark by the time they arrived—illuminated the house so that it gleamed white, seeming to glow in the darkness of the parkland surrounding it. Candlelight filled the windows of the ground and first floors, though the second floor was completely dark. As the bedchambers would be on that level, Beatrice took some comfort that they appeared not to be occupied. Yet.

The gentlemen stepped down from the carriage and turned to help the ladies out. She allowed Grace to exit first with the aid of Jeremy's hand. Gabriel reached out a hand for Beatrice and helped her down. She did not, however, relinquish his hand but pulled him close. He arched a brow.

"Please, Gabriel, whatever we find inside, do not allow Mr. Burnett to do anything rash. The last thing we need is a duel. Do what you can to stop it."

"Do not worry. I will keep him reined in. He's feeling hotheaded at the moment, but he is not a violent man. I won't let him shoot Rochdale, I promise."

"Thank you, Gabriel."

"I cannot promise, however, to stop him from blackening the man's eyes if he wants."

Jeremy had rushed ahead and reached the entrance

before the rest of them. The door opened as they approached, and Lord Rochdale himself stood there, leaning negligently against the jamb, a glass of wine in his hand. He was a handsome man with almost black hair that was worn too long and curled about his collar. Blue eyes were set off by dark lashes and eyebrows and always seemed to have a somnolent look about them. Some women called such eyes "bedroom eyes." Beatrice prayed Emily had not come to learn what that meant.

"What have we here?" he said in a lazy drawl. "A party? Lady Somerfield and the lovely Mrs. Marlowe. My, my, what a delightful surprise. Thayne and Burnett, too. How charming that you have come all the way to Twickenham to pay a call on me. Will there be more of you? Is there another carriage close behind?"

"Where is she?" Jeremy used the advantage of his height to loom over Lord Rochdale, who did not appear the least fazed.

Beatrice stepped forward and Jeremy was forced to move aside. "I have reason to believe my niece is here with you, Lord Rochdale. Is that true?"

"Perhaps you should come inside," he said. "You will find her in the Great Room. Top of the stairs to your right."

As she headed up the stairs, Beatrice heard Jeremy mutter something that sounded distinctly like a growl.

"Not to worry, old chap," she heard Rochdale say. "She is safe as milk here."

Beatrice prayed he was telling the truth as she hurried upstairs. Grace followed softly behind her. She stopped Beatrice with a touch to her arm as they arrived on the first-floor landing.

"I shall wait out here," she said, and indicated a stone bench beneath a window. You will want a few moments of privacy with Emily."

Beatrice took Grace's hand and squeezed it. "Thank you, Grace. For everything. Especially that uncomfortable journey. I believe you were the only one of us not steaming about something. How horrid to have forced such a trip on you."

"It was not as bad as all that," Grace said. "I had time to contemplate the bishop's sermons that I have been editing. Now, go on in and make sure that all is well with your niece."

She found Emily curled up in an enormous leather wing chair in front of a cozy fire. She had not heard Beatrice enter. It appeared she was dozing.

"Emily."

The girl gave a start and sat up straight. "Aunt Beatrice!" Her face flushed pink and she looked contrite and uncertain.

Beatrice held out her arms. Without a moment's hesitation, Emily leaped from the chair and flung herself into her aunt's embrace. Beatrice gathered the girl in her arms and held her close.

"I'm s-so s-sorry, Aunt Beatrice. So very s-sorry."

"Just tell me that you are unharmed, my dear. Has he touched you?"

"No. I m-mean, sort of, but n-not really. He kissed me, that is all. But he s-said there was more to come later and it fr-frightened me, the w-way he looked at me. But he hasn't touched me again, only talked to me, and I kept w-waiting and w-worrying about wh-whatever it was that was supposed to c-come later. But nothing else happened, I pr-promise you. He only kept giving me food and watching out the w-window. I think I became drowsy and must have fallen asleep. I did not hear you come at all. Where is he now, Lord Rochdale?"

Beatrice had been rubbing the girl's back as she sobbed and hiccuped through her story, but now she pulled away and reached into her reticule. She dug out a handkerchief and wiped Emily's face. "Lord

Rochdale is downstairs with Lord Thayne and Mr. Burnett.''

"*Jeremy* is here? Oh, how perfectly mortifying. What is he doing here? How did he know I'd run off?"

Beatrice handed the handkerchief to Emily, who blew her nose daintily and dabbed at her eyes. Somehow the girl managed to be beautiful even when she cried.

"I am afraid you must blame Charlotte for Mr. Burnett. The little minx sent him a note implying that Rochdale had abducted you and that you needed rescuing. He came in order to be your knight in shining armor, my dear, to save you from the evil dragon."

Emily looked up at her sheepishly. "I was not abducted."

"I know. This was your revenge on your mother and me, wasn't it?"

She nodded her head. "I thought I would ruin myself to show you how it felt to be publicly humiliated. But then I got scared. It was a stupid thing to do."

"Yes, it was. And allow me to tell you something, my girl. I know precisely how it feels to be publicly humiliated, so do not presume to teach me that lesson."

Emily dropped her eyes and blushed. "You are right. I'm sorry, Aunt Beatrice."

"As for your mother, you will not be teaching her any lessons, either, for she will not hear of this little episode if I have anything to say about it. Only imagine what sort of scene she would enact with Lord Rochdale, forcing *him* to marry you. Is that what you want? To marry Lord Rochdale?"

"No! He . . . he frightens me. I would not like to be married to him, not at all."

"Then, for God's sake, be sure your mother never learns of this. If she was willing to marry you to a

man she believes to keep a slave girl for his pleasure,
then she would have no compunction about forcing
you on a gambler and a libertine. We must keep this
a secret. Do you understand me, Emily?"

"Yes, ma'am. If I ever choose to speak to Mama
again, it will not be about Lord Rochdale. I promise."

"Good girl. Lord Thayne and Mr. Burnett are certainly to be trusted. And I believe those gentlemen
will ensure Lord Rochdale's silence." She hoped
there would be no duel, was confident that Gabriel
would not allow it; however, she also knew both gentlemen would make his lordship's life a misery if he
ever spoke of this misadventure.

"You have had a fortunate escape this time, my
girl. Many men would not have hesitated to take
your virtue in such a situation. I hope you have
learned your lesson."

"Yes, ma'am, I have indeed. I am very sorry for
all the trouble I put you to."

"All that matters is that you are safe." Beatrice
touched Emily's cheek gently. "And we can only
hope that your Mr. Burnett is not putting a bullet
into Rochdale at this moment. That is why he came,
you know. To challenge the man to a duel for daring
to touch you."

Emily's eyes nearly popped from her head, they
grew so wide. "*A duel?* Good heavens, are they
shooting at each other? My God, what if Jeremy—
Mr. Burnett, I mean—is killed?"

"Would it matter to you?"

"Of course it would! I do not want him to die.
Especially for something that is my fault."

"He is in love with you, you know."

"I know."

"He is a very charming young man, Emily. You
could do much worse. Although, of course, your
Mama would say you could do much better."

"I do not care what Mama says. Can we go now

and make sure poor Jeremy is not lying dead somewhere?''

"I could wring your pretty neck, my girl."

Emily walked with Jeremy in the moonlight while Grace and Aunt Beatrice saw to Lord Rochdale's cuts and bruises. There had been no duel, thank heaven, but Jeremy had apparently planted Lord Rochdale a facer, or two. He had done it for her, and though she did not like to think of him fighting, she felt a rush of pride that he had felt compelled to defend her honor.

"I know," she said. "It was a foolhardy thing to do and I have apologized to Aunt Beatrice."

"She was worried to death, you know. So was I. You are far too innocent to understand what a man like that would do to you. I thank God you are still innocent of that knowledge. Tell me, Emily, why did you do it?"

She shrugged. It had seemed so logical when she had planned it, but appeared so unutterably stupid now. "I know it sounds silly, but I wanted to punish Mama and Aunt Beatrice for humiliating me in public. Oh, don't roll your eyes at me—I told you it was silly."

"Worse than silly. How does it punish your aunt and mother to ruin your own life, I'd like to know? It would hurt you more than them."

"I thought it would make them feel bad. I know it was stupid, but I was mortified to learn about Aunt Beatrice and Lord Thayne. It was so embarrassing. I had wanted him for myself, you know, and to learn that he and my aunt were . . . well, I was mortified."

"Your aunt did a very courageous thing by coming forward like that and admitting she and Thayne were lovers. She could have kept quiet, but she did it to save your reputation, my girl. You ought to have thanked her rather than try to punish her."

"Oh. I suppose you're right. I never thought of it

that way. But don't you find it a bit embarrassing? I mean, she's so *old*."

"She is not so old, and she is a beautiful woman. Besides, Thayne loves her to distraction."

"He *does*?"

"He wants to marry her."

"But she has refused. I heard them argue about it."

"I hope she will come around eventually. Otherwise Thayne will be miserable and will make everyone around him miserable in the bargain. Besides, I have known him for years and never knew him to fall in love. I would like to see him happy. He deserves it. He saved my skin more than once in India."

"He did? How?"

"I owe him my life. I got caught up in a rebellion in the Punjab at one time, and sat for two hours with a dagger at my throat while Thayne negotiated with the fellow holding it. And he negotiated for more than my hide. Thayne worked like the very devil to ensure Bonaparte did not get a foothold in India, as he had been trying to do. Lord Minto, the governor-general, depended upon his skill with the languages and his diplomacy. Not to mention his courage. Well, I shall not bore you with my eternal admiration for Thayne. Suffice it to say that I hope your aunt will change her mind and make him happy."

It was strange, but listening to all the important things Lord Thayne had already done with his life made him seem older and wiser and somehow better suited to a woman like Aunt Beatrice than to a younger woman like herself. Or Lady Emmeline Standish. Such a man would not want a frivolous girl for a wife. And Emily knew that girls her own age could be terribly frivolous. Only look at what *she* had just done. No, Lord Thayne was much better off with Aunt Beatrice, even if she was a bit older than him. She really ought to marry him.

"She can be very stubborn," Emily said.

"So can he. My point, though, is that you should not be so quick to condemn your aunt for having an affair. Or to punish her for it. She is a widow, a mature woman, and can do as she pleases. And she loves you. Look how she came charging after you when you bolted."

"So did you."

"And for similar reasons."

"Would you really have killed Lord Rochdale if he'd . . . well, you know?"

"I would have tried. The thought of you with that man set my blood to boiling. Thank God he did not harm you."

"He did kiss me."

"Did he, by God? And did you enjoy it?"

"I was too busy being frightened to enjoy it."

"Are you frightened of me, Emily?"

"Only when you start talking about killing people. But no, you do not frighten me."

"So, if I kissed you, do you think you might pay attention enough to enjoy it?"

"I might."

"Let's see if you can."

He lifted her face in his hands and dipped his head until his lips very gently touched hers. They were surprisingly soft, and cool from the night air. It felt very nice. More than nice. She felt a little tingle skitter down her back, and her skin turned to gooseflesh.

He lifted his head and stared down into her eyes. And all at once, like the sun breaking over the dawn horizon, a smile spread across his face and lit his eyes.

"So?" he asked.

"I liked it," she said sheepishly.

"Good. Let's try one more time."

And they did. And she liked it even more.

Afterward, they strolled back toward the house with their arms around each other.

"Jeremy?"

"Hm?"

"Would you really love me if I weren't beautiful?"

"Yes. It pleases me that you are so pretty to look at, but I love what's inside even more."

"I thought of you a lot after that horrid ball."

"Did you? You were very cool to me when I called on you."

"I know. I didn't want to face you."

"Why?"

"Because you were right. About how my beauty would not bring me happiness. I was still pretty, but my reputation was in shambles, thanks to Mama. And it was then that I realized you were right. That in the end, beauty does not matter. Character is more important."

"And that, my girl, is why I love you. Because you are smart enough to figure that out for yourself."

He took her in his arms and kissed her again.

Chapter 17

Gabriel sat with Rochdale in a small library while the ladies and Burnett shared a cold supper in the dining room. He had asked for a moment alone.

"I want the truth, Rochdale. Were you planning to bed that girl?"

Rochdale slowly swirled the brandy in his glass and took his time answering. "I might have done, if I hadn't known to expect a rescue party. She admitted she'd told her cousins what she was doing, so I knew Lady Somerfield would come after her. As much as I'd have enjoyed it, I did not wish for her ladyship to find us in the act. A pity. But there you have it."

"And so you *had* hoped to bed her. An innocent young girl."

Rochdale smiled. "What would *you* do if an exquisite creature like that threw herself at you? She's a headstrong little vixen. She will not take no for an answer."

"You tried saying no?"

"Well, maybe not precisely. But I could see what she was up to. I was at that ball, too, you know. I saw what happened. The girl was embarrassed about your affair with her aunt. And angry enough to get back at her by doing the same thing."

"She did this because of Lady Somerfield and

me?" One more disaster to plague him with guilt. All because he'd forced his way into Beatrice's house and made love to her.

"That is what she led me to believe," Rochdale said. "She told me more than once that what she was doing by running off with me was no worse than what her aunt had done with you."

"Good God."

Rochdale grinned. "Of course, she had no idea what that meant. The girl is as innocent as a babe."

"And knowing that, you still agreed to bring her here?"

He shrugged. "She is too naive for her own good. Perhaps I have taught her a lesson. I gave her a bit of a fright, I think. Kissed her once. Nothing fancy, fairly chaste. But I hinted there was more to come, and she trembled like a leaf. That girl needs to be married off, and soon."

"Burnett will do his best to make that happen."

Rochdale uttered a disdainful snort and rubbed his eye. "Damned spindle-shanked puppy. This eye will be black for weeks, I have no doubt."

"You cannot blame him. He loves the girl. He would have killed you if you had ravished her."

Rochdale leaned over and glared at Thayne. "I do not ravish young girls. Contrary to popular opinion, I do not *ravish* anyone. They come to me willingly. If they think better of it later, that is not my concern."

"I want a promise from you, Rochdale."

"Oh?" He lifted a challenging brow.

"I want your solemn oath that no one will hear a word from you about what happened here."

"I have told you, nothing happened."

"I do not want it known that Miss Thirkill was ever here. Or that she ever concocted this scheme, or that you were ever in communication with her at all. Do I make myself clear?"

Rochdale took a long swallow of brandy. "Abundantly clear. Though I have no idea why it is any of your damned business."

"There has been enough scandal involving Lady Somerfield and her family," Thayne said. "I want this incident kept quiet. I will tell you now that if I ever hear so much as a whisper of this tale from anyone other than the six of us here tonight, I will come after you with ten times the fury you saw from Burnett."

"Egad. Such drama. I am quaking in my boots."

"I will have your word, Rochdale."

He heaved a sigh and leaned back in his chair. "You have it. My lips are sealed on the matter."

"I shall depend upon it."

"You take an uncommon interest in that family, Thayne."

"I do not wish for Lady Somerfield to suffer any more scandal."

Rochdale grinned wickedly. "It was bound to happen to one of them sooner or later, what with their secret pact. Got yourself well and truly caught up in that one, didn't you, old boy?"

"Secret pact?"

"The widows' pact. All those charity widows. She didn't tell you?"

"I have no idea what you're talking about."

"Don't you? Well, I suppose it's only fair that you know, since you got involved in it. Those pure-as-snow charity widows, two of whom are seated in the next room, are all on the hunt for lovers. Cazenove learned of it by accident, or figured it out on his own, I've forgotten which. They have a secret pact, those women, never to marry, to find the best lovers, to use the fellows for their own pleasure, and to share with the rest of the group every private detail. Rather amusing, isn't it? I suppose that's what they think *we* do at our clubs and they want to do the same."

Gabriel was speechless. A block of ice seemed to have lodged itself in his chest. She'd *used* him?

"I trust you gave Lady Somerfield the best you've got, old boy, for you can be sure the rest of the women know every move you ever made."

Good Lord. Had Beatrice regaled her friends with all those *Kama Sutra* positions? Everything they'd shared in private?

"And as for your noble gesture at that infamous ball," Rochdale continued, clearly enjoying Gabriel's discomfort, "you mustn't take her repudiation personally. None of them plan to marry. Marianne was an exception, of course, since she and Cazenove had loved each other for years, though they never admitted it. But the rest of the charity widows? All you'll ever get is a bit of pleasure and nothing more. Not that there is anything wrong with that. It's a perfectly reasonable philosophy, if you ask me. Just be sure not to have an off night with one of them. The rest are bound to hear about it."

The block of ice in Gabriel's chest exploded into a thousand angry shards. Icy hot rage filled him. How many kinds of fool had he been over her?

No more. He was through with her. He'd had enough.

The drive back to town was only marginally more comfortable than the drive out. Grace had given up her seat to Emily, which meant that she would drive back with Lord Rochdale. And so Emily and Jeremy sat side by side on the opposite bench making calf's eyes at each other. Finally, something good had come out of all that had happened. Jeremy was so charming and full of life. He would make Emily happy.

Ophelia would be furious at first, since he had no title, but she would accept the situation well enough when she learned of the fortune he'd made in India.

Emily no longer cared what her mother wanted. It seemed that her mother's inexcusable behavior had shaken her so thoroughly that she came to understand how unimportant the quest for rank and fortune was in the long run. Beatrice wondered if Emily would ever reconcile with her mother, and suspected that if she did, it would not be for a long, long time.

Sitting beside Gabriel on the drive back was worse than sitting across from him had been. Instead of only their knees bumping, now their whole bodies brushed against each other from time to time. But there was no hint of warmth between them. She might have bumped against a stone statue, he'd grown so cold and stiff.

Beatrice suspected Grace's drive back with Rochdale might be at least this uncomfortable. Poor Grace.

Gabriel's chilliness was a puzzle. Beatrice thought they had got through this episode rather well together, without coming to blows or shouting at each other. In fact there had been a few moments between them that had made her think they could eventually overcome their recent friction and at least remain friends.

But now she began to doubt it. He had not spoken a single word to her since before they had left Twickenham.

Why did men have to be such difficult, prickly creatures?

When the carriage turned into Brook Street at last, it was close to midnight. Jeremy leaped down and offered his hand to Emily. They walked up the steps to the entrance and stood close together, deep in conversation at the front door. Beatrice wanted to give them a few moments alone before interrupting them, so she lingered behind with Gabriel at the carriage door.

"May I ask," she said, "why you have grown suddenly so cold toward me? I realize we have been at odds, but this is something new."

"Perhaps it is because I learned something new, something you would rather I did not know."

She looked at him, puzzled. What could he have learned in Twickenham that he had not known before? "What is it?" she asked.

He glared down his nose at her in his most obnoxious lordly manner, as though she were an insect. "Let us just say that I learned what our love affair— correction: our sexual affair—really meant to you."

"What are you talking about? You know what it meant to me. I told you often enough."

"But you never mentioned that it was merely a game, that I was little more than your toy, your sex toy, to be played with and discarded."

"My sex toy?"

"Don't deny it, Beatrice. I know about the widows' pact."

Her mouth dropped open. Good God. How could he possibly know about the Merry Widows? And how could he have learned about it in Twickenham?

Oh, dear Lord. Rochdale. Rochdale must have told him. But how did *he* know? And how *much* did he know?

"What do you know about a pact?" she asked.

"I know that you are all on the hunt for the best lovers, and you play at kiss-and-tell. I have no doubt every move I ever made with you has been duly reported."

Beatrice blanched. She could hardly deny it. And what difference did it make if the Merry Widows shared personal secrets? Men probably talked about their mistresses to one another in the same way.

She drew herself up tall and faced him squarely. "Not *every* move."

"You little bitch. How dare you share our private intimacies with your friends?"

"So what if we share a few intimate details? What difference does it make? At least I don't keep a little slave girl at home to cater to my sexual needs."

"*What?*"

"I know all about the Indian girl you have at home. The one who probably instructs you in all those positions you taught me. I even know her name, Gabriel, so you cannot deny her existence. Chitra."

His brows lifted in surprise. "Good God. What do you know of Chitra?"

"I know that you brought her, and who knows how many other slaves, back to England with you. You probably keep an entire harem, for all I know. So don't get all righteous over a few private conversations with my friends."

He scowled furiously. "I do not know where you heard such lies, but it's ridiculous. I thought you knew me better than that. You really believe that I keep slaves?"

"So you never once bought and sold slaves while in Asia?"

"I never sold a slave in my life."

"But you bought them?"

Silence.

His hesitation almost broke her heart. Until that moment, she had believed him, believed that what Ophelia had heard was all a lie. But he could not deny buying slaves. Nor had he denied bringing them back to England with him. And he as good as admitted there was a girl named Chitra.

She groaned her disappointment aloud and looked away from him.

"So this is what you think of me." His voice had a steely edge that was almost frightening. "This is the sort of man you think I am. I wonder you can bear to be in my sight. I certainly have no wish to remain in yours." He turned away and took a step up into the carriage, but stopped, and swung back around to face her.

"I wish to say one thing before I go. I am truly sorry, Beatrice, that I have been such a disappointment and a burden to you. And I take full blame for all the business that started at that wretched ball. It was my fault, all of it, because I insisted on coming here that night. My only excuse is that I love you. Oh, yes, Beatrice. I love you." He shook his head and sighed. "But now I wonder how I could possibly love a woman who thinks so little of me. Good night, ma'am."

He stepped up into the carriage and closed the door in her face.

Beatrice walked to her front door in something of a daze. She barely noticed Jeremy and Emily jump apart as she approached. Jeremy said a quick good-bye and dashed down the walkway to join Gabriel in the carriage.

As Beatrice and Emily entered the house, Emily was agog with excitement about her new relationship with Jeremy. "He has asked me to marry him, and I have accepted. Is that not wonderful, Aunt Beatrice? I am bursting with joy." She threw her arms around Beatrice and hugged her.

And all at once, tears were streaming down Beatrice's face. She could not stop them. She hugged Emily tight, and told her how happy she was for her.

"I feel like crying, too," she said when Beatrice had released her. "For happiness. Who ever thought things could work out so well after all that has happened? It is a miracle. It is—"

"Serendipity."

"Yes! That's it. Oh, I feel like shouting the roof down!"

"Not tonight, I beg you. I am exhausted, Emily. Let's go up to bed, if you please."

It was not until much later, after Dora had finished

with Beatrice and gone to her own bed, that Beatrice was able to sit quietly and consider Gabriel's parting words.

I love you.

Such a simple thing. A simple phrase. Three little words. But in all her life, in thirty-five years, no one had ever said those words to her.

Not Somerfield. There had been affection between them, but no words of love. Her parents had never said they loved her, though she was quite certain they did. Her daughters had never said so, either, but then, she had never told them how much she loved them. Love was something that had never been spoken of in her life. Oh, she had heard it said about other people. Only tonight Jeremy had said he loved Emily. It was certainly not a foreign concept. But in *her* life, it was not spoken of. Neither to her nor by her. Love was simply there, or it was not. But it was never acknowledged. The words had never been spoken aloud.

Until tonight.

It was astonishing the difference it made to hear those words spoken *to* her. To hear them from Gabriel had shaken her to the core of her soul. Almost paralyzed her. She had not known how important those three words could be. It made love more tangible, more real. Surely words were not as important as love itself. Or were they? Did Georgie and Charlotte really, truly know that she loved them? Did Emily? Did her friends know she loved them?

Perhaps they did, but she had never told any of them—not even her much-beloved daughters—so how could they be sure?

And Gabriel. Dear Gabriel. The only person in all her life who had spoken those precious words to her. Words that took possession of her, filling her so completely that she could hardly breathe.

And now he was lost to her.

What a fool she had been. She had suspected he was a little in love with her. Would she have reacted differently to his proposal if he had said the words? Considering her reaction to them tonight, she believed she might have overlooked every objection for the possibility of hearing those words from him for the rest of her life.

I love you.

How silly, that simple words should make so much difference to her. It made no sense that words could cause such an overpowering emotion, but hearing them changed everything, painted everything in a new light. It suddenly seemed that anything was possible, any obstacle could be overcome. All that talk of domination and control suddenly seemed so much nonsense. Even all that business about slave girls. With love, love that was acknowledged out loud and was therefore somehow more powerful, none of the rest mattered. Things could be worked out. Compromises made.

Lord, what an epiphany.

But too late. The enormity of all she had rejected suddenly threatened to overwhelm her. Gabriel. Her beautiful young man. The way he looked at her and made *her* feel young and beautiful. His dry humor. His stalwart sense of honor. His passion for India. His passion in bed. His adventurous spirit. The way he seemed to know her as no one else had ever done. Even his lordly arrogance was suddenly endearing.

What a mess she had made of things. All because she had not heard three words.

I love you.

And now that she had heard them, nothing would ever be the same.

The next morning, Beatrice sat on Emily's bed with all three girls, as she so often did, discussing fashion or friends or the previous night's party. This time,

Emily had regaled them with the news of her betrothal, which delighted Charlotte in particular, as she was so fond of Jeremy. She also felt a certain smugness for having had the good sense to send him that note, for she was quite sure that having him come to Emily's rescue, so to speak, was all that was needed for her to recognize that he was the perfect man to marry. Beatrice had scolded Charlotte for having the temerity to send a note to any gentleman, ever, but the girl was so pleased with the outcome that the scolding had been shrugged off as unimportant.

"I want to tell you girls something," Beatrice said. "I want you to hear the truth from me rather than from gossip or rumor."

"What truth, Mama?" Georgie asked.

"The truth about why Emily felt the need to run away in the first place. You know something happened, but I do not think you know the whole story."

"I don't know any story at all," Charlotte said in a peevish tone. "Nobody tells me *anything*."

"Well, I am going to tell you everything," Beatrice said. "It is a very grown-up story, though, and you may not understand it all, but I want you to hear it. Do you remember when Emily and I made a visit to Doncaster House to visit the duchess? And how we also met Lord Thayne that day for the first time?"

And she went on to tell them a slightly edited version of all that had happened since that day at Doncaster House. She did not tell them about the masquerade ball, or details of when and where she and Gabriel had met. But she told them enough for them to understand that she had been involved in a very adult and very improper relationship with Lord Thayne, and how it had ultimately led to scandal.

"Are you in love with Lord Thayne, Mama?" Charlotte asked.

Beatrice took a deep breath and let the words come out into the open. "Yes, I am. I love him."

"Then why did you refuse to marry him?"

She told them all the things she had told Gabriel at the time, about being wrong for him, too old for him, how he would need an heir to ensure the succession.

"I already have you girls," she said. "And I love you both very much." There. She had said it. Now they would always know. "I cannot imagine having more children at my age."

"I always wished we had a brother," Charlotte said wistfully.

"Oh, me, too!" Georgie exclaimed. "I used to wish and wish that you would marry again, Mama, so we could have a brother."

Beatrice gazed at her daughters in shock. "I never knew that. You never mentioned it before."

"It was just dreaming," Georgie said with a shrug.

Beatrice shook her head at all the new revelations in her life. "I am too old to have more children, I fear."

"But what about Lady Hengston?" Emily said. "She is over forty and is still having children."

Too many children, in Beatrice's opinion. Twelve, at last count.

"And Lady Oscott, too," Emily continued. "She has a very young son, a toddler, and she is over forty. You are not yet forty, Aunt Beatrice. You could still have children. If you wanted. If you were married."

"Oh, having babies in the house would be such fun!" Charlotte said. "Brothers. At least one must be a brother."

"A little girl would be fun, too," Georgie said. "We could dress her up and teach her things."

"Excuse me, girls, but you may stop spinning those

fantasies right now, if you please. There will be no babies. I am not getting married."

Just like all the other objections to marrying Gabriel, the inability, or unwillingness, to give him an heir suddenly seemed as insubstantial an excuse as all the rest. It did not matter, of course. She had lost him.

"But wouldn't you like to have a child with the man you love?" Emily asked. "I do. I can't wait. A child is the truest symbol of love, is it not?

And just like that, an image sprang into her mind of holding Gabriel's child in her arms. A dark-haired little boy with a tiny cleft in his chin. And Gabriel looking down upon them with love and pride as she took their son to her breast. *The truest symbol of love.*

"Yes, Emily, it certainly is. But we shall have to look forward to *your* babies instead."

Chapter 18

"Must you always smoke that ghastly thing?"

Thayne looked up to see his mother stride into his sitting room, her nose wrinkled at the smell of tobacco. She rarely visited his apartments, so he knew she must have something serious to discuss. And he could guess what it was.

He put down the mouthpiece, wrapped the tube around the neck, and moved the pipe away to burn itself out. "Not always, Mother, but it calms my nerves."

She sat down in the chair opposite and regarded him thoughtfully. "Well, then, it is no wonder you smoke so much. I imagine your nerves are often on edge of late, considering all that has happened."

"Indeed."

She sat in silence for a moment and then said, "Not to put too fine a point on it, Gabriel, but the duke and I were still hoping for an announcement at the masquerade ball next week."

"Fine. Tell me who it should be and I shall pay my addresses to her."

"You do not really want me to choose your bride for you. You have said any number of times that you will do your own choosing."

"I did choose. She rejected me."

"Choose again."

"No. You do it. I have no interest in it whatsoever. I am sure whoever you pick will be fine. You know better than anyone what is required."

Her shoulders sagged and her brow puckered into a frown. "You are breaking my heart, Gabriel. I hate to see you so unhappy. Why do you not make one more effort with Lady Somerfield? Perhaps you have given up too easily. Perhaps a bit more persuasion—"

"No. No more." He rose from his chair and went to stand by the window. He did not want to have this conversation with his mother. He'd been having it with himself for several days and was tired of it.

She was silent for long minutes and he could feel her gaze boring into his back. He really did wish she would just name some girl and be done with it. Thayne would be more than pleased to court her, whoever she was. It was more or less what he'd expected anyway. Yes, he had preached and harangued about making his own choice, but it was always meant to be from among those girls the duchess brought to his attention. He was now prepared for her to narrow that field to one. Making his own choice had not mattered to him for quite some time now. Ever since he'd become obsessed with Beatrice.

He watched a flock of birds swoop together in one direction, then the other, drunkenly weaving their way as one across the park. Which one was their leader? Who decided when to swing left, when to swing right, when to go back the way they'd come? For once in his life, Thayne was willing to be one of the follower birds, to allow someone else to send him in a specific direction. He just wished his mother or the duke would make the damned decision for him so he could finally know where he was going. He'd been chasing his own tail for too long, getting nowhere.

"If you are concerned," the duchess said at last,

"about how your father and I would feel about an older woman, a widow with children, you need not worry on that score. She is not what we had expected from you, to be sure, but she is a fine woman and you obviously love her."

"I have been wondering why. She thinks I keep slaves. That I brought back slaves with me from India to do my bidding."

"*What?* Where did she hear such a nonsensical thing?"

"I did not ask," he said, and wondered why he hadn't. Not that it mattered. "The point is that she believed it, wherever she heard it."

"How could she believe such a hateful, wrong-headed thing about you? You would never keep slaves, for heaven's sake. You're an Englishman."

"She asked if I ever sold slaves, and I told her I had not. But when she asked if I had ever bought slaves . . ."

She gave a low groan. "And you did not tell her the truth?"

"Lady Somerfield already had her opinion of me. I had neither the desire nor the inclination to defend myself. The fact that she believed it was all that mattered."

He heard the duchess heave an exasperated sigh. He did not need to turn around to clearly picture the look of irritation on her face. "Has it not occurred to you," she said, "that she was hoping you would explain? To prove wrong whatever ugly gossip she may have heard?"

"No, it has not. Because there was more, Mother. She had somehow heard about Chitra. She knew her name."

"Little Chitra? What about her?"

"She believes her to be my sex slave or my concubine or some such nonsense. She seems to think I might even have a harem."

"But that is ridiculous, Gabriel." Her voice rose in outrage. "Where could she possibly have heard such stories? You might want to make it your business to find out, you know. Lady Somerfield may not be the only one who has heard them and believes them."

He turned to face her. "I have thought of that. But I prefer, I think, to allow my actions to speak for me. I have nothing to hide. Nothing of which I am ashamed. I certainly have no slaves."

"Of course not. Well, you must do as you please, my boy. But I do wish you could settle things with Lady Somerfield. If she is the one you want, then you must fight for her."

Restless, he walked back to where he'd been smoking and plopped down in the chair again. "I used to think I could have everything I wanted, Mother, and it was true. Nothing was ever denied me, and I have grown accustomed to getting my way in all things. But I am finally learning that I can't have everything, after all. I cannot have Beatrice. She does not want me. And at the moment, I am not sure I want her anymore."

"Then for God's sake, find someone else! Soon." She rose and walked to the door. "I want that announcement at the ball, Gabriel."

"Then name the girl!" he said to her back as she left.

An instant later, she had returned to stand in the doorway. "If I do in fact name the girl, you will accept my choice?"

"Have I not said as much? Yes, Mother, I will accept your choice."

"I have your word on it?"

"You have my word."

"All right, then. Consider it done." She turned on her heel and left.

As soon as she was gone, Ramesh stepped into the sitting room from the adjacent dressing room. He

JUST ONE OF THOSE FLINGS 283

bowed and said, "Forgive me, my lord Thayne. I did not mean to listen, but I could not help hearing. You are not a trader in slaves. You must not allow anyone to believe that you are. It is wrong."

"It doesn't matter," Thayne said, with a dismissive wave. "Have my horse brought round, Ramesh. I am going for a long ride." He needed to get away. The walls seemed to be closing in on him. Fresh air. Space. He needed room to breathe.

"Rochdale knows about the Merry Widows. He knows about our pact. *Everything.*"

Her friends stared at Beatrice in astonishment. They were gathered in her otherwise empty drawing room on Brook Street. Once again, no other guests arrived. Beatrice was still something of a social pariah. Thank heaven the Merry Widows still came round; else she would turn into a recluse. Grace was the only one missing today.

"How do you know that?" Penelope asked. "Did he say something to you?"

"No, but he apparently said quite a lot to Thayne. He knew about the pact, about our candid discussions, all of it. He was furious with me—said I'd used him, played with him like some kind of . . . of . . . sex toy. And he did not appreciate knowing that I might have shared with all of you the intimate details of our sexual encounters. I could hardly deny it, could I?"

"I don't see what is so unusual about friends sharing intimate secrets," Penelope said. "I am sure men do it all the time, telling each other about the particular abilities of this highflier or that opera dancer."

"It is threatening to them," Wilhelmina said. "They don't like to think that women may talk behind their backs about size and performance and stamina and such. What if they were to . . . come up short, so to speak? Or were unable to perform? Men are much more vain about such things than women. Only imagine their anxiety if, after a less-than-satisfactory performance, their failure was reported to other women? It is that fear, Beatrice, that made Thayne so angry. A typical male response."

"But how did Rochdale know?" Beatrice asked. "I am sure none of us has told anyone. Have we?" She looked around at each woman. Wilhelmina shook her head; Penelope did the same.

"Oh, dear." Marianne's face was pinched with concern. "I think Adam may have told him."

"You told Adam about our pact?" Penelope asked.

"No! I never told him. Not even since we married. We promised to keep it secret and I have honored that promise. But I have often wondered how much he actually overheard that morning at Ossing Park. He might have been on that staircase longer than we know."

"If that is true," Wilhelmina said, "then, as I recall, he would have heard nothing but praise for his lovemaking."

"But I think we may have mentioned our pact," Marianne said. "Or perhaps he only heard enough to figure it out for himself. And then, while I was still punishing him by pretending I believed someone else had been my lover that night, he spent a great deal of time with Rochdale. He may very well have had too much to drink one night and admitted to Rochdale what he knew. Or thought he knew. That is the only explanation I can think of."

"You may be right," Beatrice said. "Unless Grace confessed to someone, and I sincerely doubt that."

Penelope grinned. "She can hardly bear listening to us talk about our lovers. I cannot imagine she would dream of telling anyone else about it. No, I think Marianne has hit upon the answer. Rochdale learned it from Adam. Well, let us hope he is not telling tales of us all over London."

"I doubt that," Wilhelmina said. "I have some . . . experience with Rochdale. He has his faults, but he is not entirely dishonorable. Consider his restraint with young Emily. He might have ruined her, but did not. I suspect he must have deliberately teased Lord Thayne with what he knew because of that unfortunate public airing of your affair, Beatrice."

"You're probably right," Beatrice said. "It hardly matters. Thayne and I have ended things between us. We parted with considerable bitterness, with hateful words spoken by both of us. And I have never been more miserable." She felt the sting of tears build up behind her eyes and made an effort to hold them in check.

"Endings are never easy," Wilhelmina said in a gentle voice.

"Especially this one," Beatrice said. "I fear I have made the biggest mistake of my life. He loves me. Or did. And I love him. I ought never to have refused him."

"You believe you should have married him?" Penelope stared at her incredulously. "Is this the same Beatrice who encouraged us all to forsake marriage and relish our independence?"

"I was wrong. Love changes everything."

"It certainly does," Marianne agreed. "I never thought I wanted to marry again, but I have never been happier. It is sometimes wrong, I think, to stay so fixed on an idea, to be so inflexible in one's thinking. Things change. People change. Love comes into our lives and turns everything topsy-turvy. We cannot assume that the things we want today will make sense for us tomorrow. The freedom we have all talked about and relished so much as widows, the freedom to live our lives as we please, also means freedom to change."

"Beautifully stated, my dear," Wilhelmina said. She sat next to Marianne on the sofa, and patted her gently on the arm. "I have always lived my life in the moment. I have never presumed to know what tomorrow may bring. Or whom."

"I wish I had moderated my own philosophy a bit earlier," Beatrice said. "Because I was inflexible, as Marianne said, I have lost what I now realize I most wanted. Love."

"But you must have known Thayne loved you," Wilhelmina said. "He would not have asked you to marry him otherwise. Now, if he had betrothed himself to some young girl in her first Season, we would know it was a match based on fortune or rank or dynastic alignment. The usual reasons. But to marry a widow with children, an older woman . . . such an unexpected decision has to be based on love."

"I suspected," Beatrice said. "But I did not know. Until he said the words. That changed everything for me."

"It always does," Wilhelmina said.

"And so now I realize what a fool I've been," Beatrice said, "and there's not a damned thing I can do about it. The final Widows Fund ball is approaching. The masquerade at Doncaster House. He is to announce his betrothal at the ball."

"Is he?" Wilhelmina said. "Are you certain?"

"The duke and duchess are determined on it, he told me. Knowing Her Grace, I have little doubt she will insist upon it."

"But who—"

They were interrupted by Cheevers, Beatrice's butler, who had entered the room quietly and now bent close to her ear.

"There are two persons downstairs, my lady, who insist upon speaking to you."

"What sort of persons?"

"I am not certain, but they are foreign, to be sure. The man is wearing an orange turban. He is most adamant that you see him. I fear, my lady, that they will not leave until they have spoken with you."

"Do you have any idea what they wish to speak to me about?"

"No, my lady. The man will not say."

"I suppose I had better go and see what he wants." She turned to her friends. "I fear I am needed downstairs. You will please forgive me for calling short our visit. Thank you so much for coming. Truly. You are all very dear to me."

The Merry Widows rose, collected their things, and made their farewells. Marianne had almost blurted out that she loved them, but recollected that Cheevers stood behind her, and thought better of it.

Beatrice followed him downstairs to the housekeeper's sitting room, where the two strangers had been asked to wait. She walked in to find a tall, dark, good-looking young man standing at attention by the hearth. A pretty young girl of about twelve or thirteen with enormous dark eyes sat at a table. And most extraordinary of all, Charlotte sat across from her.

"Mama! You'll never guess. These people are from India! They have come from Lord Thayne's house. That is Mr. Ramesh, and this is his sister, Chitra."

Chitra. A little girl no older, and probably younger, than Charlotte. Beatrice's heart sank. Another enormous mistake was about to be revealed to her, she was quite sure.

Both the man and his sister were dressed in ordinary English-looking clothes. But he wore an elaborately twisted saffron-colored turban, and the girl wore a scarf covering her glossy long hair.

"Mr. Ramesh, Chitra. I am pleased to meet you. I am told you wish to speak to me."

"We are here to tell you a truth, my lady Somerfield," Mr. Ramesh said. "To right a wrong." He had a delightfully musical voice, and though his English was good, his accent was very pronounced.

"Well, then," she said, and took a seat on the housekeeper's sofa. "What is it you wish to tell me?"

"It is about how we came to know my Lord Thayne."

And he proceeded to tell a tale that brought tears to her eyes, but not for the reasons they might have thought. No, it was because she had listened to gossip from a source with no right to be trusted, and had deliberately used that dreadful lie to inflict pain when she'd known in her heart it could not be true. She had used what she knew in her heart to be a lie to push Gabriel out of her life forever.

Mr. Ramesh told of how he and his entire family had been taken into slavery by some Indian prince with a long name. After a time, they had been bought from the prince by Dutch traders, who packed them onto a ship carrying hundreds of other slaves to southern Africa. It had been a harrowing trip, and at least half the slaves died from disease before reaching the Cape. Ramesh and Chitra were the only members of their family to survive the trip. He had been a boy of seventeen; Chitra had been only five years old.

Ramesh never knew all the details of what happened next, and what little he did know he learned much later, apparently from Jeremy Burnett. Their Dutch slave ship had arrived at the Cape at the same time Gabriel had arrived from England as a very young man. He had witnessed the herding of the slaves from the ship to the place where they would be sold again, primarily to white farmers in Africa. Ramesh remembered actually catching the eye of the young man on the docks who seemed so moved by their misery. Gabriel bought the entire lot of them from the Dutch trader. Then, with the help of an East India Company clerk on his way to Calcutta, Gabriel had created emancipation papers for every one of them. Many of them, including Ramesh and Chitra, returned to India on the same ship as Thayne. Ramesh had sought out their savior, and pledged his life to him. By the time they reached Bombay, he had managed to secure a position for himself in Gabriel's employ.

Gabriel had provided education for both Ramesh and Chitra as well as the protection afforded his rank and position. Although Gabriel had moved about India the entire time he was there, never establishing a home base in any one city for longer than a year, Ramesh and Chitra had traveled with him, along with a larger staff he had collected over the years. Ramesh was a paid member of that staff, helping out in whatever way he could. When Gabriel had announced his plans to return home to England, Ramesh had pleaded for him to take him and Chitra along. The group of slaves Gabriel was purported to have brought home with him consisted of two individuals only, one who became his valet, and one who was given work in the kitchens at Doncaster House.

And the slaves on Ramesh's ship were not the only ones Gabriel had bought and freed. He despised the Dutch and had made it his business to interfere in their slave trafficking. Gabriel or his agents bought shipload after shipload of slaves from India, often intercepting the ships before they reached the Cape, and sent them back home or provided the freed slaves with papers in order to find legitimate employment in Africa or Madagascar or whatever port they were near. By the time Gabriel and his two companions had passed through the Cape on their way back to England, the trade in slaves from India and Southeast Asia had almost completely dried up. Thanks in large part to Gabriel's efforts.

"Neither I nor my sister are slaves, my lady Somerfield. We are paid handsomely to work for my lord

Thayne. He is good to us, and we would give our lives for him."

Beatrice sat stunned and silent. Charlotte, too, had been affected. She wore a look of confusion and anger, and reached shyly across the table to touch Chitra's hand.

"I believe," Ramesh continued, "that you have been told another story about my lord Thayne that paints a different picture. It is not true. You must know this. My sister and I, we are—what is the word?—testament to the truth. We are proof of his goodness."

"Yes," Beatrice said, "you certainly are. Thank you for telling me."

"Your pardon, my lady." One of the housemaids had stepped into the room and bobbed a curtsy. "Mr. Cheevers asked me to tell you that a guest has arrived and awaits you in the drawing room."

A guest? It was her afternoon at home, so it should not surprise her, though no one but the Merry Widows had deigned to make an appearance lately. Perhaps it was Grace. She had been absent earlier.

Beatrice rose from the couch. "Thank you again for coming, Mr. Ramesh. I appreciate what you have told me. And it was lovely to meet you, Chitra."

"May Chitra stay a while, Mama?" Charlotte asked. "Perhaps she would play a game of jackstraws with me. And tell me all about the interesting bracelet she is wearing."

Beatrice looked to Mr. Ramesh. "May your sister be spared from her work for a few more minutes?"

"Only a few minutes," Mr. Ramesh said. "Mr. Bernier, the chef, will be wanting her back soon."

"Do not keep her long, then, Charlotte."

Beatrice returned back upstairs with a heavy heart. She had done a terrible thing, to accuse Gabriel of owning slaves when he had done so much to stop the slave trade. It was too late to redeem herself with

Gabriel, but by the time she had climbed the stairs to the drawing room, Beatrice had made a firm decision to locate the couple that had been on the ship with Gabriel—the Padgetts?—and make certain that they never again spread such lies about him.

She walked through the open drawing room door and said, "I am so sorry to have— Your Grace!" Beatrice came to a halt, brought up short by the sight of the Duchess of Doncaster standing tall and straight beside one of the windows. She was fashionably attired in a high-necked white muslin dress sprigged with yellow and green flowers, and a green mantle in the latest Pyrenean style gathered in a graceful fold on one shoulder. Her hands rested on the end of a long-handled parasol.

"I thought I had recalled correctly," she said, "that this was your afternoon at home, Lady Somerfield. I seem to have been mistaken."

Beatrice collected her scattered wits, dipped a curtsy, and walked across the room. She gestured for the duchess to take a chair. "You are not mistaken," she said, and waited for the duchess to be seated before taking her own chair. "I am afraid that I no longer receive many visitors, Your Grace."

"Because of that beastly business over Thayne, I presume."

Beatrice offered a small shrug, but did not confirm the statement.

"Well, it is for the best in this case," the duchess said, "for I wish to speak with you privately." She sat very straight, her back never touching the chair, and kept one hand propped on the handle of her parasol, the tip of which was jabbed hard into the carpet. "I shall get straight to the point. I want you to reconsider my son's offer of marriage."

Beatrice blinked. "I beg your pardon."

"You have refused him, rather publicly, I might add, which is of no great consequence to a man of such strong character. Nor is it to me. That is not why I wish you to reconsider. I want his betrothal announced at your Widows Fund masquerade on Saturday, and he will not commit to any particular girl. No, he wants you. But he thinks he cannot have you and has therefore asked me to choose his bride. I am doing so. I want you to marry him, Lady Somerfield."

Beatrice gave a rueful smile. "I have no reason to believe the offer is still open, Your Grace. In fact, I suspect your son wishes me to the devil. I said some rather hateful things to him."

"Yes, I know." Her eyes narrowed and her lips thinned. "That idiotic business about little Chitra. I would certainly love to know where you heard such a vile story. It is not true, you know."

"I know. I have just now heard the real story from Ramesh. He and Chitra are downstairs in my house-keeper's sitting room at this moment."

The duchess lifted her brows in surprise. "How extraordinary. That young man is very devoted to Thayne. I will confess, though, to being rather shocked that Thayne would send him."

"I don't believe he did. I had the impression that he came on his own initiative."

"Ah. He must have overheard my conversation with Thayne. He came to put a halt to any such stories about his employer. Or about his sister. Pretty little thing, is she not? Such eyes! But hardly a . . . a concubine." She spit out the word in disgust.

Beatrice flushed that she had dared to suggest such a thing to Gabriel. "I know she is neither a concubine nor a slave. And I have every intention of confronting the persons spreading that unsavory tale and putting a stop to it."

"Do that," the duchess said. "Now, back to my original point. You said you do not believe Thayne's offer is still open to you. What if it were?"

Beatrice felt her heart begin to race. "I don't understand."

"Don't be obtuse. I have no time to dance around the subject. Would you accept if he offered again?"

Beatrice had been fantasizing about just such an occurrence and had no hesitation in giving an answer. "Yes."

"Then why in heaven," the duchess said, punctuating each word with a stab of the parasol on the carpet, "did you not accept him the first time?"

"I thought I was all wrong for him. I am older. I have had my family. I am too stubborn and would not be a biddable wife. A thousand stupid reasons."

"All of which you are now ready to dismiss?"

"Yes."

"Why? What changed your mind?"

Beatrice grinned and said, "He told me he loved me. That changed everything."

"That's *it*? That's all it took? A declaration of love?"

"Yes. I have never had one, you see. It was rather devastating. And allowed me to put matters into better perspective. All of my earlier concerns still exist. I have not grown younger or more biddable. But I realize now that when there is love, any obstacle can be faced."

The duchess gazed at her intently for a long while, and then smiled. "You will make a fine wife for my son, Lady Somerfield. I can see why he has been so indifferent to all those young misses I have trotted out for his inspection. A docile, complaisant bride would bore him to death over time and ultimately make his life a misery. Thayne is not the sort of man to thrive with a woman who jumps when he says to jump. A woman like you, more self-assured, is precisely what he needs. I ought to have known that. You will challenge him, Lady Somerfield, and make him a better man."

"Thank you for saying so, Your Grace. I would like to believe you are right. But the fact is, Lord Thayne may not make me another offer. He is very angry with me."

"Was I not clear on the matter?" Her Grace said, leaning forward and putting her weight on the parasol handle. "*I* am offering on Thayne's behalf. He abdicated to me his right to choose a bride. I have made my choice. And, if I understood you correctly, you are willing to accept my offer as his proxy."

"I am." Beatrice smiled broadly as her heart filled with joy. Was it really going to happen? So easily? "But are you certain, Your Grace, that he will not want to murder us both for pulling such a trick on him?"

"I do not care how loudly he roars. He has vowed to accept my decision and he will do so. But in the end, he will thank me for this. Now, I have devised a little plan. Here is what I want you to do. . . . "

Chapter 19

Thayne took another swallow of claret. Though he would like nothing more than to get roaring drunk, he really must take care not to imbibe too heavily. It would not do to approach his future bride on unsteady legs, nor to slur his offer. Even so, he needed fortification to face the ordeal.

There would be a great deal less anxiety if only his mother had told him which young lady she had selected for him. The single hint she would give him was that he had met her on more than one occasion and had not found her offensive, which narrowed it down to only about several dozen or so girls.

He did not understand all the secrecy. It made no sense. He could have more properly prepared a speech if he at least knew the girl's name. And if he had known her identity even as late as yesterday, he could at least have met with the young lady in his normal attire as a gentleman. Instead, he was to make his offer while in full costume for the masquerade. His only hope was that the girl would at least be unmasked when he met her. It would be just like his mother, in her current playful mood, to have him make an offer to a masked stranger, only to reveal her identity at midnight when the masks were removed and his announcement was to be made. No, he would not allow the duchess to take her game that far. He would insist on seeing the young lady's face when he made his offer.

And so here he was, dressed in all his Punjabi finery—just as he had done on one other memorable occasion—waiting for his mother to come and take him to his bride. She had insisted that he wait here in his own sitting room until the girl's arrival. It was all very mysterious, and yet Thayne was still unable to conjure up more than a modicum of interest in the whole business. He just wanted it over and done with so he could move on with his life. A life without the only woman he had ever wanted.

Knowing she was probably downstairs at this very moment, standing in the receiving line with the other Benevolent Widows Fund patronesses, added fuel to his surly mood. Thayne had no wish to face Beatrice tonight. His anger and disappointment were still too raw, the marks of her claws too deep on his heart. Parading his new bride in her face would give him no joy.

And yet, if he had never proposed marriage to her, if their affair had simply proceeded in the normal way of such things, tonight would have been the end of it. She had told him often enough that she would not continue as his lover once he committed himself to another woman, and he'd accepted that decision. It was bound to have been an awkward evening at best, with both lover and bride in attendance, and his ending the affair and announcing his betrothal at the same time. As it happened, the break with Beatrice had come sooner, which should have made it easier to get through the evening.

Yet somehow, it was much worse.

He stood at the window and watched the hustle and bustle in the courtyard below as carriage after carriage pulled through the entry gates and guests in all manner of costume spilled out and approached the front doors. Was one of those masked figures his future bride?

Damn the duchess for making him wait like this.

Thayne eyed the hookah and considered firing it up, but the decanter of claret required less effort and so he poured himself another glass. He knocked back the wine in a single swallow. If his mother did not arrive soon, he would indeed be foxed by the time he met his future bride.

He sank onto the sofa, propped his elbows on his knees, and dropped his face into his hands. A bone-deep weariness settled on him, and he heaved a sigh.

And finally. The sound of the sitting room door opening. It was time to meet his bride. Before he could summon the energy to lift his head, there was an odd *thwack* and then a whistling *whoosh* of air as something passed by his shoulder. Thayne jerked to a start in that instant, just as a small golden arrow pierced the cushion at his side.

He stared incredulously at it, then turned sharply to face the door.

"I've been practicing that for days. Nice shot, eh?"

Artemis.

She walked into the room looking as beautiful as ever, wearing the same costume she'd worn the first time he ever saw her, except that her hair was its natural red and not powdered. She held the miniature bow in her hand. Yellow pleated silk clung to every curve as she moved, and his groin tightened at the sight.

He stood, glanced down at the little arrow, and said, "That depends. If you meant to shoot *me*, it fell a bit wide of the mark."

"No, I did not intend to shoot you. I have, I fear, inflicted too many wounds already, with all the barbs I have flung at you lately." She tossed the bow onto the couch and stood straight and tall before him.

Lord, she looked glorious. His eyes feasted on her; he wanted her as much as ever. Why had she come? Was she here simply to torment him while he waited for his bride? To remind him of what he could not have?

"Why are you here, Beatrice? Shouldn't you be downstairs welcoming the guests?"

"It is not my place to welcome them. I am no longer a trustee of the charity. My recent notoriety made it impossible for me to continue in that role."

"One more misfortune to lay at my feet. I am truly sorry, Beatrice. I know how important the Widows Fund is to you."

She shrugged her shoulders. "I'll survive. And once the scandal blows over, perhaps they will allow me to join them once again."

"Why are you here?" he repeated.

"The duchess sent me." She gave a tentative smile and watched his eyes closely.

"But why would she—" The truth slammed into him with the force of a charging elephant. She saw it in his face, and her smile broadened.

She raised her hands, palms out, and said, "I am not what you expected, am I? Too old. Too stubborn. Too stupid. As incredible as it sounds, though, the duchess chose me."

Thayne narrowed his eyes, and studied her. "I was under the impression, madam, that you wanted no part of me."

"I changed my mind," she said, throwing back at him those same words he'd said to her when he first asked her to marry him. Her face became more serious, concerned, contrite, as she reached out and took both his hands.

"I said terrible things to you, Gabriel, hateful things. Please forgive me. Please. I've been such a fool. I know the truth about your 'slaves.' I never truly believed it. I knew you were a better man than that. I knew it, but when you did not deny buying slaves . . . well, I didn't know what to believe. But I know the truth now, the full truth about how you fought the slave trade, and knowing it, I have never admired you more. And I know about Chitra. That was the worst accusation of all, and I am more than ashamed of it. Especially now that I've met her."

"You met Chitra?"

"Yes. She and Charlotte are great friends."

Thayne shook his head, not understanding any of this. His heart thudded loud in his chest at the very idea of having Beatrice back in his life. But it was not that easy. Despite his mother's damnable interference, he was not certain he wished to capitulate.

"None of this is making sense to me, Beatrice. Let me see if I have it straight. You have changed your mind and now wish to marry me?"

"Yes, very much so."

His heart did a little dance in his chest, but he kept his well-honed reserve in place.

"If you will have me," she said.

"I am rather surprised that *you* are willing to have *me*. You have been rather clear on the point, as I recall. You hated the idea of marriage, and most especially to me."

She grimaced. "I was wrong."

"You no longer believe I keep a sex slave."

"No, of course not. I never truly believed it. Deep in my heart."

"You no longer think I will try to dominate you, to take control of your life?"

She quirked a smile. "You will try. But I will fight you on it."

Yes, he rather imagined she would. "And you no longer think you are too old?"

"I cannot change my age, Gabriel. But it no longer matters to me. I have enjoyed having a vigorous younger man as my lover. Why not as my husband?"

"And there was, as I recall, an objection to starting a family. You did not want more children, and yet I will want an heir."

"It has occurred to me that making a child with you would be a wonderful thing indeed. My daughters tell me they would like a little brother, if you please."

He could no longer hold back a smile. He squeezed her hands and pulled her closer.

"You were so adamantly against marriage before. And against me. What changed your mind?"

"You told me you loved me."

"But you *knew* I loved you. You had to have known."

"You never said it."

He wrapped his arms around her. "I am sorry if I didn't. I thought you knew. But I suppose it is good to hear the words now and then, is it not?"

"You have no idea how good it is."

"Then allow me to say it again. I love you, Beatrice. I love you."

Her eyes suddenly grew bright with tears. The words really were important to her. He held her tight and whispered them over and over in her ear until the tears turned to laughter.

I love you I love you I love you.

Her heart swelled and she laughed with joy. She had not been entirely convinced the duchess's plan would work. She had been prepared for Gabriel to toss her out on her ear. But to have him hold her again and declare his love . . . oh, this was bliss. All-encompassing, mind-shattering, life-altering bliss.

It was an overwhelming sensation to love a man with your whole heart and soul, to want him so badly you ached with it. To discover such love at her age, after marriage and children and a respectable widowhood, was quite simply breathtaking.

"Oh, Gabriel. I love you." To say the words aloud

was almost as powerful as hearing them said. "I am consumed with love for you."

And he kissed her. It was the kiss of a lifetime, a kiss that marked the before and after of their lives, the first kiss wrapped in love fully acknowledged and a promise for the future. When it ended, while she was still dizzy with the potency of it, Gabriel took her face in his hands.

"Will you marry me, Lady Somerfield?"

"Gladly. But you must accept me as I am, Gabriel. I am too old to change."

"I do not want you to change. I love you just the way you are. Well, maybe except for one small thing. You must stop telling me you are too old. We shall banish the word 'old' from our vocabulary. You are no schoolgirl, for which I am grateful. You are in the prime of your life, my love. The very best time of your life. You are not an unformed young lady just out of the schoolroom, thank God. You are a complete woman, Beatrice, and that's one of the things I love best about you. So, my one and only order is that there will be no more talk of you being too old. Agreed?"

Beatrice rolled her eyes. "He's ordering me about already. All right, then. I am no longer too old. But do not ask me to change anything else, for I cannot promise I will acquiesce so easily and without a fight."

He grinned and kissed her nose. "No more changes, my little ingenue. And I can't change my spots, either, you know. I am quite aware that I am arrogant and demanding and controlling. I was raised to be a duke. Arrogance comes with the territory. But I will try to be accommodating, I promise. I may not succeed as much as you'd like, but I will try."

"I know you will. We'll both try. And we'll be better people for it."

They kissed again and it grew more passionate, urgent, a little wild.

"Dear God," he said at last, "I am desperate to make love to you. Right now. But you look so beautiful, my Artemis, and we have to make an appearance soon downstairs at the ball. I don't want to ruin this lovely Grecian hairstyle or wrinkle your gown. But we can sneak up here after midnight and I'll make love to you all night long."

"We don't have to muss my hair, you know."

"If I toss you on this sofa, or carry you to my bed in the next room, I guarantee you that your hair will be mussed."

"I am surprised, Gabriel, at your lack of resourcefulness. There are a thousand ways to make love."

She pulled him roughly by the sash around his waist as she walked backward to the nearest wall and fell back against it. Lifting a leg to wrap around his thigh, she said, "*Jataveshtitaka*. The twining of the creeper."

He laughed joyfully. "You are a fast learner, my love. Your pronunciation is quite perfect."

"I learned more than the pronunciation." She felt inside the Indian coat and found the ties that held the trousers in place. "I seem to recall these were easily removed." She fumbled with the ties until they came undone. With a quick shake of his hips, they slithered down his legs. She reached inside his smallclothes and freed his erection at the same time that he hiked the skirts of her chiton to her waist.

She held him in her hands and positioned him at the already damp entrance to her sex. Lifting her thigh higher and wrapping it around his back, she achieved a better angle. With one thrust forward of her hips, she took him inside her.

"Ahhhhh." He gripped her bottom and held her in place, not moving. "Paradise. Home."

She began to move her hips and he set up a fast

rhythm, driving harder and harder so that the wall shook with each thump of her backside. She would be bruised tomorrow, and did not care.

He somehow managed to insert a hand between them and, while still thrusting into her, began to massage the apex of her sex. It sent her over the edge in an instant and she cried out her release. His climax followed closely behind hers as his thrusts became short and frantic. He moaned and started to jerk free, but Beatrice gripped his buttocks, clenched her inner muscles, and held him tight inside her. "Stay."

He had no choice as his climax rocked him in that moment, and he pumped and pumped until his whole body went limp against her.

Panting, he gathered her in his arms and held her close. "Are you sure?"

"Of course. We need to start working on the heir. I'm not getting any younger, you know. Oops, I'm not supposed to mention that."

He laughed and kissed the top of her head. "I promise to keep working on that heir. Often."

He pushed himself away and they both straightened their clothes. Beatrice walked to the mirror above the fireplace to check her hair. He stepped up behind her, wrapping his arms around her.

"You were right," he said. "We can make love without mussing your hair. It still looks perfect."

"Yes, it—oh!" Her gaze had dropped to the mantel, where a tiny gold arrow had been placed right in the center. She looked in the mirror again and clearly saw the other arrow still lodged in the cushion. Then she looked up into Gabriel's eyes in the reflection. "What is this?"

"You dropped it that night we first met. I have kept it as a memento ever since. Cupid's arrow. Sent straight to my heart."

"Oh, Gabriel." He'd really kept it all this time? It was the sweetest thing she'd ever heard. She went to the sofa and extracted the arrow she'd shot into the cushion. Returning to the mantel, she placed it across the first arrow, so they formed a sort of X.

"Cupid shot me, too," she said. "Now they are like hearts entwined." She gave a sheepish laugh at such sentimentality, but she was feeling very romantic and sentimental and full of joy.

He turned her around to face him and wrapped her in his arms again. They could not seem to stop touching each other, as though every caress was a new discovery. This, from two people who knew each other's bodies intimately.

"You know," he said, "you might have killed me tonight with that damned arrow."

"Not a chance. I told you: I practiced. I have always had a bit of skill at archery. Somerfield hated it, but I have taken it up in earnest since he died. It was simply a matter of becoming accustomed to the smaller size of the bow. If I had wanted to shoot you, Gabriel, I could easily have done so. Which was my whole point. I wanted you to know that even though I was prepared to marry you, I was not a woman to be trifled with. If you try to bully me, I will fight back." She grinned. "I might even shoot you if you're not careful."

"Egad, you terrify me."

"I just want you to know what you're getting in this bargain, my lord. I will not be managed."

He stroked her cheek with the back of a finger. "I know. I'll try not to, but it's in my nature to be in charge. You may have to cut me down to size now and then. But I will promise you this: you may manage all our investments till your heart's content. I took your advice on that mining stock and made a quick bundle on it. Quite remarkable. You really do know what you're doing, don't you?"

"I do."

"Then I am happy to yield to you in all matters of business, if you like. At least, I'll try."

"We'll work side by side, Gabriel. We'll share the burden and make decisions together."

"I'd like that." He kissed her again. "You may find, though, that I tend to get my way most of the time."

"We'll see."

His expression grew serious, intense. "It won't be like your first marriage, Beatrice. I will guarantee you that. I will not shut you out or put checks on your behavior. I won't be another Somerfield. Believe that."

"I do."

"Besides, Somerfield didn't love you, whereas I love you to distraction. That has to count for something."

"My dear Gabriel, it counts for everything."

Later that evening in the ballroom of Doncaster House, brilliant with the light of a thousand candles in the famous chandeliers, the duke and duchess announced the betrothal of their son to Lady Somerfield, and led the guests in a toast to their future happiness.

The announcement was received politely but with quiet reservation. The betrothed couple, after all, had only recently been the focus of a rather interesting scandal.

"Hell and damnation," Thayne whispered to Beatrice. "They think we are simply trying to redeem ourselves, that we are marrying merely to placate the gossip. Well, blast them all, I'll show them what this is really about."

He pulled her into a shockingly tight embrace. After a few feminine gasps, the room went silent. He pulled her even closer.

"There you go," Beatrice said, smiling, "bullying me already."

"On this matter, madam, you will simply have to get used to it."

And in front of all their guests, the Marquess of Thayne kissed his bride-to-be soundly. At first there were a few gasps of shock, followed by hushed conversations, and then someone began to applaud.

The Dowager Duchess of Hertford, beaming at the engaged couple, clapped her hands enthusiastically. Mrs. Marianne Cazenove came to stand beside her and did the same. So did Penelope, Lady Gosforth, and Mrs. Grace Marlowe. Miss Emily Thirkill joined in with enthusiasm, as did the two gentlemen who flanked her. Mr. Burnett shouted huzzahs at his friend. The other gentleman, whom some recognized as Sir Albert Thirkill, watched his future son-in-law with amusement twinkling in his eyes, then looked down at his daughter and smiled. It was whispered about town that, having heard of the shocking display at the last Widows Fund ball, he had come to take his wife back to the country with him.

When it was noticed that the Duchess of Doncaster herself was beaming with approval, others joined in the clapping, and then more, until the room rang out with thunderous applause, cheering, whistles, hooting, and general merriment.

Lord Thayne smiled broadly at the crowd, bowed an acknowledgment, then pulled his betrothed close and kissed her again.

London, May 1813

"There is not a woman in London whose bed I could not seduce my way into with very little effort."

John Grayston, seventh Viscount Rochdale, was a bit the worse for drink, having spent the past hour and a half in the card room at Oscott House, where obliging footmen kept his glass filled. But his statement was no idle boast fueled by too much claret. It was a fact, pure and simple.

His companion, Lord Sheane, had commented that some women would never allow themselves to be enticed into a love affair, and Rochdale could not allow the comment to stand unchallenged. Women, all women, were hungry for seduction—some quite openly, others unwittingly. It was no great accomplishment to get any one of them between the sheets. All it took was a quick assessment of the game, to determine whether she wanted the Great Lover or the Notorious Libertine. In his considerable experience, he'd found that most women of the *ton* were intrigued by the wicked nature of his reputation, by the unsavory tales associated with him, most of which were true. Even the highest-ranking ladies of the aristocracy enjoyed the notion of flirting with danger.

No, it had been no idle boast. He knew precisely how to make any woman desire him.

Over the rim of his wineglass, Lord Sheane narrowed his eyes at Rochdale. "Is that so?" He had to raise his voice to be heard over the music in the adjacent ballroom, and the general hubbub of voices and laughter in the card room. "No woman in London can resist you?"

Rochdale shrugged his shoulders. It was not a subject that required debate. Of course, a man like Sheane, who'd gone a bit soft in the belly and jowly around the mouth, would label Rochdale arrogant rather than admit to his own jealousy.

"Shall we put it to the test, old boy?"

Rochdale arched an eyebrow. "I beg your pardon?"

"You said you could seduce any woman in London." Lord Sheane's mouth twisted into a sneer. "Are you willing to prove it?"

A familiar prickle of anticipation settled in the base of Rochdale's spine. He braced himself for the irresistible siren call of a wager. Donning an air of supreme indifference, he said, "What did you have in mind?"

"I'll stake Albion that I can name a woman you cannot seduce."

Albion? Damnation. Sheane, the blackguard, knew Rochdale had coveted that particular horse ever since he'd won the second class at Oatlands last year. He'd twice offered to buy the bay gelding, but Sheane had refused. Albion was a winner and the star of Sheane's stables. And yet here he was now, offering the horse as stakes in a wager he was bound to lose. It was almost too good to be true.

"Has Albion suffered an injury?" Rochdale asked. "You seem anxious to be rid of him."

Sheane threw back his head and laughed. "Damn me, but you are an arrogant bastard. So much so that I am sure you would have no qualms in offering Serenity as your stakes in our little wager."

"You think to win Serenity off me?" Rochdale chuckled. "I don't think so." Serenity was his best horse, his favorite horse. The little chestnut mare had won more races—including the king's plate at Nottingham and two cups at Newmarket—than any other horse in Rochdale's stables. He would as soon cut off his arm than give away Serenity to Lord Sheane.

But of course, if he accepted the wager, he would have to do no such thing, for he could not lose.

"If you are so confident," Sheane said, "then you will have no qualms about offering her as stakes. My Albion against your Serenity that you cannot seduce a woman of my choosing. What do you say?"

It was too easy. Rochdale studied the man closely, wondering what trick he had up his sleeve. He had lost a fair amount of money to Rochdale that evening, but for an inveterate gambler like Sheane, it meant nothing. And he would no doubt win it all back, and more, tomorrow night, or the night after that. Such was the life of a gambler.

But a gambler never bet against a sure thing. What was Sheane up to?

Rochdale held out his glass while a footman refilled it, then took a swallow of claret. "You have a particular woman in mind, I suppose."

"One or two, actually."

Rochdale gave a crack of laughter, and several heads turned in his direction. He lowered his voice and said, "One or two? You believe there is more than one woman immune to my charms?"

"Your arrogance will be your undoing, Rochdale. I am certain there are several women at this very ball whom even you could not seduce."

"Then let us be more specific in the wager. You must name a woman in attendance here tonight." Rochdale could not imagine a single woman among those in the ballroom whom he could not coax into bed. It might prove to be unpleasant if the chosen woman was a gnarled and wizened antique, or had a face that would curdle cream. But he could do it. For the chance to add Albion to his stables, he could do it.

"All right," Sheane said. "One of the guests at this ball. Excellent. So here is the wager: I shall name a woman and charge you with seducing her. If you fail, I get Serenity. If you succeed, you get Albion."

"How long do I have? These things can take time, you know. It is to be a seduction, after all, not a ravishment."

"Until the end of the Season?"

"Hmm. That is less than two months. It may not be enough time."

Sheane scowled. "Good God, you astonish me. I thought you were a master at wooing women into your bed. And yet two months is not enough time?"

"A master knows that a true seduction can take two minutes or two years, depending on the woman. Certain delicate creatures require more seducing than others. Since I do not yet know the identity of the woman, how can I say how long it will take?"

Lord Sheane snorted. "There must be a time frame. Where is the sport in an open-ended wager?"

"Indeed. Then let us name a date."

"It cannot be years, Rochdale. The horses will not be worth winning if we drag this thing out too long. Suppose we use the Goodwood Races as a deadline? You are planning to run Serenity for the cup, are you not? If it takes longer than three months to bed a woman, then you are not the man you claim to be."

"All right, then. Goodwood it is. I will seduce the woman you name by then, or forfeit Serenity. But if I succeed before Goodwood, I win Albion. Agreed?"

"Agreed."

Rochdale offered his hand, and Sheane shook it with a level of enthusiasm that boded ill. Rochdale did not trust him. What harpy was the man going to inflict upon him?

"Let us survey the ballroom," Sheane said, "shall we?"

Lord Sheane placed his empty glass on a side table and made his way through the maze of card tables. Rochdale upended his own glass and finished the last of his claret. He followed Sheane and saw that on his way he spoke to several gentlemen, each of them laughing and turning to gaze at Rochdale.

Damnation. He was making their wager known. Rochdale had had enough public scandal in his life. He had no desire to play out another seduction under the eyes of every gambler and club man in London. How was he to seduce a woman if it was public knowledge that a wager was involved? No woman in her right mind would succumb to him under such circumstances.

He caught up with Sheane as he was laughing with Sir Giles Clitheroe. "A word with you, Sheane." He caught the man by the sleeve and led him out of the room.

When they were in the main corridor, Rochdale turned to him and said, "I will not have this wager made public, Sheane."

"Since when have you developed such fine sensibilities?"

"Since I wagered my best horse. I will not have you jeopardize my chances by trumpeting the wager to the world." He lowered his voice as a couple in conversation walked past. "If the woman got wind of it, you cannot imagine she would welcome my advances."

"Ah, but you said *any* woman in London. Correction: You amended your boast to encompass only those women in attendance tonight. But you said nothing about what they may or may not know of the wager."

Rochdale put his face so close to Sheane's that their noses almost touched. "Let us say that I would not consider it sporting if you were to make the wager public. Do you take my meaning, sir?"

Sheane raised his eyes to the ceiling and stepped back. "Dammit, Rochdale, there is no need to threaten me. All right, then. I promise to keep the wager in confidence."

"How many men in the card room already know?"

Sheane heaved a sigh. "Clitheroe, Dewesbury, and Haltwhitsle."

"Confound it. Do they know which woman you will name?"

"No."

"Good. Let's keep it that way. Do we understand each other?"

"Yes, yes. What a fusspot of an old woman you've become, Rochdale. But I suppose that business last year with Serena Underwood took a bit of the wind out of your sails, eh?"

Rochdale would not be baited by reminders of his most notorious indiscretion. "Name your woman, Sheane. Let me see how easy this is going to be."

"All right, then."

He made a show of surveying the room, which was filled with pretty young girls in white dresses. There were just as many older women, mothers and chaperones of the pretty dancing girls. Some of them handsome. Some of them gone to seed. There were the dowagers, too, the grandmotherly types in plumed turbans, gathered in gossipy groups along the walls. God help him if Sheane chose one of those. And there were the wallflowers—spinsters growing a bit long in the tooth after too many Seasons, or younger women too unattractive to entice a dance partner.

Rochdale eyed every one of them, judging how he might woo her into his bed, regardless of how distasteful an exercise it would be.

"Her," Sheane announced. "I name her."

Rochdale followed the man's gaze and groaned aloud. "Mrs. Marlowe? The bishop's widow?"

"The very one. There's your challenge, Rochdale. And what a challenge she will be." He cackled in glee as they watched Mrs. Grace Marlowe walk past chatting with Lady Gosforth. She glanced in his direction, caught him staring at her, pursed her lips in disapproval, and turned away.

Rochdale shook his head in disgust. He ought to have known Sheane would pick the most prim and proper woman in the room. As straitlaced a prude as ever lived. The widow of that old windbag Bishop Marlowe, for God's sake.

Grace Marlowe was young and attractive, to be sure. If Rochdale had not known who she was, he would no doubt have found her quite desirable, with all that honey blond hair, those smoky gray eyes, and that perfectly sculpted profile. But he did know her, and no amount of beauty could change the fact that she was the Widow Marlowe, hailed by one and all as a Good Woman. A God-fearing woman. A do-gooder. The sort of woman who despised men like him.

But he had broken down the defenses of more than one so-called virtuous woman in his long career. He knew how to get around their fine scruples and tenacious morality. Mrs. Marlowe might be a more difficult case, but he had no doubts about his success.

"A challenge, indeed," he said. "I shall find no joy in it, but seduce her I will."

Sheane raised his eyebrows. "You think so, do you?"

"I know so. I have no intention of handing my best horse over to you. And I covet that bay gelding of yours. I shall alert my head groom to make room for him in the stables."

"I would not get your hopes up, Rochdale. That woman will not be seduced. I guarantee it."

"Yes, she will." He watched her walk away and detected the merest hint of a sway in the hips beneath her silk skirts. "She will be one of those delicate cases who will take a bit longer than others. But I shall have her before Goodwood. *I* guarantee it."